To m

r·J   Er)

DISCARDED

Best,

By

Keith E. Burns

A Marathon Torres Novel

Copyright © 2020 by Keith E. Burns
Registration Number TXu 2-217-400
United States Copyright Office

Summary: Detective Marathon Torres of the 73rd precinct in Brooklyn, stumbles upon a haunting cold case file linked to her past. When things spiral out of control, Marathon must confront her demons to expose the circumstances behind the tragic death of a young girl.

ISBN- 978-1-7357088-0-5 – Hardcover
ISBN- 978-1-7357088-1-2 – Softcover
ISBN- 978-1-7357088-2-9 – eBook

Discarded: A Marathon Torres Novel by Keith E. Burns

Published by Keitheburns.com
1st Edition

Cover by Sam Aalam from Sam_Designs1 at Fiverr

Acknowledgements

Writing is tough. As a writing teacher, I often pair students together with the hopes they read and revise their own work. It's essential for writers to receive peer review for feedback on how to improve. Many students dislike writing because of the amount of time that goes into the process. From drafting, to rereading, to rewriting, to editing, everything takes time and at each step an author can feel discouraged by their own work. Self-doubt creeps in and the writing process could easily stall into obscurity. I now know this first hand having started this project well over a year ago. During my writing process I conferred a lot with a good friend, Jared Morgenstern, who read most of the early writings. He suffered through the grammar, punctuation and spelling mistakes to see there was something and encouraged me to continue on this journey. He has been a vital ally and a dear friend that certainly helped complete this novel. Jared, also, happens to be a clinical therapist. His insight into emotional trauma helped Marathon Torres come to life in ways I couldn't put on paper. Marathon is more real because of our conversations and I would like to thank him dearly for our numerous text messages. I'm sure he's sick of my name popping up on his phone.

Special Thanks

To my dear wife and best friend, thank you for all the love and support over the years. Your strength and caring nature has provided the necessary inspiration to tackle a project like this.

To Tina Giambastiani, a dear friend who graciously accepted the task of reading an early version of the book. She took the time to read, react and discuss the content of the book with me while battling the numerous spelling and grammar mistakes the early version had. Tina's feedback has been vital towards shaping Marathon's character.

To my cousin Bryan, who also accepted the tedious task of reading an early version of the book. Your early review of the book helped propel this project forward, thank you!

To Joshua, my friend and conceptual editor, without you this project would not exist in its final form. Thank you for challenging me, my characters, and my writing. You have made me a better writer. If given the opportunity, I cannot wait to return the favor.

To my brother-in-law, Stephen D'Ambrosia, who's early reviews helped shape the plot and main character. For once, band aids were not needed.

To my friend, Amanda Morgenstern, for graciously reading an advanced release copy of the novel. Your early critique helped shape this novel. Thank you!

To all my friends and family for believing in me and providing the support and encouragement necessary to undertake such a time consuming project.

For my daughters Kelsey and Alexandra, this book is written for you (when you're older).

Preface

Let's get a few things out of the way first, before you dive into this book. I am going to use a quote from an artist I grew up listening to because his words put it best (I'm just going to update it for 2020). If you, in any way, hate the LGBTQ+ community, women, people of a different religion, race, color, or if you don't think Black Lives Matter, please do not read or buy this book. Stop here and do not continue reading. You are not welcome to go any further.

Now that we got that out of the way, I hope you enjoy my first attempt at writing a novel. The writing process is extremely challenging, especially for first time writers like myself. For the record, I am a white male, who has lived in privilege most of my life. I fully understand this, and I am here to help make the world a better place. If this book brings joy or entertainment to people, then I feel this will be an accomplishment of some sorts.

The subject of mental health comes up many times through character thoughts and actions. Post-Traumatic Stress Disorder and wartime trauma are real, and I have only begun to understand how traumatic events manifest in people who suffer from PTSD. Our armed forces deserve way more credit than they are given, especially when their military careers have ended and they move onto civilian life. While their uniform comes off, their scars and sacrifices do not. We, as a nation, need to do a better job supporting our veterans.

As a male writer writing a female lead character, I believe there is room for criticism and I welcome it. In no way do I pretend to know how women are treated differently, especially in the situations covered in this book. In many ways this can be interpreted as a male's point of view of what women go through in a man's world. I hope one day my two amazing daughters can appreciate this novel. It is okay to cry and show emotion, it is okay to show weakness and accept help from others. This, deep down, is what makes us humanity strong and we are better for it. Understanding this has helped me become a better father, and a better teacher.

I hope you enjoy this as much as I have.

"Coming home from war, pieces don't fit anymore"
– James Hetfield

DISCARDED

M

Prologue

"Come on, we're going to be late!" Isabella said.

"Who cares? It's a dumb New Year's Eve party," Marathon said as she focused on her eyeliner with her face inches from the brightly lit mirror.

Her friend sat impatiently on the bed twirling her hair. Marathon's room looked like it was back when they used to sneak out of their houses to attend neighborhood parties. There as a gigantic poster of a sweaty Ricky Martin displayed on the wall beside the bed. His chest hair almost seemed life like as his hand suggestively rested on the belt barely holding up his pants.

"Why do you even bother putting make up on?" Isabella asked.

Marathon didn't respond, she wanted to get it just right. She was out of practice.

"Hey, what's this?" Isabella asked.

Marathon turned her attention away from the mirror and noticed Isabella holding a medal display case. She immediately turned her attention back towards the mirror to finish her eyeliner and purposely didn't respond.

"Is this the medal?" Isabella asked.

"Si," Marathon responded. Her face moved closer to the mirror.

"Why is there a boat on it? Weren't you in the mountains or something?"

"It's a Navy Cross," Marathon responded with a slight hint of annoyance.

"Wait, you were in the Navy?" Isabella asked. Marathon was getting annoyed with the rapid fire questions.

"A Navy Cross is awarded to the Navy, Coast Guard, and The Marines," Marathon responded.

"Oh, is this like, a big deal?" Isabella asked.

"It is, kinda," Marathon responded nodding.

"Then why is it in this crappy box, shouldn't this be on your wall or something?"

"If you keep asking me questions, we'll be here all night," Marathon responded.

"We don't want that," Isabella responded. "You know, Mark is going to be there."

"Yeah, so is half our graduating class," Marathon said.

"It'll be good for you," Isabella said.

"If you say so," Marathon replied.

"You don't seem that excited to go," Isabella said sounding a little let down.

"I'm going because you're going," Marathon said.

"So then why are you taking so long? Mark is probably there already," Isabella said. "Wait a second, you plan on meeting that guy again? That's why you're dolling yourself up."

"No," Marathon responded.

"Bullshit, I can see it in your eyes," Isabella said.

She looked back at her with a glare. Their friendship usually involved a competition to see who would end up with who by the end of the night. Marathon's stare was intentional and meant to send daggers at the line of questioning.

"Vete a la mierda!" Marathon exclaimed.

"Since when you curse in Spanish?" Isabella asked.

"Since someone started asking stupid questions," Marathon snapped back.

"Well, well, someone has a boyfriend," Isabella taunted.

"Ugh," she grunted turning back towards the mirror. Marathon's legs crossed as she sat at her vanity desk with scattered perfume and makeup spread without any organization.

"Wait, he ain't your boyfriend, he's your papi chulo," Isabella said playfully.

"My what?" Marathon asked impatiently.

"Oh come on Marathon Torres, where's your inner Latina?" Isabella playfully asked. Marathon glanced at her friend through the mirror.

"He's your sugar daddy," Isabella repeated, this time in English.

Marathon sent more glares reflected in the mirror and regretted inviting her friend over to get ready together. Her friend had figured out she was going to eventually ditch the party and go out with Danny later that evening.

"This is the one from the support group you've been going to?"

"Ugh, can we change the subject?" Marathon responded.

"Hell no! I wanna hear about this!"

"Well you ain't hearing shit," Marathon snapped back.

"Oh come on, you can't live with your uncle forever."

"What does that mean?" Marathon asked. She knew her friend was a master at getting people to spill information without directly asking, but she couldn't let this turn into a rumor amongst her friends. She was already on broken glass with them since she got back from Afghanistan.

"You have a sugar daddy, he gives you money, you can move out. That's what you are trying to do here, right?"

"Eh," she responded. "You make it sound like I'm getting paid to fuck him, like some sort of prostitute," she responded.

"If you put it that way," there was a brief pause. "I mean you aren't fucking him just to fuck him, right?" Isabella asked.

Marathon slammed her make up down on the vanity table. "If you keep asking me stupid questions, we're never going to the party," she barked.

III

"So, when are you going to see him? Before or after midnight?" Isabella asked.

"None of your damn business," Marathon said.

"You're going to sneak out of the party. And leave me there," Isabella said.

"Can you stop?" she barked back. "Besides, you're gonna be hooking up with Mark anyway."

"Make sure you bring some condoms," Isabella said.

Marathon finished the eyeliner and started patting powder on her cheeks. She wasn't satisfied with the way she looked and wanted to start over, but Isabella would kill her if they missed any more of the party.

"Come on! You're done, he's not going to care what you look like. He's like fifty and you're twenty-three, he just thinks he's the luckiest guy in the world," Isabella said. Marathon knew she threw her age in there for effect, and it pissed her off.

"He's forty-four," she snapped back.

"Still, nearly double your age."

"You just want to get to the party for Mark!" she said.

"You're just jealous that I claimed him first!" Isabella said.

"Please!"

"You're trying to change the subject!" Isabella said. "I have Mark and you have some old guy, Danny. You just call him Danny to make him sound younger."

"What? I'm just stating the fact that you are trying to get laid also!" Marathon said in response.

"Ugh, at least Mark is our age!" Isabella said.

"Yeah and we know him from high school!" Marathon said.

"So?"

"So, it's time to expand your pallet," Marathon said.

"Well, I didn't go to overseas and have random hookups with exotic men from around the world."

"Come on, you know what I mean," Marathon said. "Mark is like, a high school thing. I don't think he's that into you anyway." She knew this would send her a back the fuck off message.

"Your just jealous I got to him first!"

"That was high school! Why would I be jealous now?" Marathon asked.

"You've got an old man," Isabella said.

"You're right, Mark is such a hot commodity," she said sarcastically. "The boy hasn't even left Queens. Do me a favor, when you're going down on him, check to see if his balls have dropped."

"Why is this a big deal?" Isabella snapped back.

"Time to live a little, get out there, meet new people," she said. "Trust me, Mark ain't going anywhere."

"It's easy for you to say, you got the looks."

"Says the girl who could literally be on the cover of sports illustrated swimsuit. You're impossible," Marathon proudly said.

"Me? Please, you've always been the one who everyone wanted to be friends with. Guys always lost their minds around you and ignored the rest of us."

"The good old days," Marathon said.

There was a pause in the conversation as Marathon started to put the makeup away. She wasn't going to be satisfied with the way she looked this evening. Her friend was right, why did she care so much about seeing this guy Danny. She met him at a veteran's support group of all places.

"Wait a second, you're fucking considering his offer? It's not just about Danny, it's about what he wants you to do."

"What? No," she said.

She was.

"You are! You want to be a fucking pig, don't you? That's why you're gravitating towards him. It reminds you of the Marines."

"No!"

"For sure, I thought you started fucking him to help you out with the law. Maybe he was giving you more than just dick, maybe he was your sugar daddy or something. But now, I think you are going to take him up on his offer, aren't you?"

"That's not how you join the police force," she responded.

"Oh, so tell me how?"

"There's an application process, and being a veteran, I can use the GI Bill to help," she said.

"You see, you are interested," Isabella said.

"So what," she said.

"So now this makes sense."

"Ugh, you suck," Marathon responded, annoyed.

"It's a good career move for you," Isabella said.

"What?" she asked. She wasn't expecting that comment as she was already prepared to defend her decision to enroll in the police academy.

"You can't keep doing what you're doing," Isabella said.

"What does that mean?" Marathon asked defensively.

"You know what it means. You're letting what happened to you take over," Isabella said.

"What?" Marathon said getting angry. "Since when did you get like this? You've been with me, every time we go out, every step of the way."

"Yeah, I am an enabler, I've seen first-hand how everything is in excess," Isabella said as she tried to move closer to Marathon.

"You've seen shit," Marathon said. She stood and turned towards Isabella as if to confront her head on.

VI

"I've seen you blacked out drunk, seen you hook up with random guys while we were still at the bar, carried your ass home so you wouldn't end up in a ditch. Yeah I've been with you every step of the way," Isabella said.

"What the fuck Isabella!" Marathon said as she crossed her arms just under her chest.

"You're different, you don't even know it," Isabella said.

"Isabella! Is this how you truly feel or has my uncle put you up to this?" Marathon questioned.

"Your uncle loves you! And I would have said this with or without him," Isabella said.

"So he has talked to you!" Marathon said.

"What does it matter? You can't keep doing this," Isabella said.

"We're young, we're supposed to enjoy life and do whatever to whomever, whenever," she said.

"Marathon, you don't see it! Everything is in excess, everything is taken beyond what you've normally done. You haven't been yourself!"

"Like what? Tell me!" Marathon said trying to defend herself.

"Two weeks ago, we were at that bar in Brooklyn, the one you insisted on going to. Remember that?"

"No," she said.

"No shit you don't remember because I carried your ass to a cab and brought you home."

"I've carried your ass home also, don't fucking forget that!"

"Don't deflect Marathon!"

"We look out for each other. That's what we do. I got your back and you got mine, just like old times!" Marathon said.

"Yeah we do look out for each other, but since you've been back, you haven't been the same. You fucked a random ass dude in the bathroom of that shitty bar, you get shit faced every time we go out and how you're getting serious with a man nearly twice your age," Isabella said.

"You're just fucking jealous that I can walk into a bar and all the attention is on me!" Marathon said.

"Yeah, that's it, you nailed it. I am super jealous of you, looking like a tramp, fucking random guys in the bathroom. Yep, that's what I want out of life."

"Fuck you!" Marathon said. "You don't get to judge me!"

"No, I don't. I have no idea what happened to you. I have no idea what hell you've seen or what you've done. But I know you are not the same Marathon Torres I went to school with," Isabella said as a tear streamed down her cheek.

"Go to the fucking party yourself!" Marathon said. "and get the fuck out of my house."

More tears started to flow from her friend's face, but Marathon refused to back down. Her friend then grabbed her purse and left the room. Marathon looked again at the mirror and saw that her makeup smeared from the water dripping from her own eyes. She pushed the mirror away and sat down on the bed where her friend was just sitting. Isabella was her only friend who called her by her full name, Marathon.

She picked up the medal display case Isabella forgot to put back on her bookshelf. She took out the Navy Cross and held it in her hand. Marathon caressed the intricate details of a Navy ship at the center of the bronze cross as tears obscured her vision. She then stood and threw the Navy Cross on her dresser. It slid across the top of the dresser picking up dust along the way. It stopped just before it plunged over back edge of old piece of furniture.

She heard muffled voices below, her Uncle and Isabella were probably talking about her. No doubt he heard what happened, the walls in this house were thin. She waited for Uncle Dave to come up and console her like he's done in the past. But he didn't come and Isabella didn't come back. No one came, so she left to go see Danny.

Chapter
One

Marathon Jessica Torres sat timidly at her desk in the center of the large open floor precinct. She stared glossy-eyed at a stack of cold case files as they rose above her like a tidal wave waiting to break. She had been addressing these files all day and for the better part of the week. Marathon slowly chewed the remaining bits her egg-salad sandwich and desperately tried to refocus her efforts. Her first week as a detective was completely unremarkable.

The excitement of a promotion was quelled by the near endless stack of files before her. Like most cold case files she came across, Marathon, Mara for short, was able to officially stamp case closed for the simple fact that the statute of limitations ran out. Once she entered the information into the archaic computer system, the folder could then be dead-filed in a record room somewhere in the bowls of the precinct. She marveled at the sight of so many unsolved cases and questioned her ability. She wondered how many cases were actually solved.

Marathon found the term dead-file to be grotesque. The way it was used to discard crimes made it seem like it never happened. People's lives were altered when these files were created; altered enough for the police to get involved. Now these records sat in front of her waiting to be dead-filed if the statute of limitations expired. Assault, robbery, even rape, all had an expiration date that let the government off the hook. Marathon wondered if the victims in these files knew their case was being discarded. With most of the assigned detectives long gone, she was certainly not going to try and track anyone down to let them know the terrible news.

She was on her last pile of the seemingly endless folders that filled the old rust covered cabinet close to her desk. Determined to finish, Marathon struggled through the dust and paper cuts and tried to energize her waning spirit on the last stack of faded folders. She wanted nothing more than for the day to end and to celebrate her promotion at her favorite bar in Manhattan, but this overwhelming task irritated her.

What a way to start a new position, she thought. Spending most of the week reading cases the precinct long since forgot about. Mara wondered if any of the officers were even stationed here when these files were even opened. Most of the files predated her employment in the NYPD, some even going back to the 80's when things were carbon copied or written with a typewriter. The detective Marathon replaced was a veteran of the force and loved by many. He was probably here when most of these files were created. That troubled her, was she going to meet the same fate and forced to abandon hope on cases she couldn't close? Most of the folders were assault or domestic violence cases that were at a standstill because people stopped talking. No one wanted to talk to the police, there was no trust.

She had heard stories about the old detective who previously occupied her desk. He was one of the best. She was told he had a keen sense of how the world in Brownsville worked. Marathon had an opportunity to speak with him before her promotion. His advice was simple enough, but at the same time a bit discouraging. During their brief conversation, he repeated "you can't solve them all" a few times over. Now that she had gone through so many cold case files, she knew why he had said that.

2

He also gave some solid advice for interacting with the community at large. The way things tend to work in Brownsville is simple, he said. The residents do not trust the police and they are only called to restore order when a crime is in progress. Most of the callers are anonymous so the police are left to gather statements and evidence from what they find at the scene. Once order is restored, the police offers are no longer welcome and it's as if nothing ever happened. Suddenly everyone forgot something just went down and the collective amnesia spreads like a rumor in high school. Officers and detectives had similar experiences in the neighboring precincts, but nothing like the lack of regard found in Brownsville.

After speaking with the older timer, she got a sense of regret. Like he was leaving the job unfinished for the next person to come along and fuck it up even more. You can't solve them all, those words had new meaning and she now understood his regret.

Mara rubbed her eyes, sat up straight, pushed herself forward and reengaged in the tedious task. She could almost taste a freshly poured ice cold beer from happy hour and used that as motivation to push forward. At the beginning of the week, Marathon was given her first direct order from her former mentor and now commanding officer as sort of a welcome to the precinct assignment. Inspector Frank Davidson had a weird sense of humor. Review every cold case in the precinct, categorize them by crime and dead-file the closed cases and the ones that expired. Marathon was determined to impress the Inspector and wanted to finish before the end of her shift.

Frank Davidson wasn't even at the station this week. He had a series of council meetings that demanded his attention. Election season made everything political and city council members seized his time with every event they could conjure just to gather votes. Everyone wants to appear tough on crime during elections. Mara knew this was more busy work because he wasn't there to adequately introduce her to the precinct. She forgot his exact words, but it definitely sounded more pomp and circumstance than what Marathon was

3

accustomed to. He also mentioned that he hadn't selected a partner for her yet and he wanted to personally match her with someone that could keep up with her wit, or at least he said something like that. She always got the sense that he was very protective of her, she knew some would say overly protective.

When the old timer retired, his partner transferred to midtown south for a desk job before he was eligible for retirement. Instead of a seamless transition for a new detective, Frank Davidson had to find another detective and partner them up. He basically had to play matchmaker and hope a working relationship would develop.

Marathon needed to navigate the politics of this precinct carefully. She respected Frank Davidson and appreciated all that he had done for her career, but at the same time, she knew she could take care of herself. Frank had a lot on his plate and the last thing she wanted was for him to worry about her adjusting to a new precinct.

After 9/11, she enlisted and spent four years stationed in Afghanistan hunting Al Qaeda, the Taliban and Bin Laden. She was one of the first female Marines in Afghanistan to see combat in active duty. Marathon returned home after two tours of duty and a Navy Cross for an act of heroism on the battlefield. Yet, Frank Davidson was usually the one looking out for her. She knew he had pulled some strings to get her under his command after she was promoted.

Marathon picked up what she thought was the last file on her desk. Under it was a very thin dust faded manila envelope that seemed to have gotten shoved in the drawer without the proper filing sequence or case number attached to it. This sparked her curiosity and she placed the larger file in her hand down on her desk next to her computer and examined the manila folder closely. The color had faded and the envelop had that old draw string that sealed the envelope shut so no papers could fall out. It had looked like it hadn't been opened in years. The string felt like it could crumble in her hand as she unraveled it from its circular seal and opened it. Mara peered inside and found it rather barren with only a single sheet of paper and some photographs inside.

The astute detective thought this envelope must have been part of a larger file that seemingly got misplaced. That would explain why only a few items were in the envelope and why it was at the bottom of this stack without the proper identification. Marathon let gravity take hold of the inner contents and the pictures fell out first landing face up on her desk. Her heart froze, time stood still as she instantly recognized the color faded 4x6 photo.

She was the officer that took those pictures with a disposable camera back when she was a rookie in the 75th precinct. A flood of memories engulfed her as she recalled that eventful day on the boarder of East New York and Brownsville.

"Officer, officer," the bodega owner yelled as he frantically emerged from this corner store. Mara recalled the desperate look on his face as he flagged her and her partner down.

"You have to go to the back," the owner said in broken English. He mainly gestured with his hands pointing to where they should go. The owner refused to follow as Marathon slowly crept around the side of the bodega. She remembered the suspense slowly build as the dark alley reluctantly revealed its secret.

The alley between the back of the bodega and a pharmacy was long and narrow; it took her eyes a while to adjust to the reduced light. The shadows from the two buildings prevent the sun from reaching the moss covered cement ground and Marathon wondered how anyone could find anything in this area. But then she saw it. What the bodega owner was freaking out over.

Marathon instinctively reached for her radio and called for her partner who was still back with the owner. She couldn't recall the exact words she used, but the image of what she found was burned into her mind. Like when you stare at the sun too long, when you close your eyes the image remains. There was the body of Marley Williams, a seventeen year-old girl discarded in a dumpster on top of black garbage bags.

5

Marathon returned to the picture in her hand, but the moment she found Marley Williams all those years ago permeated her thoughts. This popular young girl from a high school just down the street from the bodega was motionless in a dumpster.

Mara's instincts about taking pictures turned out to be the correct call. There was a shit storm that followed once other students got wind of what happened. Teachers, friends, and parents came down to the bodega and demanded answers. They arrived there before forensics could seal off the area, which left Marathon and her partner in a tense situation.

The mob's grief turned to anger and rival gangs started to square up in the streets surrounding the crime scene. Marley Williams was loved by many. She was a good student, a friendly person, and was in good standing with her school. Rival gangs blamed each other for what happened, as it clearly looked like a gang related crime with the body being displayed on rival gang boarders. The bodega was considered neutral territory, almost like the 38th parallel that separated North Korea from South Korea.

With the picture still in her hand, she recalled some of the events after when detectives eventually took over the scene. Mara had moved to crowd control as detectives from both the 73rd and the 75th argued whose jurisdiction it was. No one wanted this case and it must have changed precincts a half dozen times while Marathon and her partner Officer John Stroman tried their best to calm the crowd and prevent a gang war from engulfing the neighborhood. She remembered developing the pictures later that day and gave them to her commanding officer at the 75th. That was the last she saw of them until now.

She had taken various pictures of the crime scene and used the entire roll of the disposable camera she grabbed from the bodega. Only a handful of pictures were in this envelope, most of the others were probably lost with the rest of the file. Marathon put the remaining pictures back into the envelope, as if she were trying to erase the events that just happened.

Before she could get all the remaining pictures in, one of them slipped out from hey shaking hand and landed back on her desk. It was a picture of Marley's shoe. She thought back to why she took that picture and realized there was something odd about it. The film failed to capture the fine white powdery sand covering her sneakers, but Marathon remembered that was out of the ordinary. No playground in the surrounding area had sand, and there wasn't a beach for miles. But, there was sand all over her socks and shoes. It looked like it was wet sand that had dried around the rubber tread that lined the bottom of the shoe like she had walked along the water at Coney Island.

Marathon returned the picture back to the stack inside the envelope and took out a single sheet of paper. She recognized this as the old chain of custody form for evidence collection. Her name was at the top being the officer who took the pictures and a case number appeared in clear handwritten ink next to a detective's name who was eventually assigned the case. Mara fired up her computer and searched for that case number, but nothing came up. Thinking there was a clerical error, she changed her search parameters and typed the name of the detective and the year the crime took place. A few cases popped up, but none of them were about Marley Williams. Again, she changed the search parameters to go city wide instead of limiting her search to the 73rd precinct, maybe the file was transferred back to the 75th and somehow this envelope got separated.

Still Nothing.

Mara then looked at the numbers closely. They were clearly labelled and recorded properly. The chair creaked as if it were annoyed when she shifted her weight backwards. She tried to remember all the details from the Marley Williams case, but she was missing huge gaps of information. She knew that the case was eventually assigned to the 73rd, that is probably how this particular envelope ended up here. She also knew that the detectives assigned to this case transferred to different precincts shortly after. That's what officers did in the 73rd. This precinct was usually a stepping stone for something bigger and better.

7

After that, as time when on, Marathon lost track of the case. She sort of let time bury her memories of this event. Growing up in Queens, Mara was forced to emotionally bury large portions of her life. She was a product of love and rage which made for an unstable childhood where she often spent time with her uncle.

She had a tough time relating to her family because she didn't look like her family. Her father was from the West Indies and was multiracial himself. Her mother was Irish and from Long Island. With her dark olive-toned skin and Irish freckles under her eyes, she looked nothing like her parents. Her uncle often said she inherited the best qualities from her mother and father, but she only had his word on that. Marathon never got to experience their best qualities, at least not in any meaningful way she could remember.

How her mother and father met was speculation on her part and she never had the maturity to ask her parents before they split. Her uncle eventually told her the truth, but Marathon was more comfortable with her version of how her parents met even though it was more fantasy than reality.

The manila envelope stared back at her as if it was calling out. She couldn't resist and reached back in. She took the photo of the deceased out of the envelope, gave it a quick glance and folded it into her inner suit jacket pocket. Marathon then threw the envelop down on the desk and stood up quickly. She decided she was done for the day as her shift had ended over an hour ago. She quickly grabbed her things, said her few goodbyes and headed for the door. She needed to get to the bar, get a few drinks in her, and mingle with people that she cared about. Her version of the past was resurfacing, the flood of emotions was becoming intense. A picture of Marley Williams discarded in the dumpster struct an emotional cord she hoped she would never hear again. She felt her mind drift off as the darkness of her past crept back in.

This wasn't the first time she felt like society had discarded its harsh reality. While serving overseas in the war in Afghanistan, she had witnessed the worst in humanity. With those thoughts also creeping back into her mind, she took

8

out her cell phone and sent a quick text to confirm her therapy appointment over the weekend. With the drastic change in her schedule from her promotion to detective, Marathon had cancelled the last two sessions. Her therapist, Dr. Sandra Lee, sent her a text earlier that day to confirm an opening she had on Sunday morning. She knew Dr. Lee reserved her Sundays for her family, but she said she would make an exception this one time to hold a session on Sunday morning to make up for the previous missed sessions.

When Dr. Lee sent the confirmation text earlier, Mara was going to cancel and reschedule the regular session next week, but she had gotten carried away with her dead-filing task. The photo of Marley Williams, now sitting in her suit pocket, made her crave someone to talk to. Mara sent a quick confirming text to Dr. Lee who immediately replied with a thumb's up emoji.

M

Chapter
Two

73ʳᵈ Precinct
July 19th, 2019
5:30pm

Marathon's commanding officer was waiting for her as she approached the exit. Senior Detective Morales was an eighteen year veteran at the 73rd and head of the department. Marathon reported directly to him and he reported directly to Inspector Frank Davidson. The chain of command at the 73rd was much easier to navigate than her previous post. At the 75th, she had many supervisors and was outranked by most officers in her division. As she approached Senior Detective Morales, she wasn't so sure a change in scenery was welcome. At least at the 75th, she could do her job and skate under the radar of scrutiny.

"Hey Torres," Morales said. "Do you have a sec?"

"Oh, hey, Detective Morales. I was just leaving," Marathon replied. Senior Detective Morales was dressed in a used car salesman's suit that looked a little big on him. The first day she met him, he spoke to her in Spanish expecting her to understand him, but she had to remind him that not all Hispanics from Queens spoke the language.

"Did you finish those cold case files?" He asked.

"Yeah, I finished all but one. I'll take care of the last one on Monday morning," she replied.

"Did you find anything worth noting in those old files?" he inquired.

Marathon hesitated for a moment. She didn't want to bring up Marley Williams, but not mentioning it now might eventually bite her in the ass later. Frank was expecting a report and Marathon knew it wasn't wise to go above her commanding officer.

"Yeah, actually," Marathon said. Detective Morales suddenly seemed more interested.

"I came across a case file that I remember from days on morning patrol," Marathon said. Morales responded with a puzzle look on his face.

"You weren't in the 73rd," he stated.

"No, you're right," she said. "This file started over at the 75th and got transferred over here."

"Oh, what case was that?" Detective Morales asked. He seemed interested, like a true detective when given only a snippet of information.

"The Marley Williams murder, over by Blake Avenue near the L Train," Marathon said.

"That name doesn't ring a bell," Detective Morales responded. "What year was this?"

"2006," Marathon said.

"Well before my time here," Detective Morales said. "I started my career in the Bronx."

"There was no record of the case being in the computer system," Marathon stated.

"Blake Avenue runs into 75th territory, you sure that the file isn't over there?" Detective Morales asked.

"Either way there would be record of it in the database," Marathon responded stating how odd it was for the case not to have a digital footprint.

"I've come across a few cases from back then that got lost in the merger. Back in 2012, we upgraded our system and during the data migration, many of our cases got fucked up," Morales said.

11

"Is there a backup from before the migration?" Marathon questioned.

"Of course there is. That's on a separate drive, you have to go through central to get that. Special request from the help desk," Detective Morales said.

"So that's what I'll do," Marathon said. She then turned towards the door but sensed the conversation wasn't over, and that Detective Morales still had something to say. She paused and looked at him.

Next to Frank Davidson, Detective Morales was the 2nd longest active duty veteran at the 73rd. He had a good decade on Marathon and had spent most of his career as a detective. Marathon noted that he wore the same version of his tan colored suit throughout the week. Men were typically allowed to wear the same colors over and over again without much scrutiny. She wondered how many tan suits he had sitting in his closet.

"Detective," Morales said. "I also wanted to touch base with you before you left."

"Oh, okay," Marathon said.

He then motioned her away from the exit as a steady stream of officers came and went signaling a Friday evening shift change. Marathon interpreted the gesture as being an off the record conversation.

"Listen, kid," Detective Morales stared. "We wanna make this transition as smooth as possible."

"Yeah, I know," Marathon replied not knowing where this was going.

"Good," Detective Morales said. "You know, you're replacing someone who was well liked here. And when he retired, his partner also left."

"Yeah, I had a chance to speak with him before he retired," Marathon said.

"Oh, good," Detective Morales stated. "Did Inspector Davidson set that up?"

Marathon studied his face, she sensed that there was some politics driving the conversation. She didn't know how to answer the question so she simply nodded stating the truth. Frank Davidson had arranged for Marathon to meet with the retiring detective before everything was made official. Detective Morales should have known about this. Maybe this was the source of his concern. Things were happening in his department and he wasn't directly involved in the decision making process. Marathon knew Frank sometimes had breakdowns in communication. He would get this idea in his head and run with it. Sometimes key players were left out of the loop and it made things worse in the long run.

"Hey, listen, I'll be sure to include you in things," Marathon said as she sensed he was not pleased about how things went down.

"Yeah, it's not your fault, sometimes I would just like a consult on things that happen in my department," he said.

"I get it, I really do," Marathon said. She also sensed that he was well aware of her relationship with Frank Davidson, and how her career started under his leadership over in the 75th when he was Captain.

"I know it was not on purpose or anything. Inspector Davidson has the right intentions, but sometimes he neglects to include the people that need to know," Detective Morales said.

"I'll be sure to include the people that need to know," Marathon said.

"Great, I can see we'll get along great then," Detective Morales responded.

"I'm gonna be late," Marathon said as she motioned towards the door.

"Oh, yes, have a great weekend Detective Torres," he said.

M

Chapter
Three

"I can't believe you're actually going through with this," Marathon said as she sat down next to John with a set of freshly poured drafts. They touched glasses and each took long sips.

"It's time, kid. You'll know it when you get there," John Stroman said.

"How are things with Nancy?" Mara asked.

"I think they will get better, but only time will tell," he responded. He never liked discussing his relationship with his estranged wife.

Frank Davidson came over and sat down next to them. He clearly had too many and was on the verge of having another when the waitress came over. Mara gave her a glance and she knew he was now cut off.

"You gotta slow down, your shift starts in a few hours" Mara stated.

"This guy here, he's a cop, he knows how we used to do this in the old days," Frank said slurring his speech and ignoring Mara's statement as if he had never heard her.

"Those days are long gone," John said after he took another sip.

"So, I hear you plan on working in a bar after retirement," Frank stated.

"Yeah, well, I figured if I don't keep myself busy, Nancy will go forward with those divorce papers," he said.

"You know, men who retire, men of your age that is, if they don't keep busy, their mind starts to rot away," Mara said as her speech started to slur as well.

"Don't you fucking worry about that," Frank said. "This boy ain't got anything to rot away."

The three of them started chuckling as if Frank were a stand-up comedian. Their drunken laugh echoed the tiny Irish pub as each glance given to each other set off a new string of bellowing laughter. Some of the after-retirement party guests had filed their way into the establishment to wish John one last farewell before he turned his badge in the next day.

Mara secretly planned this evening out carefully. John was technically not on duty the next day because he was using his remaining vacation time. All he had to do was turn in his badge, so the plan was to keep him out until the commanding officer of the 75th precinct showed up the next morning, and she would get him over there all plastered to formally retire.

After the laughter had calmed down, John held his glass up to thank all of his friends who had stuck with him. He said a few misarticulate words that ultimately made sense and Mara ordered another round for everyone, making sure Frank received something less potent.

Frank then wished everyone farewell and reminded the crowd that his shift started in a few hours when they bashed him for leaving early. Mara took a break from the action to see him out. She used her cell phone as a light to hail a cab in the middle of the empty Manhattan boulevard.

"Do you know who my new partner is going to be?" she brazenly asked Frank Davidson as the cab approached. Being a captain, he could pull a few strings and get her a new partner.

"There are a few cadets coming out of the academy in a few months, I would like you to be their senior officer," he responded.

15

"Now I know you have been drinking too much!" she said in response.

Frank simply stared at her with an are you kidding me kind of look.

"You are fucking serious," she responded thinking she was too young and inexperienced for the role.

"We'll talk more about it as the new cadets get closer to graduation," he said as he got into the cab.

Marathon saw him off and then slowly strolled back into the pub. There were a number of guys still drinking at the bar, one of them was John who had relocated his seat to chat with the cute bar tender whose shirt was three sizes too small. There was an empty seat next to him, so she took advantage of the space and sat down.

John didn't notice her at first, he was occupied by a pair of double ds directly in front of him. Mara caught up to their conversation, but her thoughts slowly drifted away from the seemingly innocent flirting. She was way too inexperienced to train new cadets during their probationary period in the NYPD.

She remembered an assignment in the Marines when she had to train a replacement who just joined their company in the field. A few days before, one of her friends was wounded in a firefight. He suffered some significant injuries and had to be air lifted to Germany bypassing the field hospital in Kabul for immediate surgery. A few days later, his replacement came along, a demolitions specialist. Her commanding officer chose her to train the newbie and get him up to speed on intel and his role in the company. She hated the assignment, all he wanted to do was get in her pants.

Marathon had just earned the unwritten role of being one of the guys in the 75th. The men stopped treating her like a princess, stopped ogling her every move, and saw her as an equal. It took three years to get to that point where she didn't feel sexualized in a man's world. Part of it was thanks to John who shut a lot of it down with the other officers, but a lot of it was how she reacted to being treated differently. Her Marine style approach worked well in the department. Men love to compare the size of their dicks, and it was very intimidating when she revealed a bigger dick than all of them.

"Hey kid," John said.

"What?" Mara responded.

"Have you heard a word I said?"

"You were talking to Double D," she responded.

"I said you need to specialize in something, take a few tests and move up," John said. He loved to provide career advice. This was funny coming from someone who never took a test in his life.

"Why?" she responded.

"When you get to retirement, your pension will thank you," he said.

"Why haven't you moved up?" she asked. "You could have been a captain by now."

"I can't pass a test to save my life, you know that," he responded. "Besides, I train rooks and that floated my pension just enough over the years."

"You haven't trained a rook since me," Mara responded.

"Yeah, I was set after that. Retirement was all planned out," he said.

"So I'm the one who broke the great John Stroman," Mara said with a smile.

"Yeah," he said with a chuckle. "Don't get cocky."

Double D came back over to check on John and gave a jealous look towards Mara. What the fuck? She hated the subtle threats other women sent her way. She wanted to respond, but she wasn't drunk enough to start a fight this early in the morning.

"I think I am done sweetheart," he said to Double D.

"Shall I close out your tab?" she asked.

"Put all of his on mine," Marathon said.

Double D turned and complied with the request.

"I'm serious, I have a few connections I want you to look into," John said.

"What does that mean?" she asked.

17

"Specialists, they're recruiting. Could use a cop with your expertise," he said.

"Expertise?"

"You're cool under pressure and your reliable," he said.

"Okay," she responded.

"They need people they can trust," he said. "You're also a heck of a shot."

"Are they SWAT?" Mara asked.

"Something like that," he responded.

"Ugh, you're always so vague," Marathon said. Double D came back and put a slip of paper in front of her to sign. Mara checked the balance over and determined the price to be fair. She signed the credit card statement and left a generous tip.

"For someone who keeps to himself, you sure have a lot of connections," Mara responded.

"When you get to my age, kid, you'll see," he responded.

"Frank gave me an assignment already," Mara stated.

"Mine's better, but you might be able to do both. Just hit them up," he said.

John wrote a number down on a napkin and passed it over to her. "Call this number and ask for Dan," he said.

"I know that name," she said as she stared at the number on the napkin. She also recognized the number.

"Oh, you've met him?" John said. "I don't remember introducing you."

"No, I don't know him through you," she said. Mara didn't want to air dirty laundry and get into how she knew him. John turned and looked her over as if he were questioning her with his eyes. He then turned back to his drink after she shrugged him off.

"Well, call him," he said.

"Okay," she said as she stuffed the napkin into her bra under her tank top. Double D behind the bar caught this and sent another dirty look her way. She

18

simply sipped her beer in response. Marathon wasn't going to tell John that she had no intention of making contact with Danny. That relationship ended poorly and she had no desire go backwards.

M

Chapter
Four

Manhattan, New York
Financial District
July 19th, 2019
7:15pm

Marathon got off the 2 line at Fulton Street in Lower Manhattan, the financial center of the world. Typically, these streets would be bustling with foot traffic trying to get to their evening destinations. However, summer weekends in Manhattan saw a mass exodus of the wealthy class that normally inhabited these streets. The mass migration out of the Financial District would start around noon, when wealthy CEOs and business executives would charter helicopters to the Hamptons out on the south shore of Long Island. The rest of the business class would slowly start their journey out once their bosses left the city. Mara's apartment was just north of the Financial District and she appreciated the lack of foot traffic on her commute home during the summer months.

Mara's multiracial background gave the appearance she needed to fit into most neighborhoods, but her looks made her stand out regardless. She walked like a cop, talked like a cop, but she did not look like a cop. No matter how she dressed, acted, or presented herself, her looks dominated the presentation. The attention she got usually was for the wrong reasons, as her therapist had pointed out on numerous occasions.

Recently, people would often compare her looks to the Congresswoman, Alexandria Ocasio-Cortez. The comparison was uncanny, and she definitely saw the connection, especially when she smiled. Deep down she didn't mind the comparison, AOC was nine years younger, very pretty and very successful. However, Mara's dating life drastically changed during that election season in 2018 when AOC took congress by storm. Her Tinder profile exploded to the point where she needed to delete the app completely. For some reason, after a few dates, the extreme right-wing republican mentality surfaced in the men she dated and it was painfully obvious they had this strange obsession with her resemblance to Alexandria Ocasio-Cortez.

During a political event, back when Marathon was still on patrol, she had met Alexandria briefly and they two shared a laugh when AOC asked if she would be her body double. The congresswoman also jokingly asked if her life drastically changed because of the political climate. A few days after the event, Mara had received a bouquet of flowers from the congresswoman thanking her for her service that day and apologizing for all the publicity.

As Marathon walked towards her destination, a text popped up on her cell phone from a former colleague at the 75th. He had arranged this little get together to celebrate Mara's promotion to detective. He was asking for her estimated time of arrival, clearly they had something planned for her.

She enjoyed going to John Street bar. It was cop friendly now that John was in charge. It was also a home away from home that dated back to her early 20's when she attended college and had some roommates in the area. Before enlisting in the Marines after 9/11, she would find herself down at John Street Bar using her fake ID to land drinks. John Street was on the fringe of Wall Street but did not cater to the Wall Street crowd. Located in the basement of a laundromat, John Street Bar had little curb side appeal that big shot businessmen needed to massage a deal or get laid.

She replied, "omw" which auto corrected to "On my way!" and sent the message. Mara shook her head in disgust as her phone seemingly knew that she needed correction. She shoved her cell phone away in her suit jacket and turned

21

the corner onto William Street. Marathon caught a glimpse of her reflection in a car window and paused to check her appearance. Her long black hair was down, the way she liked it, and her business suit gave off a very specific vibe that she sort of liked.

Marathon realized she was way overdressed and the cops in the bar would bust her balls all night and then try to take her home. For some odd reason, men thought that insulting women and making lude remarks would increase their chances of getting laid. The crowd Marathon was meeting were long time colleagues, so she knew how to manage them and their remarks. A few of them, also knew how to manage her in return. There's a reason why cops are known for cheating on their wives.

Mara arrived at the bar and navigated the wide staircase with ease in her one-inch heels. She hated wearing them, especially while commuting. She made a mental note to leave her heels at work in her locker and commute with her sneakers instead. Standing at 5'10", she was tall enough without them.

The bouncer seated outside the door leading to the basement bar recognized her and held the door open for her as she entered. She gave him a quick hug and peck on the cheek. The old bouncer was always kind to her, he would often call her a cab and sit to keep her company as she waited outside for the ride home.

Marathon wasn't sure what to expect as she crossed the threshold into the establishment. Things appeared normal, but not one person looked her way as she entered; she knew something was up. A girl, any girl for that matter, who walked into this bar would receive attention.

The bar itself was dimly lit and took up a quarter of the main area. There was table seating, a pool table, a dart board, and an aging jukebox in the back where a few patrons were drowning themselves after a long hot work week. Marathon recognized her co-workers and started to make her way towards them. The place then became eerily silent as the everyone in the bar turned towards her like she was a celebrity. With one loud voice, the entire bar erupted with "Congratulations Detective Torres!"

The unified sound startled her and the applause afterwards broke the decibel warning on her watch. Mara gave an awkward, I'm going to kill you smile towards her co-workers and hastened her pace towards them. Out of the corner of her eye she caught John Stroman clapping behind the bar. Her first partner at the 75th, and now retired police officer was eating this moment up. He probably planned this and got the locals involved as well. Bartenders have a lot of power in establishments like this. They could get anyone to do just about anything for a free round of drinks.

Her former colleagues at the 75th precinct each embraced her as they said their hellos and individual congratulations. The inevitable ball-busting began with the comments on her attire. Mara knew that if she were in the business world, her suit would have been considered more casual, but appropriate for a Friday evening get together. Here, with a room full of cops, Mara was treated like her shit didn't stink and was openly mocked with exaggerated impressions of her status. This, of course, was all done in a playful manner amongst friends. She simply took it all in and enjoyed the roasting. It was a rite of passage that separated their profession from others.

After some lengthy greetings, Mara needed a drink. She excused herself to the bar and found John serving a beer to a local patron Mara recognized but never interacted with. This is what John loved doing, his malicious smile confirmed that he had a heavy hand in what had just transpired. John was the behind the scenes type, who liked controlling things without getting directly involved in any overhead. He ran the bar, successfully, but had no financial stake in the business. He came in after retirement, ran the day to day operations at the bar and was paid handsomely for his work while the owner didn't have to worry about anything. It was the perfect retirement gig and it kept him active and out of Nancy's hair.

23

John still looked young for his age. He was always stocky and wore his weight well. His thinning white hair was neatly combed back and his service tattoos were proudly displayed on his forearm.

"Hey Torres," said John as he instinctively poured her a whiskey on the rocks.

"Hey John," she said taking a seat at the stool opposite him.

"I hear congratulations are in order?" He jokingly stated.

"Yeah, I finally made something of myself," she said in response.

John placed the drink in front of her and motioned that this one was on the house. He then poured himself water and motioned to click glasses. Mara grabbed her whiskey and followed suit. She took a sip and then placed the drink in front of her. The familiar taste of alcohol hit the spot.

"How was your first week on the job?" John asked as he poured himself some more water. John was a patrol officer his entire career who now spent his days and nights gossiping at a bar and serving drinks to former colleagues and local patrons who wanted to drown their sorrows. Ever since he retired, Marathon had a sense that he missed the job.

"Did you orchestrate this?" Mara asked ignoring his question.

"What? You think I did this? No," he said then paused. "Well, yes, maybe," he continued. "I mean, it was easy. You mention your name around here and people listen. Shit I could get anyone in here to do almost anything for you."

Marathon smirked knowing that John could probably get anyone to do anything he asked, but not because he mentioned her name. John had this way about him, when he spoke, people listened. His baritone voice and horseshoe style moustache commanded attention. Mara always questioned why John didn't ascend the ranks in the department. He had this air of leadership around him that would have made a great commanding officer. Instead, he retired never seeking promotion. Maybe it was his bad back, or bum knee, she couldn't quite figure out why John never aspired for anything more than a patrol officer.

24

As Marathon made small talk with John, her friends started to arrive at the bar seeking more alcohol. They each greeted her with more congratulations as if they forgot they had already sent their blessing when they embraced her entrance. Marathon remained at the bar and after a few drinks she started to feel the effect kicking in.

"John, can I get a burger and fries," she asked.

"Really?" he said with a confused look on his face.

"Yeah, John, I do eat you know," she said as he took her order.

"You've been here for years and you have only ordered the grilled chicken and a salad," he stated as he plugged the burger and fries into the computer system with his large beefy fingers. The space on the touch screen seemed to collapse with the weight of each press. Mara smirked at the sight.

"Careful, you don't want to put a hole through the screen," Mara jokingly said as John struggled with the interface.

"Go, on, laugh it up. These damn screens. Oh, this will make life easier they said, this will make things faster," John annoyingly stated has each press on the screen agitated him more. "You know how easy it is to yell to the back?"

"People want to eat and drink in peace," she responded.

"This stupid thing wants to know if you want cheese," he stated.

"Sure why not," Mara responded.

"What the fuck is this? It now wants to know what kind of cheese you want," he said.

"American," Mara said as she tried to contain her laughter.

"Every time I enter a part of the order, it wants me to confirm, yes I want to fucking confirm," he stated. "Fucking American Cheese."

His fingers clumsily finished the order as he looked bewildered at the machine. He then looked at Mara with a confused look on his face.

"I think I fucking cancelled the order," he said. Just then a receipt printed out from behind the bar.

"Wait, I think it worked," he said as his eyes squinted to read the receipt. "you can never tell with these damn machines."

"Thanks John," Marathon said as she took another sip of her third whiskey.

"So what's the deal Torres?" He asked still focused on her choice of food on the receipt.

"Comfort food I guess," she responded wanting to drop the subject.

"Well, we've all had those days. I could usually tell when something is wrong. Most of the time you're out there mingling with your colleagues."

"You keeping tabs?" She glanced at him as he had a concerned look on his face.

"That's my job."

The bar seemed to grow quiet as if only the two of them were in the crowded bar. She could sense that John knew something was bothering her. He was a very smart cop and would have made a fine detective if he ever applied. In fact, it was John's suggestion that initially set her on the path to apply for the promotion.

"You can do this kid," John said leaning forward.

The picture of Marley Williams still rested in her suit jacket pocket. It's weight seemed to grow as the evening went on. Marathon knew this was a celebration, but there was nothing to celebrate with Marley's picture inches from her heart.

Mara liked completion and when she noticed just how many cases had gone unsolved, she started to worry about her ability to do the job. If seasoned veterans couldn't solve these cases, how should she? That worried her immensely. The number of unsolved cases that got tossed were statistics the public never saw, they were often buried under mountains of data hidden in more data when it was time to go public.

She glanced back up at him with her drink touching her lips and smiled. She knew she could do the job, but that was not the issue. This past week was an adjustment for sure and the weight of the position took its initial toll on her, but finding Marley Williams' case file, or what was left of it, was the issue.

"You wanna tell me about it?" John finally said to break the silence as both of them stared at their drinks.

"Why didn't you take the test?" She responded with a question.

"Ahh, you are getting the hang of the job already," John replied. "I never took the test because it wasn't a test I needed to take. Listen, kid, this job does a number on you. Men…"

"Men," Mara interrupted with a smile on her face.

"I mean, you know, people of the force," John stated trying to correct himself with an awkward pause in his advice.

"Oh John, you always fall for it, but yes, I do know what this job does."

"Of course you do, I am not in the presence of a rook anymore," John stated and then paused. He looked at her as if he were deep in thought. "You've been on the force for, what, sixteen years now?"

"Fourteen, but who's counting anyway?"

"Six more until retirement," John had to state the obvious next phrase that went along with the number of years on the force.

"I'm glad you can still do the math John," Mara replied looking at him.

He was much younger when they first met and she wondered where the time went. John was her first partner and senior officer. He was already eligible for retirement when she had met him. He truly loved what he was doing and training rookies made him feel invigorated. As their partnership grew, so did their friendship. Mara would often be invited over for dinner or to other family events. She became close with John's wife Nancy and their kids.

"Mara, so what's really bothering you?" John knew her all too well.

"John, remember that morning on patrol during my first year on the force," there was a pause in her voice as if she was summoning the strength to continue. "The one with the kid found in the dumpster?"

27

"How could I forget? Marley Williams, seventeen-years old found in the dumpster over by the tracks behind the bodega," John recalled, looking down at his drink. "Right smack middle of our patrol."

"Well, I found that file in the 73rd," Mara said as she emptied her glass.

John reached behind him, grabbed a bottle of whiskey, another glass and poured the remaining contents for both of them. Mara waved off the ice and took another sip. The cook in the back emerged with the burger Mara had ordered.

"There's a memory that should stay buried Mara," John stated as he stole a fry from her plate.

"It's a cold case without the proper identifying tags and it's sitting in a filing cabinet with no one assigned to it," Mara said looking at her drink as if it were calling back to her. "I was shocked to find it in the cold case files of the 73rd, wasn't this case originally assigned to our precinct?"

"The crime was committed between precinct boundaries by the train. I remember the 75th originally took the case and I was questioned by detectives about what we had found. I don't know much about what happened next," John stated as he looked off into the distance.

"I remember, I had an appointment with Detective Jacobs and then it was suddenly cancelled when I showed up for the appointment. He said that it was not his case anymore and that I would be contacted by a different detective. Well that never happened," Mara recalled as she continued sipping her drink.

"I had done some digging for us, remember? Found out that the case was transferred to the 73rd and that detectives over there had a lead on the case. That was that and it was out of our hands," John stated as if he were trying to remember more details. Mara did not recall John talking much about this case back then.

"I plugged the case number into the computer, and nothing came up. It was like the case never existed. I searched for the date, searched the names, searched our names as officers on scene. Nothing," Mara stated. "It's like the murder never happened, like Marley Williams never existed."

"I suggest that you leave that case alone Mara. Let's start your career off right and gets some wins under your belt," John suggested. "The case file was probably transferred back to the 75th and buried in their cold case files. Back then, we were still using a DOS based filing system that clerical needed to manually enter file information. It was probably never filed properly, or it never transferred to the new system," He added.

Mara thought John was right. When she first started in the 75th, she was shocked by how old and outdated their filing system was. The archaic computer system got a recent update when the DOS system became web-based through the departments intranet, but it was still DOS based. All they did was move the system online without actually updating anything. With the major update, there was many instances were data in the system spontaneously became corrupt from the migration.

This meant a clerical secretary was still needed to manually enter in each case from the physical file as a form of redundancy. MS DOS had limited memory and storage, a code system was used to categorize data for reporting statistics, good clerical secretaries memorized the code system and used the platform with ease. Without an expert who knew the system well, someone would never find any relevant information on a case file. She suspected that was done by design. The NYPD kept their numbers close and away from prying eyes. Brass also wanted to keep data from uniformed officers so the precinct's message to the community remained intact.

Marathon agreed that a case like this and her connection to it was not a good way to start off her career as a detective. Yet, the image of the teenage girl tossed out as if she were trash was still in her suit pocket. She wanted justice for Marley fourteen-years ago and tried to be as helpful as possible in the early days of the investigation. Today, those feelings resurfaced like a runaway freight train bent on destroying anything in its path.

29

Mara's thoughts were interrupted by a former colleague as he sat next to her at the bar. John used this moment to excuse himself and actually go back to tend to his bar.

"Hey Mara, you looked like you could use some rescuing. John talking your ear off again?" Jason was clearly intoxicated, and his speech slurred as he tried to engage in conversation.

"John and I were just catching up," Mara said in response and tried to keep this conversation as brief as possible. She knew how Jason got when he was drunk. Marathon had made the mistake of going out with him after hours a few times. He was a good officer and a gentleman on the job. This changed with a few drinks and his feelings for her became less than pure.

"You two don't need to catch up, come join us for a round of pool," Jason said as he led her by the arm away from the bar. As they left the bar area, Mara swiped away his guiding hand from her ass and put some distance between them as they joined the rest of her colleagues. She tried addressing the status of their relationship numerous times, but he never really understood boundaries, maybe a knee to the groin would fix that next time.

In Johns Street Bar, time moves at a different pace and before long only a few patrons remained. Jason tried to steal Mara away from the larger crowd they were with. Mara guessed at his obvious intentions and resisted his advances. He was drunk, she was not in the mood and wanted to end the night alone regardless of who was pursuing her. Jason clearly wasn't on the same wavelength and took their past obscure relationship as an invitation for more.

Marathon wasn't uncomfortable, she was used to this type of interaction with her drunk male colleagues. This was a common theme throughout her career in the Marines and in the NYPD. In the past, she would get close with her colleagues and it would often lead to something she would either have to address or let happen naturally. The parameters of her relations were often undefined and considered them to be situationships, at least that is what her therapist called them.

Upon recent reflection, Marathon realized she needed a change. Her free spirit attitude towards men and relationships were going to conflict with her recent promotion. She also felt that chapter of her life needed to close, it probably should have years ago. After her career in the Marines, she went on a binge. Not with just recreational drugs and alcohol, but with men and needing physical connection. Therapy has been a key staple in her life after the Marines. Something Uncle Dave, her surrogate father, pushed her towards when she came back home.

While Jason used the bathroom, Mara took advantage of his absence and said her goodbyes as the bouncer hailed a car service to take her home. Avoiding him would quell any temptation she might have about going back to her old ways. The remaining officers at the bar wished her well and asked her to remain in touch. With her pleasantries out of the way, Marathon made her way to the bar and John walked her out to the street level, relieving the bouncer who usually accompanied her.

"You look like you want my opinion," he said as they stood waiting for her car service to show up. She would normally walk to her apartment, but John had already called for the ride.

"I always welcome it," she said.

"Forget about the Williams case," he said.

"How? It's haunted us for years."

"Compartmentalize it, box it up, lock it up, whatever you need to do," he said.

"Is that what you've done?"

"It's what I do," he said.

"Yeah, it's hard for me to do that," she said.

"I know, that's why I'm telling you it needs to be done now," he said. She saw a car turn down John Street towards them.

"All those years ago we agreed to bury that case, remember," he stated.

31

"Yeah, how could I forget," she said. "You took me to a bar, got me wasted, and told me to forget about what we had seen."

"It was for your own good," he said. "We can't let these things destroy us. You see shit every day, and now that you're a detective, you're gonna see even more shit."

"So, what I am supposed to do? Just burry it? Just forget that people do fucked up shit all the time and get away with it?"

"You can't save the world kid," he said. "You should know that by now."

"I'm not out to save the world," she snapped back. She didn't like when John referred to her as Captain America, especially when he implied it.

"I'm out to make the world a better place," she concluded.

"Yeah well, what's the difference?" he questioned.

Her ride slowly rolled up and Mara confirmed it was the driver on her phone. She opened the back door and looked at John.

"Goodnight John," she said. "Thanks for the drinks, and the advice."

"You got it kid, get home safe," he said as he closed the door. Mara saw him walk back downstairs as the driver confirmed her address.

M

Chapter
Five

The next morning, Marathon woke with a sharp hangover. If she had just kept drinking whiskey, she would have been fine, but after Jason dragged her off, beer started flowing and the night turned in a much different direction. She sat up in bed and noticed she was wearing the same clothes. Her hair smelled like sweat, beer and oily bar food. There was a nasty ketchup stain on her now wrinkled suit pants. Her decision to go home alone was very satisfying and even empowering, something she wasn't accustomed to.

Jason was a nice enough guy; their past situations were clearly not defined and there were zero expectations. Yet, Mara felt more liberated now than when she used to rebel against her Uncle's wishes. Her phone displayed numerous missed texts from him. She deleted them without reading any of his drunken booty call messages. She had power to say no to something she would have wanted in the past.

The aroma of the automatic single serve coffee machine starting its daily brew reinforced her wise decision. She was extremely thankful for her normal morning routine, which included setting up the coffee machine for the next day.

Marathon got out of bed, undressed and started the shower. She thought about burning her clothes as she brushed her teeth. Her reflection in the bathroom mirror became hazy as the steam from the shower started to fill the small room.

She looked herself over and noticed a few wrinkles under her eyes, a heavy night of drinking brought out her age. She let the mirror completely fog over and then spit the toothpaste out and got in the hot shower. She stood there for a while and time seemed to move at a different pace as she let the hot water roll off her back. The sensation of steamy pressurized water felt like a massage, something she desperately needed.

After her long hot shower, Mara liked to air dry. One of the luxuries of now living alone was walking around her apartment naked. A number of years ago, she had read that air drying was healthy, so she adopted it when she could. Her long slender body and shoulder length jet black hair wouldn't take long to dry in the mid July heat. She didn't like to use the air conditioner, even when it was humid out.

She was about to throw her suit into the hamper, then realized what she had stowed in her suit pocket. She fumbled through the jacket to retrieve the picture, keeping it face down to avoid an emotional response. She placed the picture on her dresser and threw her suit in the hamper. She would have to get it dry cleaned but realized she didn't have a system for that. She made an on the spot decision to separate clothes out at the laundromat instead of doing that at home. Making an extra trip to do more laundry was completely out of the question.

Marathon made herself Greek yogurt with freshly chopped strawberries for breakfast and sat on the couch to eat and sip her coffee while browsing news articles on her tablet. Just as she finished her last bite, she heard her cell phone ring in the other room. It wasn't her personal ringtone, which meant work was calling. Could it be, her first case? Being a detective meant being on call 24/7; in addition to normal working hours.

"Hello, Officer Torres," She answered sounding professional and forgetting her new title as she answered. Deep down her heart sunk into her chest waiting for the voice on the other side to respond.

"Detective Torres, you are needed at the station. Report directly to Inspector Davidson," the monotone dispatcher stated.

"I'll be right in," Mara replied. She hung up the phone, dressed in her only other suit and finished fixing herself up in the mirror by her front door. She nearly forgot her new detective's shield as she tried to race out of the apartment. She paused breaking her haste to check for the essentials just before she left the apartment building. Keys, check, Glock, check, ID, check, wallet, check and her mental checklist was complete.

On her way into the station, she thought about how weird the conversation with dispatch actually was. Report to Inspector Frank Davidson? Why was she required to report to the Inspector instead of Senior Detective Morales? She was told Morales was the commanding officer in charge of distributing cases. She brushed her thoughts aside as she continued her commute into Brooklyn. She also didn't have a partner yet, unless Frank was going to introduce her to her new partner, which would explain why she needed to see Frank.

Upon arrival at the 73rd, Marathon was greeted by her colleagues as she entered her station. She glanced at her smartwatch which read 10:05. Detective Morales was not at his desk, and the station seemed rather empty for a Saturday morning. Paying no mind, she walked to her desk and glanced to see if the Inspector was in his office. The light was on in his office, but the door was closed, she decided to sit at her desk and sign into her computer. She briefly checked her mail and messages; aside from the congratulation emails, there was nothing important. Her phone then rang at her desk.

"Hello, Officer Torres," She answered, still forgetting her promotion.

"I need you in my office now," Inspector Davidson stated without any formalities. There was concern in his voice and Mara suddenly thought back to her brief conversation with dispatch. Something was up.

"I'll be right there Frank," Mara responded using his first name.

Frank's door was now open and Mara walked right into his office and waited for him to acknowledge her before she sat down. His office had a window behind his desk with a view of the squad cars parked by the station. His desk was messy with seemingly random papers stacked on top of each other and post it notes scattered around him. To his left was a large bulletin board with various criminal mugshots and snapshots of suspected criminals posted on the board. They were arranged with one mugshot on the top and many pictures below. Mara knew each and every one of these faces well. Some of perps were also known in the 75th.

Frank Davidson turned around, finished his brief conversation and hung up the phone. He did not look pleased. Frank had short grey hair parted to the side and a salt and pepper mustache. He wore a tan suit and his badge was hanging out of his front pocket. It looked like he was also called into the station as this was not his normal attire. Being the commanding officer of a precinct meant a more formal white collared shirt uniform. His glasses had dug holes in the sides of his nose as he used his fingers to alleviate the soreness around his eyes. Frank stared at her and then spoke.

"Mara, did you access any case files in the computer system yesterday?" He asked as he motioned to the computer on his desk, he must of forgot the task he had ordered her to do early last week. His computer was on and hot air spewed out the back of the machine. It looked like it had not been serviced in years.

"Yes, you asked me to get familiar with the system while I dead-filed cold cases. I looked at the hard files along with the computer files to cross reference information. Why do you ask?" Marathon responded.

Frank Davidosn hesitated as if he seemed responsible for what he was about to say next. "There are two officers here to question you. They are from special investigations."

"What? Since when was doing my job a matter for special investigations?" Mara annoyingly responded.

"I couldn't get much information out of them, but they had a case flagged that you had accessed. I couldn't see which case it was, and they wouldn't tell me what this was about." Frank stated as he sounded concerned.

Mara knew this was not standard procedure. If there was a problem with her employment, it would have been internal affairs, but this was a completely different department. The Special Investigations office had oversight on many different city agencies. Officers only heard about them if something big happened, something bigger than Internal Affairs.

Thoughts about the missing case file in the computer system popped into her head. Did she accidently do something to that case file? The Marley Williams case? She remembered typing in the case file number and getting the no results response from the computer. She breached protocol by taking a picture home with her, but that picture wasn't attached the case file. She technically did nothing wrong, that case didn't electronically exist. Also, how would anyone know that?

"Did you accidentally delete any files or alter them in anyway?" he continued.

"No, I wouldn't even know how to do that without proper authorization and training," Mara responded knowing the files she had accessed where read only files.

"Listen, you are going to have to meet with them, but I was able to get you a union rep just in case there is blowback. He is waiting for you with the two officers." Frank stated as he motioned her to the door.

"Wait a second," she stated. "Union rep? I did nothing wrong. If I did, that's the job of internal affairs."

"This is different Mara," said Frank in response. "These officers need you for questioning, and to me, that is serious enough to warrant a union rep. They also agreed to have your union rep present and they didn't put up much of a fight over it."

"This makes it seem like they are investigating me!" Mara stated in protest.

"I got the same impression," Frank said in reply to Mara's concerns.

Mara briskly walked out of the office toward the interrogation room where her union rep and special investigators were waiting. She opened the door without knocking stood there waiting for the men to acknowledge her presence.

"Detective Torres, please have a seat," The younger investigator stated and motioned for her to sit, he knew who she was without asking. The older special investigator didn't bother standing while her union rep and younger special investigator stood and greeted themselves. Mara knew this tactic and the tone was set. They definitely suspected her of something.

The older officer looked like Robert Duvall with grey hair set in a semicircle around his shiny dome shaped head. The younger officer had this G.I. Joe appearance and looked like he served. The way he stood when Mara entered the room, reminded her of the Marines. She looked him over carefully, but his long sleeved shirt covered any possible military tattoos that might explain his soldier like appearance.

Marathon glanced at her union rep and sat down at the metal table. She looked up at the camera in the corner of the room. The red light under the camera indicated this wasn't being recorded, but the camera was on and she suspected Frank was in the other room watching the footage.

Mara's union rep leaned over and whispered, "Look at me before answering any questions." Mara nodded and then focused on the two men across from her.

"Detective Torres, yesterday, you accessed cold case file 2006-08-01.110 from your computer station using your login information." The younger officer asked as the older one remained motionless and fixated on Marathon's face.

38

The young officer had dark brown hair, tan skin that looked like he bathed in extra virgin olive oil. His face was angular and proportionate. He looked Israeli or Middle Eastern, she couldn't tell exactly. His hands were folded out in front of him as he looked directly at Mara. He didn't seem distracted by her appearance, like most men were during their first encounter. She would often catch them ogling her or it would be difficult to make eye contact for an extended period of time.

Marathon looked at her union rep and he nodded. She then stated that she had accessed that case with a nod. She knew exactly which case they were referring to. Case files represented the date of incident, August 1st, 2006 was a day she would never forget.

"Why did you access that particular case file?" The younger officer continued.

"I was given…" Mara glanced at her rep and he nodded so she continued "I was given an assignment to familiarize myself with the system, it is a different system and a different precinct from which I am used to. That case was in the pile I had pulled from the drawer to review."

"So out of all the cold case files, you randomly chose that particular file to review? One that you had a connection with so long ago?" The younger officer's line of questioning became more narrowed. They knew more than they were letting on. Mara's union rep interrupted before anyone else could speak.

"Excuse me, but this is well within her line of duty. She is an assigned detective in the 73rd and has complete access to both cold case files and active case files. I don't see where you are going with this line of questioning and by my understanding, Detective Torres has done nothing but do her job," her union rep said. He then stood and motioned for her to stand as well. She hesitated, wanting to find out more, why they were questioning the file. Her union rep kept motioning her to stand, she reluctantly stood up and the officers also stood. They looked at each other and then back at Mara.

Finally the older officer spoke. "I would be very careful in accessing information from the past," he stated in a raspy voice that rattled Mara's core. His piercing tone was guided, like he had a personal stake in what he was investigating.

The older officer looked as if he had dedicated his entire life to his work. He wore an old suit with a loose tie and worn leathered dress shoes. Marathon stared at him closely and noticed his eyes were emotionless and his gaze seemed to look beyond her. Mara immediately knew he meant business.

Before leaving the interrogation room, Mara turned towards the officers and said "That case file, was incomplete. It was missing information, so I tried to access the file electronically. I also accessed many electronic files last week, it's my job."

The officers said nothing in response, and this further confirmed the foul smell that emanated from this case. Mara thought quickly on her feet and gauged the situation in the interrogation room. The officers clearly knew she had accessed the case file, which meant it existed and was somehow being monitored. The case of Marley Williams was much more intricate than she thought. John had warned her about this, but his warning came late with the events from Friday already in motion.

Mara didn't turn her back to them as she exited the interrogation room. Her union rep motioned her to follow him out before she could say anything else. From her past experience with union reps, she knew they didn't like anyone saying anything more than what was needed. No one knows the right to remain silent more than a union rep for the NYPD. Mara paused at the threshold of the door and looked back at the officers.

"You never told me your names," she stated looking right at the older officer.

"I'm Officer Esposito and this is Officer Russo," The younger more polished officer responded. Mara gave them one last glance and checked their visible ID badges to confirm. She then followed her union rep who was intently trying to get her out of the room and he walked down the hall so she would follow.

"What is this about?" she asked as she caught up to him. She glanced back at the interrogation room and the two special investigators walked out and proceeded to leave the station. Mara thought they would want to talk to Frank, but that seemed like it wasn't the case as they proceeded towards the lobby.

"I don't know, but their line of questions shows that you did nothing wrong. I wouldn't worry about it," he stated as he walked away towards the Inspector's office.

Marathon's union rep was a well-known and liked by many officers at the 73rd. She had briefly met him last week when he introduced himself at her desk. He was about her age, stocky like a football player, and shorter than her. Officer Terrence Morgan was also supposed to be off duty, but he was called in to represent her this morning. He was always ready to defend his fellow officers and would go to any lengths to do so. Morgan was in street clothes and probably rushed in at the inspector's request. He wore a light blue polo shirt with light tan khaki pants. His polo shirt was untucked and form fitted his stocky physique.

How could I not worry about it, Mara thought as she slowly followed him to the Inspectors office. Mara had been around long enough to know when something was going down in a station. There was a certain vibe in the air as these situations usually meant someone was in trouble. That vibe did not exist here. Marathon concluded that this was either common place or other officers didn't even know they were in the building. The latter scared her; they were like ghosts.

Mara entered Frank's office and her union rep was already debriefing him about the line of questioning. She was lost in her thoughts and only caught the tail end of their conversation before she came back to reality.

"That's it, they summoned you down here to ask those ridiculous questions?" Frank stated picking up the phone. He quickly dialed a number and waited. "Hello, yes, this is Inspector Davidson from the 73rd. Two of your officers were down here today questioning one of my detectives. It was completely inappropriate and implied wrongdoing without any evidence," Frank paused as he was listening to the person on the other end. His head nodded and then looked confused.

"What do you mean you are not aware of this situation? Your officers just left here. An officer…" Frank was motioning for their names. Mara provided them.

"Officers Esposito and Officer Russo," Frank spewed into the receiver of the phone. He waited for a response.

"What? Those names are not in your system? Then who are they?" Frank questioned.

He continued going back and forth with the person on the other end as Marathon left the office towards the lobby. The officer at the front door greeted her and she asked if two men in suits walked by, he nodded and she left out the front door. Marathon looked around but couldn't see them, she spent the next few minutes looking around the exterior of the station before returning to the lobby unsuccessful.

"Hey, those two officers that came in here," Marathon said turning towards the police officer who greeted visitors who came into the main lobby of the precinct. "Did you check them in?"

"Yeah, they just signed out," he said.

"Did you run their credentials?" Mara asked.

"Sure did," the officer responded turning the monitor towards Marathon so she could see his screen. "An officer Macron Esposito and an officer Anthony Russo from Special Investigations. Entered the building at 8:45am and left at 10:20am."

The two special investigators were not who they said they were. Yet, they had all the proper identification and presented themselves as if they've done this a thousand times before. She returned to the office as Frank hung up the phone.

"Mara, do not speak with anyone about this. I am going to make some calls and find out what the fuck is going on here," Frank stated with heat in his voice.

"Frank, their identification was legit in our system. You know how hard it is to fake that?" Mara asked. Frank nodded and stared down at his desk.

He was old school and it showed when he became heated, his composure was starting to crack. Mara was keen on picking up on the slight changes in mood, even if someone was trying to hide it. Frank was not trying to put on a show, he was genuinely upset and she knew he was trying to instill confidence and promote his ability to lead.

Inspector Frank Davidson was very protective of his officers and his precinct. She knew if something happened, he would keep it inhouse and deal with it himself before sending it off to his commanding officer outside the precinct. She knew he was getting heated. Those officers had infiltrated his building under his watch, and he did their bidding without making any phone calls to confirm their credentials.

Marathon knew this was now personal for him. The more he had time to think about this, the more angry he would get. The two fake special investigators impersonated cops, which was a crime, and somehow gained access to sensitive information, which was also a crime. Yes, Mara thought, Frank was pissed, and a shit storm was coming. She was sure of that.

Frank turned and nodded to Officer Morgan who turned and motioned Mara to follow. "Go home, you are off duty. We'll get to the bottom of this, but for now enjoy the weekend," Morgan stated as he left the office.

She left the station with more questions than answers. On her way to the train station, she felt as if every eye was on her watching every move she made. What the fuck is going on here? Her thoughts raced back to her conversation with John from the night before as a trained barreled into the station like a bull trying to hit a matador.

43

Marathon got on the subway and sat down, this was all about Marley Williams, the seventeen-year-old girl murdered and discarded in a dumpster. She remembered her funeral and her family pleading for answers at the station. As those days turned to weeks, Marley's name became a number, then a file, and then a memory. She became angry and a tear fell from her cheek. She wiped her face and continued on her journey back to the safety of her own apartment.

M

Chapter
Six

Doctor Lee's Office
Manhattan, New York
Lower East Side
July 21st, 2019
10:30am

"Tell me, why the sudden text on Friday?" Dr. Lee asked as Marathon sat down in her usual comfortable chair across from her therapist.

The small office consisted of two seats in the middle of the room separated by a small coffee table. The room had large floor to ceiling windows that took up the entire wall and over looked various rooftops of the surrounding neighborhood. The room felt welcoming and safe with a large bookcase and a free standing globe made of a polished cherry wood.

The first time Mara sat in this chair, she thought she was the captain of her own ship. The nautical themed office certainly helped portray that image, but there was always something more with Dr. Lee. She had this uncanny ability to know what was going on and instead of telling Mara about her problems like she expected, Dr. Lee would lead her towards a self-realization like she was the captain of her own ship.

"I was extremely busy during the week and I forgot that we still needed to schedule this week's appointment," Marathon responded only giving a sliver of truth. Somehow, she suspected Dr. Lee knew something else was bothering her, but like most things, Mara kept her secrets close.

45

"Right, you started your new position," Dr. Lee said. "Congratulations."

"Thank you," Mara responded.

"I can now honestly say, you're my first detective," Dr. Lee said.

Mara smiled and she felt Dr. Lee had set her up for something. She hated showing emotion in front of the clinical psychologist and wanted to prove to herself that she could handle the increased pressure that came with a promotion. If a senior officer found out she was in therapy, her active duty status as a detective would be questioned and she would, in best case scenario, end up with a desk job for the rest of her career. There are strict rules when it comes to a police officer's mental health and their ability to carry a firearm. It was generally an unwritten rule not to mention anything about therapy while on or off the job.

There was an awkward silence in the room and Mara avoided eye contact as Dr. Lee sat there with her legs crossed. She was extremely patient and Marathon knew she could easily outlast her in the quietude of the moment.

"I found something," Mara stated as she shifted uncomfortably in the captain's chair. Dr. Lee brushed her silky black hair behind her ears. The middle aged woman was an expert of drawing information out of her.

"When I was going through cold case files and I found something. I shouldn't have found it. It wasn't even part of an actual file, it was just an evidence folder." Mara said. "With pictures in it."

Mara took a deep breath and retrieved a folded 4x6 picture out of her front pocket and slowly opened it to herself. She looked vacantly at the picture and felt her eyes start to water. She then, with haste, folded it up before her emotions were revealed.

"I had mentioned her name before, Marley Williams," Marathon said.

"Yes, I remember," Dr. Lee reassured her. "She was the young girl you found while on patrol back during your rookie year."

Dr. Lee's face changed ever so slightly. The usual deadpan therapist revealed the gravity of Mara's discovery. Early on, when Marathon was first paired with Dr. Lee, the Marley Williams case was a frequent topic of conversation. As they dug deeper into Mara's subconscious, there was a parallel connection between the trauma she experienced in war and the murdered young lady discarded in a dumpster. Through continued therapy, Marathon was made aware that these experiences even went back as far as her childhood when she felt abandoned by her parents.

A child's mind processes information differently than adults. When a child feels abandoned, they typically don't have enough self-awareness to verbalize their trauma. It manifests in different ways, which happens to spill into adulthood. Mara determined that broken parents led to a broken child, which then led to a broken teen, and thus a broken adult left to continue the circle. She was determined to fix herself before the cycle continued, even if it meant breaking the cycle altogether.

"Yes, just seventeen-years-old I believe" Mara said looking down at her feet. She wanted to curl into a ball and forget.

"What emotion did you feel when you saw that picture?" Dr. Lee asked. Marathon took her time responding.

"Initially, I don't know. It took me a while to register what I was seeing. Almost like I was watching myself. If that makes any sense," Mara said.

"It does," Dr. Lee said. "We often perceive traumatic events in unusual ways. Especially when they are revisited in the manner you are describing."

"I searched the precincts digital file system for the case," Marathon said. "But there was no record of Marley's case anywhere. All I had was a manila envelope and a few pictures, the ones I took when John and I secured the crime scene."

"How did you react?" Dr. Lee asked.

"I don't remember my initial reaction, but I know I left the precinct. It was the end of the day and it was well past quitting time. So I clocked out and left," Marathon said.

"Where did you go?" Dr. Lee asked.

"I met colleagues at a bar," Mara replied. "And no, I didn't take anyone home with me, nor did I go home with anyone. I spent that night alone."

She wanted to answer Dr. Lee's subsequent questions. In the past Mara would routinely follow the fight, flight, fuck routine when faced with traumatic events. She, thankfully left out the last F, feeding, from her source of self-medicating behavior. Unless drinking was considered a form of feeding, which Dr. Lee would probably associate that behavior with, then Marathon consistently nailed the four Fs of response to trauma.

Dr. Lee slightly shifted position signaling she was not ready to respond and left the door open for Marathon to continue. She didn't know what to say, without knowing it at the time, she set herself up for every self-medicating behavior in response to this event. She got out of the precinct, went to a bar where she could either find someone to fight or fuck.

"The after work plans were set way before I found this picture," Mara said in defense. She tried to explain her behavior as if Dr. Lee was judging her. "At least I didn't end up sleeping with anyone."

"Marathon, you just relived a traumatic event and you coped with it," Dr. Lee said as she took out her phone and opened her text messages.

"You had sent me a text late in the day, I assume this is the day you are talking about," Dr. Lee said as she adjusted her glasses. "I bet this text was soon after you made this discovery, and that triggered you to seek support. That's progress."

"Progress?" Mara questioned. "I've been an emotional mess this entire weekend."

"Yet, you texted me for support, went out with colleagues without falling into the pitfalls of before," Dr. Lee said.

"The urges were there," Marathon responded after a few moments of thought.

"The urges will always be there," Dr. Lee said. "Where you honest with me when you said you avoided sexual activity this weekend?"

"Yes," Mara said immediately.

"You made that choice?" Dr. Lee asked. "You weren't seeking sexual gratification and got rejected?"

"I made the choice, and I had an opportunity to engage in sexual activity, if that's what you're asking," Mara said.

"That's what I am talking about," Dr. Lee said. "You made a conscious choice, whereas in the past, you did not. Tell me, did you get drunk?"

"Yes," Marathon answered truthfully.

"Did someone have to carry you home?" Dr. Lee asked.

"No, I took a car service and I was able to get home without assistance," Mara responded.

"You see, progress," Dr. Lee said.

Mara thought for a moment and smirked slightly. She remembered her friendly competition with Isabella many years ago. Who could take home the hottest guy in the bar or who could get the cute guy's number at a party? Not getting laid was now considered progress; how far has she fallen?

M

Chapter
Seven

Monday morning arrived faster than Marathon anticipated. The events from Saturday stained her perception of the 73rd precinct. For the first time as a police officer in the NYPD, she felt like she didn't belong. This feeling reminded her of her second tour of duty over in Afghanistan, right after she received the Navy Cross. Orders changed and her perception of the war changed along with it. Soon after, she was honorably discharged and diagnosed with Post Traumatic Stress Disorder.

She walked into the station, dressed in the suit she wore on Saturday and made her way to her desk. Mara always looked professional and took pride in her appearance, but something about the events that transpired tainted her pride in the job. Wearing the same suit in a week or within days of each other was fashion suicide.

She glanced over at Frank's office, the door was shut, and she could see a few shadowy figures move about in the office. Frank was not the sit-down meeting type and liked to pace around his office. Mara could make out two addition figures inside whose shadows remained still.

She plopped her lunch bag on her desk, checked her watch and sat down. She had fifteen minutes before roll call and morning briefing. Marathon hesitated to access her computer but ultimately turned the machine on knowing it was probably being monitored. She needed to project a perception that everything was normal, at least until she figured out who she was up against. As she typed in her password, she noticed a brown saucy liquid creep under her keyboard. Her lunch bag, which was sitting next to the keyboard, had ruptured sending her Chinese food leftovers spewing out all over the inner contents of the insulated reusable lunch bag that should have been replaced years ago. The sauce had leaked out and escaped between the seams. She cursed under her breath and reached for a napkin inside her desk.

Instead of trying to salvage anything, she tossed the ruined lunch bag into the trash while making a mental note to keep leftovers for dinner and not bring them into work for lunch. She soaked up the greasy liquid with a crumpled napkin that was unequipped to handle the volume. A greasy smear of sauce remained on her desk as she heard someone approach her.

"Hey Detective Torres," Morales said as Mara continued cleaning up her ruined lunch. "I heard what happened this weekend. Frank briefed me and you're going to miss roll call this morning to meet with Frank."

Marathon looked up at him, she could tell he was being polite and considerate. "Thanks for letting me know, should I go see him now?" Marathon replied.

"No, he'll call you. I think he's on a conference call with a council member," Detective Morales said. He then turned and left towards the briefing room.

Marathon felt like she was going to be sent to the principal's office for misbehaving. She saw the crowd gathering outside the briefing room as Detective Morales had made his way over. She noted that he was very popular in the precinct as he greeted every officer along the way. He seemed to get along with everyone.

Out of the corner of her eye, the computer screen flickered, and this drew her full attention back to the screen. For a brief moment, her computer seemed frozen and the inner workings of the machine struggled to remain operational. She finished cleaning the underside of the keyboard using hand sanitizer to get rid of the Chinese food smell.

Normally, she wouldn't have paid any mind to the stuttering computer, but after her experience with Esposito and Russo over the weekend, her suspicions were warranted. Someone knew she accessed a digital file that theoretically didn't exist. This line of thinking led her to the conclusion that the file did exist. Why was it being monitored, and by whom? How were they monitoring it? Regardless of these questions, this is the most information she has had on this case since it was transferred from the 75th many years ago.

Her desk phone rang breaking her train of thought and snapped her back to the real world. Marathon composed herself and kept an eye on the computer screen looking for any more abnormalities as she answered the phone.

"Hello, Detective Torres," Mara answered, this time correctly using her title.

"My office, five minutes," Frank Davidson said and then hung up the phone not giving her time to say anything. He sounded agitated, like when crime numbers started spiking on his watch back when he was in charge of a patrol squad in the 75th.

Usually, Marathon was knee deep in something and five minutes seemed like five seconds, but this time was different. The information Frank had for her was probably about what had transpired over the weekend and she would finally have some answers. Five minutes now seemed like five hours. She glanced over at Frank's office and noticed that the blinds were drawn and that the door was still closed.

Mara got up and decided five minutes was over and started towards the office. Before she reached the door, it opened, and Officer Morgan was standing in the threshold. He noticed Marathon a few feet away and said that Frank was

52

expecting her. They crossed paths and he winked at her as their eyes met. Maybe she was about to receive good news for a change.

Marathon stood at the doorway and Frank motioned her to enter and sit. He was wearing his normal white collared uniform that made his salt and pepper hair look distinguished. He was pacing back and forth clearly still upset from the events that transpired on Saturday. After she had sat down he noticed the door was still open and closed it. He made sure the shades were still drawn and then moved behind his desk.

"Mara, I'm assigning you this case," he stated as he looked at her with fiery eyes.

"The Marley case?" Mara inquired looking back at him, but his expression changed.

"Indirectly," he stated with caution now in his voice. "I am assigning you to the case of the two imposters that impersonated special investigators and infiltrated our precinct."

"I see, I'll find out who they are, but we need to actively investigate the Marley Williams case. They are connected." Mara stated trying to sound confident.

"We will, but this is your starting point," he said.

"I'll get right on it," Marathon stated as she motioned to stand. Frank held his hand up letting her know there was more information.

"Mara, you are the only one I trust to do this," his voice lowered as if he didn't want any recording device to pick up what he was saying.

"What do you mean, Frank?" Marathon questioned him.

"I made a number of phone calls after you left on Saturday," Frank stated and then continued as he leaned in closer. "No one knew what I was speaking of. No one ever heard of these officers and they belong to no immediate agency we know about. I've called them all."

"Frank, they had detailed information about me and had access to the computer system. That is how they knew I had accessed Marley's file," Mara said in a whisper. "I didn't mention this in the interrogation, but I suspect they knew I was involved with the initial case."

"Yes, I'm sure they know that," he said.

"They have access to our system Frank," Mara reminded him. "How they got it, I don't know, but I assure you, that is how they found out."

"There is something else going on here, and it reeks like a coverup. We don't know who Esposito and Russo are. We also don't know what their intentions are," Frank paused for a second as if he was making a point. "But we do know this directly involves you and the Marley Williams case."

"That case died when it was transferred from the 75th to the 73rd," Mara said.

"Do you know anything about the assigned detective when it was transferred?"

"I just know the detective retired a month or two after he received the assignment. Then I lost track of it," Marathon said trying to explain her lack of knowledge on the case.

"It wasn't your job to track it, but I get your connection," Frank empathetically replied. "I think this is the most appropriate course of action. Investigate who Esposito and Russo are. They broke the law by impersonating city investigators and also by hacking into our computer system. We have every legal right to pursue that crime and open an investigation."

"What about Marley Williams? We need to open this up as well!" Mara said in protest.

"That would be a mistake. Until we know what we are dealing with, we will pursue Esposito and Russo," Frank stated as his voice became deeper. "We don't even have a file, Detective. Opening up her case in the system after, what fourteen-years, would send red flags straight over to internal affairs."

"So, we forget about Marley?" Mara snapped.

"Detective, we need to let this one play out a bit. Their interest in you is of great concern to me, and until we know who they are and what agenda they have, we will stick to Esposito and Russo... if that is even their real names," Frank stated.

"Where do you suggest I start?" Marathon asked.

"On Saturday, I ran their license plate from our security cameras and adjacent traffic cameras. The registration belongs to an Anthony Forsythe at 1238 Linden Boulevard," Frank stated handing over the information he had.

"Okay good, we got a lead," Marathon said as she stood up holding the paper Frank had given her.

"Mara..." there was hesitation in Frank's voice. "This case has bad news written all over it. I am having second thoughts about this."

"Frank, I am not," Mara turned toward him and leaned over his desk but didn't get up. "Remember when we first met. You had told me a story about a case that affected your career. The type of case that keeps you up at night?" Frank stared back at Marathon as if he knew where she was going with this.

"Marley is that for me Frank." Marathon said as she stood up straight and turned for the door. "There are times, when I am in between the conscious world and sleep... I see her, laying in the dumpster. Her lifeless eyes open staring back at me."

Frank remained silent and allowed her to continue.

"Even though she doesn't move, she is reaching out to me, begging me to do something."

"Have you seen someone about this?" he responded.

"That's personal business, Frank. I can be removed from the field if I am not mentally fit to perform my duty," she responded.

"It's okay, I see a therapist too," he stated. "This job, it takes a lot out of you. Sometimes it takes everything."

"Someone took her life Frank, and that person is somewhere out there. It is our job, my job, to see this through," she replied.

"At what cost?" Frank replied.

"That's a question for Marley," Marathon said as she turned towards the door to leave.

"Mara, one more thing," The door was open as she was about to exit. "I do not have a partner for you as of yet. It goes against protocol to assign a case to someone without a partner, you should consult with your union rep and possibly file a grievance," he stated as she left the office.

Mara went back to her desk and contemplated Frank's advice. Officer Morgan was not at his desk, she decided to consult with him later and run the license plate number through the system again to get more details on the make and model. The computer kicked in slowly as if it had to wake the hamster up to get the gears moving again. She knew if Esposito and Russo were monitoring her computer, they would see she was on the case. She wanted them to know that; this was a keep your enemies close type of situation.

The search engine gave the make and model of the SUV used by Esposito and Russo but it wasn't registered to them. Instead the 2015 Jeep Patriot was registered to a Dr. Anthony Forsythe of 1238 Linden Boulevard, in Brooklyn. Mara quickly googled the address and noticed it was right down the street by Brookdale Hospital. The address was for an urgent care facility attached to the hospital. She noticed another detail, it was registered as part of Brookdale Hospital as a company vehicle. She read the description of the vehicle and also found it had a GPS system built into it. Marathon jotted down this information on her notepad.

She noticed Officer Terrence Morgan cross her field of view and she quickly finished scribbling the information. She stood and approached Morgan who was now sitting at his desk sipping a cup of coffee from the corner store. Morgan hadn't noticed her approaching, and Mara paused behind him unsure of her actions.

She then remembered her trust in Inspector Davidson and how he would not put her in jeopardy.

"Hey, Morgan, you got a sec?" Marathon asked.

Morgan spun around in his chair as if he was expecting her. "Hey, Detective Torres. Let's talk in private." Morgan got up as if he had prepared for this moment and walked towards an empty room he used for union related issues.

As Officer Morgan entered the dimly lit room, he turned and waited for her holding the door. She entered and Morgan then gave a quick look outside and closed the door. Mara sat at the empty table that looked strangely like the one from interrogation.

The Police Benevolent Association room, commonly known as union only, which also served as a lounge or break room, had various postings on the wall about upcoming union events or announcements. There was a large sign which read, "United We Stand, Divided We Fall" with a union worker holding up a wrench and plenty of backup behind her. Mara loved that poster as it reminded her of democracy and power of the people.

Morgan broke the silence after he took a seat opposite her. "Frank informed me of what's going on."

"You know I am assigned to this case?" Marathon asked making sure they were on the same page.

"Yes, and that you must file a grievance with the union," he stated.

"I'm not sure this course of action will be productive. Do we really want to draw attention to this, and won't that be detrimental to my investigation?" Mara questioned.

"Listen, Marathon, you have to protect yourself here. Filing a grievance with me will force the inspector to make an exception in this case. He will assign me as a temporary partner which will satisfy the union and allow you to investigate. Our department policy is to have two detectives in the field together while on assignment."

"I see," Mara responded. She had never filed a grievance before.

Morgan leaned back in the chair and remained silent. She appreciated the space as she played out the scenarios. She needed to act but wasn't sure about the unintended consequences a decision like this would have. Sometimes, the union makes matters worse and with so many moving parts, Marathon could not predict what was going to happen next. Either way, her honeymoon as a new detective officially ended.

"Why can't he just assign you to me without this grievance bullshit?" Mara asked.

"That's not the way it works," Officer Morgan responded. "The union has to be involved in the decision making process and his hands are tied until we step in to represent you."

Marathon stayed silent and thought about her next response. She didn't like it and she thought it was the wrong move to make. Morgan interrupted the silence and stated, "I already filed the grievance. Frank is in the process of assigning me as your partner to settle the grievance as we speak."

"So I never really had a choice?" she asked.

"Marathon, this is for the best," Morgan said.

"I think we are making a mistake," she responded.

"How so?" Morgan questioned as if he and Frank have thought of every possible outcome.

"We need to keep our cards close and not reveal what we know. I know they are monitoring my computer so I can feed them the information I want to feed them, we shouldn't be airing everything out for them to see. A grievance will do that," Marathon said. "Our internal plans then beyond these walls."

"Frank and I discussed this," Morgan said being dismissive, like a parent speaking with a child. He continued, "We know little facts about who we are dealing with. Their resources are extensive, pulling off a stunt like they did on Saturday took expertise and experience. They would have fooled every precinct in the city with how convincing they appeared and acted. We need to know more and we need for them to show some of their cards."

"This puts the I know, you know that I know, in play," Mara added trying to understand his point of view. She added, "I still don't like it. I am not about to create a standoff between us and whoever has a problem with me. I want to find out what happened to this young girl. She was killed for a reason, and for the first time in over a decade we have an opportunity to find out what that reason is and provide her and her family some justice."

"Marathon, that's what we are trying to do. How can we find justice for Marley your way?" Morgan responded.

"We do it the old-fashioned way, following leads and solid detective work. We certainly don't shoot our load here by exposing ourself completely." Mara argued with authority.

"Listen, what's done is done. You don't know the inner workings of this precinct and Frank told me that there was a lead with the license plate the security cameras provided," Morgan replied trying to change the subject.

Mara knew any further protests would only cause a further divide on this approach. She was new to this role, and she wanted to be a team player in a new precinct. John had taught her when, and when not to make waves. Her heart contrastingly told her she didn't care about station politics.

"Morgan, stop trying to change the subject, you know we have a lead. I'm not happy that I wasn't consulted on this. You can't file a grievance without the person grieving the situation," Marathon stated. She turned to leave the room. She had some choice words for Frank.

"Torres, wait…" Morgan said as he stood up and followed her out of the room. "We are gonna have to tread lightly here. We also have to file the paperwork to protect you and your job."

"What?" Mara responded.

"If you are not assigned a partner, you can't be assigned new cases according to union practices. Frank can get into a lot of trouble," he said.

"Frank should then officially assign me a partner," she responded.

"It's not that easy. You're the odd detective out after Jones left for Midtown. We're waiting for a transfer to come through," he said as Marathon turned and looked back at him.

"Yeah you're right. But, you just put all our cards out there for the world to see. Whoever fucking hacked my computer now knows there's another player in the game to investigate Esposito and Russo, or whoever they are." Mara said as she felt her blood start to boil. She hated cursing at work, and always tried to keep things professional, especially since her promotion.

"Hey, wait a second!" Morgan firmly stated. "The best way to flush out someone out is to force them to react to your next move. It's not like we are going to sit with our thumbs up are asses. We have a lead, and now it's time to put the pressure on and force them to make a move."

Mara stopped halfway to Franks office and turned back towards Morgan. Other officers started to look their way. They must have sensed an argument brewing.

"I really do see your point of view," Mara responded sounding more calm than before, but that was just a façade. "You don't poke a dragon expecting them to not poke back."

"What is that supposed to mean?" Morgan questioned as Marathon got closer.

"It's tough to anticipate their response when we don't know much about them. How can we fucking prepare for what's going to happen next?"

"If we did it your way, you think that these fuckers will show themselves or make a mistake?" Morgan said.

"I don't know, but now we won't have an opportunity to find out," Mara said as she turned towards Franks office and continued her march.

60

Mara reached the office and thought about bursting through unannounced. She hesitated and then knocked. Morgan caught up to her just as Frank welcomed them both in.

"What the fuck Frank?" Mara blurted out just as the door closed behind them.

"Detective," Frank stated trying to shift the conversation more formal. "I get why you are mad, but we had to make a decision fast. Impersonating an officer and infiltrating a precinct are serious crimes. If I didn't assign someone the case immediately, it would have been a major problem for me. The only way I could assign you the case was in this manner. Otherwise you'd be sidelined for not having a partner."

"Next time bring me in on this," Mara stated almost interrupting Frank.

"I figured you'd be more pissed if I assigned this case to someone else," Frank stated. "However, Next time I will bring you in on the decision."

Mara looked at Morgan who was used to being in the middle of arguments and disputes.

"Frank, we have another option here," Morgan chimed in.

"I'm listening," he stated.

"Leave the grievance open," Morgan said.

Mara could see the wheels turning in Franks mind as he turned to look out the window, she shared Franks curiosity.

"Go on," She stated.

"Frank has 30 days to address the grievance and Detective Torres cannot work the case. It shows that she does not want the case without a partner and forces you to assign someone else," Morgan stated.

"That frees her up to work on this through another angle," Frank stated, completing Morgan's suggestion.

"Behind the scenes?" Marathon asked.

"Sort of, you won't be officially assigned, but you'll have access to everything because it is in your department," Frank said. "I'll assign you something light, like dead-filing and that will allow you to work the back end of this case while other detectives work the lead."

"What back end am I working on? The only lead we have is the SUV they used to get here," Mara replied.

"We are missing a case file on Marley Williams. I assign you to dead-file cases, you are free to look for it," Frank said.

"We do need that file," Morgan agreed.

"Okay, fine," Marathon reluctantly said.

"Good, I'll make it official," Frank added.

"This should take the focus off of you for the time being," Morgan said.

"We need a response, otherwise brass is going to be all over this like a shit storm and I don't want them breathing down my neck. When a station is breached like this, people's careers a permanently altered," Frank said. "I am comfortable with this response."

"Alright, I do think this is the best course of action," Marathon stated. "Just include me in on this next time. You know how I get when people make decision that are in my supposed best interest."

"Okay, I will do that," Frank responded.

"Good, we have a plan," Marathon said as she went for the door.

"Mara, don't do anything until I assign the case to someone," Frank said.

Mara turned and took out the scrap of paper she used to copy Dr. Forsythe's information on. "I ran those plates again, it's a company SUV belonging to Brookdale hospital. There's also a GPS system," Mara said.

"GPS?" Morgan questioned as he leaned over to look at the note. "So we can track everywhere it's been," Morgan stated.

"We need a court order for that," Frank said as he reached for the phone. "I'll work on that while you just sit tight and find the rest of Marley's case file. We're gonna need that."

"Yeah, I'll start in the dead-file basement. It might have been incorrectly transferred down there," Marathon said.

"Let me send a uniform over to Brookdale to get a statement and see if we can get eyes on the SUV," Frank said. "Remember you're grieving this Marathon, you agreed, and now you're sidelined for the time being. You only work the cold case file, you got it?"

Frank was always direct in his approach and he certainly meant she was sidelined. She knew this was the best course of action, to follow procedure and address the crime in the station first when Esposito and Russo illegally gained access to sensitive computer files and infiltrated the precinct. She was free to work the back end and was still assigned to the cold case files that haunted her last week. Not the best outcome, but certainly progress. Marathon felt like she was the wild card in this investigation.

Mara turned and left the office to her desk. She hated being sidelined, when she was in high school, she wouldn't settle for anything less than being a starter on her varsity basketball team. Every time she had to exit the game, she couldn't wait to get back in. She thrived off of adversity and competition. Sitting at her desk made her feel powerless, like a lobster sitting in a grocery tank peering out to the world. She decided to start with her former colleagues over at the 75th. Maybe they had the physical file and a simple record transfer would solve that problem quickly.

M

Chapter
Eight

73rd Precinct
July 22nd, 2019
4:30pm

Marathon waited patiently for the uniformed officers to return to the station. Inspector Frank Davidson had sent them out shortly after their meeting with specific instructions. They were gone for a while and she was having a tough time sitting still. Her phone calls to the 75th produced no results and she thought about going down the basement to look for the case file, but she didn't want to miss the officers coming back from their assignment.

She noticed Officer Morgan talking to a few of the rookie beat cops over in the corner after they had finished their foot patrol. They looked like children when compared to the seasoned veterans around them. The rookies stood there as if everything Morgan was saying was either life or death. Maybe it was, but their stary eyed expression made it almost seem like Morgan was talking to children about the rules of the playground.

Brownsville was a tough neighborhood and officers needed to get past their tough guy image to be successful on the streets. While she knew this community, she didn't know why the police in this precinct seemed to have an imaginary wall between them and the people they served. The citizens of Brownsville didn't trust the police. They were viewed as adversaries and only tolerated their involvement when it was absolutely necessary. This was much different than the neighborhood she grew up in.

Mara had yet to judge Officer Terrence Morgan. She liked that he was readily available and that he took his job seriously. Being the union rep in a precinct like the 73rd was nearly a full time job in of itself. Yet, he found the time to do his normal duties and serve the union. He was well liked and respected so there was no reason for Mara to think anything less of the man. Yet, the stunt he pulled earlier without consulting her about a decision she needed to make left a sour taste in her mouth. One that wasn't easily washed away.

After the rookies received their daily dose of advice, Marathon followed Officer Morgan from the comfort of her desk as he made his rounds checking in with his fellow officers. A fist bump usually started the brief conversation as he sipped his coffee and made small talk. She was too far away to eavesdrop on his conversation, but everything appeared to be business as usual. Union leaders constantly had to massage the union rhetoric to convey majority compliance. Officer Morgan was a really solid union leader.

Mara allowed her thoughts to travel back to when she was a beat cop with John. She must have looked like the rookies talking to Officer Morgan. They would patrol the morning commute and check in with business owners along their predetermined path. It was a nice change from her service in Afghanistan. Back in the Marines, she was young, naïve, and ready for action. Based on her service, when she entered the academy, she didn't share the change the world attitude many of her fellow cadets had. War changes everything.

The NYPD offered her a chance to restart her life, or at least distract her feelings enough to become assimilated back into society. During her second tour of duty, her life started to spiral out of control quickly. Initially, she was sent in with her company to liberate the small city of Baghlan, in northern Afghanistan. Once the city was liberated from the Taliban, it turned into an occupy and protect scenario. The Taliban were actively eradicating Shiite Muslims in the city, like the Nazi's did with the Jews.

When the Marines were sent in, the Taliban scattered and ran. They fled into the mountains and the Marines successfully liberated the city from their control. The occasional night raid on the city meant the Taliban were still in the area and Marathon's company received new orders to protect the city. After a few months, orders came down to return the city back to the Afghan government, the slaughter of Shiite Muslims resumed. The very people Mara was assigned to protect were defenseless and there was little she could about it.

Marathon was lucky to get out with an honorable discharge. Her Navy Cross medal played a major role during her insubordination court martial hearing. She was accused of violating direct orders and going AWOL. The prosecuting officer said she left her post and disobeyed direct orders. In Mara's defense, she relied heavily on her act of heroism and how she had a clean record of service. She won her case, but under certain conditions. She had to leave the Marines and accept an honorable discharge with a diagnosis of suffering from post-traumatic stress disorder. The condition was used to explain her actions during the court martial hearing.

Her troubles continued after being honorably discharged. No job, no experience, and lack of motivation created a cocktail for disaster that landed her in trouble with the law and with her family. When society reached out and offered her a helping hand, she wasn't too far gone to realize she should take it and do something with her life.

Marathon was snapped back to reality when she heard her phone vibrate on her desk. She checked the notification and it was from a blocked number with a text message that read "locker 1369." Mara looked around the station, but no one seemed to react or move differently when she scanned the room.

She stood with the phone in her hand staring at the text message, and made her way to the locker room. She continually checked the cellphone screen to see if another message would pop up. The station's locker room was dimly lit and looked like a something a high school football team would use, it also had the same smell. She navigated the narrow path between lockers and scanned their numbers.

Locker 1369 was located in the back corner of the room, away from most foot traffic and the main bulk of used lockers. Each officer was assigned their own personal locker, and the section of 1369 was not currently in use. Mara stood in front of the locker and opened it. There was a note at the bottom of the locker and she discreetly bent over to grab it.

She slipped the note into her fitted suit jacket pocket and not risk reading it out in the open. She discreetly walked back to her desk and sat down. No one seemed to notice or care about her business. Morgan was still making his rounds, detective Morales was at his desk on the computer, and Frank's door was closed. Other officers didn't pay any attention to her as she accessed the note in her pocket and slipped it out on top of her desk. The note had a series of numbers on it that looked like an IP address. Instead of using her computer, she used the internet browser on her phone and typed the numbers in.

A window popped up with a message box front and center. There was nothing else on the blank white screen. She used her finger to click on the box and her keyboard popped up to type.

"Who is this?" she typed out on the screen.

There was a delay and then a short reply. "You know who."

"Esposito?" She replied in the box typing faster than the letters appeared on the screen.

"You've got eyes on you," the next message read.

"What?" Marathon replied.

"You are being watched, be careful," the response read and then the window suddenly closed forcing her internet browser to close. Marathon reopened the window and typed the IP address back into the address bar but nothing came up. The IP address was no longer valid.

Marathon looked around again and everything appeared normal. She sat staring at the note and came to the conclusion that the NYPD was compromised. The purpose of the physical note was to display that they, whoever 'they' are, had physical eyes on her. She knew Esposito and Russo were the ones monitoring her, but Esposito, if it was him, said there was someone else involved. Why was he reaching out like this?

A cold bead of sweat dripped form her forehead down the side of her temple and onto her cheek. Mara felt her heart beating faster as if a drum was banging inside her chest. She looked around and everything still appeared normal. She then noticed the security cameras inside the station. She stared at the one directly opposite her in the corner of the room as if she tried to look at the person monitoring on the other side.

She weighed her options as a response. Mara hated being threatened and she took being watched as a direct threat to her personal safety. She thought about going directly to Frank, but that option was probably not the best course of action. Whoever was monitoring her was probably somewhere on the inside. She didn't want to sound the alarm just yet. She decided to play this out a little more before involving anyone else.

Just as she was weighing her options, the two uniformed officers Frank sent out to Brookdale walked into the station together and made their way towards Franks office. Mara stood and walked towards them and met them at his door.

"Well, what did you find out?" Mara questioned.

The two officers glanced at each other and then back at Mara. She was growing impatient.

"The inspector wants us to report back to him immediately," the older looking officer said. Mara felt him check her out as he made his intensions known.

Mara knocked on Frank's office door for them with an annoyed look on her face and then waited for a response. Both officers and Mara entered when he responded.

68

"Oh, good you two are back," Frank stated as Mara stood by waiting for them to spill the beans.

"Um, sir," the older officer stumbled on his words before Frank threw him a lifeline by introducing the officers to Mara and that she was privileged to the information. Once satisfied, the officers started telling their interaction with the doctor at Brookdale and Mara started mentally profiling him.

Dr. Forsythe, whose name is on the registration, was fairly young, as described by the younger officer. His description led Mara to believe that the doctor was freshly out of med school and probably doing his residency. The officers then spoke of their conversation about the SUV used over the weekend.

Mara would have followed a different line of questioning, but the officers were experienced enough to not lead the doctor to a possible conclusion. Apparently, Dr. Forsythe was in charge of the medical delivery system at the clinic next to Brookdale hospital and registered the Jeep under his name for that purpose. He said that any medical staff at the hospital would have clearance to use the vehicle for professional use in the field. Marathon took particular note when the older officer mentioned wanting to see the vehicle to make sure it wasn't stolen. The doctor didn't have time to show them the Jeep and had an intern walk them out. The Jeep was right where it should have been, there was also no record it was used that weekend.

The younger officer then stated that there were security cameras at the hospital and they focused on the staff parking lot where the Jeep was parked. They didn't have the footage, but Mara knew she could gain access to public video cameras using her credentials as a detective. Being that the cameras outside the hospital were not owned by the establishment, the NYPD had access without a warrant. Frank picked up on this, and nodded for her to follow the lead.

Mara quickly typed in her password before she was able to settle down in the chair at her desk. The other officers who reported back to Frank lagged behind as she navigated the ancient operating system and pulled up the public cameras surrounding the parking lot of Brookdale Hospital. The system couldn't keep up with her commands as she typed in the key information needed to access the cameras surrounding the urgent care clinic. She noticed Frank hovering over her shoulder and Detective Morales standing to his right. She was too involved with her computer to notice him arrive behind her.

After a few seconds the information Mara entered materialized on the screen. She scanned the images and pointed to a Jeep in the top right corner of the video. The two officers who took the doctors statement started to also lean forward in curiosity, they were probably amazed at how fast she was able to access this information. Frank agreed that the jeep was the suspected vehicle.

Mara accessed the date and time of the camera and noticed the Jeep leave the parking lot the morning she was called into the station to meet with Esposito and Russo. She kept the camera rolling even though Frank wanted to see that moment again to focus on the men who entered the car. She could always go back later to confirm what she already knew.

After a few moments, the Jeep appeared back in the parking spot and she saw two men get out of the car. The blurry image showed an older man dressed in a tan suit and a younger man in a grey suit walk from right to left in the field of view. Mara paused the image and studied it closely. It was Esposito and Russo, she was sure of it. She could tell by the way Esposito carried himself. He was tall, well-built and his suit fit his muscular frame perfectly. Mara continued the camera feed as the other men standing around let her follow her instincts.

As Esposito and Russo went off camera, Mara had cued another camera from a different angle that was running in parallel. Both Esposito and Russo appeared on the different camera and Detective Morales pointed them out.

"Those are the clowns that were here on Saturday right?" Detective Morales asked.

"Yeah, this is the time frame after they had questioned me," Mara replied.

70

The security camera revealed the two men getting into an older sedan parked on the street outside the parking lot. Their license plate was partially obstructed by a fire hydrant, but she made a mental image of the partial and opened a second screen and accessed the motor vehicle database. She typed in the approximate year, make and model of the car in real time and then put the partial plate in as well. After a few seconds, the computer revealed the car's registration.

"Government plates?" Frank blurted out questioning what was on the screen. "That can't be right."

Mara looked just as puzzled; she wasn't expecting that. She turned her chair to face the men standing behind her after she paused the camera footage.

"Frank, what does this mean?" she asked.

"Detectives, my office now," Frank said and then thanked the uniformed officers for the diligent work.

Mara again found herself back in Franks office with Detective Morales this time. Frank closed the door behind them and then paced behind his desk. Something was clearly bothering him.

"Frank, what is it?" Mara asked.

"This investigation needs to end here Mara," Frank said breaking the silence as he turned towards her. "I am shutting this down."

"What? You can't do that Frank," Mara said in protest. Frank turned towards Detective Morales, who looked just as shocked as her.

"Detective Morales, I am officially closing this case and you or any detective will not investigate anything related to Esposito or Russo. Anyone caught doing so will be met with disciplinary action. This is a direct order, do I make myself clear?"

"Yes sir," Detective Morales said with a stern voice. Mara looked at her direct supervisor and realized he had also served. The way he responded to the order was a dead giveaway.

"What about the Williams case?" Mara asked. "Are we going to not seek justice for her?"

Frank looked at her with but didn't see her, he was deep in thought and she knew something was bothering him.

"Detective Morales," he said, "You are the lead detective on that case. You are to treat the Marley Williams homicide as an open case on your docket."

"Yes sir," he said again, this time less enthusiastically.

"Detective Torres, I expect you find that missing case file. Your supervisor is going to need that," Frank said. She knew she was still inadvertently involved.

Marathon was stunned by the turn of events and her protest was interrupted when Frank opened the door to escort them out. The door closed behind them leaving Frank alone in his office.

"What the fuck was that about?" Marathon asked.

"It's about minding our own business and forgetting about Esposito and Russo," Detective Morales responded.

"I don't like this," Mara stated. "They are somehow connected to the Williams case."

"You don't have to like it; you just have to drop it. Now go transfer whatever you have on the Williams case to me and we'll meet tomorrow so I can review what you have," Morales stated as he made his way back to his desk.

"Fuck, I don't have anything," she said under her breath, but Detective Morales heard it.

"Frank said to find the missing file, if you want to do anything about the Williams case, I suggest you find it," he said.

Marathon felt defeated. She truly thought she was onto something when she rolled the security footage on her computer with everyone standing around her. She was onto something and now Frank was spooked. She had never seen him act like this. Mara sat back down at her desk and hesitantly closed the security camera footage and then the motor vehicle database. Whoever was monitoring her computer was definitely aware of what was going on. She didn't much care, she wanted them to know, wanted them to make a mistake. Cover ups tend to fall apart when people are forced to repeatedly cover the same thing up.

Marathon felt like she was just played, like a rookie chess player against a grand master, the game was over before it started. Esposito and Russo were probably the ones monitoring her computer. Once government plates materialized on her screen, the case would reach a dead end. Frank probably had hours upon hours of shifting through red tape just to figure out what agency Esposito and Russo worked for. He would never get to the bottom of why they were here.

The question still remained, who killed Marley Williams and it festered like an ailing wound that refused to heal. After all this she was no closer to an answer and now a new question formed in addition. How is the government involved in this? Government plates tied to the Marley Williams case opened a flood gate of questions. She found her fingers typing the name Marley Williams into google. She hesitated and then added the word conspiracy to the search. She didn't care about her computer being monitored, she wanted whoever was out there to know she was not going to let this go.

Various news sources from fourteen years ago popped up on her screen. The google search found many local articles regarding her murder and the subsequent aftermath. Most of them she had read already. According to Google's search algorithm all of them were missing the word conspiracy, but they also hinted at possible gang involvement. A few articles suggested Marley Williams was a gun runner for a gang affiliated for the Bloods. She had heard those rumors before, but like most cases in Brownsville, that rumor was used to almost justify her murder.

When a person of color is killed in the streets, public opinion is easily swayed if that person was even suspected in criminal activity. This is what happened to Marley. An innocent girl, convicted of no crimes, got good grades in

73

school, and played high school basketball, was murdered. The initial reaction was that of tragedy and a demand for justice. But, as the story developed and as the case showed evidence of gang involvement, public opinion shifted, and the news media quickly changed the narrative. Marley Williams was no longer a victim, but portrayed as someone who deserved what happened to her for suspected gang involvement.

Back when this case was still fresh on the docket, Mara got into a fierce debate with a fellow officer who suggested Marley got what she deserved. The white cop belittled her argument and acted like Marley was already found guilty and deserved her death sentence. Marayhon had to remind him that in the United States, people are innocent until proven guilty. He laughed and wrote her off as being a naïve rookie. She continued her argument towards her fellow officer by stating regardless of public opinion, a child's life was lost to an intense act of violence in the area he was sworn to protect. Even with those grim facts, he still justified her death as being her fault, and refused to acknowledge another child's life was lost to the streets.

She turned off her computer in frustration, grabbed her belongings and made her way towards the exit. She saw Morales look over at her, but she was too pissed off to stop and say anything to her commanding officer. He nodded and she felt better knowing Detective Morales was on her side.

M

Chapter Nine

After a long and stressful day at work, Marathon wanted nothing more than to enjoy Chinese food takeout and veg out in front of the television before going to bed. She had serious doubts about her promotion and her ability to do the job as she fumbled with the key to summon the elevator.

Her apartment in the Lower East Side was in an old building with a squeaky elevator that seemed to take its time whenever someone was in a rush. The door to the elevator parted and made its distinct noise that suggested the stairs were always a good alternative. As the elevator ascended to the 4th floor, the overpowering smell of the Chinese food made her stomach growl with anticipation.

She forgot to navigate the strollers stowed in the hallway as she tried to read messages on her phone while holding the greasy bag of take out. Just in the last few months, it seemed more and more families were moving in. Young couples and babies with all the baby gear that went along with it. Someone forgot to tell them that their apartments were too small for all that equipment. The jokes were now on her as she rubbed the mark left by the latest casualty with a random stroller.

John had sent her a few text messages requesting that they touch base. He was never good with technology and only recently learned how to use a smartphone. He used text messages like he was leaving a voicemail. Mara couldn't wait to bust his balls for writing the date and time out in text again.

"Hey Mara, it's John, it's 5:30pm on Thursday, give me a call when you get a chance," The text read.

Mara shook her head knowing how difficult it was for him to use the phone. She fumbled with her keys as she expertly balanced her takeout and cellphone while unlocking her apartment door. The heavy wooden door slammed behind her as she flicked on the kitchen overhead light. She placed the Chinese food on the counter and washed her hands in the sink. The grime from the subway, and all the other various germ-infested surfaces washed down the drain as she dried her hands with a fresh hand towel. She placed her badge and holstered Glock 15 on the counter next to the Chinese food. Mara couldn't be bothered grabbing a plate, and instead reached for her favorite bamboo chopsticks. She sat at the counter using the only barstool and displayed her platter to prepare for the best part of her day.

She used chopsticks to mix the soy sauce in with the chicken fried rice and prepared a massive first bite. She paused for a moment, noticing the picture of Marley Williams on the counter top. She didn't leave it there and she certainly wouldn't have left it propped up like that.

As she stared at the picture her shoulder suddenly jerked forward knocking the food out of her hand. An arm appeared in front of her and she was suddenly yanked backwards off her barstool. A man's hairy forearm dug into her neck as he applied choking pressure from behind her. Mara struggled to get her feet under her as the man's immense strength continued to throw her off balance. She felt his biceps squeeze around her ears and her vision started to narrow. He applied a simple, yet effective choke hold that would render her unconscious unless she fought back.

Gasping for breath, she knew she needed leverage to break the hold. Mara brought her knees up to her chest as the man struggled to support her full weight.

As he leaned forward, she forcefully extended her legs out towards the kitchen counter. The strength of her legs propelled both of them backwards and she felt him loose his balance and his grip weakened enough to resume the flow of oxygen.

Somehow the man remained upright and regained his footing. As he began to reapply pressure, Marathon used her momentum from the thrust backwards to move her hips to the side of his body so she wasn't directly behind him. His grip around her head morphed into a side headlock as she was now in a better position than before.

Mara saw an opening and struck like a coiled rattlesnake. Her forearm traveled up his thigh striking his groin, she repeated the motion until he was forced to react. His grip weakened, but she still couldn't break free. The continued strikes were met with success, but his grip remained firm enough to keep her in place. Before another strike, the man threw her forward causing her fall into the granite countertop. Her head narrowly missed the edge as her chest took the brunt of the impact. Mara spun around in defensive position as her hand instinctively reached for her firearm a few feet away.

Before she could extend her arm, the man was on top of her again. He landed a straight cross punch that connected with her orbital bone. The force sent her backwards onto the countertop causing the Chinese food to splatter everywhere. She used her momentum to fall completely over the counter to create a barrier between them. She stood up right on the opposite side of the counter and again reached for her gun. The man beat her to the location and knocked the gun off the counter.

"They told me you'd fight back," he said. "I like it rough."

Marathon pulled the utensil drawer open from under the counter and pulled out a kitchen knife about the size of her forearm. She held it up and brandished her weapon, showing she knew how to use it. She then saw him reach behind his waist as he brandished a weapon of his own, an M9 military grade handgun. He held it like he knew what he was doing also and motioned for her to put the knife down.

She gave him a reluctant look but dropped the knife on the counter next to her cell phone.

The M9 was held close to his chest and he used it to motion her out from behind the counter. She knew he was trained, if she were to guess, probably by the military or police. Mara kept her hands out in the open and slowly moved away from the counter and out towards the dimly lit living room. The man slowly backed up keeping his distance.

"You don't want to do this," she said.

"Shut the fuck up bitch," he replied. He slowly massaged his groin and Mara knew she had weakened him.

"I'm a detective with the NYPD," she said making her case why this was a bad idea.

"I don't give a fuck," he responded. Mara detected a slight southern accent.

He wore a black wifebeater undershirt and black cargo pants. He was older, she estimated mid-forties by the tone of his leathery white tanned skin. Various redneck tattoos were on full display as he slowly motioned her to step away from the kitchen counter and towards the living room. Mara complied moving slowly but directly towards him. He then motioned her to stop.

"You get any closer I'm gonna pop you one," he said confirming his southern accident.

"Knowingly committing a crime against a police officer adds time to your sentence," she said in response. "It's not too late to give yourself up or leave."

Mara scanned the room looking for any advantage. The couch was a few feet to her left and the television was a few feet to his right with a small coffee table separating the two of them. She knew this wasn't a simple home invasion, she knew he wasn't here to rob her. Something else was going on and she started to piece things together.

"You know the people next door heard the commotion, these walls are thin, I hear their baby cry like they are in the room. I bet they're probably calling the cops right now," she said. "Take what you want and go."

"Ain't no one calling the cops," he responded as he motioned her to turn around. "I know who the fuck you are."

Mara reluctantly complied with the non-verbal gestures to turn around from his M9 and kept her hands out in the open. The man disappeared from her field of view, but his presence flooded her senses. She felt the barrel of the M9 press up against the back of her head as he got closer. Marathon remained frozen, not knowing what his intentions were.

"I'm here to send you a message," he said. "Apparently you can't fucking take a hint. So I'm gonna have to send a different message."

Mara then felt a powerful blow to the back of her head. The force sent her forward face first into the couch. She struggled to remain conscious. Before she could turn back around the man was on top of her pinning her into the couch. The barrel of the gun pressing the back of her head again.

"Don't you fucking move," he said as she felt him grope her body. His body was pressed up against her rear as she remained face down on the couch. She knew what he was planning to do.

"Fuck you," she said in response. She felt another strike from the M9 and her vision went dark for a split second. Her body reacted like she had just touched a live wire and got electrocuted. As the room started to spin, pain from being pistol whipped started to settle. She felt warm blood pool in her hair where the pistol had struck. Marathon heard him fumble with her pants, but she was still recovering from the repeated strikes to mount a response. He was trying to get her belt off, but couldn't hold the gun steady and unbuckle her pants.

The barrel of the gun started moving from side to side and would randomly vacate the back of her head as he continued to fumble with one hand on her belt

79

buckle. His panting and heavy breathing behind her made him sound like a wild animal.

"Get your fucking pants off," he said in between grunts. Mara remained motionless on the couch and feigned unconsciousness.

"Fuck," he said as she felt the barrel of the gun release from the back of her head.

She then heard the distinct sound of metal on wood as he placed the firearm on the engineered wood floor. Her false display of unconsciousness had worked. He was no longer in possession of a firearm and she needed to keep it that way. She felt his hands return to her as he now used both hands to undo her belt. She had moments to decide on a course of action before he violated her. She felt her suit pants release around her waist as he yanked them down. She used that motion as a cue to turn her body into him with the back of her elbow striking him on the bridge of his nose. There was a soft squishy sound that emanated from the impact.

He fell backwards creating just enough space for her to grab the M9 laying on the floor. She picked it up and raised it towards him. She squeezed the trigger, but nothing happened, the trigger remained firm signaling the safety was on. This gave the man enough time to recover and lunge forward at her. Marathon instinctively flipped the safety lever into firing position and squeezed off a round before the man toppled onto her.

She didn't know exactly where she had shot him, but she knew it wasn't enough to stop him. His hands prevented the gun from firing again as he punched her again in the face. She fell back into the couch and felt him try and pry the M9 out of her hand. Knowing she was about to lose control of the firearm, she instinctively hit the clip release on the handle ejecting the remaining rounds in the clip onto the floor. She knew one round was still loaded in the chamber.

Mara kicked the clip away from them as he continued to pry the weapon out of her hand. Her white blouse started to turn red as blood dripped onto her from his bullet wound. She kept her finger in the trigger guard as she lost her grip on the firearm. Her finger bent back in the wrong direction as he tried to use the remaining bullet on her. Her fingers were able to prevent the weapon from discharging in her direction. As the man tried to pull her hand off the gun, she successfully applied enough force to pull the trigger. The single round shot back towards the kitchen shattering her coffee pot on the counter.

Mara knew the neighbors definitely heard the gunshots, which meant the next few minutes would determine her life or death. The man had failed his initial mission, which was probably to scare her and get her to back off. He had failed to rape her and had a bullet hole in his upper shoulder area to show for it. He was running out of options and it came down to one of two choices. He could either leave or try to kill her. He chose the latter and she was ready for a fight.

After the firearm was empty, it became a melee weapon but she didn't really have much of a chance to use it. Mara kicked him off of her and used the coffee table to create distance between them. With both of them now on their feet, he made the first move and charged forward into her using his strength to propel her back into the kitchen. She hit the floor hard and he was back on her quickly throwing strikes down onto her. The ground and pound style he was using was effective as she tried to recover and better her position.

His fists continually slammed down into her as he stood over while she tried to turn his punches into glancing blows. She couldn't last long in this position and she couldn't compete with his strength, so she timed his strikes and maneuvered her body out of the way sending him off balance and his fist crashing down into the wood floor.

Mara heard the deafening thud as his fist buckled from the force. Before she could maneuver her body into a better position, his knee crashed down onto her and she felt his full weight on her chest. Another strike came straight down, but this time she couldn't move out of the way and it struck her cheek bone sending her head backwards into the ground. Before she could assess the damage from the

81

impact, another strike came down from his other arm. This one crashed into the side of her face like a hook punch turning her face in the opposite direction.

She saw blood dripping from his hand, but realized it wasn't hers. His hand, the one that had just struck her, was bleeding from a compound fracture from when he missed and punched for the floor. He stared at the metacarpal bone protruding from his hand as if he were confused by what had happened.

Marathon seized the opportunity and grabbed his wounded hand by the exposed bone. She wanted to inflict as much pain as possible so he would make a mistake. He did, almost immediately, as his knee came off of her chest. She used the opportunity to better her position by wrapping her legs around his waist into a guard position. She kept the pressure on his hand as he tried to squirm and protect his injury.

Mara positioned her body carefully, knowing he was about to fight back. She needed to get him in position to end this fight. Her legs guided his hips into a lower position to take away most of his strength as he started striking her with his other hand. The hammer fist blows were intense, but she was prepared to absorb them, her life depended on it. Mara applied more pressure to the wound on his hand by pulling the fractured bone that stuck out of his skin upwards. He screamed out in agony and sent another hammer fist crashing down onto her. This time she released the broken hand and met the hammer fist on her chest just as it struck. At the same time, she moved her legs up and around his head and expertly interlocked them into a figure four position. He was stuck with one arm straight across her body while his other arm dangled on the outside of her legs trying to push them off of him.

She kept his arm close to her body as he frantically tried to pull it away. His head and his arm were now between her legs as she positioned her leg over the other in a crossing pattern. His other hand was practically useless; Marathon knew she had him and by the look on his face, he knew it as well. She started the slow squeeze with her thighs to get him to slow his movement. The triangle choke, as it's called in the martial arts world, applies pressure from three sides of the neck. It cuts off blood to the brain and oxygen to the lungs.

Back in the military, this choke hold was very effective because it used three points of pressure to render the assailant unconscious; it could even kill the person if held long enough. Two of the pressure points were from the legs wrapped around the victim's head cutting off the two carotid arteries on each side of the neck. The third pressure point came from the person's own arm conveniently placed just under the chin cutting of oxygen. The choke hold worked well when equal pressure was placed on all three points. Once this position was locked in, like it was around the man in her apartment, there was not much the victim could do to get out of the hold.

Her legs and thighs had him locked in place and his bicep was under his chin. With his head between her legs, she got a good look at him and saw he knew what was happening. He was fighting it and she tried applying more pressure. He used his broken hand to try and pry her legs off him. If this hold wasn't going to render him unconscious, it could also be used to subdue him long enough for the authorities to assist her. He was slowing down, but she knew there was more fight left in him. She just needed to hold this position a little while longer.

She tried to reposition his arm to close off the triangle and noticed a tattoo on his inner forearm. The flying eagle holding a sword and shield tattoo was a common Marine symbol and proved he was former military. Mara studied it closer and noticed there were custom alterations to the standard divisionary tattoo Marines got. Before she could study it further, he started shifting his weight, as if he were trying to stand up. Mara knew this was bad and tried to prevent him from standing, but that required her to release the hold. Something she was not comfortable doing. The man's strength again surprised her as she was being lifted off the ground. Mara started punching him in the face as she tried desperately to regain control. Using his broken hand, he grabbed his other arm and used it to pull her up into the air. Before long she was above his head inches from the ceiling.

83

She knew he stood too fast as his eyes rolled into the back of his head. She felt his body go limp into a collapse and she fell down along with him. On the way down her head clipped the edge of the countertop and everything went black.

M

Chapter
Ten

Afghanistan
130 Miles North East of Kabul
March 29th, 2003

Marathon peered out her temporary makeshift pillbox discreetly observing the surrounding area. The pillbox was the first line of defense for their bivouac camp located about a half click further down the path. Sergeant James Jackson was seated with his back to the dirt wall fortification observing her performance while on duty. The two of them had been stuck in their pillbox all day and the intense heat made it hard to focus.

"Jackson, you ready to take over?" Mara asked, not taking her eyes off the perimeter.

Jackson moved and placed his hands around Mara's hip signaling he was moving into position. The two of them traded spots numerous times the past few hours and got quite familiar with each other in this tight space. The surrounding mountainous terrain was littered with Taliban forces itching for a firefight.

Mara withdrew her M4A1 rifle and moved her body backwards while Jackson replaced her position. His rifle then focused on the horizon as he scanned the jagged mountainous terrain surrounding their camp. Mara replaced Jackson in a seated position and reached for her canteen. She sipped the warm water as a slight breeze ruffled their canopy.

"Wish we had more of a breeze," Marathon stated.

"Why? So the enemy can smell us down wind?" Jackson responded.

"You know they smell just as bad as we do. Ain't nobody got a shower out here."

Mara closed her eyes and focused her attention on the breeze before it dissipated and allowed the staunching heat to return. Being on high alert for so long was as mentally draining as it was physical. Mara and Jackson were strategically placed at the foot of the only easily accessible path to their bivouac. Mara, being the lowest on the totem pole, was ordered to stand watch and lookout for Taliban or friendly reinforcements.

Their mission started three days ago, after they left the town of Pukh and traveled north on their assignment. Originally, their orders were to resupply some Army Rangers scouting the terrain. However, their mission quickly changed when they spotted armed Taliban moving through the mountains. After engaging the enemy, they quickly realized they too were on a resupply mission somewhere in the mountains, which meant there were more of them somewhere in the surrounding area.

Fearing their position was now compromised, Sergeant Jackson ordered the platoon to setup defensive positions while waiting for reinforcements. Normally, the Corps would send a few choppers with heavily armed Marines ready to engage the enemy and provide air support. This time was different, there was no air support because that usually sent the Taliban underground making it harder to find them. The Corps was trying a new tactic.

Two days ago, Jackson distributed his orders to fortify up and assigned Mara to this position. He stated that reinforcements were already in the area and were going to link up for a resupply and provide support to hunt the remaining Taliban in region.

Mara wondered why the sudden change in mission parameters, The Army Rangers were still out there and their supplies were running low, but she knew those questions would have to wait. The enemy was close and it was her responsibility to guard her sector and protect the bivouac.

"Sergeant, why are you posted here with me? Shouldn't you be at the bivouac incase new orders come in?" Mara boldly asked breaking the silence.

"The Corporal can handle it," Jackson stated. Mara saw his intense focus stare out towards the horizon. This time of day was extremely challenging as the sun was nearly in line of sight with the horizon before it would disappear behind the mountains.

"You didn't exactly answer my question."

Marathon looked up at Jackson and waited for a reply. His hand suddenly rose signaling that there was movement. Mara grabbed her rifle and slid into defensive position adjacent to the pillbox. She let the dust settle and then used the iron sights to guide her vision. She also saw movement, shadowy figures moved gracefully as they navigated through the mountain path. Mara's field of view included part of the pillbox where Jackson remained. They had rehearsed this very scenario until Jackson stated that he was satisfied with Mara's response and actions.

She only caught glimpses of the figures moving towards them as they dipped in and out of cover from the rocks around them. She counted two distinct figures, but it was hard to tell if there were more. Jackson kept signaling her from the pillbox as he also counted two figures. A few cracks of static came over the radio, this served a signal to the company that they were about to receive friendlies. The static served as a simple message, don't shoot, we're on your side.

The two shadow figures moved at a steady pace, their weapons were at the ready and Mara remained focused on the lead figure and kept him in her sights just in case the static radio was accidental. Just then, Mara felt a presence behind her. She hesitated and looked around trying to get Jackson's attention.

"Hey looky what we have here," shouted someone behind her breaking the eerie silence.

Mara turned and looked up at a man standing over her with a devilish grin on his face. He looked like a grease monkey smeared in oily dirt as the last ditch of daylight glistened off his body.

"Damn, girl, what's-a fine young lady with a booty like that doing all the way out here?"

Mara recognized the accent and knew mission critical arrived for their resupply. She was not amused by the man's appetizing gaze. She quickly got to her feet as the two shadowy men revealed themselves. Sergeant Jackson introduced himself and started leading them back towards the bivouac.

"Corporal, come in, over," Jackson barked holding his radio close.

"This is Corporal, over."

"Send a replacement to join Private Torres in the pillbox, over."

"Affirmative."

Jackson gave Mara a glance and started to escort the men back to their camp. Mara felt uneasy as the man that surprised her offered to keep her company until her backup arrived.

"No, thank you, I can handle it,"

"I'm sure you can handle it, but I wouldn't want you to get lonely out here," the man stated as he got eerily close to her.

He looked rough and dirty like he spent a week working on a farm in hot and humid weather; he smelled the part as well. His plain clothes showed no signs of military affiliation, like he were under cover. She didn't know much about his unit, but she knew they were the real deal, and not the Army Rangers they were originally sent to resupply. These were the ones who pulled your ass out of intense situations. She would later learn that this particular unit was responsible for the most confirmed kills during the war in Afghanistan.

Mara pondered her interaction with the man and decided to play it safe. Men like this, especially in the armed forces, didn't take rejection well. They were used to taking what they want when they wanted it.

"How did you sneak up on me, the path you took must have been difficult?"

"We weren't sure if you were the enemy, so my C.O. sent me to get a drop on you," he stated.

"I thought our position was good, we had no idea," Mara responded.

"To be honest," he leaned closer and his repugnant odor nearly caused Marathon to gag. "I spotted you over a mile away. Once I saw such a fine ass Marine, I knew the path was clear."

Mara kept her composure as he stood within inches of her. His presence made her feel uneasy, vulnerable, and weak. Mara backed up and turned towards the pillbox.

"Don't worry ma'am, ain't no one around here," he said as he followed her matching her pace. She could feel his gaze penetrate her body and she tried to give him nothing to promote advancement.

Mara took her position and focused her rifle back towards the perimeter as the man remained behind her. She desperately wanted her backup to report, but she knew he was probably still a few minutes out. Mara couldn't take him ogling her any longer and she turned back towards the man.

"Don't you have to check the equipment, isn't that why you are here?" Mara asked trying to get the man away from her.

"That can be done at any time," he stated squatting down to her level while inching closer to the pillbox. Mara noticed numerous tattoos on his arms as he stowed his rifle on the rocks. Most of them were recognizable and displayed his various tours of duty. It was like a storyboard laid out for anyone to read.

"You started as a Marine," Mara stated trying to control the conversation.

"Yup, just like you darling," he replied. He moved his arms as if he were telling a story that only another service member could read.

"I recognize most of these," Mara stated, "But that one, I can only assume what that is."

89

"Ahhh," the man stated as if he were impressed. "This one is special, it represents my current assignment," the man said as he caressed the flying eagle as if it were real. Mara felt like she was flirting with the man, and immediately refocused herself.

"I see you have your standard Marine tattoo," the man stated pointing towards her exposed forearm. "I would love to do some recon to find more."

Mara knew she needed to choose her next words wisely. This man was coming on strong and she wouldn't put it past him to try and get some action right here and now.

"Hold your horses' big guy," Mara stated as she politely told the guy to back off.

"Alright pretty lady, we'll continue this back at the bivouac," he said. Mara got the impression that she handled that perfectly. The man stood and grabbed his rifle and disappeared into the shadows.

Jackson's replacement materialized moments later and took up the seated position ready to relieve Mara upon her request. Corporal Matherson looked tired, and irritated at the order to be here.

"Did you see that guy?" Mara asked.

"Who?" Matherson responded.

"The spec ops guy that was just here. He was going back to the bivouac," Mara replied.

"What? No one was out there Private," he stated.

"You must have just missed him," she said.

"When I left they were discussing intel, apparently we got some new orders coming down," he said.

"Oh?" she responded. She didn't like the sound of new orders and the tone in which they were delivered. Ever since they spotted the Taliban patrol a few days ago, orders rapidly changed their mission objectives. She felt uneasy about what was probably going to happen next.

"Apparently, we're going to be in a support role and engage the Taliban a few clicks from here," he said.

"Support them?" Mara questioned.

"More like under their command," he stated. She didn't like the sound of that.

Mara turned and gave him a puzzling look. He shook his head in response and Mara turned her attention back to her duty. She had this eldritch feeling that he was still out there watching her.

M

Chapter
Eleven

Room 302
NYU Medical Center, NY
July 29th, 2019

Marathon's eyes flickered open and she gasped for breath as she suddenly woke from a disturbing dream. The intense bright florescent lights above her felt like demonic fire fueling the pain swelling behind her eyes. She tried to shield her vision, but her arms felt like she had done hundreds of pushups. She noticed someone in the room with her but her eyes couldn't adjust fast enough to see who it was.

She tried to remain calm, but felt her body tense thinking she was still in danger. The last thing Marathon remembered falling after the man had lost consciousness from her chokehold.

"Welcome back to the land of the living," a voice said off to the side.

Mara didn't recognize it, but it sounded comforting and compassionate. Not like the man she encountered in her apartment. She felt her bicep pinch as the sound of an air pump replaced the woman's voice. She had a piercing headache that immediately set in as her eyes still struggled to adjust.

"Your vitals look good, that's promising. You're a fighter."

Mara shook her head to the side as her eyes failed to produce recognizable images in the room. They hurt, and for the brief moment they were open, her tear ducts acted like an open faucet in response to the overpowering sensations. She tried to speak but couldn't find her voice. Her mouth was dry and it felt like she had a severe sore throat. The only thing she could muster was a whisper.

"Where am I?" she asked.

"You're at NYU Medical Center, dear," the woman responded. "You've had a rough recovery, but things are starting to look better."

"What?" Mara whispered sounding confused.

"You've been through a lot, you've got severe bruising around your neck, that's why it is difficult to speak."

Mara's head was spinning, and with her eyes closed, she felt like the room was also spinning around her, a sense of nausea crept in.

"What happened?" She asked.

"You took some serious impacts to the head, and suffered some brain swelling. You have a grade four concussion, a broken orbital bone, and a detached retina."

"Oh, is that all?" Mara joked trying to regain her strength.

"That's not all," she said with compassion. "You suffered a skull fracture and we had to put a metal plate in your head."

"Oh, well, that's not good," she said. The nurse hit a button on the hospital bed that raised Marathon up to a seated position, she then handed her a plastic cup filled with cool water.

"Thank you," Mara said taking the cup. It felt as if she were holding a gallon of water. The nurse grabbed a napkin and wiped her chin as Marathon fumbled with the task. Her sight started to return as her eyes regulated the light in the room.

"Well, you fared better than the other guy at least," the nurse said.

"Sort of…" Marathon paused trying to triage her memories, her voice seemed stronger now after drinking some water. "I remember someone attacked me in my apartment. I fought back. I remember the guy had a tattoo, a military tattoo similar to mine, but I can't make out what he looked like."

She was able to produce sound slightly louder than a whisper, but now she sounded like someone who smoked for fifty years. Her memories were still scrambled. She tried to focus on the man's appearance, but his face was out of focus. She would probably need to identify him in order for criminal charges to stick. The memories were all conjured together and it was hard to picture the chain of events in any logical order.

"Pardon my manners dear, I'm Nurse Fuller," she said as she refilled Marathon's cup with water. She placed it on the tray next to her bed. Marathon saw a tall angular nurse that didn't exactly match what she imaged from her voice. Her dark skin stood in stunning contrast to her light pink nursing scrubs.

"Nice to meet you Nurse Fuller," Mara responded with a smile.

"Your colleagues are here, but outside in the waiting area. Looks like I'm gonna recommend a discharge from the ICU. Your vitals are strong and you've been in stable condition for a while. Now that you're awake and alert, we can confidently downgrade your condition and get you a bed elsewhere, somewhere more private to help with your recovery."

"How long I have been here?" Marathon asked.

"You arrived in bad shape, suffered a seizure on the operating table while they put in that titanium plate," Ms. Fuller said. "Your head injury caused some major swelling, which was why we put you in that medically induced coma. But I'll leave it up to the doctor to go over everything with you. All you need to know, is that you are on a solid path to recovery."

"Oh, it was that bad," Mara stated. Her other arm was free enough to explore the back of her head. There were numerous stitches and a lot of her hair was missing from the surgery.

"Don't you worry about the hair dear," Nurse Fuller said. "A good weave would cover that right up."

Marathon's fingers explored the stitching, she lost count after twenty and she was afraid to keep going. The nurse must have seen her reaction.

94

"It doesn't look as bad as it feels," she said as she motioned with her cell phone indicating if she wanted to see a picture of it. Marathon nodded and after a brief flash, she was staring at a large incision on the back of her head.

"Your brain was swelling, we had to relieve the pressure and address the fractured skull. That's why you have a titanium plate there," she said.

"Oh," Marathon replied unable to find words for what had happened.

"I'm gonna recommend that you get some rest before you have visitors. Your grade four concussion is very serious, we were very concerned," Ms. Fuller said.

"How long do you think I'll be here?" she asked.

"Well, now that you're stable enough to leave the ICU, the doctor should put you on a path for discharge. However, your injuries are gonna take time to heal honey. Grade four concussions can take weeks to months to recover, sometimes even years to make a full recovery. Your medical history is spotty and only shows your service record from the armed forces and NYPD. Have you had a concussion before?"

"Ummm, yeah, in high school, probably. I played all the seasonal sports," Mara responded.

"Your time overseas has a large gap of information missing. Care to fill me in?"

"No," Mara responded immediately. "It's not medically relevant."

Nurse Fuller raised an eyebrow as if she sensed something was wrong with the response. She then flipped through her notes and jotted some information down.

Mara didn't want to disclose her PTSD diagnosis. Part of the terms of her honorable discharge was to have her records sealed. She was more comfortable leaving her service history well enough alone. The nurse didn't immediately respond as she finished taking her vitals. Mara felt her nausea take over and her body sank into the bed. It was as if someone was sitting on her chest and pinning her down.

The nurse noticed what was happening and placed her warm gentle hands across Mara's checks. Mara felt the nurse's comforting touch and opened her eyes. The wave of nausea dissipated and she felt more relaxed.

"You've got a low grade fever, probably a response to fight off infection," Nurse Fuller said resting her hand on Mara's forehead.

"My head feels like its underwater," Marathon responded.

"You're going to feel like that for a while," Nurse Fuller said.

Mara turned her head towards the window and unintentionally stared out at the other buildings surrounding the hospital. She was unsuccessfully trying to clear her mind and manage her throbbing headache.

"Listen, I have to ask these next series of questions. They might be painful and spark emotion, but I am required to ask them anyway," Nurse Fuller said.

"Okay," she responded.

"When you arrived, EMS said you were half naked, missing your pants," Nurse Fuller stated. Mara knew where this line of questioning was going and she nodded in response.

"Was he trying to rape you?" she asked.

"Yes," Mara responded.

"Did he enter you?" Nurse Fuller asked directly.

"No," Mara said. "I fought back."

"Okay, then he only got your pants off then?" Nurse Fuller asked.

"Yes, unless he tried to rape me while I was unconscious," Mara stated.

The nurse stood up from her bedside stool and adjusted the blankets covering her. She checked her intravenous therapy and took out a syringe.

"Would you like something for the headache?" Nurse Fuller asked.

Mara nodded with approval. Her headache was making the room spin and she was afraid to close her eyes again.

"Was there any evidence of rape?" Mara asked knowing they probably used a rape kit to collect evidence.

"There were no signs," Nurse Fuller said. "Besides your missing pants that is."

"Okay good," Mara said feeling relieved. Nurse Fuller injected what she said was a strong pain killer into her IV and Mara felt it's immediate effects kick in. She suddenly felt like she was floating as her body seemed weightless.

"I'm gonna get the doctor to sign off on your transfer out of ICU. Then she'll discuss your prognosis and recovery."

"Thank you, Ms. Fuller," Mara said.

The nurse gently placed her hand on Mara's shoulder and smiled before taking her leave. A numbing effect spread throughout her body as the drug took hold. Her eyes became heavy. She didn't want to close them, didn't want to deal with the images that lay waiting in her subconscious. But as the wave of relaxation grew stronger, Marathon's will power to remain awake diminished. She found herself slowing, and her eyes blinked closed until she didn't have enough strength to keep them open.

M

Chapter Twelve

Room 611
NYU Medical Center, NY
July 30th, 2019

Marathon opened her eyes to strobing lights above her. She saw Nurse Fuller at her side as her hospital bed was being wheeled down a long wide hallway filled with doctors and nurses. She didn't recognize anyone as the bed rolled to a stop in front of a large elevator.

"We told everyone to leave," Nurse Fuller said. "I think they gathered in the lobby."

"Thank you," Marathon said, her voice seemed a bit stronger than before.

The elevator arrived and her bed was expertly maneuvered into place. She felt her stomach drop a little when the metal box started its journey upwards. Marathon closed her eyes, the lights started to get the better of her and the headache resurfaced.

She was slowly rolled into her new recovery room that seemed to be about the same size as the room she was in before. The room was empty, but there was definitely space for two patients. There were flowers by the window and next to her bed, but she couldn't make out the writing on the cards.

"We had them brought up from the ICU for you. It definitely adds warmth to these old rooms," Nurse Fuller said as she anchored the bed in place close to the window at the far side of the room.

Marathon's eyes wondered around the room, it did seem larger than her previous room with all the machinery checking her vitals being left behind. She brought her hand up to her face, it felt warm to the touch. She winced when her fingers ran over the stitches above her eye where her fractured orbital bone was now healing. She took a deep breath and continued to scan the room.

Various machines were brought into the room, but they were much different than the ones in the ICU. There was a widescreen television in the upper corner next to the window and the remote dangled off her bed.

"The doctor will be in momentarily," Nurse Fuller said as she continued her duties. Marathon noticed the nurse go through what seemed like a mental checklist as each machine was set into position and attached to the cacophony of wires coming off of her from under the hospital blanket. Each machine responded with beeps and flashing lights as they were individually connected.

"This old room here was just redone," Nurse Fuller said. "We had this floor renovated a good month ago and we finally got cleared to use it. That's why this is taking bit longer to set you up."

"Am I the only patient in this room?" Marathon asked. She wanted to know if she would have a roommate.

"You're the only one on this floor," Nurse Fuller said.

"Wait, what?" Mara questioned as her voice went an octave higher.

"You're under protective custody," Nurse Fuller said. "You were attacked and your colleagues think you still might be in danger."

"Oh, um, well," Marathon was at a loss for words.

"Don't worry dear," Nurse Fuller said. "I'm stationed up here with you. We were going to slowly open up this floor anyway and it would give me a chance to get my station up and running while caring for you. You're in good hands."

"I need to speak with my colleagues," Marathon said.

"Dr. Jenkins is on her way up," Nurse fuller responded. "She needs to clear that first."

"Gotcha," Marathon said and sunk her head further into the pillow. She wanted desperately to get up and walk around. She couldn't stand being off her feet for so long. Before she could muster up the courage to do something foolish, the door to her room opened. There were a number of figures standing at the threshold peering in. The silhouette of a tall angular woman started walking towards her. Various voices could be hear in the hallway, but Marathon couldn't make out who was there.

"Welcome back," the woman said as her silhouette turned into defined features of an African American woman who looked to be in her mid-thirties. Her hair looked like black silk as the light bounced off her radiant skin. The doctor greeted her with a warm smile that seemed brighter than the florescent lights above her.

"I'm Doctor Jenkins and you, Detective Torres, had us all worried."

Marathon was at a loss for words and was fixated on the doctor who seemed to command power from the large empty room.

"You were in a serious life-threatening situation," the doctor said not giving her much information. "Do you know what happened to you?"

"There was a man at my apartment complex. He attacked me in my apartment and I fought back," Mara said trying to remember what happened and avoid the pain swelling behind her eyes. She noticed Dr. Jenkins take notes on her tablet.

"Good, do you remember any specific details about what happened?" Dr. Jenkins asked.

Marathon paused for a moment, the specific details lurked in her mind but were scrambled out of chronological order. She tried to piece sequences of events together, but lacked the concept of time to formulate a narrative about what had happened. Moments before, she would have been able to state what happened to her as if she were telling a story. Now, with the pressure to perform, she couldn't even formulate a coherent thought.

"What did the man look like?" the doctor asked using a more direct question.

"Umm, he had a tattoo, he looked older," Marathon answered. She still couldn't see his face. The constant headache she experienced started to grow in intensity. Dr. Jenkins took more notes on her tablet using a stylus to write.

"Okay, I am going to pause the questioning," Dr. Jenkins said. "Based on my quick observations and the notes in my tablet, it looks like you are suffering from some memory loss and you are probably having trouble putting things together in your mind."

Marathon nodded as if Dr. Jenkins knew exactly what she was experiencing. She noticed Nurse Fuller in the background, she had finished setting up the room and was waiting for directives from Dr. Jenkins. The doctor came over to her and sat in a chair next to her. Marathon appreciated the change in eye level as she turned her head to look at the doctor.

"I reviewed your medical history and ran a ton of tests. You have a severe concussion from the impact you sustained to the back of your head. You're extremely lucky to be here. There were numerous marks on the back of your head, it looks like you were struck multiple times."

"I was," Mara said. "He pistol whipped me."

Mara looked closely at the doctor sitting next to her. Nurse Fuller checked her vitals as the doctor recorded the information on her tablet. Marathon got a good look at the Nurse, as she navigated her bedside as she read off numbers to the Doctor.

"Are you related to Nurse Fuller?" Mara asked. Dr. Jenkins looked up with a smile and then wrote some notes down on her tablet.

"Yes, we're sisters," Dr. Jenkins said. Nurse Fuller smiled and then stood by the bedside. Dr. Jenkins nodded at her and Nurse Fuller took her leave.

"Your smile," Mara said. "It's the same."

"I can see that," Dr. Jenkins said as she continued with her tablet.

"You have more to tell me?" Marathon asked.

"I had to put you in a medically induced coma Ms. Torres. Your brain swelled and was badly bruised," Dr. Jenkins said.

"I see," Mara responded as she looked out the window. Her eyes still hurt and the headache was getting sharper.

"We kept you under until the swelling subsided and then we let you wake up on your own."

"That was smart, I strongly dislike people waking me up," Mara stated getting a smile out of the doctor.

"I'm sure Nurse Fuller mentioned that you are the only one on this floor, and that you have a stationed guard outside your room," Dr. Jenkins said.

"Yes," Marathon responded. "When can I have visitors?"

"I am going to clear you for visitors, I feel that they will help you piece things together about what happened."

"Are there any signs of brain damage?" Marathon asked.

"That's a loaded question," Dr. Jenkins said. "I'm going to answer it though. Yes, brain damage sounds bad, but a concussion is technically damage to the brain. The effects of that are what is considered brain damage."

Marathon stared at the doctor as she received a more detailed explanation about what had happened to her. Her memory loss and out of sequenced events are direct results of the concussion and head injuries.

"As far as lasting effects," Dr. Jenkins concluded. "I see you making a full recovery."

"Well that's good," Marathon responded after she heard the full prognosis. "When can I get out of here?"

"Listen, your tough, I get it. Your injuries are severe, and I wouldn't be comfortable discharging you without the proper observation to monitor symptoms

102

from the concussion," Dr. Jenkins said. "I also wasn't sure what condition you'd wake up in."

"You thought I'd be a vegetable?"

"With what you've been through, we're fortunate to have this conversation," Dr. Jenkins answered sounding sincere. "Head injuries like yours are tough to diagnose and even harder to give a prognosis for, unless we monitor you directly."

Mara focused her attention at the ceiling and nodded her head in approval. She felt powerless as her headache continued lurking in the background.

"Listen, there are a lot of people that want your story. You have an Uncle out in the waiting area, and a few officers have been in and out. There was a John here to see you earlier," Dr. Jenkins said.

"Can they come in?" Mara asked with a slight smirk on her face. Dr. Jenkins looked down on her and smiled back.

"Let me just finish some notes and I'll allow a few in at a time," Dr. Jenkins replied smiling back at her.

"Have you seen my phone?" Mara asked

Dr. Jenkins looked up and walked over towards a paper bag resting on the only chair in the room. She then produced Mara's cellphone from the bag and handed it to her with an awkward smile. The front screen was shattered and had large chunks of screen completely missing exposing the inner logic board. Mara held the power button but the phone did not respond.

"I'm about to leave for the day, you were my last patient of my shift, who would you like to see first, I think I can sneak in one or two?" The doctor asked.

"Will you get in trouble?" Mara sheepishly responded.

"It'll be our little secret," Jenkins said with a devilish smile. She liked her doctor and appreciated the level of care she provided.

"When will you be back?" Mara asked.

"My shift starts at 0-800 tomorrow."

"Military time? Mara question.

"I figured you'd appreciate that. Besides, someone had to pay for medical school," Dr. Jenkins replied. "Listen, I'll be back in tomorrow morning. I'll leave you so you can catch up to the rest of the world. Your uncle has been... what's the right word?"

"Annoyingly persistent?"

"Yes, that describes him perfectly. By the sound of it, it looks like he made his way back up here," Dr. Jenkins said.

"I would like to see him," Mara responded.

"Good, I'll let him know before I leave. He'll finally be able to leave my nurses alone."

Marathon laughed as the doctor turned and left the room without a proper goodbye. She heard commotion in the hallway as Uncle Dave's distinct voice pierced through the thick wooded door that separated them. Dr. Jenkin's could barely get a word in as Dave's nervous personality had to finish the doctor's sentences.

"Oh my gosh, Marathon, Marathon," Uncle Dave said as he opened the door. "Marathon, I've been so worried."

Uncle Dave rushed over to her side next to the bed. He was wearing his usual buttoned up collared shirt with tight tan slacks. The lines around his face conveyed his tired and concerned look. Uncle Dave was the only one to use her full name in almost any context. He loved her name, mainly because he always stated her name fit her personality. Mara only understood this when she became an adult.

"Dad," Mara stated and then paused as she fought back tears. Dad was the name she had given him when her biological father left.

She immediately saw how concerned he was and she opened her arms up to him welcoming a deep embrace. Uncle Dave gave the best hugs and she needed one of those now. There were no words exchanged as the two embraced. Mara always knew Uncle Dave was unconditionally there for her. He was the most responsible man in her life, and treated her like his daughter. He was flamboyantly warm and welcoming, and his personality filled a room.

Uncle Dave had taken her in when Mara was very young. Dave's brother, Mara's biological father, was in and out of jail for drug related crimes. Mara grew up in a very turbulent household during the first few years of her life. She constantly heard her mother and father argue, many times their arguments turned physical. If it wasn't for Uncle Dave, Mara's life would have turned out much differently. Uncle Dave officially adopted Mara when she was old enough to understand what it meant.

"I got the call no parent ever wants to get Mara," Uncle Dave said as Marathon didn't want to let go.

"Dad, I..."

"I know you're a tough kid. I know you can handle yourself," Uncle Dave paused and took a deep breath as if this was the only thing that mattered to him in the world. "You had Adam and I so worried."

"Is Adam here?" Marathon asked.

"No, he went to get you a new cell phone. The doctor told us yours was broken," Uncle Dave Responded.

"Oh, that's so nice of him," Marathon responded. "I'm so happy you are here."

"I wanted to be the one you saw when you woke up, but that damn doctor wouldn't let you have any visitors while your room was being prepped."

Mara smiled as she played out the conversation Uncle Dave probably had with the Dr. Jenkins. She would have loved to have witnessed that.

"So, tell me what happened," Dave said as he sat on the bed next to her, not taking up much room.

"I don't know where to begin," Mara said.

"The doctor said you might have some memory loss."

"It's not that," Mara stated. "The whole event is crystal clear in my mind, yet, his face is a blur. Almost like a phantom at the edge of shadows."

A tear rolled down Mara's cheek as she remembered more details about that night. Flashes of events sparked her memory about how the man violated her. Uncle Dave took out a handkerchief and caught her tear before it fell off her chin. Her hands started trembling as more details began to surface.

Uncle Dave grabbed her hand and put his other hand on her forehead. "Marathon, it's okay, I'm here. You're safe, people who care about you are here and will let nothing happen to you."

Uncle Dave's words helped, but the feeling lingered. Marathon realized that she was intensely squeezing his hand and felt beads of sweet build up and roll down her back.

"I'm sorry Marathon, I shouldn't have asked you that," Uncle Dave said.

"No, I am going to need to do this soon, and I want you to help me through his," she said.

She was counting on his decades of experience as a licensed clinician working with adolescent trauma. Back when Uncle Dave was part of the work force, he was a member of the United Federation of Teachers as a licensed social worker in the New York City Department of Education.

"I see how much this has affected you," Uncle Dave said. "I don't think now is the time to relive what you have been through."

"Well, I am going to have to identify the guy and make a statement to make sure the guy stays locked up," Mara said but Dave didn't respond. He simply smiled and nodded.

"What? Did they let that guy go? Is that why they are keeping me here, because I'm not safe?" Mara nervously asked.

"No Marathon, the man that attacked you is dead," Uncle Dave said.

"Dead?" Mara said trying to recall the last thing she remembered from that evening. "No, that can't be. The last thing I remember was being slammed to the ground. He lost consciousness, how could he be dead?"

"Officers found you unconscious in a pool of blood," Dave started and then continued when Mara gave him a nod to tell the story. She needed to hear this.

"He was on top of you in a choke hold position, like the ones you used to do in your martial art tournaments. The officers who found you said that your body tensed up when you were unconscious, like your muscles were locked in place."

"Oh," she said.

Mara was stunned by the news. She knew what type of choke hold she put on the man. A triangle choke that cuts off blood to the brain and oxygen to the body. She remembered placing that hold on him to subdue him, but when he picked her up, he had lost consciousness. Uncle Dave went on to explain how the force of impact caused a chain reaction that led to his death by strangulation.

Mara turned and looked out the window. The night sky was filled with spotted lights from the apartment building across street. Her vision was still blurry from the swelling tears and the creeping headache.

"I killed someone," she said.

Uncle Dave didn't respond, but the warmth of his hand gently let her know he was there.

"I know you are going to say it was either me or him," Mara said trying to build up justification for taking a life.

"The officers I spoke with determined he was trying to kill you," Uncle Dave stated.

"No... No, he wasn't trying to do that, at least not at first," Marathon said. The details seemed to materialize in her mind as if they were always there but hidden from her conscious thoughts.

"Marathon," Uncle Dave said squeezing her hand tighter.

"When I fought back, he had to match my intensity. I remember fighting for my life with everything I had. He was bigger, stronger, and well trained. I had to..." Mara stated.

"Stop," Uncle Dave said. "Stop this, Marathon. Don't go there. Don't you ever go there! You don't need to justify what happened. He got what he deserved."

Mara could sense the frustration in his voice build. She was starting to internalize her actions that lead to the man's death. She felt fissures forming in her psychological foundation that took years of therapy to build.

"His actions were his own Marathon," Uncle Dave demanded. "You reacted to his aggression and defended yourself."

Mara heard the pain in his voice and focused on the fact that she had survived the encounter. Her psychological tool belt was activated thanks to her uncle and she separated this instance from her past traumatic events. This man tried to rape her like she was an object to be manipulated. She had no choice but to defend herself and it cost him his life.

"Has he been identified yet?" Mara asked.

"I don't know, your buddies tell me nothing," Uncle Dave responded.

"He was military," Mara said.

"What? How do you know?" Dave asked.

"He had military tattoos all over his forearms, and his fighting style was a dead giveaway," she stated. "He also had this one particular tattoo, only spec ops had them."

"Spec Ops?" Uncle Dave questioned.

"Former, I think," Mara answered. "He seemed familiar to me."

"Familiar how?" Uncle Dave asked.

"Like I've met him before somewhere," She responded.

"Maybe from the military?" Uncle Dave asked.

"His name is William Bowden, or Billy Bo Boxer as his friends call him," Frank Davidson stated as he entered the room without warning. He always had a flare for the dramatic entrance. Mara suspected he was outside the door waiting for the right moment to enter.

"He was a career criminal and wanted in Florida for rape, and theft. He nearly beat his latest victim to death," Frank stated. "His rap sheet is longer than most dissertations."

Uncle Dave stood up from the edge of the bed and shook Frank's hand. The two of them had made acquaintances over the years.

"It's good to see you Frank," Uncle Dave said.

"I wish it were under different circumstances," he replied and then turned his attention back to Marathon. "I overheard you state he was former military. Are you sure?"

"Yes I'm sure, I've seen that tattoo before," Mara replied. "When you did a background check, didn't that come up?"

"No, there was no indication of any service record," Frank stated.

"What? How could that be?" Mara asked.

"This detail is troubling," Frank hesitantly stated.

"I know you don't like unexplained clues, but what exactly is troubling you?" Uncle Dave asked.

"There might be a connection between me and the perp," Marathon answered. "I definitely saw that tattoo before, during one of my tours in Afghanistan."

"If this is a connection," Frank continued. "Then this confirms this was not a random attack. I'm going to inspect the body later and officially make the connection."

"Are you saying Marathon was targeted?" Uncle Dave blurted out.

"It is a possibility, and it is one we need to act on," Frank stated. "This has all the markings of a home invasion gone wrong, but this new detail has me worried."

"Well, what are you going to do?" Uncle Dave asked. His voice rose an octave higher that sounded both concerned and anxious.

"Dave, your daughter is safe here," Frank said. "I am going to post a uniform outside your room. Only approved people are allowed in for visitations. We are going to tighten the security we already have in place."

"Thank you, Frank," Uncle Dave said.

Mara starred out the window while Frank and Dave continued their conversation. Mara knew what the men were talking about and knew they had her best interest at heart. Her mind drifted back to the man, who now had a name. William Bowden, at least that was the name on file. His criminal record suggested this could have been a random crime, but Marathon knew it sounded more like a targeted hit. The mere thought of having a target on her back was utterly terrifying.

"Frank," Mara interrupted. "William Bowden, if my memory serves me correctly, was there to send me a message."

Frank paused his conversation with Uncle Dave and moved closer to her. Mara could see the fire in his eyes as clearly took an attack on a fellow officer personal. When someone harms one of your own, everyone suffers. This happened under Frank's watch and Mara knew him well enough to know he took responsibility for the officers who served under him.

"He was there to send you a message?" Frank confirmed.

"Yes," Mara said. "I don't think he was there to kill me, he had a gun and he could have easily accomplished that when he snuck up on me in my apartment."

"What message was he trying to send?" Uncle Dave chimed in.

"I think this has to do with the Marley Williams case," Mara said. Her thoughts were more clear now.

"What? That was over a decade ago," Uncle Dave said as he was trying to connect the dots and catch up. Frank looked at him to suggest there was more to it than that.

"We had stumbled upon new evidence in the case," Frank said. Uncle Dave nodded and sat down in the chair. He gave off the impression he was waiting for someone to tell him what was going on.

Frank filled in the missing details as Uncle Dave asked a few clarifying details. Mara's mind slipped away from their conversation to avoid reliving the details she already knew. She felt fatigued and her eyes heavy.

"Marathon," Uncle Dave said interrupting Mara's quest for tranquility. "Frank is going to follow a few leads."

Frank waved as he walked towards the door. He then stopped and turned back towards them. "You should let John know you're alive and well. He's been calling me non-stop since the news broke."

"I'll do that," Mara replied as Frank Davidson left the room.

Uncle Dave returned to Mara's bedside and took a seat in the chair next to her. "Get some rest kiddo," he said as he accessed his phone. "I'm going to let Adam know how you're doing."

"Say hi for me," Mara replied as she turned over to her side trying not to rip out the IV. She laid facing the window again, with her back towards Uncle Dave. She could hear him mashing the virtual keypad on his cellphone. She felt comfortable now that Uncle Dave sat by her side. Her eyes became heavy and she slowly drifted off to sleep to the beat of the rapid fire text messages.

M

Chapter
Thirteen

Parris Island, South Carolina
November 12th, 2001
3:52am

"Welcome to the Marines, recruits!" The Staff Sergeant said as Mara and the rest of her class stood at attention as the bus that brought them puttered off into the misty fog.

The swampy surroundings emitted a damp rotten smell that lingered in the stagnant air. The dimly lit broken road was lined with various one story buildings that housed various offices and officer quarters at The Depot. The vibe oddly reminded her of her old stomping grounds in Queens, NY.

"You will... from this point... refer to me... as sir," the Staff Sergeant barked.

The intensity in his voice matched each stride he took as he paced back and forth. He occasionally glared at the soldiers around Marathon as if he were planning on fighting them. His muscular frame and stature was intimidating, she expected nothing less.

"Sir, yes sir," The recruits in unison answered loud and proud.

"I can in turn... refer to you... however I damn well please."

"Sir, yes sir!"

"You will speak… only when spoken to… you will eat… only when I tell you to," the Sergeant barked as he continued pacing up and down the ranks in front of him. Marathon stood tall and kept her focus straight ahead.

"You will piss… only when I tell you to," he continued.

"Sir, yes sir!"

"You will change..." he paused and stared at a soldier to Marathon's right. "Only when I tell you to."

She tried to focus on the sole streetlight directly ahead across the mud-stricken broken concrete road. She hoped her neatly tucked hair was hidden well enough under her service issue hat to not draw any unwanted attention.

"Sir, yes sir!"

"I want your crap… off my lawn in two minutes. I want your sorry behinds… back out here in three," The Sergeant ordered and then held up his watch.

"Sir, yes sir!"

The Staff Sergeant clicked a button for all to see and the response was a mad scramble of soldiers picking up their belongings. Mara grabbed her bag and hoisted it over her shoulder. The Staff Sergeant walked over to her and held out his hand.

"Private," he pointed to the nearest soldier next to Marathon. "Are you going to let a lady carry her own bags?"

The private jumped to attention. "Sir, no sir!"

He dropped his belongings and went to grab Mara's. She took a step back and the private had a puzzled look on his face.

"I can carry my own shit," Marathon exclaimed.

"Excuse me private?" The Staff Sergeant stated turning towards her.

"I can carry my own shit, sir!" she repeated with more enthusiasm.

The Staff Sergeant waved the helpful private off and he scurried back towards the barracks trying to make up for lost time. Marathon remained at attention. The Staff Sergeant got within inches of her face. Mara remained still and looked forward not making eye contact. The Staff Sergeant was only a few inches taller than her, so it was difficult for her to completely avoid his gaze.

"I gave you a direct order!" He barked as Mara felt his spit bounce off her face.

"Sir, no sir!" She responded.

"Excuse me Private?"

"Sir, you gave a direct order to Recruit Duncan, sir!" Mara responded.

The Staff Sergeant got even closer, she felt like he wanted to rip her soul out of her body. He stood there for what seemed like a moment in time that lasted way longer than it should have.

"Private, turn and get your sorry tail ready. You have less than two minutes to get back out here," he stated as his attention started to shift to recruits storming out of the barracks.

"Sir, yes sir!" Mara yelled and ran towards the barracks with her duffle bag in tow.

"Where the hell do you think you're going?" the Staff Sergeant said. Mara froze in place at attention.

"The *fe*-male barracks are over there," he said as he pointed to the small building about 50 yards down the road. Mara looked where he was pointing and wished she hadn't opened her big mouth.

"Tic-toc, tic-toc, recruit," he said as Mara scrambled with her duffle bag down the road towards the smaller building.

She barely made it back in time after she found the last remaining bunk bed in the small barracks. The Staff Sergeant was looking over his ranks with a look of displeasure. He paced back and forth with anger. He glanced at Mara who was breathing heavy from the fifty yard dash back to the lineup. The fog was thickening, and a light drizzle formed as the recruits outside the barracks remained at attention.

"This here is Corporal Miller, he is going to lead you on your morning stroll."

"Sir, yes sir!"

"All except you, Torres," The Staff Sergeant stated turning towards Mara. "You're gonna give me fifty and then join them."

"Sir, yes sir," Mara yelled and dropped down in pushup position and proceeded to pound out as many pushups she could before her squad ran off and got too far away from her.

"I don't know where you come from, and frankly I don't care," The Staff Sergeant stated standing directly over her. Mara heard the Corporal line the recruits up. She then heard them march off in a brisk jog towards the tree line adjacent to the barracks. The Staff Sergeant leaned over her like a catcher trying to smother a baseball in the dirt. He was inches from her face as her pushups slowed and her arms felt like jelly.

"You cuss again Private Torres, you'll be outta here so fast the pencil necks in the office won't have time to process your paperwork. Do I make myself clear?"

"Sir, yes sir!" Mara yelled trying to keep pace with her pushups.

"Good! Now make sure you catch up with your squad, I would hate for the Corporal to realize you were left behind," The Staff Sergeant stated.

Mara finished her fiftieth pushup and stood and took off in a sprint towards the direction the recruits went. They had disappeared from her field of view and Marathon assumed there was a path beyond the tree line. She made her best guess at which direction they took and charged at near full sprint to make up for the lost time.

It was nearly 5:00 am when she returned with the other recruits back to the barracks. They were drenched in sweat and most of them were gathered around the water pump outside the barracks filling their canteen. The Corporal disappeared towards the officer's quarters and left the soldiers without orders. Mara stood in line to get water, her pale green fatigues were drenched, she smelled like she had just ran through a swamp.

"You did good," a soldier said as he passed by her after refilling his canteen. Mara nodded in reply, still trying to catch her wind.

"If you didn't catch up to us, we'd be still out there until you did," he said. "I heard this happens every time, someone gets left behind and the Corporal keeps the group out in the woods until the unit is whole again."

Mara took a deep breath and checked the line for her position. He then offered her a sip from his canteen. Mara grabbed the canteen and chugged a large portion of its contents.

"You should have seen the corporals face when you showed up. I reckon he had a lot more planned for us," he said allowing his southern accent to shine through.

Mara noticed the Corporal exit out of the officer's quarters as three men in plain clothes approached. They looked like people you would not want to meet under any circumstance. Their rough appearance gave a don't fuck with us vibe and she pointed them out to the soldiers around her.

"Who are they?" Marathon asked.

"They are the best of the best and you do not want to get in their way," Recruit Duncan said as he stood behind her in line.

"They're spec ops, you can tell by the way they dress… and the way they walk," another recruit said as he grabbed his canteen back from Mara.

"Spec ops?" Mara questioned. "What are they doing here?"

"Clearly, they are here to meet with the Staff Sergeant," the other recruit stated in a sarcastic tone.

"No shit, asshole," Mara snapped back.

"Hey, you wanna get us in trouble?"

116

"Stop cursing," another soldier said.

"Fuck," Mara said under her breath rolling her eyes. She knew where she was, and cursing wasn't the issue. They would find any excuse to break them down.

It was now Mara's turn to fill her canteen and her focus remained on the Corporal who had just encountered the men entering the Staff Sergeant's barracks. The Corporal was walking towards them and Mara noticed his pace was brisk, as if he were about to bark orders at them. Mara barely finished filling her canteen when the Corporal reached their position.

"Attention!"

The soldiers dropped what they were doing and stood at attention in place ready to receive orders.

"You are to report back here in full garb at 0900 hours. The mess hall is expecting you now," the Corporal stated pointing to a large building behind their barracks. "The Staff Sergeant is expecting you to clean yourselves up. You have guests. Dismissed!"

M

Chapter Fourteen

Uncle Dave's Ranch
Quincy, Pennsylvania
August 2019

After Marathon was discharged from the hospital, she decided to take leave from the NYPD and get out of the city to recover at her uncle's place in Quincy, Pennsylvania. She knew it wasn't really her decision, when Uncle Dave insists, it's not something that could be turned down. Dr. Jenkins said she had a long road to a full recovery, and refused to sign any paperwork stating she could return to active duty until she made that full recovery. Strick doctor's orders was something the Police Benevolent Association didn't take lightly.

The NYPD granted her paid leave after the department determined she was attacked while on the job and quite possibly targeted for her work. Officer Terrance Morgan filed all the paperwork on her behalf and easily got the leave approved thanks to Dr. Jenkins signature on the medical form.

It was a straight forward process, also considering the department didn't want any negative press from an officer being forced to return to work after being attacked in her own apartment. The press was all over this already and the NYPD had some public relations work to do to reassure the public that Detective Marathon Torres was targeted for a very specific reason. A reason they conveniently couldn't reveal at the time due to the pending investigation.

Upon her discharge from the hospital, a line of uniformed officers welcomed her as the Mayor of New York City shook her hand before she got in Uncle Dave's SUV. They exchanged a few words and the press was able to grab a quick statement as she transitioned out of the hospital. The segment played on every major news channel and made her an overnight hero in New York City. Just another reason for her to get as far away as possible. She was tired of seeing the same segment on the news.

Frank Davidson also didn't provide her an option to return to work, usually he would consult with the PBA and human resources to determine details of the leave, but in this case, he just signed the paperwork and sent her a quick get well soon text without having her return to the precinct. He would check in from time to time with some updates, but the case was at a standstill with all leads resulting in dead ends. The case died when Bowden died.

Initially, Marathon was given a protective detail at Uncle Dave's ranch in Quincy. The NYPD coordinated with local law enforcement to keep a patrol car parked outside the ranch. This lasted for about a month and with no further threats or developments in the case, the department rescinded their protective detail and left Marathon to recover on her own.

Mara's return to duty was contingent on doctor approval, and based on her current status, that wasn't going to be happening for quite some time. She spent a week in the hospital and was discharged solely under the condition she would receive bed rest with some light activity through the summer. Dr. Jenkins was adamant about this, citing how bad her concussion was and citing the metal plate in her head needed to heal properly so she would be able to manage her headaches. She was right, her pain was intense, sometimes unbearable. The pain meds she was on only took off the edge, a subtle throbbing remained just behind her eyes.

Adam joined Uncle Dave to help Mara move out of her apartment. Being attacked in her own place allowed her to get out of her lease. Adam arranged for all her belongs to be moved in with them in Quincy. She never stepped foot in her apartment again and allowed Adam to handle all the details with the move. Their ranch in Quincy had plenty of room and she even had plenty of space to call her own.

Adam was an amazing partner for the high strung Uncle Dave. He was always calm and collected. Uncle Dave and Adam met when Mara first moved in after her parents gave her up and left. At the time, she didn't comprehend that Adam and her uncle were romantic, she thought they were just friends. As time went on, Marathon began to understand their relationship and told them she was happy living with her uncle. Adam eventually moved in and they created a new nuclear family.

Mara was introduced to Quincy, Pennsylvania when Uncle Dave and Adam suddenly retired and sold their house in Queens. This all happened while Mara was in the police academy. When she moved out of the house and in with one of her friends from the force, Uncle Dave and Adam took that as a sign to get out of the city. Uncle Dave retired from the Department of Education and Adam took a buyout from his firm and dissolved the partnership. Their combined income and the sale of the house in Queens allowed them purchase property and build a lavish ranch with all the modern accommodations needed for a luxurious retirement.

Quincy was a small-town north of Maryland and about fifteen minutes east of route 81. It was barely big enough to have its own post office and that's the way the Torres family liked it. The sounds and smells of the big city were replaced with fresh country air, rolling hills, and wild life. The summer heat was as intense and the humidity made it uncomfortable, but the Torres Ranch, as Mara liked to call it, had its own in ground swimming pool complete with a diving board and waterfall. More importantly, it had its own completely stocked poolside bar, something they could never have in Queens.

Uncle Dave and Adam had to design and build their dream home from scratch. That's what Adam did for a living before retirement. He was an architect and had lavish plans to design and build a home for his family. Mara envied them for acting on a lifelong dream. Adam had a rough childhood as well, he came out to his family when he met Uncle Dave, and that event created distance between himself and his own family. Mara suspected his family always knew, which was why he was treated so poorly growing up but, when he came out to them, they couldn't accept their new reality.

Mara remembered Adam enthusiastically showing off the property when she first arrived after graduating from the academy. He was beaming with pride and provided an excellent tour of the Ranch with exquisite detail highlighted. Everything was pristinely new; Mara never thought she would ever see such luxury, let alone be a part of a family that owned it. Adam had provided for a family he always wanted to have. He treated Mara like a daughter and she often returned the love by calling her dad. When she was younger, she did this on purpose to see who would respond first. She got a kick out of it and sensed they did as well.

Uncle Dave and Adam made sure to stay north when they left the city where their lifestyle was more accepted. The people of Quincy were accepting and welcomed them into the community with open arms. Uncle Dave and Adam didn't advertise their relationship to the community, but they didn't shy away from it either. The thing about discrimination, it tends to break down and become foolish once you actually get to know your neighbor. Both Uncle Dave and Adam were good people and good neighbors. It wasn't long before the community swallowed them up as one of their own. It also helps that the surrounding community is less than one hundred people, not too many walls to break down. Plus, Uncle Dave and Adam loved to entertain.

Their Ranch was now the hot ticket in town and being invited to one of their parties was the highlight of summer. They would kick things off proper with a 4th of July blow out party complete with fireworks and catered BBQ. There would be a party mid-summer in early August and then a final one Labor Day weekend. Small get togethers would happen in between the over the top events. The Torres family had made a name for themselves and they did it by welcoming people into their lives and in turn the community welcomed them back in appreciation.

Marathon stayed in her old bedroom, which happened to be roughly the size of her apartment in the city. It was late August and the summer heat was in full force during the dog days of summer. She enjoyed her time of healing, having spent most of August out by the pool and taking in the sun and responding to social media posts. Her headaches still persisted, and she would often become dizzy if she physically asserted herself in the pool, or even when she cleaned up around the house. She felt tired and sluggish most of the time and missed her workout routine she developed over the years.

She gained a few pounds, one of the side effects of not being as active and living at home with parents that always thought she was too skinny anyway. She tracked her recovery closely, each day taking a selfie to track progress. Her face was scared, but Dr. Jenkins recommended an excellent plastic surgeon to deal with the scaring around her eyes. Her orbital bone healed nicely without any further intervention she received in the hospital. The break was clean above her eye just under her brow and after the doctor determined it was set right, it healed naturally.

Marathon posted her progress on social media, her account blew up since the life changing events in late July. Her initial post that showed the true extent of the injuries and received thousands of likes and comments. The social media site even sent her emails about her "influencer status" and how she could maximize her potential if she changed her account to a public figure.

She ignored those and simply documented her progress in recovery. It was more a photo diary to help her cope with the traumatic events. Dr. Lee provided therapy sessions remotely and suggested she pay close attention to the details of her recovery instead of basking in the woe is me mentality of recovery.

She got a kick out of some of the comments and used that as a way to keep herself busy while lounging by the pool. Her favorite comment was someone who went by the name of TreCoolio22, "Imagine being so hot that your face gets smashed and you still look good."

Just because she left the city didn't mean she escaped the public eye. She received calls from numerous late night television hosts and TV personalities to appear on their show for a sit down interview. She turned them down and wanted to avoid the spot light. Her stint with fame was overwhelming and couldn't imagine it being a thing in her life.

In mid-August, Frank had called with an update, well at least that's what it appeared to be. Brass reviewed her case and decided to offer her early retirement. This caught her off guard and she told Frank that she would have to think about it. Retirement wasn't even a thought in her mind. It seemed to even take him by surprise.

One late August afternoon, Mara was relaxing in the blistering heat baking in her own thoughts. She placed a cold damp towel over her head, which helped calm the headaches and clear her mind. Uncle Dave was at the outdoor pool bar making drinks while Adam swam laps. She had developed a nice end of season tan, that darkened her olive skin tone.

"Here ya go Marathon," Uncle Dave said as he placed her whiskey on the rocks on the table next to her chaise lounge. If this was what retirement was like, she wanted to sign the papers immediately.

"Thanks," Marathon said sitting up to take a sip. The ice was melting fast, but she enjoyed the added cold water, it provided a smoother taste with more defined notes.

"You got a letter in the mail today from the department," Uncle Dave said.

"Oh, was it addressed here or to my old apartment?" Mara asked.

"Your old apartment," Uncle Dave said.

"It's probably union stuff, or standard info for my leave," Mara responded.

"Or it could be retirement papers," Adam said from the pool clearly eavesdropping in on their conversation.

Marathon laid back down and rested her whiskey on her chest between her breasts. The cold beverage cooled the skin just above her bikini top right by her heart. She didn't want to deal with this now, she wanted to go back to her daydreams and not make any adult decisions, especially now that her headache was gone.

"Can we treat that as junk mail?" Mara stated.

"Marathon, it's time you made a decision," Uncle Dave said. He was seated upright, which signaled it was time to talk. Marathon couldn't avoid this conversation any longer. Since the department offered retirement, she knew this conversation was coming.

"You might not like the decision I make," she stated after taking a sip of her whiskey.

"You know we support you. We just don't want you to live your life and be happy," he said.

"Unless you make the wrong decision," Adam yelled from the pool.

"So if I told you I was going back to work, you'd support that decision?" Mara asked. She knew they would completely support her without question, but she needed to hear it for her own reassurance.

"I would, we both would. Even though we don't think it's the best choice," Uncle Dave said. Mara always appreciated his honesty.

"I don't even know if I want to go back," Marathon stated. "Part of me never wants to step foot in the city again."

She sat up and held the whiskey in her hand. Marathon stared down at it and swirled the remaining ice cubes in her glass before taking another large sip. Uncle Dave got up and sat next to her. He put his arm around her shoulder and brought her in close like he used to do when she was kid after a rough day at school.

"I know you want to go back and finish this," he stated. "I know you well enough to see this eat away at you. And... I'm not entirely sure it's the attack that's causing this."

"You know me well," she responded. "Sometimes better than I know myself."

"That is not true!" Uncle Dave stated immediately. "Remember that argument we had after you had snuck off to the recruiting center and signed your life away to the Marines? Remember how mad I was?"

"How could I forget that? Adam had to physically separate us from killing each other," Marathon stated.

"I did want to kill you too," Adam said from the pool.

"I was more angry with myself for not taking your decisions seriously. You had mentioned the armed forces after 9/11 and I shrugged them off," Uncle Dave said.

"I think I joined because you wouldn't approve of it," Mara said. "I was a much different person back then."

"I had thought, how could someone so smart be so stupid," Uncle Dave said.

"I know you told me," Mara said.

"Well, what I didn't tell you was that you had made me extremely proud," he said.

"You did dad, in your own way. You too, Dad," She yelled over at Adam who was taking a breather by the diving board.

"The point is, you make the right decisions," Uncle Dave said and then immediately retracted his statement "well, your taste in men is extremely questionable."

Mara sat up straight and leaned back to get a better look at him.

"Oh come on, you've liked the guys I've brought around."

Marathon heard Adam make choking sounds from the pool. She looked to make sure he wasn't drowning, but saw him swim closer to them at the edge of the pool. His face seemed to light up from the topic of conversation. Adam was a stocky fella with a warm heart. His round welcoming face was just above the edge of the pool as he rested it on his massive folded arms. He was the type of person who was always willing to help.

"Liked is a strong word," Adam said.

Mara turned towards Uncle Dave with a shocked expression. "What? You always said they were nice guys!"

"They were nice guys, I mean they were cute and all," Uncle Dave stated in defense.

"But not nice guys for you," Adam said, finishing Uncle Dave's confession.

"Okay, so Jeremy, what was wrong with him?" Mara asked.

"Was he the one who never had a hair out of place?" Adam asked.

"No, he was the one who always wore those muscle shirts, and had those tribal tattoos," Uncle Dave responded.

"Oh, right. Didn't he cheat on you?" Adam said.

"No, that was Timothy," Uncle Dave said.

"Oh, the white boy," Adam said. "Fucking Timothy."

"Yeah, fuck that guy," Uncle Dave said.

Mara's face showed a hint of laughter as she remembered specific details from her past boyfriends. The truth was, they were right. If you took those details as a singular moment in time, yes they were extremely funny and damning to an extremely opinionated gay couple. One wrong move from one of her boyfriends turned into a damning meme that would last forever and lived in moments like these.

"Okay, forget Jeremy, and yes, fuck Timothy," Marathon stated.

"What were we talking about," Dave stated with a snarky, playful attitude. Clearly the whiskey was doing what it was supposed to.

"Mara's taste in men," Adam reminded him.

"What about Keshawn?" Marathon said as she thought about the one that got away, the guy she had the most regrets about.

126

"The football player from college?" Uncle Dave asked. Mara nodded and tilted her head as if there was nothing wrong with him.

"I think we really liked Keshawn, didn't we?" Adam said.

"No, no," Dave said waving his finger in the air. "Keshawn appeared to be a good guy. He was not a good guy for Marathon."

"That's true," Adam said in agreement. "We did talk about that."

"What?" Mara questioned.

"He was a baby, and you were well set in your career in the NYPD."

"So?" she said.

"You two weren't on the same page about anything," Uncle Dave said.

"He's got a point Mara," Adam said with his head peering out from the pool.

"He was a frat boy who needed to mature," Uncle Dave said.

"He was cute though," Adam said.

"Yes he was." Uncle Dave agreed.

"Ugh, I can't win with you two," Mara stated in frustration.

"Marathon, you're thirty-eight, you've got plenty of time to find a guy and settle down," Uncle Dave said. "You know, Adam and I met when we were about your age."

"How could I forget that? You stumbled over every word trying to explain your relationship to me. It also didn't help that you told that ridiculous story," Mara said.

"What was I supposed to do, you had no idea about the birds and the bees," Uncle Dave said in defense.

"You mean the bees and the bees," Adam said from the pool.

"Yeah, that too," Uncle Dave agreed.

Marathon desperately wanted to change the subject. She always felt uneasy discussing her love life and wanted to avoid the topic of conversation altogether.

"Honey, remember the time we had to change our house number because boys were calling constantly," Adam said as his legs made splashing sounds behind him. Dave sat up from his lounge chair.

"Of course I do, I mean, how could I forget. You and I were just becoming serious, and we had this hormone ranging teenager giving out our home number to anyone that looked her way in school," Uncle Dave responded.

"Oh come on, it wasn't that bad," Marathon protested.

"What about the time a boy called in the middle of the night trying to get you to sneak out of the house?" Uncle Dave asked.

"Oh, I remember that!" Adam stated. "You forgot that we screened your calls using the other phone in the house."

"You mean the time you followed me? Spied on me?" Mara answered adding a bit of frustration to her voice.

"Oh the look on your face when I caught up with you right after you met that boy, what was his name?" Uncle Dave asked.

"Jaquan," Adam said.

"Yes, when you met up with Jaquan," Uncle Dave continued. "You two were getting hot and heavy in the playground, on those slides, then I sent that intense beam of light from that high-powered flashlight. The one I got for Christmas that year. Remember that thing?"

"I got that for you!" Marathon exclaimed.

"Oh right, how perfect was that? The look on that young man's face was priceless," Uncle Dave said.

"You told the entire neighborhood! I was so embarrassed," Mara stated. "He was a nice boy!"

"Yeah, he was," Adam said. "His mom worked at the bodega on Rockaway right?"

"No, it was on 97th," Mara added. "That's how I would meet him. He worked there stocking the bottles at night. After school, we used to sneak in the basement of the bodega and make out."

"Oh really? The truth comes out," Uncle Dave responded with a glance of admiration.

"So he wasn't intimidated enough to stay away?" Adam asked looking back at Dave with a glance.

"There are a lot of things I did in high school you don't know about," Mara blatantly stated with a smirk on her face. She decided to push the envelope a little in hope they would backdown. She didn't think they wanted to hear the details just like she didn't want to share them.

"Oh, great…" Dave said sarcastically. "Our daughter lied to us in high school."

"Yeah, I'm also not a virgin anymore," Mara abruptly stated.

"Uh, my ears…. Okay, it is time to change the subject," Uncle Dave said as he stood and moved towards the outdoor bar.

"Oh, you don't want to hear about that?" Mara pressed hoping to end all future conversations about this topic. "You don't want to hear about who has my v-card?"

"V-card?" Uncle Dave asked as he stood to freshen up his drink.

"Oh my god Dave," Adam said from the pool. "She is referring to who took her virginity."

Dave didn't immediately respond and futzed around with his drink. Marathon got a kick out of how frazzled he looked. He looked like he regretted ever bringing up the topic and she knew he desperately wanted to change the topic. Mara pressed on.

"Yeah, the boy," Mara paused looking directly at her dad. "The boy who took my virginity…"

"Okay! You win! Enough, please," Uncle Dave said.

He took a large sip and held his head in defeat. Mara stood from her sunbathing position and in one graceful motion jumped into the pool next to Adam. The stark temperature difference engulfed her body like daggers. When she surfaced, Mara half expected steam to come off of her like when a hot frying pan hits cool tap water from the faucet.

Mara spent the remaining afternoon doing laps with Adam while Uncle Dave lounged on the patio by the pool. She swam slowly, but found she was not as winded as she thought she was going to be. Her strength in the water surprised her and she increased her pace to match Adam's breast stroke. Mara was afraid to push herself further, but she knew there was more in the tank. She could crank it up a gear or two and could sustain an increased workload on her body.

For the first time since the attack, Marathon thought she was recovering. Everything up until this point seemed to take forever. The stitches in her head and the bruising around her face, the metal plate bridging the gap in her skull, her fractured orbital bone all took weeks to heal. Now here she was, swimming laps and increasing her heart rate to aerobic exercise and sustaining it. She would judge how she felt later and tomorrow she would determine if she could try anaerobic exercise and really push herself the next time she swam in the pool. She wasn't going to wait for doctor approval to swim laps and get her heart rate going again.

M

Chapter
Fifteen

The next morning, Marathon tried to follow her typical routine but, the hype she had after her exercise yesterday invigorated her to change things up. She went for a short walk following a trail she made while exploring the surrounding land. After a light workout, and being satisfied she was headache free, Mara decided to out to the market and get some fresh groceries. She hadn't been out on her own since before the attack and she was getting cabin fever. She showered quickly and decided to combine breakfast and lunch into one big meal.

Uncle Dave had mentioned the local market had a great farmer's deli where you could get fresh sandwiches and hot food while grocery shopping. Her mouth watered at the thought of an egg sandwich with fresh avocado and bacon. Adam and Uncle Dave usually slept in and would probably not even notice Mara had left. She grabbed keys to the Jeep Wrangler, quickly checked her appearance in the mirror and sprang out the door with an extra spring in her step. The late August heat was gaining steam, and Marathon felt sweat form on her brow as the black Wrangler struggled to cool the interior.

The market was about ten minutes outside of Quincy and more towards route 81. Nothing but country music was on the radio as she flipped through the stations trying to find something that resembled civilization. She noticed Uncle Dave didn't have any presets and she smirked at the fact that he hated country as well. She took after him in many ways and inherited his taste in music. For better or for worse, Mara enjoyed a wide variety of 90s hip hop and teen angst music from that genre. She would find none of that here.

After a brief search, she found compact discs in the visor above her head. She placed a random Broadway musical into the player and let it blast as she drove the winding roads towards the market. The interior cabin refused to cool down and she decided to roll down all of the windows instead. At this time of day she would normally be in or around the pool waiting for her parents to wake and make lunch, or their breakfast.

Mara pulled into a local grocery store and parked the four door Jeep Wrangler close to the entrance. The heatwave they were experiencing was supposed to peak, last a few more days and then slowly dissipate back to normal temperatures later in the week. The humid air felt sticky and made her cotton clothes feel damp with moisture. The rush of cold air felt great as she entered the grocery store.

Typically, everyone knows each other in small town America. The local store was a social hub and gathering place for news and gossip. Going to the store also meant running into people who knew you just as much as you knew them. Mara didn't know anyone, and no one knew her, but they knew of her. Her city wardrobe stood out in the country small town. What she considered casual attire certainly did not fit in as casual attire here. She couldn't tell if people were staring at her because she was an unknown or because of the way she dressed, or because the bruises on her face still had that disgusting shade of purple. There was also a possibility that someone recognized her from the news. In New York, she was used to people staring at her, here, it felt different.

Being tall and lengthy, Mara had a difficult time shopping for her figure and generally relied on the yoga pants and a spaghetti strapped tank top. This look caught the attention of other patrons who typically wore more conservative attire. She took note for future reference.

Lately, Mara didn't wear makeup, even when she went out with her friends. She typically wore makeup to blend in more, and to tone down her features, but that required more work than what it was worth. Even with her scared face and fading bruises, being out and about, she regretted not toning down her looks. The combination of her natural beauty and the way her clothes clung to her body made her feel self-conscious and slightly embarrassed.

Marathon went to the deli counter where a young man, maybe just out of high school was waiting behind the counter. As they made eye contact, Mara thought his jaw was going to smack off the countertop. The young man's coworker, a female clerk was standing to his side and smacked his arm as Mara smiled awkwardly as she approached.

"Excuse me, do you make egg sandwiches here?" She asked. It was like a scene from a Looney Tunes cartoon where the Yosemite Sam notices a dolled-up Bugs Bunny for the first time. Yosemite Sam's eyes would pop out of his head and his tongue would hang from his mouth has he panted out loud. This is how the young man looked and she wondered if he had even heard her.

"Yes, what would you like," the young lady said rolling her eyes at her coworker who still had not recovered from Marathon's approach.

"Can I get two eggs on a roll with avocado and bacon?" Mara asked in response. "Oh, can you make the eggs sunny side up?"

The young lady looked like she was on summer break from college and wore a University of Virginia t-shirt with her dark brown hair in a high tight ponytail. The freckle cheeked young lady smiled at Mara as if she approved of her choice.

"Your sandwich comes with coffee," the clerk said handing her a small cup. The clerk then ordered the young man standing next to her to make the sandwich.

"I bet you didn't think we made egg sandwiches out here in Quincy," the clerk said.

"How did you know I was not from around here?" Mara asked with a smile on her face.

"Besides being blatantly obvious that you aren't from around here, you kinda have your father's eyes," she said as Mara heard the young man crack eggs behind the counter. He was still glancing at her, but this time being more discreet about it.

"Do I stand out that much?" Mara jokingly asked.

"Any new comer stands out here in Quincy. I remember when your father and his husband moved in, they stood out nearly as much as you do, but people around here get used to things fast. You, on the other hand, stand out for other reasons," the young lady said as she accessed the cash register.

"Yeah, I get that a lot." Marathon replied.

When Mara left the store, she felt the hot humid air rush towards her like stepping onto another planet where the environment was hostile towards human life. She got in the Jeep and started the engine. Hot air came blasting out as she rolled down the windows again.

"Detective Torres, don't move," a voice came from the backseat directly behind her.

Marathon kicked herself for not checking the car before entering the vehicle. She kept her hands on the wheel and pondered her next move.

"I am not going to hurt you, but I need you to stay here in the car," the voice continued.

"Who are you?" Mara asked with authority.

"You know who I am," the voice in the back said.

Mara recognized the voice, but she couldn't place where she heard it. She desperately wanted to turn around and confront whoever was behind her.

"I want you to drive away from here and park in the lot across the street," the voice said.

Mara looked across where she saw the open space of a baseball field and playground. The parking lot was empty, no one in their right mind would be out there playing baseball in weather like this.

"I am not going anywhere with you," Mara defiantly said. She moved her hand towards the door and prepped for a dash back into the store.

"You leave, and the truth about Marley Williams leaves with you, and you never see me again," The voice said.

She paused in her seat and stopped herself from opening the door. "Who the fuck are you?"

Marathon could feel the stranger in the back sift his weight as she glanced in the rear-view mirror. A face emerged and Officer Esposito appeared in her line of sight. Marathon's face turned to rage as she was prepared for a fight.

"Detective, I am not here to hurt you," he said putting his hands in the air to show he wasn't armed.

"Then why the fuck did you send that man to kill me?" Mara said when she turned towards him to look at him directly. People in the parking lot began to stare as her voice became heated. Esposito looked around nervously.

"Can we not do this here?" he stated.

"Fuck you," she said.

"I had nothing to do with that," Esposito protested. "If I knew you were in that kind of danger, I would have taken different actions."

"You have a lot of explaining to do," Mara said as she reached for her cell phone. Esposito noticed this and put his arm out towards her in protest.

"Don't do that, you'll be dead before nightfall," he said motioning her to put down the cell phone. "There are certain things we cannot undo; if you make that phone call, you'll set in motion things that cannot be undone."

"What the fuck are you talking about?"

"When you searched for Marley Williams from your computer, you set in motion a series of events that led you to this moment," Esposito said as he relaxed his arms at his side. "You're lucky to be alive, you have to be smart now."

"Start from the top then," Mara responded.

"We need to leave here first, too many people to track, too many variables," Esposito said nervously as he looked around at the comings and goings of employees and shoppers.

"Listen, Mara, if I wanted to harm you, or kill you, you'd already be dead. You're not a hard person to track or find," he said with a desperate look on his face. The parking lot they were in was clearly making him nervous.

That made sense, he easily infiltrated her life and completely caught her off guard, again. Mara wasn't even carrying her gun or badge. She looked around and then put the car in gear. She navigated the parking lot and pulled out onto the street. However, she didn't trust him enough to go into the parking lot across the street. Instead she continued down the street and studied him in the rear-view mirror to gauge his reaction.

Mara wanted to be in control of the vehicle and noticed Esposito was not wearing a seatbelt. If she needed to crash the car to protect herself, she was prepared to do that.

"Start talking," she said as she spent half her focus on him in the back seat.

"I am Lieutenant Macron Esposito with special operations."

"Lieutenant, yeah right, you're too young," Mara snapped back noting his youthful appearance.

"I was promoted to lieutenant because I accepted this assignment, now may I continue?" He snapped back at Mara who was looking through the rear view mirror.

Lieutenant Esposito was strikingly attractive and looked younger than her. His hair was neatly styled, and this stubbled beard gave him a rough looking appearance in contrast. He was not dressed in a suit like she remembered him, instead he wore a light pink form fitting polo shirt.

"I was recruited by special operations to partner with who you know as Lieutenant Russo. My assignment was to investigate corruption in city agencies including the NYPD. Russo and I started to notice a pattern of corruption. When we pieced things together, there seemed to be a common denominator. The events that led us to you were strikingly random at first appearance." Esposito said.

"So you're undercover? Like Leonardo DiCaprio in The Departed undercover?"

"It didn't start that way, but I guess that's a good frame of reference," Esposito responded. "May I continue?"

Mara remained silent, still frustrated that someone got the better of her so easily.

"Most of my work is done from following a paper trail or transactions from the safety of my own computer. Russo and I rarely get out of the office, but when we saw someone accessed the Marley Williams file, especially in the manner it was accessed, we knew we needed to act."

She sensed honesty in his voice, but something was off like he was purposely leaving out information. Something was off about his explanation as he told her more about the specific case she was working on. The fact that someone as athletic looking as Esposito sticking with a desk job following computer crimes was a stretch. She didn't believe the details of his story, but she still decided to play along.

"What's up with the Marley Williams case?"

"Marley Williams didn't die from gang violence, she was killed because she either witnessed something or threatened to expose something. Something happened with her that left a lot of loose ends in the criminal underworld and if you follow the surrounding events closely, you'd see a pattern surrounding her death."

"A pattern, that's what your theory is based off of?"

137

"It's more than that, but it's the part that involves you," He responded. Marathon confirmed he was withholding information. He was telling her what she wanted to hear.

"So, you investigate me for accessing the file?"

"At first, you looked like a random detective accessing a cold case file, so when I flagged your account for review, I noticed…"

"That I was the officer who found Marley's body."

"That's suspicious, but then, upon further digging, I noticed that you were recently promoted to detective. Within a week of your new assignment, you accessed, well tried to access Marley's file."

"So that gave you grounds to interrogate me and make it look like special investigations was onto me?"

"If that was a lead that came your way detective, how would you have handled it?"

Mara realized that she would have done the same thing, but decided to remain silent and not give Esposito the satisfaction that his course of action was correct.

"William Bowden was hired to either scare or kill you. It was supposed to look like a random home invasion that led to murder if it got that far," Esposito said as his voice cracked at the grim details.

"He tried to fucking rape me," she interjected.

"Bowden was a career criminal who had no problem killing someone for the right price," he continued. "The people behind this brought him up from Florida, where he was on the run for a similar crime. I'm thinking that is how they chose him."

Mara knew there was a deeper connection. The tattoo on his arm was significant and Bowden wasn't just a thug Esposito made him out to be. He was far more dangerous than that and Marathon knew she barely escaped that encounter with her life.

"You keep saying they, who are THEY," She asked intently.

"We have an idea of who they are, but there are still many unknowns and their network is so interconnected and obscure that it is really hard to track. The reason Russo and I paid you a visit at the station was because we thought you were one of them," Esposito said.

"You figured you could put pressure on me so I would either rat or make a mistake," she said.

"That's generally how it works," he responded. "You were either a new recruit or a loose end."

Mara found herself going well over 60 miles per hour. She eased off the gas and slowed down to try and match the speed limit on the winding roads in the back country.

"So when did you realized you fucked up?" Marathon asked. "Is that why you're here? To say you're sorry for fucking up my life?"

"You tend to fuck up your life on your own," he snapped back showing his balls. Mara liked the comeback, if this conversation took place in a bar, she'd send clues of interest his way to see if he'd pick up on them. She found him strangely attractive, and this back and forth was turning her on.

"When I found Marley Williams, you weren't even on the force," Mara snapped to poke fun at his age and inexperience.

"Russo was, he was a detective from the 73rd."

"What? Bullshit, I would have recognized the name," Mara said.

"Detective Torres, do you really think Russo would use the same name?"

"If you're not here to apologize, then what the fuck are you here for?" she asked as she focused her eyes ahead on the curvy road that seemed to visually convey her thoughts.

"Officer Russo had me convinced that you were part of the underground network which infiltrated the 73rd and the department. The evidence pointed that way, you were recently promoted, transferred and even accessed the one file we thought tied everything together."

"You took a major risk coming out to the station to question me," Mara stated. "And you still didn't answer my fucking question."

"No wonder you're single, do you curse like this all the time?" he scolded.

"Only when I'm pissed off," she snapped back with a glare in the mirror.

"Okay, I'll get to your question. You know, we did take a risk, but now we have solid leads to follow up on."

"You mean the fact that I nearly got my head bashed in by a psychopath pervert?"

"You've proven that you could handle yourself," he responded.

"You missed a key detail," Mara said, thinking it was now time to share her information. Something inside her told her to trust Esposito even though he was withholding information and possibly being deceitful.

Marathon saw his face perk up in the back seat. His chiseled features expressed intrigue and waited for her to continue. Marathon paused to be more dramatic and appreciated his interest. As she stared at him through the rearview mirror, his dark eyes stared back at her.

"Bowden wasn't your average thug hired to scare or take someone out," Marathon stated. Esposito didn't respond and waited for her to continue.

"He is former Military, special forces," Mara said.

"What? There's literally nothing in his file that would suggest that," he protested.

"He had a tattoo, I've seen it before," Mara stated. She described the incident in Afghanistan where she encountered special forces while on a resupply mission. She then described how Bowden's tattoo was oddly similar to the one she encountered in the mountains. Marathon saw the gears turn in Esposito's head as if he were given another piece to a vast puzzle.

"You're sure?" he said.

"Have you ever served Macron?" Mara asked.

"Please call me Mac, and no I haven't," he said. She knew that was a lie. She could spot another soldier a mile away.

"Then you should know that many soldiers get tattoos to show a sense of group bondage and loyalty. Mara pointed to her exposed tattoo. "His tattoo matched the one I saw in Afghanistan."

"This changes things," he said.

"What do you mean?"

"This is not the first former military to come up in our investigation," Esposito answered. Lieutenant Esposito looked puzzled and worried.

"Can you please answer my question now? Why the fuck are you out here?"

"I heard rumors that you might be retiring," he said.

"Are you monitoring my phone calls? You know that's illegal without a warrant!"

"Mara, I am not about to defend my actions, and yes I have been monitoring you," he said. Marathon paused for a second and looked at him directly through the rear view mirror.

"You just used my nickname," she said.

"I'm sorry Detective," he said. "I've been monitoring you for a while."

"How long?" Mara asked as a wave of embarrassment came over her.

"Long enough to know many details about your life," he responded.

"You've got a lot of nerve," she said.

"It's my job," he said. "Detective, I need your help."

"I know you do. I can tell asking for help is very hard for you because you've been pissing around the pot the entire car ride," Mara sharply responded.

Mara saw a gas station on her right and decided to pull into an empty spot on the side of the station. She put the Jeep in park but kept the engine running.

"I know you are not telling me the whole story Lieutenant," she said.

"I'm not," he said as Mara observed him looking out the window. "I don't know if you can handle the information I know and the conclusion I've drawn based on the evidence I've collected. This has been my entire career."

"What do you think this has been for me? You know I was there when Marley Williams was found. Don't fucking do that," she said. "If You've observed me long enough to realize that I am not some weak dame who needs to be protected, then you should fucking know to just get on with it and not insult my intelligence," Mara responded making sure he wasn't going to play the knight in shining armor routine with her.

"You are many things Detective, but weak would not describe you," Esposito said.

Mara got out of the car and walked over towards the passenger door and opened it. She motioned for Lieutenant Esposito to get out. Mara now had a chance to fully size him up. Lieutenant Esposito was slightly taller than her, with broader shoulders and more defined frame. He was thin, and his light pink polo shirt was tight enough to accent his pectoral muscles. His arms were also well defined with clear cuts that showed he was into weight lifting. Esposito had roughly the same skin tone as her but it seemed to glisten in the sunlight.

Marathon thought this have looked like a fragrance commercial with the two of them standing on the side of the road together next to a typical small-town gas station without a soul in sight. She half expected a photographer to come out and start photographing them as a director order them to pose for the camera.

Esposito looked annoyed. Perspiration already started forming on his brow from the midday heat and he put his hands on his hips showing a smaller waist that what his shorts defined.

"Marathon, what are you doing?" He asked.

"We are done, find your own fucking way home," Mara said as she turned towards the driver's side.

"Are you kidding me? You're going to leave me here?"

"Sure," she said opening the car door.

"Hold on, hold on."

"Unless you have any other information for me, or you want to actually answer my fucking question, we are done and it is time for us to part ways," Mara said getting back into the car.

She shifted into gear and started to speed off. Before she could exit the gas station, she heard Esposito yell for her to stop. Marathon grinned and slowed to a stop and allowed Esposito to catch up to her. He tried to open the rear driver side door, but it was purposely locked. Mara looked out her window waiting for him to speak.

"I'll tell you what I know, just let me back in the car," he pleaded.

"And get to the fucking point," she said.

She unlocked the door and Esposito climbed in. She adjusted the rear view mirror to look at him, he was sweating and looked unhappy. Mara shifted into gear, turned back the way she came.

"Well lieutenant, start talking," she said.

"Since you want the truth, here it is. Russo and I believe Inspector Frank Davidson is a member of this underground department that has infiltrated every agency in New York City." Esposito paused as Mara processed the information.

"Frank?" Mara finally said, "You think Frank is behind this?"

"Maybe not behind this, but certainly caught up in it," he said. "He is certainly aware of what's going on."

"What proof do you have?"

"Observations, recordings, emails," Esposito said.

"You collected all of this yourself?" Marathon questioned.

"Russo and I, together," he responded. "We thought you were either in on it or being recruited by Frank. That's why we observed you for so long."

"Recruited? What to join a club?" Mara asked.

"Yes, ruling you out as a conspirator, you were set up to either be a fall guy or for recruitment, or maybe whatever was convenient for them. However, based on my dossier of Frank, I think he was recruiting you," Esposito stated.

"I think you are making a leap," Mara stated in protest.

"Frank is former military right?"

"Yes, but that doesn't mean he knew Bowden, or had any connection to Marley Williams," she stated. "Fuck, Frank served in the Army, not the Marines or Special Forces."

"We think Frank was suspicious and carefully planned this scenario. Frank knew you would recognize the name Marley Williams. He knew you would access the online database for any updates on the case file. He probably suspected that the case was flagged. You served as bait for Russo and I," Esposito said.

"If Frank wanted to recruit me, then why send Bowden to kill me?" Mara asked impatiently. "Your narrative doesn't make sense Lieutenant."

"That is what I was trying to figure out as well. Why would Frank send Bowden to kill you, or even scare you?" He asked. "Until you mentioned the military connection, I wouldn't have pieced this together."

"Piece what together?"

"I don't think they were ready to recruit you, or they determined you weren't going to be recruited. Your service record is exceptional, I don't think you match what they are looking for," he said.

"So they send Bowden to get me to back off the Williams case?"

"Also, to lure Russo and I out. I am now convinced that their objective was to bring Russo and I out in the open," Esposito stated. "We are getting close and I think they know we are onto them."

"Are you getting close? Because it sounds to me like you got a shit full of nothing," Mara said.

"Russo shares your line of thinking. We still think Frank is somehow involved, but since your attack and Bowden's death, everything went quiet. Frank is the only one asking questions and the only one pressing the issue. It either means he's calling the shots and playing the game, or he is not involved and trying to legitimately find out what's going on."

"You must know my relationship with Frank goes way back and simple circumstantial pieces of evidence will not get me to go against my friend."

"You're right, I am here against Russo's better judgement," he said.

"If you think you can use me to get to Frank, you can go fuck yourself."

"That's not my goal," Esposito said. "I am here because you have access I don't."

"Ahh, finally…" Mara stated.

"You're a pain in the ass you know that," he said.

"Yeah I get that a lot," Mara responded.

"You have access to the 73rd, you are a target and I don't think they will stop coming for you."

"You want to use my relationship with Frank to see who's involved? Wait, you think Frank and I are more than just colleagues?" Mara question.

"That thought crossed my mind," Esposito said.

"Fuck you!"

"Listen, if it were true, you would not be the first beautiful woman to fuck her way to the top. It's a plausible scenario. Besides, you have a questionable background."

"Fuck you," she said again.

"What? Do you really think your service record wouldn't be investigated?" he questioned.

"I was honorably discharged, you piece of shit!"

"Yeah, the official version," Esposito said.

"Go on, keep going," Mara baited him. "You're the fucking moron who couldn't find shit out about Bowden."

"You're a piece of shit," he said in response. "I am not here to get into a character debate with you."

"But you did when you suggested I fucked Frank, right!" she said.

"While we're on that topic, you wanna explain fraternizing with a superior officer just before deployment?" he snapped back.

Those records were sealed conditionally as part of her honorable discharge. How the fuck did he know this? Where was he getting this information? "Fuck you," she said again as her anger spilled over to her lack of vocabulary.

"Don't fucking question me about my motives, when you've done some shady shit yourself," he said.

There was an awkward silence in the car as she tried to maintain the speed limit. She never expected her past to come roaring back like this and wanted history to remain where it belonged.

"Do you think it's true Lieutenant?" Marathon finally asked in a much calmer tone as she looked directly into his eyes through the rear-view mirror.

"No," he said not breaking eye contact in the mirror. "I think you got where you are today on your own accord."

"You don't know what it's like dealing with this every single goddamn day," Mara responded as the car continued back towards the market.

"I don't, but you seem to be doing just fine on your own," Esposito said.

The market was just ahead, and Mara slowed down scouting out the place before she pulled into the parking lot. Everything looked normal for small town America.

"Where's your car?" She asked as Mara was unsure of which way to turn.

"To the right, back of the lot," he said.

Mara pulled the Jeep right next to his car and backed into the parking spot. Esposito didn't move from the backseat. He looked deep in thought.

"Why did you join the force?" he finally asked.

146

Mara didn't reply and felt that was a personal question. She had her reasons, but wanted to keep this line of questioning to herself. For her the NYPD was life line to a more secure path. The department offered stability, a career, a pension, and a sense of belonging she had missed overseas.

"You could have done anything, model, act, your SAT scores were through the roof, and you could have gone into engineering, or became a doctor. Why the force?"

Mara turned around and looked directly at him. "You have no idea what it's like," Mara said with fire in her eyes. "If you know so much about me, then you tell me why the fuck I joined the force!"

"Mara, listen, I need an answer from you," Esposito finally said. "I need to know if you are willing to see this through."

"I don't know Lieutenant. I was offered early retirement and I am seriously considering it," Mara said in response.

"I know," Esposito responded.

"You trying to talk me out of it?" she asked.

"Yes," he said.

Mara looked straight ahead. She couldn't respond to that question at this time because she was unsure herself. She had no idea what she wanted, the thought retirement made her feel old and washed up. While the thought of going back to the 73rd and back into the city frightened her. She wanted more time, she needed more time, but she felt time was about to run out and the world she left in NY was about to come for her again.

"I'll be in town for a bit longer," he said breaking the silence.

"How do I get in contact with you?" Mara asked.

"You don't, I'll get in contact with you," he said. "Your phone is probably being monitored."

"Lieutenant, next time you try and recruit someone, take them out to dinner," Marathon said as he opened the door.

He got out of the car and she watched him slowly walk away towards his sedan. She studied him closely and determined he was a man of action and resolve. Marathon knew he didn't reveal everything he knew. He simply fed her details she needed to know to get the ball rolling. It worked, and now she was intrigued.

She wanted to get away from everything. Her head hurt and the painful memories of the attack in her own apartment were still fresh. She looked at Esposito in her rear-view mirror before she pulled out of the parking lot. She liked him, even though he was still hiding things from her. She sensed that he only spoke to her in partial truths.

Something bothered her. Russo was a detective at the 73rd back when Marley Williams was murdered. Bullshit! She would have recognized him, or someone would have recognized him at the 73rd. The turnover at the precinct was high, but Detective Morales would have recognized him from the surveillance video. She knew Esposito and Russo were not special investigators for the NYPD. Something else was going on and she wondered if she was ready to get involved. Could she see this through, she seriously questioned her resolve.

M

Chapter
Sixteen

Uncle Dave's Ranch
Quincy Pennsylvania
August 29th, 2019

A few days passed since Lieutenant Esposito entered her life again. Mara couldn't stop thinking about him, about what he said as she relaxed by the pool. Was he really suggesting a big conspiracy within the department? Was Frank involved somehow? These questions shook the perception of her career and questioned the very foundation of what she believed. Her belief in the Marines suffered a similar fate when her company was ordered to turn the city of Baghlan over to the Afghan Army. She was court martialed for going against orders, which settled with her conditional honorable discharge from the armed services.

There was also the fact that someone felt threatened by her enough to send a former spec ops soldier to her apartment to intimidate her. It was over the Marley Williams case; something about that case was supposed to remain buried and whoever was behind it went through great lengths to cover up what was going on.

Mara wanted to call Terrence Morgan, her union rep, and let him know what had transpired, but each time she went to dial his number, she paused. Mara never second guessed herself before, she never questioned her actions, but now, her entire life was turned upside down. Macron Esposito planted the seed of doubt in her mind and her circle of trust shrunk considerably. She held her department issued cell phone in her hand and looked at it closely, and opened to the home screen and noticed the GPS symbol was active, like it usually was; her location was being tracked somewhere and by someone. She noticed data being sent both to and from the device. This occurs all the time, but with all that has happened, she wasn't sure who was on the other end monitoring the information it sent.

Mara turned the cellphone over and inspected the back of it. There was a plastic cover that protected the SIM card and battery. She could easily open the device up and remove the battery, thus shutting off the phone and leaving it with no power, but her inner voice told her not to do that yet. If someone was monitoring her, she didn't want to tip them off and suddenly go dark. Best to keep the status quo for the time being.

The only advantage she had now was to act naive to the situation. If Frank really was behind this, and if there really was a secret organization deep underground running the department, Mara would need to be smart and hold her cards tight to her chest. This was like organized crime. However, the I know, that you know, that I know sort of deal would not work in this situation like it would with the mob. Those rules did not apply with this syndicate. If these people knew you knew about them, Mara suspected it would be dealt with as swiftly as possible. Like what happened in her apartment. That is why no one has ever heard of them and they've remained hidden for so long.

It was getting late, Adam and Uncle Dave were still out running errands. Mara made a stiff drink to help clear her head as she relaxed the rest of the day by the pool. The summer heat melted the ice before she could even get halfway through her drink. The sun baked her tanned olive skin to the point where she thought she couldn't get any darker. She stared up at the clouds drifting aimlessly in the sky. Her sunglasses felt like weights on her eyes as the effects of the whiskey started to take hold. Lost in her thoughts, Mara drifted off to sleep.

The sound of her cellphone startled her awake. It was her personal cell phone and she reached beneath her to retrieved it. It took her awhile for her eyes to adjust to the brightness and she didn't recognize the number on the phone when her eyes finally focused on the screen. Mara let the call go to voicemail, but noted that it was a local number. She saw that the sun was much lower in the sky and wondered how long she'd been asleep. The time read 5:12 on her phone. The whiskey glass was nearly empty beside her.

The phone rang again, it was the same number.

"Hello?" Mara answered.

"Detective Torres."

Mara heard Esposito's voice on the other end of the phone. There was panic in his deep masculine voice and loud noises in the background. She heard what sounded like an 18 wheeler drive by and horns honking in the distance.

"What? Where are you?"

"Rest stop off of 81," Esposito said. "I'm glad you decided to retire."

He paused and Mara thought carefully about this statement. How did he know about her decision, especially when she didn't share it with anyone? Why was he calling from a rest stop?

"I'm heading back to New York. Sorry we couldn't do business," he said.

"Umm yeah," Mara said thinking on her feet.

"I hope you reconsider," he said as the phone went dead.

Marathon slowly lowered the phone knowing something was wrong. As she pieced the conversation together she realized the brief conversation was a warning. She was compromised and something has changed, which probably put her in danger. He knew her phone was monitored and he was desperate enough to contact her which meant *she* was in immediate danger.

Marathon sat up from her relaxed position realizing her current situation. She looked around her and saw the same peaceful environment as before. Nothing out of the ordinary, the pool was calm, the trees across the field swayed in the slight summer breeze, the clouds materialized over the rolling hills around the ranch. Yet, something seemed different. Like a virus entering the body, Mara felt like her safe space was compromised.

Marathon's phone rang again, this time it was her department issued phone. Frank's number was displayed on the home screen. The buzzing continued as she found it odd that Frank was calling right after Esposito had hung up with her.

"Hello, Detective Torres here," Mara said holding the up to her head.

"Hey, Mara, just checking in to see how you're doing," Inspector Frank Davidson said.

"Hey Frank! It's good to hear from you," Mara blurted out surprising herself with how sincere it sounded.

"Have the headaches gone away?" He asked.

"They come and go, some days are better than others, some are much worse than both," she responded trying to act like her normal self. She wanted to ask him directly, but her better judgement told her to remain in the shadows as long as possible.

"I wanted to speak with you about the offer your received," Frank said interrupting her thoughts.

"I've been giving it a lot of thought Frank," she said.

"You've been through a lot Mara, no one expects you to return any time soon. You should take your time and make an informed decision," Frank said.

Mara thought for a moment and realized Frank was trying to mentor her into a decision. Not knowing exactly how to proceed, she decided to play along with Frank's train of thought.

"I am leaning towards retirement Frank. As you know, I got out of my lease and I am moving," Mara stated. "Why not move down here and enjoy life?"

"I heard, John had told me you were gonna stay out of the city for a while, I guess a while might be permanent then," he said.

What was Frank doing talking to John, sure they spoke from time to time but they were never that close and it wasn't like them to call each other out of the blue. Frank was definitely doing the rounds and checking on Mara. Like a true cop, he started with known associates to get the backstory before asking direct questions to check for deception. She felt like he had an ulterior motive to call her.

"Yeah, I cannot go back after what had happened," Mara responded not letting onto the fact that she knew what was happening.

"That's probably for the best," Frank said. "How's Pennsylvania?"

"Oh it's beautiful here. I am relaxing by the pool as we speak and enjoying every moment of it," She said stating a half truth.

"How are your uncles doing?" Frank asked.

Mara suspected he was fishing for something, but then she heard what sounded like someone else on the line. She heard some background noise that was not consistent to the sounds that came from Frank's end. She ignored that and answered the question. She would have missed it if Esposito hadn't altered her to a possible wiretap.

"They are fine, just running errands," Mara responded.

"Well, I have a busy evening in front of me. Call me when you've decided what you want to do. Remember, I'm here if you want to talk things out," Frank said.

They said their goodbyes and Mara hung up the phone and held her personal cell phone to see if any additional message came through. She wanted to call Esposito but refrained.

Mara heard sounds coming from inside the house. She dropped the phone on the chair and went to check. As she approached the sliding glass door that led to the kitchen, Mara saw Uncle Dave walk past the refrigerator. She stopped and turned around to retrieve her phone. Then something caught her eye off in the distance east of her location. There was a brief shine of shimmering light, like a mirror reflecting in the sunlight. She knew exactly what that was and tried to act normal. She casually retrieved her phone. She wasn't just being watched, the reflection was from a high powered scope off in the distance by the trees at the edge of the property, just beyond the open field.

Mara casually moved about the pool and dove in. She wasn't doing this to cool off, she wanted to act as normal as possible for show. Somewhere beyond her Uncle's property line, there was definitely someone watching her. It was a hot day and even though the sun was going down, the heat refused to concede. Mara wanted to give off the impression that she was talking to a friend and that they had just hung up. The timing of phone calls and Esposito's warning was very suspect.

She knew the reflection well, having seen it in Afghanistan right before incoming rounds sent her flying behind cover. In the mountainous region, while hunting the Taliban, she warned her platoon of incoming sniper fire before any shots were fired, possibly saving herself and the Marines around her. The Navy Cross was awarded for her act of bravery under hostile fire. She often wondered if a sniper had her in his scopes before she noticed the reflected light. That brief moment where a single shot could have ended her life without warning often lingered in her thoughts.

As Mara made her laps in the pool, she reminded herself that they were just watching. She must remain calm and be careful not to tip her cards just yet. She didn't know how long they've been out there, watching. Which meant the status quo was still intact. Mara swam back and forth in the water and her view of the tree line was generally obstructed by the edge of the pool. Esposito's call was definitely a danger close warning.

The house and surrounding property were on the same level, which made it difficult for her to see what was happening outside the pool towards the trees. She knew that if a sniper was out in the woods, he couldn't see her easily either. The sniper would have to either wait for her to get out of the pool or get a better position if he was ordered to take the shot. The timing of Frank's phone call worried her immensely. If he was in contact with the sniper, then the outcome of their phone call determined her fate. The fact that she wasn't shot in that moment confirmed her thoughts on the status quo.

Mara did some quick mental math and decided that the tree line was roughly three hundred yards from the pool. A good distance, but not terrible for a sniper. Mara would be doomed if the order was given and she kept low in the pool with just her head above water. What factors determined her termination? Sending Bowden to make it look like a random sexual assault was something entirely different than a sniper shooting a cop in broad daylight while she recovered.

She thought back to the conversation she had with Frank, was it sincere enough? Was it convincing enough? She wasn't sure, Frank had good instincts which worried her. She trembled in the pool, afraid to get out. Afraid to continue on with her normal routine. She was talking herself out of believing the status quo still remained.

Marathon waited in the pool until she mustered up enough courage to get out. She knew she had to break line of sight to make sure there was no clear shot for the sniper. He would have to work if he wanted to take her out. But she also didn't want to tip him off and let him know she was onto him.

She swam to the deep end of the pool and got out using the table and chairs to block line of sight from the trees. She didn't bother grabbing her towel and moved swiftly towards the sliding doors. Nothing happened, no shattering glass of sniper fire, no echoing bang from off in the distance, and she entered the house dripping wet. Uncle Dave and Jacob were standing in the kitchen making dinner. Their eyes met and they both knew something was wrong.

M

Chapter
Seventeen

Parris Island, South Carolina
November 20th, 2001
6:30pm

Mara's head was spinning, tracer rounds whipped over her as she crawled under barbed wire obstacle. She felt the jagged wire rip at her fatigues as mud clung to the brim of her helmet. Sounds of explosions and gun fire drowned out everything as the intense combat training exceeded anything she experienced.

The days leading up to this were intense. Special Forces were on site conducting training operations to help weed out the potential dropouts and make them break under pressure. They were good at their job, and one by one, her fellow recruits were buckling under the intense training regimen.

They enjoyed watching the dropouts leave the barracks and often taunted them before the bus picked them up. Before any dropout was permitted to leave, the officers would rip their insignia off their uniform and staple it to the wall by the barracks door. It was like an end of the day ceremony that would ultimately conclude with a bet as to who was going to be next. Without fail, each day her name was mentioned as a potential dropout. The biggest and meanest looking officer often picked Mara as the next drop out and would stare her down until she looked away. The spec ops soldiers did this out in the open, they wanted the trainees to know they were rooting against them.

When someone drops out of the Marine Corps Boot Camp, they don't actually drop out. They don't have a choice to leave; you're actually considered a washout and discharged for physical incompatibility or medical reasons. Your status would follow suit, something other than an honorable discharge, but certainly not a dishonorable discharge.

The objective for this evenings live fire exercise was to make it through an obstacle course to the other side and ring a bell. Simple enough, but Marine bootcamp made the most simple tasks difficult. In addition to munitions flying over the course simulating combat, the special forces soldiers were entrenched at the end of the course picking recruits off with tasers or training rounds that resembled paintballs.

Mara was in the middle of the pack, and even allowed a few recruits to pass her in the course. This was the type of training obstacle you didn't want to finish first. Even with the heavy rain, she should have heard recruits ahead of her ring the bell signaling they've completed the course. But she didn't hear any bells, only distant laughter and munitions fire.

She paused mid-way through the last part of the course, where she was stuck in prone position with barbed wire directly above her. She noticed the parameters of engagement had changed. Not only were the spec ops soldiers picking the off with simulated gun fire, they were engaging them in hand to hand combat as they made it the end. They were literally beating them into the ground and kicking them while they were down unbeknownst to the other recruits making their way to the objective. With the way things were going, no one was going to ring that bell.

Mara studied the situation as her fellow soldiers reached the end only to fail the task. She saw the special ops soldiers at the end of the course picking off recruits as they emerged from the trench. They were using tasers to incapacitate the soldiers and then beat them to the ground only to mock them as they fell flat on

157

their faces withering in pain. The Staff Sergeant was there yelling at the recruits for failing.

She assessed her situation, if she pushed forward, she would have to deal with the spec ops soldiers waiting for her. Her chance of success was less than desirable at best. The spec ops soldier who constantly stared her down was waiting for her. She knew he would personally see to her failure.

To her right, there was a break in the course where the terrain dipped down just enough to take a wide angle to get behind the spec ops officers without them noticing her. This section of the course was not being monitored, but still active enough not to draw too much attention. Recruits didn't like going this route because of the big water trap that extended the length of the course. The water was deceptively deep, icy cold, and thick with heavy mud and soot below the water line.

Mara rolled to her right and dropped about a foot down and into the icy cold brown water. She slowed her pace through the mud to not draw attention, like a lion stalking her prey. It felt like she was crawling through glass as the frigged water pierced her uniform and numbed her body. Marathon kept her focus on the location of the spec ops soldiers as they tased her fellow recruits one by one. They looked as if they were enjoying themselves as they stunned the latest recruit who emerged from the course and then beat him down to the ground.

Mara saw her window of opportunity as a recruit warranted the attention of multiple spec ops officers as he tried to put up a fight. Their initial taser shot missed its mark and allowed the recruit to engage in more of a fair fight with one of the soldiers. That quickly changed when the larger spec ops soldier picked him up from behind and slammed him into the ground. The other spec ops soldiers then continued to beat him as if he had personally offended them by fighting back.

Mara crawled out of the course and rolled over the embankment and onto the grass. Her uniform clung to her body as she remained prone on the ground. A heavy rain had set in and the mud from her uniform slowly washed away from the down pour. Her helmet was soaked and the added weight from the water caused it to lean forward obscuring her vision. She took it off and retired her hair in a high ponytail.

The spec ops soldiers were now having fun with the bold recruit who managed to serve as the distraction Mara needed. The soldiers laughed at him as he looked like a fish out of water flopping around on the ground from the multiple taser shocks. The taser shots were sent as a message, not because he was still trying to ring the bell. One of the soldiers kicked him in the chest and then turned up the intensity to continually shock him, he screamed out in pain.

Marathon inched forward and saw an opening. She readied her practice rifle. It fired non-lethal paint-based rounds used for combat training. She emerged from prone position and fired numerous rounds into the backs of the spec ops soldiers catching them by surprise. Mara successfully hit three out of the five officers before she had to adjust her position to reload, giving the spec ops soldiers time to react. They readied their tasers and fired. Mara had already begun her roll and the taser wire whisked by her former position as she regained her footing and fired an additional spray towards the soldiers.

One round connected and signaled that soldier was out of commission. Mara's clip was now empty again and she charged the remaining spec ops soldier with her rifle as a melee weapon. It was the big beefy guy who frequently targeted her the weeks leading up to this event. The soldier immediately disarmed her and sent her flying over his hip as he used her momentum against her. She landed hard on the ground and was now staring up at an M9 handgun as his knee pinned her rib cage to the ground preventing any lateral movement. She saw the inside of the barrel and a live 9mm round at the other end.

"Get that fucking gun out of my face," Mara demanded.

"You dead, bitch," the beefy soldier said in a thick southern accent.

"So are your mates' dumb ass," she said as a bell rang in the background. "We fucking won."

159

His eyes squinted and he held the gun firmly at her. She wanted to swipe it away and get him off of her, but she knew she was at his mercy. He was one of the main assholes who loved to mess with the recruits. He had a nasty reputation and was sadistically pursuant of pain and torture to anyone he crossed paths with.

Being a spicy girl from Queens, Mara didn't have time for his bullshit and saw right through his masculinity. She knew what type of man he was and knew he felt threatened by her presence. Once he started targeting her, fighting back was her only option.

Mara tried to move but the spec ops soldier's knee dug in further preventing her from gaining any leverage to improve her situation. The gun was still focused on her and their eyes were locked. She saw his intense stare try and pierce through hers. He looked fierce; with an intensity she had never experienced before.

"Get that fucking thing out of my face," she repeated.

The gun moved to the right and then discharged inches from its previous location. Mara felt the gunpowder burn the side of her face as deafening sounds from multiple shots ruptured her eardrum. Mud from the impacts got in her eyes and mouth as she struggled to get out of his grasp. No one dared intervene, fearing they'd become victims themselves.

He finally let go by her using his massive frame to push off of her to stand up. Mara got to her feet and instinctively charged him striking wildly in a fit of rage. The soldier ate the initial blows and spun her around using one motion to apply a standing choke hold. He was much bigger than her, much stronger and his grasp was like an iron vice pinning her against his solid frame.

"Look at this bitch," he said to the crowd that had gathered.

Mara threw her elbow back into the chest of the soldier, it was like hitting a concrete wall. He didn't flinch or react to her strike. His grip grew tighter as if he was trying to squeeze the life out of her. She knew she was on the verge of losing

160

consciousness as her vision started to narrow like driving into a tunnel. She felt her feet leave the ground as soldiers standing around them murmured for him to stop.

Just before she lost consciousness, the man let go and Mara fell to the ground. Her body was limp, and she gasped for air as she remained on the ground and tried to recover. Her heart beat like a drum trying to get her engine started again. She was not out of this fight yet.

Mara saw the other recruits try and get to her, but the other spec ops soldiers prevented anyone from assisting. The Staff Sergeant was standing over her and allowed this to continue.

"Stay down," the beefy spec ops soldier said when he noticed she was trying to get to her feet.

Mara's arms pulled in close and started to push her body up until she was able to get her knees under. She sat back using her bent legs to balance herself upright.

"Fuck you, asshole."

The man got close and grabbed her uniform, and pulled her in. His rancid breath helped her regain her senses. Grasping her opportunity, Mara sent her forehead into the bridge of the man's nose. Marathon didn't feel a thing, it was like hitting a baseball on the sweet spot of the bat. The man fell backwards as Mara felt his blood trickle down her face. His nose had exploded outwards in all directions like a bug hitting the windshield of a speeding car.

Mara stood up, like someone else was in control of her body and she was a mere spectator. The Staff Sergeant barked orders calling for attention as Mara continued forward. The beefy man with the broken nose had regained his footing and stood upright. She kept advancing towards him as he stood ready. Just before Mara was in striking distance, another spec ops soldier grabbed her and took her back to the ground.

"Get the fuck off of me!" Mara screamed as she tried to force her way out of his grasp.

The Staff Sergeant shouted out a few more orders, but Mara couldn't comprehend what he was saying over her ringing ears. She was in a fit of rage, a switch had gone off in her head, allowing her wrath and frustration to control her. This asshole had been targeting her and push other recruits to their breaking point. The Staff Sergeant called for attention again and the soldiers responded leaving Mara free on the ground. She stood up, rage inflicted and reengaged her target. The Staff Sergeant stepped in front of her and shouted for attention. Mara couldn't hear his words, the combination of her ire intent and the gunshot that blew out her eardrum made her world silent around her. The only thing she heard was her inner blood lust calling out.

The Staff Sergeant had to take a step back as Mara kept trying to advance. He grabbed Mara's face and squeezed her cheeks. He turned her gaze towards his own and their eyes met.

"Private! STAND DOWN!" he yelled. "STAND DOWN!"

Mara eased her advance; her senses started to return. The physical redirection snapped her out of her rage induced state. She then stood at attention as the Staff Sergeant released his grasp. He turned and dismissed the spec ops soldiers and then turned back towards her. The beefy soldier wiped blood off his face as he stared her down. His nose already started to swell. She saw his lips move but could only imagine what he was saying. He then turned and walked off with his fellow soldiers.

"Private, what in the holy hell do you think you're doing?"

Mara remained silent trying to regain her composure and control her heavy breathing. Her fit of rage turned to an overwhelming wave of emotion that crashed through her body. She bent over from her statuesque stance and threw up all over the ground in front of the Staff Sergeant. Her body heaved and tears swelled under her eyes. This incident produced her most intense moment. She knew she was completely out of control and questioned what would have happened if the Staff Sergeant wasn't there to intervene.

The Staff Sergeant bent down after she was done and helped her to her feet. Tears were now streaming down her face. Mara tried to speak but her chin quivered violently, preventing any sound from escaping.

"What in the holy hell is wrong with you?" the Staff Sergeant asked, with a more sympathetic tone. She barely heard him over the ringing echo bouncing in her head.

Still no words could escape. She felt trapped in her own body as she searched for words to convey her emotions. The muted sound of heavy rain continued around her. Soon they were replaced with a high pitched ringing and she could hear the Staff Sergeant more clearly now as her hearing adjusted.

"If you can't control yourself soldier, you need to quit. You need to get on out of here," the Staff Sergeant said in a relaxed tone. "The Marines are not for you."

Mara took a deep breath and held in an outburst of emotion, almost like she was trying to swallow it down. "Sir, no sir!"

"What?" the Staff Sergeant said.

"Sir, I do not quit, sir," Mara blurted out. He stared at her hovering inches from her face.

"Then get your sorry self over to the infirmary. You've got blood coming out of your ear."

"Sir, yes sir!"

M

Chapter Eighteen

Uncle Dave's Ranch
Quincy Pennsylvania
August 29th, 2019

"Get away from the windows!" Mara yelled as she burst through the sliding glass doors that lead to the patio. Her bikini still soaking wet from the pool as a puddle of water formed at her feet.

Adam and Uncle Dave had Broadway music playing loud enough to drown out most sound. Mara had startled them, but they couldn't hear what she was saying. Mara darted over and motioned for them to get away from the kitchen window that overlooked the pool. She knew eyes were on her, which meant masking her actions as casually as possible. If a sniper suspected something or if the target found out, there might be standing orders to take action.

"Marathon, what the hell?" Uncle Dave said as he met her halfway. "Where's your towel?"

"Stay away from the windows. Someone is out there, just beyond the tree line," she said.

"Mara, take a deep breath," Adam said as he turned down the Broadway music.

"Listen!" Marathon said at a volume that was meant to speak over the music. "I saw a flash of light out there in the woods. It was light refracting in this direction from either binoculars or a high powered scope. The kind that attaches to rifles."

"So someone is out there bird watching or hunting," Uncle Dave said as he moved closer. "There are a bunch of trails in the woods, hunters use them all time."

Marathon took a deep breath, she was agitated, her headache resurfaced and she felt her heart pound in her chest. Pool water dripped off her body as the distinct smell of chlorine filled the air masking the garlic scent from the dinner Adam was preparing.

"Listen, you're going to have to trust me on this," she stated as she began retelling her encounter with Macron Esposito and her recent conversation with Frank. Both Uncle Dave and Adam listened intently and reacted to her encounter with Esposito like they believed her. She mentioned their lengthy conversation in the Jeep and she told the complete story leaving nothing out, including her suspicions about Lieutenant Esposito. Some of it seemed to fantastic to be true.

"No police?" Uncle Dave said after Mara concluded her story.

"No, I don't think they know I am onto them," Mara responded. After retelling her encounter with Esposito, her conspiracy theory sounded radical and even made up. Sometimes, when a story is retold, the details get lost in the moment and personal feelings influence the way the story is told. Marathon herself had a tough time believing what had transpired with Esposito.

Uncle Dave and Adam glanced at each other, and Mara got the suspicion that they didn't believe her. A symptom of PTSD was reliving traumatic events in real time. Usually there was a trigger, like fireworks exploding, or a backfiring muffler that would trigger an event from the past. In this case, a refracted light from the woods would be considered a triggering event. The soldier would then be transported back to that moment and sometimes it would activate their fight or flight instincts. Marathon was aware that both Uncle Dave and Adam were thinking this was the most likely scenario.

"Hey, this is real. There is someone out there!" she stated.

"Listen, honey, you have been through a lot. Please just sit down," Uncle Dave said as he motioned Adam to get a glass of water. Mara sat down at the countertop bar as Dave embraced her.

"Oh dear, you're burning up," Uncle Dave said. A symptom of PTSD and a lingering brain injury.

Psychogenic fevers are symptoms of traumatic events where the experience manifests itself through a physical response. Uncle Dave and Adam knew the symptoms well and knew what to look for. Marathon was experiencing a traumatic event that definitely had links to her past, but she knew what she saw in the woods. She didn't conjure that up out of nowhere. She knew her conversation with Esposito was real and his warnings were substantial, but she didn't know how to make her uncle and Adam believe her.

"Dad, I know what I saw…" she said taking a sip of water. "I don't think I'm safe here."

Adam had the cordless phone in his hand as he searched through a bunch of papers resting on a dresser by the vestibule. Adam knocked a bunch of papers on the floor as continued searching for something.

"Where's the number?" Adam asked.

"What?" Uncle Dave responded.

"The number for her doctor," he replied. "Dr. Lee!"

"I don't need Dr. Lee," Mara stated.

"Take it easy, you should probably go lay down," Uncle Dave said.

"Lay down?" she questioned.

"We'll get the doctor on the phone and we'll relay the new symptoms to her," Adam stated while glancing at Uncle Dave.

"You think I'm making this up, that it's all in my head?" she responded.

"No, no, we think you need rest. You're flushed, you might have a fever. Please go lay down," Adam said.

166

Mara looked at both of them and studied their expression. They looked concerned and afraid, but not from an exterior threat or bodily harm from a sniper in the woods. They were afraid for her and her wellbeing. Dr. Lee and Dr. Jenkins, during a joint consultation warned of how brain injuries affected post-traumatic stress disorder. Marathon was displaying symptoms of both, and that was grounds for a medical intervention.

Uncle Dave and Adam had the same look on their face when Mara returned home from Afghanistan. Her night terrors scared the shit out of them, and they forced her to get help. Marathon, being stubborn and arrogant, refused at first, but as she spiraled out of control, she was left with no choice but to accept professional help. By the look on their face now, Mara thought they were reliving those moments. Maybe they thought she regressed or the trauma from Afghanistan resurfaced, which was definitely a plausible scenario considering the circumstances. She didn't know how to tell them that this was different. This was not the same thing and she was not experiencing a relapse. She knew what she saw and she knew she was in danger.

"Do you want us to contact Dr. Lee, or Dr. Jenkins?" Uncle Dave asked.

"No, please, you're probably right. I'll go lay down and get some rest," she responded knowing that would hold them off for a bit.

Adam looked back over at Uncle Dave and shrugged his shoulders. Mara knew they were parents first; acting out of concern for their daughter. She also knew the danger that lurked just beyond their property line, in the woods at the edge of the field. She needed to do something, but at this point, any heed to warning would be taken as a symptom of PTSD or traumatic brain injury.

Mara stood slowly and walked towards her bedroom at the end of the hall beyond the dining room. She paused knowing what she must do to convince them she was okay. She never thought she would utter the words retirement, like she was giving up, but she was ready.

"I'm going to get some rest," she said turning slightly towards them. "I'll call Frank in the morning and let him know I am going to accept retirement."

M

Chapter Nineteen

Uncle Dave's Ranch
Quincy Pennsylvania
August 30th, 2019

The next morning, Marathon woke early. Uncle Dave and Adam were still very much asleep as she snuck out of the house. She wore her morning workout attire to make it look like she got up to go for a run. She wanted to confirm her suspicions and wanted to prove to herself and to her parents that she wasn't paranoid, that there really was someone out in the woods. She knew this was a huge risk, but she figured if she broke her routine by getting up early enough, whoever was out there was probably not in position.

She made a conscious decision to leave her Glock in her night stand. Her work out attire had no way to conceal the weapon and it would be a dead giveaway that she was onto whoever was out there. Plus, she was only going see if there was evidence of someone being out in the woods the day before, she wasn't expecting to find someone this early in the morning.

Mara did, however, leave a voicemail on Frank's office line stating that she was going to come in and sign the retirement papers. Even if she wanted to remain in law enforcement, she was done with the New York City Police Department. They offered her an early retirement, basically paying her to go away. In sports, aging athletes are often bought out of their remaining contract as a way of politely saying your services are no longer needed. This early retirement thing seemed oddly similar.

The early morning sun hung low just above the tree line as she started her light jog down the path that led towards the tree line. She paused for a moment to confirm where she saw the refracted light. She made it look like she was stretching just in case someone was watching her.

Marathon decided to follow the winding path, which snaked off to the right from where she spotted the reflection. She kept a steady pace to make it look like she was doing a light workout. Mara was good at masking her intensions, especially when she knew eyes were upon her. Her tight bike shorts and sweat whisking tank top that exposed more cleavage than she was comfortable with made her stand out in Manhattan. Out here, the dark colored wardrobe would be more concealed than her typical bright neon green workout clothes. She needed to blend in with her environment as much as possible. This outfit was the closest she could put together while pretending to exercise.

She made it to the tree line within a few minutes and found a path that took her in the general direction she needed to go. If there was a sniper out here, he would have used this path to gain access to the property without being noticed. Mara jogged a few more minutes until she came up to the spot where she suspected the sniper might have been; about where she saw the flicker of refracted light the afternoon before. She looked through the trees towards the ranch to narrow down the exact location.

She walked a few more yards and then noticed something out of place. The dirt terrain around the path showed unusual markings on it, like someone had dragged something large that pushed the dirt to the sides. She studied the path closely, this was the only spot those markings existed. She then appraised the surrounding foliage for signs disturbance. She noticed the vines and ivy on the ground were trampled, as if they were brushed to the side from something moving on top of them. Further up, she saw broken branches and disturbed leaves

170

indicating someone has been through here recently. She glanced up towards the ranch and started to inch forward following the newly formed path regretting her decision to leave her Glock behind.

Marathon approached the area cautiously but didn't see or hear anything. No insects, no birds, nothing. The new path led to a small man-made clearing. Mara's suspicions were dead on as she recognized a sniper's nest, one an expert marksman would make to stalk their target. She looked up out towards the ranch to see a perfect view of the pool and patio on an even plane. Her line of sight continued towards the house where she saw the windows that led towards the kitchen and dining room. From this position, Marathon knew anyone on the receiving end of the barrel would not stand a chance. By her estimation, a target standing out by the pool would be about three-hundred meters away. Well within the effective range of a sniper's rifle.

Marathon searched the surrounding area, the nest had been there for a while. She found markings on the ground that looked like someone camped out recently, probably last night by the looks of it. There were various candy wrappers and empty bottles scattered around. She then saw a large army green bag under one of the trees, just at the edge of the makeshift sniper's nest. Mara froze and wondered if anyone was around. She heard nothing and cautiously proceeded towards the duffle bag. With great finesse, she made her way across the opening without making a sound.

She knelt by the bag and examined the exterior. The army green canvas looked worn and ridged as if something inside was giving it shape. She grabbed the zipper and pulled it open. Inside the bag was a rifle. She recognized it immediately as being a modified Remington M24 sniper rifle fashioned for active duty. Marahon had trained on a similar rifle at The Depot on Parris Island. She lifted the rifle out of the bag, it was surprisingly light compared to the standard issue version. She checked the bolt action chamber to find a custom .338 round loaded and ready to fire. She took the .338 round out of the chamber and stuffed it in her sports bra tank top, this was all the proof she needed. Checking to make sure the safety was on, Mara aimed down sights towards the Ranch. The scope had various settings and was tuned to the 320 meter range.

She focused the scope towards the pool in the back yard. She could see the kitchen window and the sliding glass doors that led to the dining room. There was a clear line of sight with only open field between the tree line and the house. Mara then became worried, a high-powered military grade sniper rifle was sitting alone out here in the woods. Its owner must be nearby. She paused and listened closely, she still only heard the rustle of the leaves above her as the trees swayed to the gentle breeze.

She wondered how many times the sniper had her in his scope as she recovered by the pool or prepared meals in the kitchen. Was his finger on the trigger ready to end her life if he received the order to do so? Was this sniper ready to take out the rest of her family as well?

Uncle Dave and Adam were certainly in great danger. She took out her cellphone snapped a few pictures and queued up the land line to the house. She paused, there was no way they were not monitoring Uncle Dave's communications. They must be monitoring the house lines, her cellphone, Uncle Dave's cell, and Adam's cell. One wrong move would mean a certain end. She put her cell phone back in the lining of her bike shorts after snapping a few more pictures.

Marathon stared at the open bag and saw clothes, rations, an M9 hand gun and a range finder. She placed the canvas bag back where she found it. Suddenly she heard a sound coming from the trail. Marathon froze and her heart sank in her chest. She knew she couldn't stay there out in the open. She saw a break in the vegetation to the right of the canvas duffle bag.

It was a small opening in the surrounding space, enough for her to go prone and crawl into under the thick vegetation into the ivy. Mara laid on her stomach as the thick foliage covered her body and used her arms to pull herself into the void underneath large bush to further conceal herself. She hoped there was a way out once she was in there. If not, it wouldn't be long before she was discovered.

The sound grew closer. Marathon searched the area and saw a smaller opening on the other side, she wouldn't fit without disturbing the bushes, which would give away her position if the sniper was close enough. Mara moved towards the opening and remained in prone position. She took the risk, she had to, staying in her current position certainly meant getting caught. She made a mental note to never leave home without her weapon again.

Marathon successfully navigated the tight exit out from under the large rhododendron and was in the thick of the forest growth. She stayed prone and listened. Hearing movement and leaves shuffle behind her caused her to hold her breath and focus her attention to remain perfectly still. She heard a male's voice, it sounded one sided as if he were talking on a cell phone.

"How long to do think I need to stay out here?" the unknown man said. Mara recognized his deep southernly accented voice. It was one she would never forget, one that haunted her for a long time. The sniper sounded only a few feet away from her position.

"Yeah, I had my eyes on her all day. After she got off the phone, she went inside and remained indoors all night," the sniper said.

Mara believed he was giving his daily report. She tried to tune her ears to make out the loud voice on the other end of the phone, but she couldn't make it out or what was being said. She only could piece together the conversation she heard from the sniper's end.

"Hey, listen, I've had worse assignments, this broad is something to look at... remember that Marine from The Depot?" the sniper said. "Yeah the bitch that broke my nose."

Marathon Torres knew him and what type of monster this guy was. The armed forces loved people like him. No conscience, no morals, no ethics, just a pure killing machine that the army exploited to do some real nasty shit. Her time in

Afghanistan showed just how ruthless men like him could be. She witnessed their destruction firsthand, and knew exactly what they were capable of.

Marathon thought he was moving closer. Then she heard him open the canvas bag. Moments later, she heard the distinct sound of a rifle being readied. The bolt action weapon made distinct sounds as it went through its setup phase.

"Why don't you come out here?" he spoke again. "I'm sure the order will come down soon. Then we can have some fun like o'l time's sake."

The order will come down soon? Does that mean they are getting ready to take her out? Mara needed an exit strategy, she was still too close to make a clean break. She focused on her movement and slowly inched backwards as the sniper continued his conversation. She saw his beefy frame maneuver around the tight space as he was setting up his position.

"Fuck, you can't make it?" the sniper asked sounding disappointed. "I heard she is going back to New York soon. I intercepted a call saying she was going to sign some paperwork for retirement. If she's still alive by then, why don't we meet up? We can then properly honor Billy."

Mara knew this guy was only waiting for the order out of courtesy, he was out to revenge his friend Billy also known as William Bowden. He planned on coming after her regardless if he had permission or not. This type of soldier wouldn't stand by when one of their own was taken out. Marathon desperately wished she had her firearm on her. She would have ended this right here and now. She also had the opportunity to take the M9 from the bag but didn't. She can't make these mistakes. These were people that operated outside the law, outside government rule. Any more mistakes like this would cost her dearly.

"Alright, we'll meet in New York!," the sniper enthusiastically said. "We'll trace her credit card and find out where she is staying."

Shit! Run my credit card? Holy fuck, Mara thought as she needed to find a way out of here. This went beyond what the military could typically do. She knew they could easily monitor communications, movement, and go undetected while

174

stalking their prey, but to track someone's financial information. That was beyond the standard capabilities an active unit could perform.

"Damn," the sniper said. "She's not at the pool, normally she's there right now. She's probably out running. Oh, wait, there's movement in the house."

Shit, Uncle Dave and Adam were probably up making breakfast. He knew their morning routine well. He's been watching them for quite some time.

"If I get the order now? No, I won't snipe her," the sniper said into his cell. "I'd go in there at night, off the gays, and then fucking have my way with that whore until she begged me to kill her. Besides, we gotta do right by Billy... Yeah that cunt is going to pay."

The web of obscurity was starting to take shape and missing pieces were falling into place. She was missing a key detail though, what was the connection that brought them back into her life? Marley Williams? How are they related, what is the connection? She needed to put more thought into this and now wasn't the time to start piecing things together.

Well, at least she knew how he was planning to kill her. She certainly preferred the fighting chance a one to one confrontation permitted compared to being sniped without warning.

"Hold on, I'm getting a call from The Farm," the sniper said. Mara listened closely and focused.

"Pasture one here," the sniper said and then paused, waiting for orders.

"Copy that, heading to New York," he replied. Mara heard him switch back to his cell phone.

"Hey, looks like you're in luck. The Farm wants me to report to New York," the beefy sniper said. "Oh you're trailing him? Gotcha, well keep on him, there might be a play for the both of us. I'll hit you up when I get to New York."

Mara was relieved as she heard the sniper start packing up. She remained motionless and intently listened to his conversation.

"Oh good, you just got a call also? Yeah, we're probably going to take out the bitch and your mark together," the sniper said. "I hope the boss doesn't puss out. You know he's had a hard on for her for a while now."

What? What the fuck was going on? She wished for names but she had to fill in the gaps the best she could. Were they talking about Frank?

"Yep, see ya in New York," the sniper said has the line disconnected. He finished packing up his gear and made his way back the way he came.

Mara remained perfectly still, deep in thought. She wanted to give him time to clear the area before she went back to the ranch. Who was this boss? Was it Frank? Mara had to go on the assumption that Frank was the boss. She interpreted the "hard on" comment as a reference to their relationship at work. Frank was always partial to her and they had flirted in the past.

After she was sure the sniper was gone, she stood up and made her way back towards the ranch. Marathon knew what would happen if she returned to New York. Her movements were being tracked, and there was little she could do to remain undetected. She wanted to run, get as far away as possible, never to return. But as she made her way back, something compelled her to move forward. An inner voice crept in that told her to see this through, to not let them win.

M

Chapter
Twenty

Penn Station
New Jersey
August 30th, 2019

Adam and Uncle Dave had a significant freak out moment when Marathon explained what transpired in the woods just beyond their property line. At first, they didn't take it seriously, and were more concerned for Mara's mental state than someone trying to kill her. Finally, she produced the .338 round form her sports bra in dramatic fashion. It took her most of the morning to calm them down and prevent them from calling the police, especially after showing them the pictures of the sniper's nest. Uncle Dave nearly had a heart attack while Adam nervously paced around the living room.

Mara put on a masterful performance explaining how they were in danger but not immediate danger, that this was more of a message to get Mara to retire and move on with her life. They bought the story that she would go back to New York and formally retire, then join them on vacation somewhere out of the country in Europe. Adam booked tickets to Paris immediately by calling his travel agent. In a matter of hours, they secured travel arrangements for the next month.

The fib was easy, because like most expertly conjured lies, there was an element of truth woven carefully into the lie. Mara was going to retire, she was going to join them on vacation, but the part in between those events was conveniently left out. Uncle Dave wanted more assurances, so she exaggerated the truth to show that the retirement process took time and that she needed to meet with Dr. Lee for therapy sessions while she was in New York. She figured after all was said and done, it would take about a week. That was the deception both Uncle Dave and Adam bought. Everything was then arranged through their travel agent. Uncle Dave and Adam would fly out of Newark International Airport to Paris and Mara would tidy up things in New York before joining them a week later.

Uncle Dave initially refused to get on a plane without her, but she convinced him that this was the best course of action by emphasizing the status quo. That she wasn't in any danger if she was going to retire and leave town afterwards. She was surprised he bought that, but then again, he was usually gullible enough to believe stories grounded in truth.

While all those things needed to happen, they could have been done in a day or two as they were just formalities. The department was offering her retirement, she wasn't requesting it. She could be in and out of the station fully retired before lunch the next day, but that wouldn't solve a thing. There'd still be the sniper. Marathon knew he would still hunt her down, with or without permission from the so-called Farm. The sniper owned his comrade Bowden for what she did to him. As twisted as this group was, that was the one thing Mara fully understood. Someone wrongs your boy, you wrong them back. Funny how the code of the streets easily translated to the code of the armed forces.

Marathon sealed the exaggerated truth when she had Adam purchase her flight to Paris to meet them in a weeks' time. She also had to convince Uncle Dave she was cleared to fly. For some reason, a plane ticket left like solid plans, something people didn't miss. Like when you travel to a foreign country, they want to make sure you have a return ticket out before you pass customs. She also had the added benefit of possibly confusing the people trying to kill her. They would see the purchased plane tickets in her name and formulate a conclusion. Keeping them guessing was her ultimate goal. She couldn't be predictable, unless she needed to be.

After frantic packing and heavy conversational car ride to Newark, Uncle Dave and Adam dropped her off at New Jersey's version of Penn Station just outside of Newark before they boarded a plane to Paris. Mara paid cash for her train ticket back to New York and would only make herself known when she wanted.

Her first priority, upon arrival in New York, was to find a place to stay. She couldn't stay with her friends or colleagues for they would be in danger. She couldn't check into a hotel for fear of being detected when she swiped her credit card. What she needed was a cash only establishment, and those were shady places. Luckily, she knew of a place close to her old neighborhood. She kept reassuring herself that she was making the best decision she could. Her instinct was to run, get the fuck out of dodge and never return. She didn't owe Russo or Esposito anything. She could have easily justified running, it made more sense than what she was doing. But how long could she stay hidden from a special forces soldier who had more confirmed kills than the population of Quincy, PA.

Her train pulled into New York's Penn Station and came to a squealing stop. She got off the train like the rest of the passengers and carefully focused on her surroundings. In a city like New York, surveillance was everywhere, especially at major transit hubs. She hoped facial recognition wasn't fully operational yet, but she was prepared just in case. She wore a Yankees baseball cap and dark sunglasses as she navigated her way through New York's underground.

She made her way downtown taking the C train to her old neighborhood and arrived at a hotel on Bowery. It was a small, cheap, pay by the hour sort of place with a sign written in Mandarin above the smaller print English version. The clientele of this establishment were people looking to get a fix, usually drugs or sex. Mara spotted a few call girls in the alley next to the motel. There was no doubt this place was used for illegal activities. To not draw attention to herself, Marathon wore jean shorts and a t-shirt. Her long, dark olive skin toned legs reflected the lights of the neon green sign above the hotel as she stood outside

179

assessing the environment she was about to enter. Mara detected slight hesitation in her actions moving forward as if her own body was telling her to turn around and get on the first plane to Paris.

The lobby was empty except for a couple sitting at the bar off to the right. Mara looked at them, and they looked ordinary enough for what she was walking into. She knew the man in the black button down shirt with black dress pants ran the facility. Sitting next to him was a young woman who had breasts the size of her head and a dress two sizes two small. She looked like a plastic Barbie and she was holding onto the man at the bar as if he were a crutch keeping her upright. Her hands moved around his body like someone touching silk for the first time. The hotel manager waited for her to approach and smiled. Mara knew the man at the bar was checking her out.

"I'll take a room for the night," Marathon said when she was close enough to speak, she was tired from the long days travel to get here, but she questioned if she could even rest in a place like this.

"We have rooms available, will you be using one by the hour or do you plan on staying the entire night?" The manager asked. Mara thought this was a common question for this kind of place, but never once heard that as an option at the places she stayed.

"I'll be using it for the night," Mara said. The manager then looked down and searched for a room key. He had no computer, only the pencil and paper format to book and reserve rooms. Mara suspected this information was destroyed the next morning or at least by the end of the week and replaced with more tax friendly books with fake names attached to each sale.

She then noticed the man from the bar walk towards her. She knew her gun was behind her, holstered at the small of her back hidden by her low hanging backpack and slightly oversized t-shirt. The man closed the distance between them and Mara saw his eyes look her up and down as if he were debating on purchasing her for the night.

"My.. my, what brings a specimen like you here tonight?" The man said as he got uncomfortably close. Mara could smell his overpowering cologne as he started to pace around her. He looked of Asian descent, with some mixed features that made him surprisingly attractive for a man in his profession.

"I am renting a room," Mara replied and turned back towards the manager, who seemed to have conveniently misplaced the keys to the room.

"Plan on making some money tonight?" The man asked as he made it to her backside. Mara felt his gaze burn holes in her as he licked his lips.

"Excuse me?" Mara replied turning towards him.

"There is a service charge if you decide to work here," the man said.

Mara decided to play dumb, but she knew exactly what he was speaking of. These types of establishments received a percentage of what a call girl would make in a night, it was a lucrative source of revenue. The call girl would advertise her location and book appointments throughout the night. Johns would come and go, and the call girl would be free to charge whatever they wanted, but the establishment would get a cut, usually half. What the call girl got in return was a safe place to work, free internet to conduct business, and security in case things got rough. Marathon had spotted the muscle outside. If the hooker had a pimp, this arrangement was already predetermined and the hooker would not be involved in this transaction.

"Oh, no, I am not working here tonight," Marathon replied.

The man stepped closer, she could feel his body heat as he leaned in. "That's a shame, you'd make a shit ton of money," he said. "Maybe, I could offer you some company tonight? Maybe show you the ropes?"

Mara knew these questions were dangerous. Outright refusal would insult him, and he wasn't the type of man to be outright rejected. She had to gently say she was pre-occupied tonight.

"I am just looking for a place to stay and get away from my boyfriend," Marathon said. The man held out his hand towards the manager and two keys appeared.

"Here you go beautiful," the man said as he pocketed one of the keys for himself. "In case you change your mind."

Mara reached out and grabbed the other key from his front pants pocket. His pants where form fitting and she could feel more than she wanted to. He had a smirk on his face she wanted to wipe off, but contained herself just long enough to retrieve the key card.

"Not tonight big guy," she said. "I'm here to get away from men, not have another in my bed." Mara remained strong, but kept her innocent face fixated on him.

"Well, well, this boyfriend of yours, if he comes around here looking for you, he will not find you," he said as Mara thought those words could go either way, but she took them as a friendly gesture. The man was now joined by the woman who was caressing him by the bar. She looked clearly jealous of her and hung on her man. Her arms moved around his chest like water rolling over rock.

"You forgot to leave your name," the man said as Mara tried to walk away.

"I'm Jessica," Mara said turning back around.

"Does Jessica have a last name?" he asked.

"Jones, Jessica Jones," she said as the she quickly tried to come up with a name on the spot. Of all the names, she chose Jessica Jones? Ugh, hopefully he wouldn't get the pop culture reference.

"Do you have any ID, Jessica Jones?" he asked. She knew he didn't need ID and that he was playing a different kind of game, he wanted her address.

"I seemed to have left it at my boyfriend's place," she said continuing the lie and placing additional cash on the counter for the manager to collect. "But, I don't think that'll be a problem here."

He didn't respond and she could tell he suspected something.

182

"Have a good evening, Jessica Jones," he finally said.

Mara pocketed both keys and turned towards the manager and thanked him. Mara felt dirty, his cologne was still pungent in her nostrils and she couldn't shake the clammy feeling she got when she touched him. Even when she got to the 2nd floor, she still felt his presence behind her.

Once inside the room, she noticed there wasn't a safety lock on the inside of the door; literally anyone could have a key to her room. The door opened inwards, which was a good thing. She knew how to prevent unwanted entry and jammed the rooms sole chair under the door handle. It would take some time to get through that, just long enough for her to have her Glock trained on whoever her unwanted guest was, in case it came to that.

Being satisfied with her safety, Marathon scanned the room. The bed was in the center and had plain white sheets. The room was very ordinary, nothing on the walls except peeling grey paint and brown stains splattered throughout the carpet in the room. Mara could only imagine what this room had seen over the years.

She reluctantly put her bag down on the bed and sat on the couch. She took out her suit and laid it out for the next day. Marathon then took off her gun and placed it on the bed, her badge rested next to it. Next came her pajamas. Mara had packed a loose fitting t-shirt a couple of sizes too big and a pair of boy shorts. She walked into the bathroom with her toothbrush, turned on the light and froze. The bathroom looked like it's seen its final days as mold grew unrestricted on the walls of the shower as chips in the tile clung on the ceiling ready to fall at any time.

The sink had strands of hair scattered throughout the bowl and soap scum crusted throughout the fixtures. Marathon was immediately grossed out as her eyes fixated on the disgusting bathroom. She carefully brushed her teeth, trying not to touch anything she didn't have to. She used the toilet by hovering over the bowl. When she was finished with the bathroom, she never wanted to go in there again.

Marathon continued getting ready for bed by removing her clothes and placing them back in her bag. She took off her bra, but kept her panties on. She threw on the large t-shirt and hesitated before getting into bed. She knew this would not be a good night's sleep. The walls were thin and the sounds were plenty. The room above hers sounded like the NY Giants decided to hold practice in there and the room to the left of hers sounded like porn was being filmed. Mara put in her headphones, found her favorite playlist and closed her eyes without going under the covers.

She woke the next morning with an eerie silence in the hotel. It was like the light had washed the filth from the night before away. Marathon got out of bed and went towards the window. Her view was of the alley between the hotel and the Chinese restaurant next door where the hookers gathered the night before to meet their clients. The alley was quiet now, only rats rummaged the area looking for scraps.

Mara refused to shower so she decided to dress after using only water from the sink to freshen up. She wore her suit, folded her other clothes into her backpack and tried to fix herself up as best she could. Her hair, while usually being straight and thick was matted and curly because she had tied it back the night before. She decided to keep her hair tied back and retied a tight ponytail. She gave herself a quick look in the mirror, decided it was better to leave this place than to try and fix herself up even more. She grabbed her overnight bad, checked her Glock 15, holstered it, and put her detective badge in her suit pocket.

Mara had the keys to the hotel in her hand as she walked towards the lobby. The same manager was standing at the counter, he looked tired and Mara wondered when his shift ended.

"Checking out," Mara said handing the man the keys.

"Ahh yes," the hotel manager said looking Mara over. "We don't get many cops in here hiding from their boyfriends."

"You probably hear all kinds of stories, maybe a few of them are true, but most are deceitful." Mara replied.

"That'll be eighty bucks ma'am," the hotel manager said as he put the keys back into the drawer.

Mara opened her wallet and paid the manager, as she was turning to leave, she saw the man by the bar look over at her. It was the same guy from last night, wearing the same clothing. He smiled at her as she made her way towards the exit. In here, time seemed to move at its own pace. For some people, time moved way to fast and their night of fun was over before it started. For others, time held them hostage like an inmate on death row. Mara couldn't get out of there fast enough.

M

Chapter
Twenty-One

73rd Precinct
Brownsville, Brooklyn
August 31st, 2019

Standing outside the 73rd precinct felt foreign, like running into an old boyfriend and quickly realizing why the relationship ended. Officers came and went, most only glanced at her along the way. If this were the 75th, there would have been a grand to do upon her return. Officers returning to work after being injured on the job was a cause for celebration. She was new at this precinct, only a few officers recognized her and fewer officers even knew her name. Her 15 minutes of fame came and went as fast as a New York minute. She had no doubt the officers knew who she was, but without proper notice, there was little to do or say when she showed up randomly in front of the precinct.

Marathon's phone buzzed, it was from Frank asking what time he could expect her. Frank didn't like surprises and liked to plan out his day. Mara texted him back that she was on her way in while she was actually standing outside. He didn't reply but on her phone showed that he read the message. She gave him a few minutes before she entered.

Marathon wanted no part of this precinct, she had nothing in her desk, nothing in her locker, she didn't even have a partner to say goodbye to. The stain of the past events were fresh, but also soaked deep like when marinara sauce spills

186

on a new white t-shirt. You wipe it away, but the stain remains, something that's nearly impossible to be undone.

She wondered if the sniper was watching her, no doubt he was out there somewhere. Mara needed to take this calculated risk and directly expose herself to formally retire. She knew if the sniper was given a kill order, he would come for her in a more intimate setting, not at a precinct full of cops. He had unfinished business with her anyway which superseded any kill order. She was the subject of his infatuation probably to the point of obsession. The more Mara thought about it, the more she felt his scope bearing down on her, if not literally. No doubt he was enjoying this, no doubt he was savoring what he had planned.

She was surprised that Lieutenant Esposito hadn't made contact. Maybe she hid herself too well by going to that hotel last night. Marathon waited on the corner of East New York and Thomas Boyland and then decided Frank had plenty of time to get ready to meet with her. Besides, it was just a paperwork formality, nothing time consuming. Knowing him, he had everything prepared the night before and it sat in a folder on his desk waiting for her.

She was stopped by a uniformed officer at the reception area who only wished her a hearty welcome back. She typed in her code to get in beyond the security door and then proceeded to her destination. She saw Terrence sitting at his desk and when he noticed her, he immediately stood and closed the distance between them.

"Torres, my god it's good to see you!" Officer Morgan said as he gave her a big hug. Mara returned the hug and gave him a peck on the cheek. Other officers in the room started clapping and cheering her return. The warm feeling was tainted by the sour scars left from the attack a few months ago. An attack that might have originated in this very precinct.

"Morgan, how are you doing?" Mara asked.

"Same old, but I wanna hear about you!"

"I'm fine, I gather you heard why I am here?" she said.

"Yeah, smart on your part. Get out when you can!" he said. "With short notice, there wasn't much I could do to make your return eventful. I am going to gather the troops for a proper sendoff though. I heard you like John Street bar? Maybe something there at the end of the week?"

"Hey, you!" Detective Morales said as he saw Mara from across the room. He also walked over and didn't mind interrupting her conversation with Morgan. "It's good to see you Detective."

"Oh hey, Detective Morales," She responded.

Mara hated when colleagues came back and everyone had to play nice when they returned. Now she was the one returning, no matter how brief her return to active duty was, she still had to have those awkward conversations with people to answer the same question a thousand times. Marathon made small talk with the two men, and everyone seemed to like each other as they did before. She did like Detective Morales and Officer Morgan, they seemed like good people. The shadow of doubt that emanated from this place cast uncertainty on everything.

"We were just discussing Detective Torres' retirement party," Morgan said to steer the conversation back towards why she was here.

"I heard you like John Street Bar." Detective Morales said. "It's a cop friendly bar, and I heard rumors that your party is going to be held there."

"Yeah, Morgan was just asking me," Mara said. "In that case, I might actually have to go."

"We're gonna do this right, Detective Torres," Officer Morgan said. "I guess we'll invite some of your people from the 75th."

"We have to?" Detective Morales asked sarcastically. The competition between precincts felt like rival schools in the same division.

Marathon kept looking over at Franks office, his blinds and door were closed. However, she knew he was aware that she was in the building. The cheering and subsequent clapping upon her return was probably hard to miss.

"We should go over your retirement plans," Officer Morgan said as he noticed Mara was distracted by the status of Frank's office.

"I can't believe you're actually retiring," Detective Morales said. Mara wanted to respond but sensed she needed a more in-depth explanation than what she was willing to give.

"I still get headaches and I cannot see myself getting back out there anytime soon. I am at that awkward stage where it's either take the early retirement package or go on disability." She settled on the medical explanation.

"Yeah you right," Officer Morgan said with his Brooklyn accent. "Take the fucking money and run, amiright?"

"Well, you would have made a fine detective. I was looking forward to working with you," Detective Morales said sounding authentic.

"Really?" Mara boldly responded.

"You would have," Morales repeated.

"So, being that I am technically not retired yet, what's going on with the Williams case, and the fake internal affair officers?"

"Well," Morales leaned in and whispered. "I just got a lead."

"Do tell!" she blurted out.

"Not yet, I have to cross reference a few things, but I think it could be a solid lead."

"Is this about the internal affairs officers?" Mara asked.

"No, well, maybe. I think it is more to do with Marley Williams though," Morales responded.

"Please share it with me when you find something," Mara stated. After all this time, something new developed in the Marley Williams case? That seemed odd. She needed more information.

"You know I can't do that," he said glancing towards Frank's office.

Mara smiled and noticed Frank's office door open. She got the sense that he was not in his office and she looked around to found him handing paperwork to his secretary. Mara excused herself from the conversation and walked towards Frank's office, she wanted to get this over with. They met at the threshold and he invited her in.

"Hey Marathon, thank you for coming in. How are you doing?" He asked as he sat down behind his desk. There was an awkward tension in the air, like neither of them knew how to act in this situation.

"I'm doing well Frank, still getting headaches here and there," Marathon said trying to keep the talking to a minimum. She really wanted to get up and close the door and lay everything on the table so she could get to the bottom of what was going on. Her better judgement had convinced her that was too much of a risk. Especially with a sniper out there somewhere waiting for her status to change to kill on sight.

"You're doing the right thing Torres," he said as if he were giving her fatherly advice like he had done in the past.

She was taken back by this statement. The Frank she knew would have tried to change her mind, convince her to heal up and then come back before making a rash decision like retirement.

"I do think it's for the best," she stated. "I mean, who gets a deal like this?"

"These deals are very rare indeed. In fact, I haven't seen one of these pass my desk in a long time," Frank stated. He looked again at the paperwork as if he were puzzled by something.

"Mara, take my advice, this deal is a golden ticket, take it and get out. You opened a can of worms when you accessed Marley Williams' file," he said.

Mara was surprised he said her name. Frank's advice sounded like he had said too much, like he knew something was up and he was trying to shield her from it. Frank was hard to read now, and she had to stay focused and not read into anything in case he was being deceptive. She decided to change the topic to gauge his reaction.

"Anything on the officers that posed as internal affairs?" Mara asked. He paused and looked at her with a smile.

"Not yet, but we are close. We believe they were the ones that sent William Bowden to kill you," Frank said. "Plus there was a lead this morning."

"Really?" Mara stated. That came out of left field. What made him think that and what was the lead? Detective Morales also hinted at something before.

"Listen, you're about to be retired, let it go. Besides, after you sign your name, you're a civilian. I cannot share any information on pending investigations with you," Frank said.

"I want to know who sent William Bowden to try and kill me Frank!" Mara demanded and he nodded in response.

"We think it was the two fake officers that showed up here to question you. When I opened a full investigation, after your attack, we cross referenced Bowden's prints to prints we pulled from the Jeep the fake investigators used. There was a match."

"What? That seems odd." Mara stated. "Who's working the case?"

"Detective Morales and his partner, I needed someone with experience. He also would have been pissed at me if I opened it and gave it to someone else."

"Doesn't he assign cases?" Mara asked.

"Yes, but I have discretion over all the cases my detectives take on, especially after you were attacked in your apartment."

Marathon didn't reply, and her perception of Frank was changing. Why was he pushing so hard into the case? Marathon figured he would want it buried since she was about to enter retirement. Frank had signed her paperwork and gave it a quick review. He then handed it to Mara from across the desk.

"Mara, I want you to know, your family is always here for you," Frank said. Marathon thought that sounded sincere as she looked everything over and signed her name at the bottom of the document. Retirement officially started.

"It's the right thing for me to do," Mara said while looking directly at Frank. Mara thought he had a great poker face, she couldn't read him.

"So what is the next step?" she asked.

"Well, I need your badge and service weapon," he replied.

"I am going to keep my weapon," Mara said in quick response. "I applied for a permit while I was on leave and it should already be in the system."

"Oh good, you'll need to submit additional paperwork through the department, but I can have that prepared for you and mailed to your Uncle's address. Do you plan on staying with him for the time being?"

"I do, but I'll be in the city taking care of some loose ends before I leave for Paris to celebrate my retirement," Mara said closely monitoring Frank facial expressions.

"Right, you had mentioned you have things in storage from your old apartment," Frank said. Again, Mara couldn't read him. His cellphone then rang and he stood and took the call leaving Mara seated in his office.

She looked at his desk, papers were scattered everywhere. She knew the paperwork part of this was done, the rest of this was just being polite. She got his signature and all she had to do now was turn it in, which she would let Officer Morgan do for her as union rep.

As Mara stood, she noticed an odd number on Frank's desk on a file with Morales' name attached to it. She recognized it as a GPS coordinate, 40.6157 - 73.8303. She often used coordinates like that in the military when rendezvousing with other companies while scouting the mountains in Afghanistan. Mara took a post-it note off of Frank's desk and quickly jotted the number down. Frank came back having concluded his conversation.

"Where were we?" he asked.

"I think we were just wrapping things up," Mara said.

"Listen, Detective Morales is going to follow up on a lead," Frank said as he sat back down. "I'll keep you apprised on the situation. It's the least I can do."

"Well, I am not officially retired until Morgan submits the paperwork, maybe I should accompany him?" Mara asked.

"You are officially retired. Your signature and mine are on the page. You're officially a civilian now," he said.

Mara decided to be bold and ask about the GPS numbers. "Is that where Morals is going?" Mara pointed at the file.

"Ummm yeah," Frank said. Mara waited for an explanation.

"After we pulled Bowden's print off the Jeep we submitted a warrant for the GPS location data stored in its navigation system. I wanted to know where that Jeep has been. Well, this morning, we got the results back," Frank said.

"This morning?"

"Yeah, when we first submitted the request after you were attacked the company managing the GPS sent us the wrong information. We resubmitted the request and it came through," Frank said.

Mara found that strangely coincidental and became immediately concerned for Detective Morales. She looked out of Frank's office to see if Detective Morales was at his desk or still in the station.

"We have no idea why this car was there, or if Bowden or the fake cops were even there with the Jeep. This is a long shot, but it's the only lead we have. Detective Morales is going to head out there and call it in if he finds anything," He said.

"Where are these coordinates?" Marathon asked.

"Some nature preserve off of Cross Bay Boulevard," he said.

"He's going alone?" she asked.

"We had a few call outs today and he decided to go himself," Frank responded. Call outs? All these circumstances were building up to a disaster.

"I wish I could be out there with him," Mara stated as she stood to take her leave. Frank stood also and offered her a hug goodbye.

193

"I understand, I'm just glad you're safe Mara. That perp nearly got the better of you. You're training and instincts saved your life," he said, looking directly at her. "I saw the crime scene personally. You put up one hell of a fight. I'm so thankful you're still here with us."

As they embraced, he whispered to her to check in from time to time. She nodded and then left the office. She heard Frank's door close as she scanned the large open room for Detective Morales. Marathon did not like how things were stacking up. As a Senior Detective, Morales was free to conduct operating procedure for Detectives under his command. He wasn't required to have a partner, even though a field assignment warranted one. If a convenient number of officers hadn't called out sick, Detective Morales would be out there with his partner to back him up.

A thought crossed her mind, what if Frank wasn't behind this? He was very forthcoming with information. Mara walked towards Terrance's desk as she dialed Detective Morales' number, but it went straight to voicemail. Holding her phone out, Marathon decided to look up the location on her smart phone. It was the coordinates of a jetty just south of the West Pond by the Broad Channel community. The location was centered within the domains of a wildlife refuge just off of Cross Bay Boulevard, like Frank had mentioned.

Going to satellite view provided a better sense of the surrounding area. Something caught her eye; white sand clearly outlined the jetty as it stuck out like a finger poking the bay. She zoomed in on the location and found a small beach looking area close to the jetty depicted on the GPS coordinates.

Mara's heart sunk deep in her chest. Her hands became clammy as her finger navigated the map on her phone. White fucking sand! It hit her, the unexplained clue from Marley Williams' shoes. White fucking sand stared back at her square in the face as the clue from her shoes finally made sense. Was Marley Williams at this location when she died? There was plenty of evidence

194

surrounding the fact that she wasn't killed in the immediate area, that the dumpster was just a drop site for her body to send a message.

The going theory, at the time, was a gang war brewing between NYCHA houses. The body of Marley Williams was dumped on the border, and was thought to be a message not to cross gang territories.

She pulled directions to this location and focused on the mass transit routes to this section of Jamaica Bay. At Broadway Junction she could pick up the A train heading south to Rockaway Beach. She could get off at Broad Channel, where there was a small community on that finger island near the red dot on the GPS. Being that it was late summer, Marathon knew the A train had extra service heading that way to accommodate beach goers. On a hot summer day, there would be many people heading to the beach and the trains would be running peak service to get them to their destination. She might even beat Detective Morales there if she got a move on it.

Mara printed the screens from her cell phone to the color printer by her desk. She knew the cellphone needed to remain here and shoved it in her empty desk. At the very least, they wouldn't be able to know her precise location. If the sniper was out there, she did not want him knowing exactly where she was at all times, that would be too easy. She would need to be on high alert from this point out. She also left her backpack at her desk, knowing it's bulky design would slow her down if things got heated. She thought about changing out of her business suit, but decided she needed to get to Broad Channel as fast as possible, plus she needed to conceal her firearm and at least look like a cop.

Officer Morgan wasn't at his desk, so Mara left her retirement paperwork in his interoffice mailbox. Being the union rep, he checked his mailbox frequently enough where it wouldn't get lost. Then without any formal goodbye, she snuck out of the precinct.

On her way to the A-train, she studied the printed terrain surrounding the GPS location. There were numerous dirt paths that weaved in and out of the wooded area that framed the nature preserve. Her pace hastened towards the train, it was only a few blocks from the station down East New York Avenue.

On her way she considered that this was probably a trap. The evidence was very enticing, and it was something she could not ignore. Morales had already taken the bait and he was the lead detective on the case. She wasn't sure who was the target, but went under the instinct that both of them were in danger. She at least knew what she was walking into. The sniper hinted at an additional target when she eavesdropped on his conversation. Marathon suspected Morales was the additional target.

She remembered Frank stating they got the info that morning, and Detective Morales was on his way to investigate it. The coordinates were even sitting out in the open when she sat at Frank's desk. Where they counting on this to lure her out to Jamaica Bay? Was this a test to see if she should live or die? If she ventured out to investigate this clue, she knew there would be a target on her and the order to take her out would be given. Detective Morales was the unknown in this equation. If he was a target, he stood no chance without her help. Her choice was clear.

Detective Morales probably made the same conclusion about the white sand after reviewing the original evidence collected from the Williams case. Mara's pictures got a good shot of the sand around Marley's shoes. Mara's path was now clear, get to Jamaica Bay.

Marathon had turned in her badge, but her Glock 15 was still in her possession. She felt the pistol and two spare clips rest against the small of her back in a holster designed to carry everything she needed. Her black suit jacket concealed everything nicely as the firearm rested just above her rear. She knew a Glock 15 was no match for the modified M24 sniper rifle, which was most likely waiting for her at the wild life preserve.

A confrontation with the sniper was inevitable, he was going to act on revenge regardless if he was ordered to or not. Mara would rather know he was out there and prepare for their encounter than to be caught off guard. The survival rate was extremely low if a sniper caught their target off guard.

Marathon stood patiently on the Broadway Junction platform as an A train pulled into the station. She got on and didn't notice anyone or anything out of the ordinary. The beefy sniper certainly would stand out in any crowd, but there potentially was another threat out there somewhere. The sniper's friend who also wanted in on the action. He could be on the same train, in the same car, standing right next to her and she wouldn't even know it.

The train doors pretended to close a half dozen times before they finally decided to remain that way. The train was crowded with beach goers and the semi air-conditioned car reeked like stale sunscreen and body odor as it raced south while making sure it hit every stop along the way.

M

Chapter
Twenty-Two

"Hey Private, ya gonna let me in?" Marathon said twirling her hair as she used her womanly charm of persuasion.

The recent graduate eyed her closely as she played with her hair and angled her body in just the right way to accent her features hidden under her form fitting hoodie. The after graduation party was invite only. The private eyed her for a short moment, he then stood aside and allowed her to proceed to the keg party. Success, yet again.

She scanned the surroundings in the enclosed fenced in backyard and recognized a few Marines lounging over by the firepit. The reason she was here stood in the middle of the group of graduates. He was a senior officer and he caught her eye back when she first arrived at The Depot.

She decided to make her way to the beer keg first and muster up courage to approach the good looking Corporal. She picked up a plastic cup and poured herself a cold one from the keg and then made her way to the firepit. The boys around the pit immediately turned their attention towards her. Whatever conversation they were having was immediately dropped and the attention was now solely on her.

"How long you going to be in New York?"

"Probably for the weekend, then ship out," Mara responded standing close to the fire to keep warm. Even thought it was unusually warm for this time of year, she still needed the open flames to keep her from wanting to go in doors. She refused to wear a jacket and it paid off with her admittance to the party. In addition to her hoodie, she wore skinny jeans that highlighted her southern features. Her hair was down and it flowed loosely in the breeze.

After basic training at The Depot, Marines shipped out for specialized training. Some soldiers became experts in explosives, others went for marksman training, a select few were chosen for aviation school. During basic training, Marathon didn't excel in any particular area. She was going into mobile infantry.

One of the guys put his arm around her and proceeded to rub his palms up and down her arm trying to warm her up. Too bad it wasn't the guy she was interested in, but the warmth it provided felt good enough for it to continue.

"I'm going back home as well," One of the soldiers said. "Got my girl back there who wants to see me."

"She sure does want to see you," Mara said as she made a presumptuous gestures using her hands to insinuate sex. She caught her Corporal's eye

The group around her laughed causing the private to blush a little. Mara was successfully noticed by her target. She averted her eyes to not make eye contact yet. She knew how to play the game.

Out of the corner of her eye she noticed him check her out. If she were back home, there would be a lot of competition from talented girls all going for the same guy. Here it was different. She thought it would be easier, but that was not the case though. With the guy to girl ratio heavily in her favor, she had to weed through all the nonsense for the guy she was after to be interested. Mara didn't like aggressive men, she wanted to be the aggressor in the courtship. This made it difficult to land the guy she wanted. Guys that weren't aggressively seeking her out typically took a back seat during these types of gatherings.

She had seen the Corporal around The Depot since the moment she arrived, usually ran into him in the most awkward moments. Like when she was forced to do pushups because her bed had a wrinkle in her bedsheets, he would walk by as she was about to finish her last pushup, or when she was forced to run around The Depot because her uniform wasn't neatly tucked in for roll call. He would be there at the end of the run when she was ready to drop dead from exhaustion, covered in sweat and smelled like the horse stable she had just ran by.

After doing some recon after graduation, Marathon suspected he was here at this party and used that as an excuse not to go back to NY with Adam and Uncle Dave. Well she didn't put like that. Telling her dad she wanted to fuck a guy after the ceremony would not have gone over so well, so she said she wanted to celebrate with her friends and she would be on the flight back to New York the next morning. This was probably her last chance to bed him and she was going to do everything in her power to make sure that happened.

She knew he stayed somewhere on base, but she couldn't figure out where exactly. She knew he was an officer, but her limited access to that area prevented her from successfully finding him in social situations until now. Graduation parties brought everyone together. This party, was more exclusive and reserved for invites only.

Mara saw an opening in the conversation when the topic of 9/11 came up. She stepped forward releasing herself from the warmth of the soldier behind her. Most Marines enlisted as a response to the terrorist attacks. Marathon was no different, she put her college career on hold and signed up at her local recruitment office in Queens. She will never forget he look on Uncle Dave's face when she told him she was shipping out in a week. His freak out moment was short lived as she saw nothing but admiration from him today.

"I was in New York City when the towers fell," she said as the attention immediately turned towards her. "I was attending the Borough of Manhattan Community College when the planes struck the towers," Mara proceeded to tell her story of fright and despair. She kept a close eye on her officer as she sent subtle messages his way. A glance here, position her body there, request another drink but only if he got it for her. She wondered why she had to try so hard to get his attention but as the night progressed, her investment seemed promising, and she was ready to collect her dividends.

The fire was winding down as the late night turned to early morning. Marathon was now close enough to her officer to allow him to keep her warm. He smelled delicious as she burrowed under his jacket between his arms. Even though he wasn't much taller than her, she found ways to fit into his arms.

"Let's get out of here," he whispered. Mara nodded allowing him to lead her out of the backyard. Success! She was aggressive enough to get this far and now she let him lead. She was hoping he was sober enough to drive, but he had left his car back at The Depot, so they walked the mile or so back to base. Mara clung to him like a crutch, the beer had hit her harder than she thought, but this set up a nice walk with her arms around his muscular frame.

Marathon's hands wondered a bit, she wanted to see how far she could go to gauge his reaction. Her aggressiveness was resurfacing. She let her hands roll over his abs while they walked hip to hip keeping each other warm. She was thankful she remembered the pack of icy fresh pack of gum in her pocket before they left the party as she rested her head on his shoulders. His hands became frisky as well, they started around her waist, but slowly inched down to the curve of her thigh towards her backside. She welcomed him and wanted him to go further.

When they reached The Depot, Marathon was hot and ready, she hoped his place was close, she hoped it was private. Sometimes officers bunked with others, that would be awkward. They turned off the main road and he pointed to his quarters just ahead. Mara saw a group of men hanging outside the building adjacent to the place he pointed out.

"Is your room private?" she asked him as she whispered in his ear. They stopped and he pulled her in close, Mara leaned in and kissed him deeply sucking on his lower lip. Her heart was pounding in excitement and his hands explored her body further. Mara thought the men in the distance would notice them, but they were between streetlights and lost in the shadows.

Her hands found the bulge in his pants and it jumped slightly when she grabbed it. She knew both of them were on the same page.

"It's private," he said.

"Let's go," She demanded.

He then guided her along the side of the road until they reached the building where the men were. Mara avoided direct eye contact and only wanted to get her man inside so she guided him away from any conversation. She heard some whistling but didn't care.

Once the door closed behind them, the two of them frantically began stripping their clothes off. They embraced being partially successful and fell onto the bed. Mara was not one to lay on her back and give up control right away. She took matters into her own hands before allowing him to have his way with her.

Marathon snuck out of his place just before dawn. She had an early flight and needed to get herself together before heading to the airport. As she emerged from his place, she noticed the same group of soldiers huddled outside their quarters. Mara didn't want to disturb whatever they were doing so she turned and walked towards her barracks taking the long way around. She didn't get very far when one of the men spotted her.

"Look at this walk of shame boys," Mara instantly recognized the voice. The deep southernly accent from the beefy spec ops soldier she confronted during live fire training.

"Where you going sweetheart, there's more where that came from right here," Mara kept walking, but she heard footsteps behind her and before she could react they had caught up to her.

"Come on sugar tits, we got something for you," the beefy soldier said as he made his way around her blocking her path forward. Marathon looked up at him and he realized who it was. His breath wreaked of alcohol as she pushed passed him.

"What the fuck?" he said out of surprise.

"Get the fuck out of my way," Mara said in a stern voice.

"Hey guys, look, it's the fucking whore from the live fire training," he said as the other men started to make their way over to her. She felt them creep up behind her like puss oozing out of an infected wound.

Mara tried to step to the side, but the beefy man matched her move. His stature made him seem as tall as he was wide, which made it extremely difficult for Mara to get around him.

"Whatcha doing out here? Trying to fuck your way to the top," another spec ops soldier said.

Mara turned and two other soldiers blocked her retreat. She took a defensive posture and turned back towards the beefy man blocking her path forward.

"Wanna get out of the way? Or do you want another broken nose?" Mara stated as the two other men reacted with taunting gestures.

The beefy man leaned in close, Mara smelled his rotten breath mixed with vodka and cigarettes. She desperately wanted to lash out and strike the man, but she knew that's what he wanted. Striking a superior officer outside of training purposes was a serious offense and that would probably ruin her career before it even started.

"Did you spread nicely for the Corporal?" he said. His voice sounded twistingly creepy as he seemed to enjoy making her feel uncomfortable. Mara refused to acknowledge that question and again tried to move around him.

"Oh come on sugar, we got plenty of time to have some fun. Why don't you come back with us and we'll show you how you can be all that you can be? We'll let the past remain in the past."

The beefy soldier put his arm around Mara and started to physically guide her back towards where the men had gathered.

"No, get the fuck off me," she yelled out making it clear that she wanted no part in what they wanted.

Mara knew that if they didn't honor that statement, she would be allowed to fight, and she would get a chance to get her shots in before men would eventually beat her down. But it would be their careers on the line, not her's. They were dangerously close to crossing that line.

"Oh come on, you know you want this," The beefy soldier said as he grabbed his crotch and thrusted it up towards Mara in a repeatable motion. "Whores like you with daddy issues can't get enough dick."

"What the fuck did you just say? Daddy issues?"

"Your daddy left you, and now like most girls, you can't get enough dick in you to fill that void in your life."

Mara heard the two other soldiers react to the insults as Mara used every bit of restraint to refrain from striking him. She knew he was baiting her, but she also knew her breaking point and she was close.

"You don't fucking know me," Marathon stated with anger in her voice. Mara had been described like that before, but in less vulgar vernacular. She suspected that this guy had done his homework and looked up her file after she embarrassed him during live fire training.

"I got some daddy dick right here for you," the beefy soldier said. Mara knew he sensed blood in the water, and he kept pressing the issue. She needed an exit strategy that didn't involve rape.

"Get the fuck out of my way," Mara stated.

The beefy man grabbed her like he did during the live training session. Her cheeks squeezed together as the beefy man leaned in close. "Why don't we put that mouth of yours to better use?" He then shoved her face to the side while remaining dangerously close.

"I'd rather suck on a barrel than do anything with you," Mara firmly stated with fire in her eyes. The other soldiers had stopped laughing. Mara sensed that they were not willing to cross the line.

"Can you tell your boy to get off me before I report him for sexual assault!" Mara stated looking at the bystanders.

"If we ever run into each other again, sweet cheeks, you're gonna wish I fucked you."

"Good thing we'll never see each other again because I'd hate to be dissatisfied," Mara said hoping he would get the reference. His friends did though as they reacted appropriately to what she implied. The two other soldiers enticed the brawly man off of her and Mara now had enough space to get passed them.

"Afghanistan is a small country," he said as he pointed to a tattoo on his arm. It was a marksman tattoo showing how many confirmed kills. Mara did a quick count only to determine he was very good at his job. The beefy soldier took a step back and turned towards his friends.

"You know how bad you struck out? She'd rather have a .338 penetrate her," one of the other soldiers said making a joke out of the situation. Mara kept walking knowing the men were staring her down. She continued hearing them talk about her as she made her way back to the barracks.

M

Chapter
Twenty-Three

Jamaica Bay Wildlife Refuge
West Pond, Queens
August 31st, 2019

Marathon got off the A train at Broad Channel, a narrow jetty that was constructed for Cross Bay Boulevard to connect to the Rockaways making beach access easier. Broad Channel became popular for summer homes when the subway was expanded to follow Cross Bay Boulevard and connect mass transit to the Rockaways allowing greater access to the beaches.

Each block of houses had a manmade canal for boats to dock in their backyard. The houses were generally on stilts, with many of them looking brand new. Marathon remembered Hurricane Sandy devastated areas like this and wondered how long it took to rebuild this area. As she looked around, it seemed like they were still in the rebuilding process nearly seven years later.

She walked north following Cross Bay Boulevard until she reached the wildlife refuge and the matched the surroundings to the landmarks on the printed map. The mid-afternoon sun was bearing down, baking her black suit like she was in an oven.

As she walked north on the bike path that ran next to the boulevard, she noticed the woods to her left thicken and the distance to the bay increased. She knew she was getting close to the main wildlife refuge building she saw on the satellite images. She studied the map of the surrounding area again. The satellite view she printed back at the station showed the immediate area was littered with paths and dirt roads that snaked around the preserve. The path she needed was just up ahead. The last thing she wanted to do was announce her presence, so she found a path on the map just beyond the bike trail. The map showed that it ran parallel to Cross Bay Boulevard. The path required her to transverse a few yards of wooded terrain, but from there the larger dirt path would ultimately lead to her destination.

Marathon pulled out her Glock 15, inspected it and took it off safety, chambered a round and placed the firearm back in its leather holster. She had two extra clips with fifteen rounds in each. The math was not in her favor. The sniper, if he was out there, had at least an M24 long gun with an effective range well beyond what she could see in the distance. He was probably also carrying additional weapons, and if they were also military grade, she would certainly be out gunned at close range as well.

Mara scored well during her firearms training. She was extremely accurate at close range which was less than five meters. Very accurate at mid-range, between five and thirty meters, and accurate at fifty meters which pushed the effective range to her firearm to max, but the sniper she was up against had an effective range of one-thousand meters, depending on the scope he was using. The environment she was walking into was a sniper's wet dream. Her only advantage was knowing he was out there. Snipers thrive on the element of surprise.

She needed to bring the odds in her favor and that required drawing him in close. The odds were more even at close range, if it came to a hand to hand fight, she would be back at a disadvantage. He was tall, built like an ox, and psychopathically aggressive. Mara hoped Morales had a field package with him to narrow the advantage gap.

Marathon also had to consider the possibility of the sniper having back up as well. He was speaking to someone when she eavesdropped on his conversation back at Uncle Dave's ranch, and that person was probably tailing Morales. Mara had to consider that his friend was now with him, and that he was armed as well, probably covering the sniper's blind spots.

She pushed forward in a crouched position, using the overgrowth around the dirt path as cover. She checked the satellite image again, the main path intersected the trail she was on and that would take her to the white sandy beach section of this preserve. She could see the Brooklyn's skyline off in the distance which reminded her she was still in city limits.

The main path was wider than the trail she was on, which made her more exposed. There were tire marks embedded in the dirt leading towards her destination. The tread width indicated trucks came through here, and based on the indentations they made, it was quite frequently.

Marathon looked ahead and couldn't see much from her vantage point. There was a slight bend in the trail that concealed her target location. The sound from the busy boulevard dissipated the further she ventured down this path. The trees and overgrowth seemed to swallow up the existence of civilization. She had to remind herself that an expert killer was out there and not let her guard down. One misstep would be the end, the problem is, she wouldn't know it's a misstep until it was too late. She needed to keep low, follow her instincts, and use the vegetation as a visual cover.

Mara used the larger overgrowth on the right side of the path to remain as concealed as she could be. She paused for a moment to study the terrain on the paper map printed from the precinct. She was now on the path that wrapped around towards the white sandy beach jetty. The path was curved because West Pond was on the other side of the foliage to her right. West Pond, as named on the map was completely enclosed and not actually part of Jamaica Bay. Based on what she assumed was her location and the way the pond outlined the jetty, Marathon figured the sniper was set up north of her location on the other side of the pond. That would give him the greatest vantage point without any obstruction.

208

She once again checked the path she was on and determined the tree line ended just beyond the foliage up ahead. She would be exposed if she ventured out further with the West Pond on her right and Jamaica Bay on her left. If she were a sniper setting up an ambush, that's the point she would focus on.

Her senses were now in overdrive, she heard water lapping as the bay met the sandy beach and rocks, she heard seagulls off in the distance, bees buzzing around the foliage and the bushes swaying in the summer breeze. She also heard what sounded like a car engine running directly ahead, just out of view from the bend in the path.

Marathon pressed forward and reached the apex of the curve in the road. She carefully stretched herself out to look ahead. The hazy heat distorted her vision, but she was able to make out a grey sedan parked at the end of the path. The trunk was open and there was a figure standing over the trunk. She drew her Glock, kept it pointed towards the ground as she inched forward towards the clearing.

Mara now noticed the figure in greater detail as she slowly advanced further. It was Detective Morales by the way he stood and brown suit he was wearing even though his suit jacket was off. She remained concealed, obscuring her location behind the foliage next to the path. Mara needed to get his attention without startling him or giving away her position. There was little doubt that the sniper was out there somewhere, this was certainly a trap. She wasn't sure if he was there to take out Morales though, he could be considered collateral damage. She couldn't chance it, she had to warn him.

Marathon needed to act, but the options she had were terrible. She moved closer to the detective who was now about fifty feet from her position. The sniper's position probably gave him a clear shot at anything in this area. While Mara was visually concealed, she was not protected from sniper fire, and giving away her position would defeat the purpose of trying to remain alive. The bushes around her would do little to stop a .338 traveling at one-thousand meters per second.

If she called out to him, the sniper would pick up on what was happening and be more inclined to take the shot if he had a standing kill order. Marathon couldn't risk that, she needed to gain his attention without alerting the sniper of her presence. Plus she was concerned the sniper wasn't alone.

She decided to use a visual sign to gain the detective's attention. She holstered her firearm and used her watch to reflect light his way. With any luck, she should be able to draw his attention without giving away her position. There was enough light coming through the brush to achieve her goal, but her aim needed refinement. Mara saw the reflected light on the side of the car and then moved it up and back towards the detective. The light caught his eye and he looked directly over at Mara. Mara quickly held up the universal sign to shut up by placing a finger in front of her mouth. Morales looked baffled and Mara knew she needed to get him over to her as soon as possible so she gestured him to approach her. The sniper definitely suspected something was up, but no incoming fire was sent their way.

Mara placed her hand to her eye as if she was looking through a monocular, the military sign for sniper and then pointed directly at him signaling that he was in danger from sniper fire. Detective Morales understood what she was saying and rushed towards her and ducking down once he reached her position.

"Torres, what the fuck are you doing out here?" Morales said. The detective was sweating heavily in the summer heat.

"There is a lot to explain, but right now, we're in danger," Mara responded.

"From?" he responded.

"Sniper, probably on the other side of the pond," Mara said keeping her voice at a whisper.

"Sniper? Are you serious?"

Mara nodded. "You got the GPS coordinates from the Jeep, right?"

"Yeah, how did you get out here?"

"I saw the coordinates on Franks desk. When I looked it up, I noticed the connection," Mara said.

"The white sand…" Morales said. Mara looked at him knowing they were on the same page.

"While you were on leave, I studied what remained in the Williams file; that one picture with her shoes having dried white sand on them made me think she was at a beach not a playground," Morales said. "Then when we got these coordinates from the Jeep, it was an easy connection."

"I took that photo," she said.

"I know," he responded.

"I have a sample of the sand," Morales said. "It's in the evidence back over by the trunk."

"We have nothing to compare it to," Mara stated.

"We might, I have been following the chain of custody on the file. Apparently, the file was transferred out and landed in the hands of the FBI," he said.

"FBI?" Marathon questioned.

Morales nodded and turned his head back towards the jetty where is unmarked car was parked. "There's more evidence here, tire tracks. It looks like a truck or something big. Actually, this whole area looks like it has much more traffic coming through here than there should be," Morales said pointing to the dirt path.

Mara looked where he was pointing and had noted the path looked worn when she found it. The path had deep tire tracks with a raised center, like when trucks use the side roads and the road eventually warps to the weight of the truck. She shared his suspicions about what was going on here.

"There's also a small dock at the end of the road just beyond the jetty. Looks like it is used frequently," the detective said. "I was about to call it in, but my radio wasn't working."

"This feels like a trap," Mara said. "How convenient is it for GPS coordinates to show up the day I come back to NY?"

"It does, let's call for backup," he responded.

"I left my phone at the station. Where's your phone?" Mara asked.

He looked at her puzzled and took out his phone. Detective Morales dialed the station, but the call would not connect. He tried texting a fellow detective, but the message came up as undelivered.

"I don't have cell service," he said.

"He must be using a cellular jamming device," Mara said. "Which is why the radio wouldn't work as well. He's jamming all radio signals in the area."

"Who is he?"

Mara told him about her encounter with the sniper in the woods by Uncle Dave's ranch and how he was connected to William Bowden. Detective Morales now realized the full gravity of the situation.

"Is that why you left your phone at the station? Afraid of being tracked?"

"Yes, they are tracking me," she said. "They have access to my credit card, access to my Uncle's house lines, and monitored my computer at work."

"Fuck, you requested backup right?"

"I'm your backup," she said.

"You've got to be fucking kidding me? The two of us against a spec ops soldier?"

"I think there might be another person out there as well,"

"You're kidding, right?"

"No," Marathon said.

"Fuck, please tell me you're carrying." Morales stated.

Mara pulled out her gun and indicated she had two spare clips on her. Morales took out his Glock checked the weapon. He only had one extra clip. He then pointed to the trunk of the car.

"There's a shotgun in the trunk along with body armor," he said. "Standard field package."

"We won't make it that far. The sniper has a modified M24," Mara said.

"And you thought only to just bring yourself?"

"I don't trust anyone Detective. Not even Frank."

"Frank? You think Frank is behind this?" Morales questioned.

"Those two officers, you know the fake ones, that came to question me?"

"Yeah the ones that started this whole fucking shitshow," Morales immediately answered.

"Well, I made contact with one of them while I was on leave. He seemed to think Frank was a suspect," Mara stated.

"Wait, those two agents, they might actually be legit," Morales said. Mara saw the gears turn in his head as he pieced this new information together.

"Yes, and Frank is a focal point in their investigation," Mara stated.

"So why would Frank send me out here? Look at this place... This has smuggling written all over it. This is a drop off location. Whatever it is, drugs, guns, prostitutes.... They are dropped off here by boat and shipped by truck into the city," Morales stated. "That's why I was going to call it in to get forensics down here. Why would he want me to go here?"

"It's a fucking trap," Mara said. "You were baited out here, you are getting too close," Marathon continued. "Plus, they wanted to see if I would take the bait and come out here as well. That's why this is happening today, I'm back in town and you are actively engaged in the investigation. Do you think it's a coincidence?"

"In our line of work, coincidences don't exist," he said. "Two birds, one stone."

"Exactly, also consider that half your department called out sick today," Marathon said.

"Fuck! Ever since you foolishly accessed that file, you sparked this shit storm, and now I am fucking right smack in the middle of it," he said.

"Yeah, fuck me, right?" Mara responded.

Detective Morales was getting antsy, Mara could see it in his eyes and demeanor. She motioned him to remain calm, but he wasn't listening. He started peeking through the trees and looking at his surroundings. "If I can get to the car, we can get out of here," he said.

"That's about forty feet, maybe fifty to the driver's side," Mara responded.

She was always good at judging distance and she quickly determined that distance was too great to cross. Any good sniper would have them dead to rights before they made it halfway. Mara knew this guy was good without ever having seen him shoot. This kind of recon and planning proved he was the real deal; he was a few chess moves ahead of them and about to call check mate. She knew the car was not an option. He would be on them once they broke for the car and down before having reached it. Mara grabbed his arm and shook her head.

"I can make it," Morales said.

"Detective, forget it. You'll be dead before you make it halfway," Mara said.

"There's a field package in the trunk. Shotgun, body armor, evidence kits, the works," he said.

"How are we going to get to that? The moment he sees us, we're dead," Mara said.

Mara thought about going back the way she came. Take the path by foot using the brush as cover and then go down the narrow path, the way she entered. However, she didn't know where the sniper's partner was, but could assume he was covering the exit. She was sure of that, but which exit. She pulled out the map again and the two officers analyzed the paper.

"The sniper is probably positioned here," Mara said pointing at a spot slightly north of the pond.

Detective Morales translated the map location to the real world and pointed beyond their cover. Marathon then followed the path with her finger and showed that he had line of sight towards the exit where a gate blocked off the dirt road to the parking lot by the maintenance building.

"He has a limited field of view of this exit and cannot cover two positions," he said.

"I'm worried about the other guy," Mara said. "The sniper has the car covered, and part of our exit. I'm sure of that, but where would the other guy set up?"

"At this exit," Morales said. "A good sniper can cover a lot of ground, but the parts the sniper can't cover, that is where he would need support."

"If this guy is here, they can cover both exits," Morales pointed out.

"Fuck!" Mara said showing some frustration.

"What If I go out alone and get the car?" Morales said. "You haven't been spotted, and we are not 100 percent sure they are after me."

"No, that's a huge risk detective, you do that, and you're wrong, there is no way you make it out alive."

"It's our best option," he said.

"No it's not! They are jamming us! Do you really think they are jamming us for no reason?"

"They are jamming us because they are expecting you to show up, and that is why I am still here. If I go to the car and you are not spotted, I can get out of here and call for backup. I was out there doing just fine because they haven't seen you yet. They are not going to gun down an officer in broad daylight."

Morales holstered his gun showing he was convinced of his assessment of the situation.

"What the fuck are you doing?"

215

"Meet me here," he said, pointing to the path to the south that ended close to Cross Bay Boulevard. "I'll pick you up and we'll get backup once we get in town."

"Fuck no," Mara protested. "We get out of here together."

Morales stood, breaking cover and walked casually towards the car. He made it look like he had collected a sample for evidence as he made his way back to the car. Mara waited for a shot to break the eerie silence. Morales reached the trunk and put what was in his hand in an evidence bag and then closed the trunk. He then looked around and walked towards the driver's side of the car. He opened the door and got in.

He fucking made it, Mara thought. This is going to fucking work. Mara turned and assessed her exit. Go back the way she came. Follow her exact path and the two of them would meet up at the location Detective Morales chose. Mara cautiously retraced her steps. She heard the detective's car shift into gear. She kept walking towards her exit as the sedan casually passed her on the dirt road and disappeared around the bend towards the paved parking lot.

M

Chapter
Twenty-Four

Jamaica Bay Wildlife Refuge
West Pond, Queens
August 31st, 2019
Mid-Afternoon

Marathon advanced forward down the path that brought her in; she never liked going back the way she came. It felt redundant, like a bad design. She listened carefully as she heard the detective's car slow down and stop. He must be at the gate and she continued to their rendezvous location.

She saw the path she came in on and dashed across the dirt road trying to keep her cover intact. She was now close enough to hear the running engine of the detective's sedan, additionally she heard what sounded like metal clanging together. Mara stopped in her tracks and turned towards the sound. Detective Morales should have been clear by now, what was his car still doing there? She paused and listened intently. She heard voices through the thick growth, raised voices, but she couldn't make out what they were saying. Mara pulled out her map and focused on her current location. She found a path that split off of hers that brought her to the maintenance facility next to the exit into the parking lot.

She made a snap decision and took that path. Her pace quickened as she heard the voices get louder. She heard Morales barking orders.

"Put your hands where I can see them, HANDS," he exclaimed.

Shit, he was in trouble. Mara got to the edge of the path and saw Morales pointing a gun at a man a few yards away from him. The man wore a tan shirt and

217

dark brown pants with hiking boots. She thought this was probably the sniper's partner. He looked stocky, not like a soldier. Mara crouched down and raised her firearm, she was concealed enough to remain hidden.

"Where is she?" The man said. He looked calm and collected, even with a gun pointed at him.

From her vantage point, she saw a Berretta 9mm sticking out of his belt behind his back. Detective Morales was seemingly in control of the situation, but Mara knew this was just an allusion. Spec ops soldiers were killing machines that took calculated risks only when they had the greatest chance for success. Detective Morales was in grave danger. The sniper also had direct line of sight to this location. Detective Morales was no doubt in his cross hairs. Marathon suspected that the sniper was waiting for her to make a move, which was why Detective Morales was still alive.

"I am a NYC detective; I am police officer, and this is a crime scene. Leave the area immediately," Detective Morales said as he held his Glock firmly but not pointed at the man.

"Where is Detective Torres?" the man asked again.

"Who?" Morales returned with a question of his own.

"I know who the fuck you are, Detective Morales of the 73rd," the man said in response. "Where is the now retired Detective Torres?"

"Clearly not here," Morales said.

"Bullshit, she was seen getting on an A train heading south to this location," the man said.

"Funny, I haven't seen anyone out here," Morales said.

Mara looked around trying to figure out her next course of action. Any sudden movement would certainly expose her and start a chain of events in which she could not control. Marathon was sure that the sniper was scanning the area for her and was waiting for her to make a move. This standoff was deliberate and calculated. She knew this tactic well and knew tensions would escalate quickly to draw her out. She would be forced to make a tough choice if she wanted to save Detective Morales.

Marathon carefully went prone in the brush being careful not to make any noise or sudden movement. She had to take off her suit jacket because of its restrictive movement. She knew her white blouse, which was now stained with sweat and dirt would stand out in contrast to the dark green background. While in prone position, Mara focused her Glock 15 at the man, at this range, she could easily take him out before the man could even draw his gun. However, doing so, would expose her position to the sniper on overwatch. The sniper would most likely drop Detective Morales before turning his sites on her.

Mara knew she had to be patient and let the conversation play out a bit before she could act. She was counting on Detective being safe as long as she remained hidden, however she couldn't hide for long. This stalemate would not end in their favor as time was certainly not on their side. Mara looked at Detective Morales, who was becoming agitated. She knew this was going to go south quickly, but she hoped he would keep his cool, both their lives depended on it.

"Detective Morales, this will be the last time I ask you, where is Marathon Torres?" The man said.

"Clearly she ain't here. You know what, fuck this! Hands up, turn around and get on your knees! Your under arrest for threatening an officer," Detective Morales said.

The detective started to close the distance and ordered the man onto the ground. Mara wanted to yell out, this was the wrong play. The man slowly kept his hands in the air and started to move to the ground, but he did not turn around. Out of nowhere, a mound of dirt kicked up and a second later a loud bang cracked through the swampy forest. Birds flew out from the trees and everything became eerily silent. The sniper had made his move.

Detective Morales turned and faced the direction from where the shot came. The bullet traveled much faster than the sound it made and Detective Morales looked far off in the distance. That gave the man enough time to draw his Berretta and when Morales turned back, he was shocked to find the tables had turned and he was completely caught off guard.

"The next words to come out of your mouth better be the location of Marathon Torres," the man said with great focus in his voice. Mara knew he was serious, she knew he would not hesitate to pull the trigger. If he didn't suspect she was here, he would have already been killed.

"Detective Torres isn't here!" Morales said. "She's probably on her way out of the city now that she's retired."

"Her GPS location says she is still at the precinct, but we can confirm she is no longer there. So I am going to ask you one more time, where is Detective Torres?"

Marathon was glad she remembered to leave her cell phone at the station, but in hindsight it didn't really matter. They knew she was here.

"Well, as you can see, she ain't with me," Morales said in defense.

The man held his finger to an earpiece, Mara knew he was receiving instructions from someone. She steadied her firearm and focused her line of fire. From this range, and angle, her accuracy was near 100 percent. She needed this to play out a bit longer. She needed to give Morales time to find cover and needed the sniper to focus his attention elsewhere.

"What's in the car?" the man asked.

"She's not in there," Morales responded.

The man motioned for the detective to drop his sidearm and he complied throwing the weapon in the dirt between them. The man did not react and kept his focus on Detective Morales as the line of questioning continued.

"You collected samples out by the jetty, why?" the man asked. Mara knew the sniper had relayed questions to the man and they were clearly concerned with what Morales found. Any chance of letting him go was now out the window.

Mara suspected the man and the sniper were communicating through short wave radio immune to the jamming device.

"I collected samples of sand and took pictures," Morales said truthfully.

Shit, this was going to be over soon, Mara thought. Mara focused her breathing, she hoped that taking the man out was enough to draw the sniper away from Morales giving him time to find cover. She hoped her position was concealed enough for the sniper not to notice where the shot came from.

"Show me," he said.

"I'm going to reach for my keys," Morales said. Mara saw them walk towards the old Crown Victoria. This was the cover he would need. She would let them get closer before she had to act.

When she thought Morales was close enough, Mara placed her finger on the trigger and breathed out slowly. Her heart beat steadied and her hand slowly contracted squeezing the handle of her gun. It jumped slightly from the recoil and a split moment later she saw a cloudy mist of red disperse into the air around the man's head. He fell.

"MORALES, GET TO COVER!" Mara yelled.

Mara heard the sound of a sniper shot land feet from her position giving Morales time to get to cover. The sniper was now scanning for her and his cross hairs were not fixed on Detective Morales otherwise he would have been shot immediately. Mara saw the detective dart towards the car where he took cover behind the passenger side. She then rolled to her right into the bushes. Another shot came within inches of her position. The sniper was onto her and she was compromised. She jolted up, knowing the bolt action weapon would be ready in moments. Another shot narrowly missed her head as it split a tree open next to her like a bursting balloon.

Mara saw cover feet away, towards the parking lot, where trees became bigger and provided more solid cover. She made her way towards them as another tree exploded next to her. She dove behind a thicker tree and successfully used its cover to shield an incoming round.

More shots could be heard, but this time bullets were not flying in her direction. She peaked out from her cover and saw the sedan through the trees. She saw Detective Morales crouch behind the car as incoming rounds sent large chunks of metal ripping through the air. She heard the distinct sound of his Glock returning fire as more incoming .338 rounds were sent his way. The Glock stopped firing first.

"Detective?" Mara yelled out as she heard him struggling behind the car.

"Mara, I'm hit," Morales said. The sunlight exposed the Detective's position as Mara saw blood pour out from his leg. The sniper round had pierced his upper thigh and took out a large chunk of his leg. Fuck, that wound looked bad, Mara thought. She looked around for options. The maintenance building was now just beyond the tree line to her right.

"Mara, it's bad, I'm losing a lot of blood," he said.

"Tie your belt around your upper thigh, as tight as you can," she said.

She watched Morales fumble with his belt as blood continued to ooze out of his leg. Mara knew the sight well, the femoral artery was probably ruptured. Morales maybe had less than a minute of consciousness. She watched helplessly as Morales placed the belt around his upper thigh. He was slowing down and was on the verge of passing out.

"Come On!" She yelled. "Tie the fucking belt!"

Morales jolted at the instructions. He looped the belt through and had one end ready to pull tight like a zip tie.

"Detective, fucking put everything you got into this," Mara yelled.

Morales pulled at the belt using his full body weight. Mara saw the leather dig into his pant leg and squeeze the flow of blood down to a trickle. However, Morales was laying on the ground, he was grasping at the leather trying to tie it off. She knew he was about to lose consciousness. Morales looped the leather through,

222

preventing it from loosening and then went still. He lost consciousness, but flow of blood stopped indicating his triaged tourniquet worked. She hoped it was enough to keep him alive. None of it mattered if she couldn't survive herself. She was now in a one on one battle with an experienced killer who had every advantage over her.

Mara noticed the tranquil environment was absent of sniper fire. He was either baiting her out or changing position. She was concealed behind a tree thicker than she was, but any sudden movement might jeopardize her location. She observed the distant pond where the shots came from; she knew his general location and focused on what his field of view was in relation to her current position. The folded, dirt ridden computer paper was making the map difficult to read as she assessed her options.

If he was baiting her out, the sniper was still over the pond. While he had a direct line of sight towards the sedan, Mara's position was narrow with plenty of trees to absorb incoming fire. She only needed to move towards the maintenance building to conceal herself and move out of line of sight. If he was changing position, he would be on top of her in a few minutes and she wouldn't even have a chance to make it to cover.

Mara checked her firearm, only one bullet had been discharged. She made sure her clips were still secure and surveyed the landscape to the building. She had decided to make a break for it, she charted a direct path using trees as cover. She would know immediately if the sniper was still looking down scope. If he was good as Mara thought he was, she gave herself about a twenty five percent chance of making the building in one piece. If she stayed here and he was moving to get a better angle, she had a zero percent chance of survival. Both scenarios fucking sucked, but the choice was clear.

She knew time was running out and darted out, lunging for the maintenance building at full sprint through the thick vegetation. Tree branches, bushes and undergrowth teared at her clothes, shredding her blouse and slashing her exposed

223

skin. Mara used her forearms as a shield to protect her face as she burst through the tree line and stumbled onto the dirt path that ran along the back of the maintenance building. No shots were heard, he was changing position and Mara knew she only had a few minutes before he would reacquire his target.

She was on borrowed time being exposed out in the open like this. Her long legs carried her around the building, she was looking for an entrance. The doors in back were locked and she couldn't spend time trying to get them open. She sprinted around the front of the building towards the parking lot. An older pickup truck with a wildlife emblem embedded on the side was standing lonesome in the middle of the empty lot. She decided to make a run for it, as she didn't have time to try the front doors of the building. They were most likely locked and that would be a waste of precious time.

With any luck she could get the truck started. It was an older model and well within her skill to hotwire. She estimated she could cover the distance to the truck in mere seconds and she hoped there would be enough time to accomplish her task.

At full sprint, she retreated towards the truck and slid over the hood feet first. She heard a shot come from behind her as a round grazed her neck and sailed off into the blacktop on the other side of the parking lot in front of her. Mara couldn't gracefully land on her feet, so she let her momentum carry her flat to the ground and skid a few feet beyond the side of the truck. Her Glock made a scraping noise as the metal dragged across the concrete as she braced her fall.

Marathon crouched behind the rusted red Ford F250. The pickup was massive and the top of the hood stood four feet off the ground. If Mara hadn't jumped to get over the pickup, the bullet that grazed her neck would have been a headshot. She felt the truck vibrate as subsequent rounds littered the vehicle. She felt rounds sail straight over her head and land in the blacktop about fifty feet away. The rounds came from a semiautomatic rifle, he must have switched weapons upon approach. The sound the rifle made was distinct, an M4 carbine was now hunting her. She knew this weapon well and had been her weapon of choice overseas.

Her Glock was simply no match. She was out of position, stranded out by the Ford F250 and severely outgunned. The incoming fire stopped, she figured he was switching back to the M24 now that she was pinned down. Mara made sure the wheels of the truck hid her position and searched around for options. She noticed her white blouse had splattered blood all along her collar. She felt the side of her neck and felt a deep wound that was slightly more than a bullet graze. As if on cue, the wound started to hurt and she saw more blood on her hands than she expected.

The abrasion wasn't serious, but the pain and amount of blood reminded her how close to death she was. Mara figured the sniper was in a slightly elevated position, and ready to react to her movements. He was probably near the tree line close to where she came from. The sun was now at his back, which gave him another advantage, as if he needed another one.

Mara needed to stay low and behind cover. She held her hand over the wound and blood started to seep between her fingers. The pain was intense, like a combination of being burned and hit with a fastball while standing in a batter's box. She felt as if their cat and mouse game was coming to an end. He had her right where he wanted, and she was running out options.

M

Chapter
Twenty-Five

```
Jamaica Bay Wildlife Refuge
West Pond, Queens
August 31st, 2019
Early Evening
```

The sniper kept his barrage of bullets focused on the truck. He would spray rounds from his M4 and then switch to the long barrel to see if he could detect movement. This tactic was familiar, spray the target with enough fire to either break their will to fight or they'll get nervous and make a mistake, then the m24 would end the firefight. Occasionally, the intended target would be killed as bullets destroyed cover, or a lucky ricochet would do the job. Mara needed to keep her cool; she needed to weigh her extremely limited options. The .338 rounds were getting close, like a pitcher sniffing the strike zone.

Next to the pickup truck was a light pole with a solid concrete base. The shadows were now elongated to the point where they seemed parallel to the ground. Mara looked to her left, about fifty feet behind the truck was the maintenance building for the Jamaica Bay Preserve. To her right was the exit towards Cross Bay Blvd. She watched as cars flooded past the barren parking lot. The sniper must be using some sort of sound suppressant. She heard the shots, but they definitely sounded different now that they were closer to the street. She would never make it to the boulevard, the building was her only option.

The truck she leaned against could be used as mobile cover. If she could get the truck into neutral, it would roll down the slight decline towards the building. The ford was an older model, looked like it was well past its lifespan and a true staple of someone who worked in the upkeep department. Marathon quickly decided this was her best option and reached up awkwardly as she tried to remain crouched behind the wheels. Her fingers felt the door handle as her long arms stretched to maximize her reach. She felt the rusted handle and found the button to open the door, it sunk into the handle and the door opened but she remained in her position.

Marathon now needed to finagle her way around the open door without exposing herself. The truck was high off the ground and Mara thought the sniper possibly had a shot at her legs if they were exposed from behind the wheels. No doubt he saw the front driver side door open.

Mara took a deep breath; she needed a distraction. Something that would give her a chance to get into the truck. She just needed have something draw fire from the M24. If the first shot missed, she knew the bolt action rifle would give her the time needed to get into the front seat. She thought a second and then decided to remove her sweat stained blouse and use that as a distraction. She unbuttoned her top and removed it, careful not to expose any body parts from cover. Mara examined it, there was blood stained on the side collar where the M24 .338 magnum round nearly ended her life.

She was now shirtless and in a bra that matched her skin tone. The bra was stained in blood and sweat as she carefully positioned her blouse for maximum effect. She needed the blouse to soar outwards like she was on the move, trying to break cover and run. She knew that any movement like that would certainly send a round that way. Usually snipers would shoot and then immediately chamber another round before confirming a hit. He would most likely follow the target with his scope leaving her a narrow window to get into the truck. She would probably have 2-3 seconds before he reacquired her if he took the bait.

227

She had to be quick, once she heard the shot, she needed to be in motion towards the front seat. Mara crouched like a coiled rattlesnake and braced her back leg against the tire. She would use that to propel herself towards the door, giving the momentum she needed to slingshot herself around the door and into the cabin. Mara held the collar of her shirt, as if she were hanging it up in her closet. She lowered her arm, prepping the toss out to her right.

She counted to three internally and then launched the white blouse outwards parallel to the ground as if she were making a break for it. Without fail, she heard a rifle go off. She sprung from her position keeping her body as low to the ground as possible. Her left arm extended out and grabbed the end of the door and she used it to spin herself around. Like a spear being thrown, she launched herself back and into the cabin of the truck head first. She stayed low and landed horizontal across the couch style seating in the cabin. She then heard the window break above her head as she faced the passenger door. Another round hit the passenger side door with only inches separating her from the bullet as it passed straight through into the cabin.

Mara rolled off the of seats and onto the floor of the cabin. In the Ford F-250, there was no center console and the gear shift was located on the steering column. She heard another round pierce the interior of the cabin where she was laying before. The .338 round was clearly strong enough to penetrate the rusted exterior. Mara knew she needed to act fast. She turned on her back and grabbed the gear shift next to the wheel and manipulated it into neutral. The truck released from the parked position.

The Ford started to roll backwards, it was on a slight slope where water drained from the parking lot. She waited patiently as the truck slowly inched down the slight slope towards the building. After a few moments it began picking up speed; then Mara felt the truck jolt upwards. She knew it hit the curb of the sidewalk that separated the parking lot from the south side of the building. Its momentum continued it backwards, then with a slight thud, the vehicle smacked into the side of the building. She placed the truck back in park and contemplated her next move.

The truck only traveled about forty-five feet, but she was still in the same predicament as she was in before. Another round ripped through the truck passing inches from her head. She needed to get out of the cabin fast. Marathon sat up keeping her head below the window. She lurched forward, peered through the still open door and looked at the ground. Her entire position was now in the shadow of the building. This would make it tough for the sniper to acquire a clean shot. She took advantage of the opportunity and crawled out of the truck and regained her cover behind the wheel.

Another round ripped through the cabin where Mara would have been and ricocheted off the concrete having gone straight through the truck. She timed the next shot, knowing it was coming right after he chambered another round. The truck had rolled to the middle section of the building. Large windows littered the front wall and she knew what she had to do. She drew her Glock and waited for the right moment.

Marathon heard a bullet pierce through the cabin; this was her chance, she leapt out from behind the truck knowing he was in the process of lining up another shot as she extended her Glock forward and repeatedly squeezed the handle. The bullets ripped through the window as she sprang forward headfirst into the shattering glass. Mara hit harder than she expected and crashed straight through onto the tile floor below inside the building. She slid for a few feet after the dive as a glass continued to break around her.

Pain quickly overcame her senses as numerous lacerations started to materialize all over her body. A Trickle of blood flowed over her eyebrow and obscured her vision as she got back to a crouched position. Her shoulder had a few shards of glass embedded into it and her bra and a large tare just under her arm with a deep scratch behind it. She quickly checked her wounds and determined nothing was life threatening, but she would certainly need stitches in numerous places. Hopefully, a mortician wouldn't be the one stitching her up.

After a quick survey of the empty room, Mara determined she was in the front lobby with the main entrance about thirty feet to her right and a hallway straight ahead. Keeping her head down, she decided to go straight down the hallway past a reception desk. Marathon checked the multiple doors and found an open door to her left. She remained low, and kept her Glock focused on potential targets as she crossed the threshold and cleared the room. She had to assume that the sniper was in transition and was closing in on her position.

The room was filled with desks, office chairs, computers, and other various office staples. Mara's eyes fixated on a desk, a large black office phone was positioned next to a computer. Mara leapt from her crouched position and picked up the phone. There was a dial tone.

"911, what's your emergency?"

"I am Detective Marathon Torres, I have an officer down at the nature preserve in Broad Channel! I repeat, officer down! Nature preserve Broad Channel," Mara yelled into the microphone.

She waited for the operator to say something, but all she heard was emptiness.

"Hello, I have an officer down!"

Nothing.

"FUCK," she yelled out as she slammed her hand down on the switch hook repeatedly hoping a tone would resurface.

Nothing.

Mara heard a loud crash come from the lobby area, like someone had just kicked in a door. The sniper was now in the building. Mara hoped she could hold out long enough to find out if the operator caught part of her emergency call. An officer down emergency sends all available units to the target location with an average response time being five to six minutes. She took cover behind one of the desks on the opposite side of the room from where she entered. The medium sized office had about six desks void of any materials. It looked like more of a show room than an active office. Each desk had an old big and bulky computer tower with a CRT monitor next to it. Some of them weren't even from this century.

She decided that her current position was good enough for a last stand. She trained her Glock towards the only door in the room and focused her breathing. The shadows outside the room drifted as if they were floating, signaling movement on the outside. Her Glock remained focused on the door. Blood continued to flow from her brow and she cautiously cleared her vision from the distraction.

The big brawly sniper' shadow peered through the door and Mara squeezed her Glock sending the remaining bullets in the clip towards the wall where he was probably standing. The Glock was strong enough to penetrate interior walls. She heard the sniper grunt signaling her tactic had worked. She definitely hit him but wasn't sure if it was enough. She stayed in position and focused thoroughly at the door looking for any sign of movement. She quickly hit the clip release and loaded a fresh clip into her Glock and chambered a round.

A cylinder bottle like object flew through the opening and landed just beyond her cover. Mara dropped down as the cylinder exploded in a cacophony of sound and light that penetrated all of her senses simultaneously. Marathon remained behind cover as bursts of gunfire replaced the ringing in her ears. The sniper had entered the room with his M4 blazing the path. Her cover disintegrated around her as wood splinters from the particle board desks exploded. Mara dropped into prone position and rolled away from the barrage of heated metal.

She heard the distinct sound of a magazine hit the floor. While her instincts told her to return fire, she knew he wasn't exposed while he was reloading, and she would only waste the remaining bullets she had left.

"Hey Bitch, you still alive?"

The sound of a fresh clip locked into place echoed the sniper's taunt.

"More alive than your little friend outside," Mara yelled back.

"You fucking cunt," he replied.

Mara heard him move and she changed her position as well. The beefy man's movement was easily understood from her position. She knew she couldn't out gun him so getting in close was her only option, she had to stay a few steps ahead of him. She scurried from desk to desk as the sniper sent random bullets towards whatever sound she made.

"What's the matter sweet tits? Out of ammo?"

"Oh don't worry, I got something right here for you," Mara replied as she gracefully turned a corner and navigated her body towards his flank position. She was able to remain crouched as her nimble body kept her a few moves ahead of the bulky sniper. She almost had him, like a game of chess, only a few more moves were needed for checkmate.

"I'm glad I get to do you like this," he said. "I've been waiting for this moment ever since The Depot."

"I bet this is the most action you've had in a long time," Mara snapped back.

"There was a point when you could have come out on top," he said. "But your dumb ass never made it that far."

Mara needed to keep him talking as she needed to maneuver herself to get the angle needed to take him out.

"You couldn't let things go," he continued. "If it were up to me, your ass would have been dealt with a long time ago."

"I don't think they leave anything up to you, you're just a blunt object doing only what you are told," She said.

"You have no idea what you are dealing with sweet tits," he responded as Mara heard him swiftly turn a corner thinking she was there. She remained a few steps ahead of him. His movements easily gave away his position. Her advantage continued.

"I've been watching you for years, you're about as predictable as a stripper in a strip club," he said.

Mara sensed that he stopped moving, she held her position and remained perfectly sill, he was changing tactics. Any movement or sound would end their little game in his favor. She then heard the M4 crack off a few rounds in random directions. He was becoming frustrated. He then continued his search pattern.

"Yet, it was Bowden who was sent instead of you," Mara said getting back to their cat and mouse game.

"He was sent to give you a message. When they send me, they are done sending messages," he said.

"Were you jealous? Bowden was going to have all the fun with me and you got sidelined?"

"Bowden was just going to keep you warm."

"Awe, isn't that sweet," Marathon said as she stood up, aimed her Glock, and fired. The sniper spun her way and a round struck him in the upper body sending him backwards towards the wall. He was wearing tactical gear, which probably included body armor. She continued firing and heard some of her shots connect, but he didn't fall. The wall behind him kept him upright and he raised his M4. Mara dove down as bullets sprayed in her direction. His aim was wild and erratic as chunks of shrapnel erupted like a volcano around her. The familiar sound of an empty magazine thirsty for more ammo replaced the drum beat of bullets.

Mara heard the M4 hit the ground as she regained her footing. The sniper was now in motion towards her. He was still upright with some of her shots connecting around the body armor. He was hurt and loosing blood. Their little exchange caused her to expend her entire clip, she had no chance to reload in time. Mara turned for the door and sprung from her crouched position. Before she could reach the threshold, she felt his arm grab her from behind.

Mara instinctively spun around and was met with a combat knife bearing down on her. She instinctively raised her arm to block the attack sending the knife straight through her forearm between the Ulna and Radius bones. She stared up at the exit wound where the knife protruded out and hung inches from her face. She braced her forearm with her other hand as the sniper tried to force edge of the blade down into her.

Mara needed to regain control and shifted her weight backwards just enough to send the sniper lunging forward. His grip on the knife loosened just enough for Mara to roll her forearm. With the knife still firmly embedded, she freed the hilt of the knife from the sniper's grip and spun away along the wall. He turned and was now blocking the door. Mara saw he was losing a lot of blood, his pale green muscle shirt was saturated beneath his body armor. His movements were slowing.

"Looks like you're going to end up like your friends," Mara said as she backed up. The pain in her forearm was intense. She needed to create distance in case he decided to lunge at her again, she still couldn't match his strength. She had no time to deal with the knife wound in her forearm as her entire focus was on the deadly spec ops soldier trying to kill her.

The sniper seemed to be at a loss for words as he got closer. He then lunged forward as Mara predicted he would. She leaned backwards and let his momentum carry over onto a desk behind her. His movement was slow, and Mara sensed he was losing his grip on this world. She would help him let go.

Before the sniper could regain his footing, Marathon grabbed him from behind and applied a rear naked choke hold to finish him off. To prevent him from standing upright, she leaned backwards which allowed both of them to fall to the ground. Mara then wrapped her legs around his waist to control his legs. His arms started to flail as she put pressure on his jugular by squeezing her arms together, much like the choke hold she used on Bowden, but this time with her arms. The knife, still embedded in her forearm was now by this throat as she continued to apply the choking technique. It started to sink into his neck as she squeezed.

"You're going to die just like Bowden," Mara whispered in his ear.

"Fuck you bitch," he blurted out sending spit and blood flying in the air. Mara squeezed tighter. His arms tried to reach back and grab her but he didn't have the range of motion needed to be successful. She squeezed tighter. He tried elbowing her side, but the blows weren't strong enough to break her hold.

The combat knife still stuck in her forearm was now digging in under his chin as she continued to squeeze. The sniper's movement became more erratic, more frantic. He tried to roll but lacked the leverage needed as Mara controlled his hips with her legs. She knew it would be over soon, but she enjoyed this moment and wanted it to last. She beat him at his own game, she won, and she wanted him to live in his failure forever.

The sniper tried to speak but only grunts and mispronounced words exited. For a moment, she thought she should question him further and find out who he was working for, but she enjoyed this too much and increased the pressure. She also couldn't risk him getting a second wind. She needed to end this now.

She felt him gasp for breath, but no oxygen would enter his lungs. Her forearm closed his windpipe as the combat knife in her forearm continued to dig deeper. His movement slowed and his arms stopped flailing and then stopped moving altogether. Mara squeezed harder until blood ceased to flow from the bullet holes in his chest, until she felt no signs of life left in his body.

Marathon released her hold on the sniper and his head fell awkwardly to the side. She kicked him off and his body rolled lifeless as his head made a deafening thud off the floor. She held the choke hold tight for so long that her arms felt like they were locked in place. The combat knife was still protruding from her arm, but the pain it should have caused was barely present. Her hand was also numb, which probably meant the knife might have caused nerve damage.

Marathon got to her feet, found her Glock and went for the door that led out of the building. She rushed towards the dirt road where she had last seen Detective Morales. As she approached the unmarked car, she noticed the driver side door was open. Detective Morales propped up against the door with the car's CB radio in his hand.

"Holy fuck," he said as he noticed Mara approaching. "What the fuck happened to you?"

His voice sounded weak as Mara sat down next to him utterly exhausted. She checked his tourniquet, his leg was a chalky color white compared to the rest of his light brown skin. Blood was still trickling out.

"I'm gonna release the tourniquet a bit to allow blood to circulate again," Mara said as she eased the belt. Morales winced in pain and blood started to flow again from his gaping wound. She knew he couldn't afford to lose any more blood so she tightened the tourniquet back quickly after letting some blood back into his leg. Detective Morales noticed the combat knife sticking out of her forearm as she tended to his wound.

"What the fuck? You look worse than I do," he said jokingly.

Mara smirked as she finished tightening the belt causing Morales to scream out in pain.

"At least I'm not crying about it," she responded. The sun had just set behind them as they heard the radio flicker as if it were being brought back to life. Detective Morales reached for the receiver and held it up to his mouth.

"We got officers down, at the Broad Chanel Wildlife Refuge. Repeat, officers down. Over," Morales yelled into the push to talk microphone.

The radio barked back, but Mara didn't pay attention. Morales issued further commands as Mara heard sirens erupt off in the distance. How the fuck was she going to explain this? Morales dropped the radio.

"Well, now the shit hits the fan," Detective Morales said.

"How's your leg?" Mara asked.

"Better than your arm," Morales replied.

"I thought you were fucking dead," Marathon said.

"I thought you were dead," Morales also stated. "Did you get him?"

"Yeah, I got him."

"You're one bad ass bitch," Morales said with a laugh.

"Before this place gets overturned, what the fuck are we going to tell brass?" Marathon asked.

"What do you mean?" Morales replied.

"We were set up, this was a fucking hit!" Mara replied.

"Are you suggesting there's a mole?"

"I'm saying this is not over. Whoever sent Beavis and Butthead over here to kill us still wants us dead," Mara stated. "We have to cover our asses Detective."

The sirens sounded closer.

"How do we do that?" Detective Morales questioned.

"You know those two fake internal affairs officers?"

"Don't fucking tell me," Morales said.

"They are with special operations, deep undercover. At least that's what they told me," Mara said.

"Fuck, Mara. What the fuck?"

"Lieutenant Esposito," Mara continued but was then interrupted again.

"The G I Joe wannabe?"

"Yeah, him," Mara said with a smile. "Now, may I continue?"

Detective Morales nodded as the sirens sounded like they were just down the boulevard.

"Esposito suspects an underground network of cops running outside the law. They suspect Inspector Davidson is involved," Mara said.

"Frank? No fucking way Mara! I told you it's not him," he said.

"I said the same thing!" Marathon agreed.

"I served with him, there's no fucking way he would ever be involved in something like this. He's like a fucking father to you and thinks the world of you," Morales protested.

"Where did you get the coordinates for this location from?"

"What?" he said.

"Frank said that the GPS coordinates from the Jeep Esposito and Russo used gave these coordinates. Where did they come from?"

"Once I found out the Jeep had a navigation system, I got a court order to retrieve the information from the Department of Health and Human Services. Standard operating procedure. The coordinates came from the manufacturer," Morales stated.

"Anything strange?"

"Besides the delay in getting the data, no."

"Delay?" Mara asked.

"Yeah, they sent me the wrong GPS data for a Jeep with a completely different VIN number. I had to redo the entire court order just to get the company to send the correct data over."

"And that came in this morning?"

Morales nodded.

"Why these coordinates? That Jeep was probably all over the city," Mara said.

"They came up multiple times a month in the entire GPS data report."

"Don't you see, whoever sent that data over to you baited us here," Mara said. "Maybe that Jeep was used to run drugs or something, but they wanted us to find that GPS data today, because I was back in town."

"Fuck," Morales stated. "Still doesn't prove anything about Frank!"

"No, but it shows you what we're dealing with," Marathon said. "There's a good chance the original data was correct, and the faulty VIN was just there to render the data useless so the case would remain in limbo. They could have planted evidence any number of ways to set us up like this."

Morales rolled up his sleeve and exposed his service tattoo.

"You see this kid? This here lets me ask Frank anything."

"I know what it means Morales," Marathon said showing her tattoo.

"Good, because that's what I intend to do."

"Okay, that's our plan? Just ask him?" she asked.

"Do you have a better plan?" Morales asked her back.

Mara saw the first patrol car enter the parking lot. The car sped towards them as an endless stream of marked cars entered behind. Mara stood and signaled their location. "I guess that's our course of action," Mara said looking down at the detective without a better plan in place.

"We tell the truth about what happened here," Morales added.

"Right," Mara responded not liking where it could lead.

"But first, we need medical attention. Follow union protocol and everything will be fine," he said.

"I'm retired," Mara said.

"Good, that gives you added protection as a civilian. The right to remain silent and all."

A patrol car stopped a few feet from their unmarked car. Mara waved the responding officers over as they got out of their car. An ambulance pulled up alongside.

"You follow union protocols and I have the right to remain silent, got it," Mara said back to Morales as the officers approached.

They both nodded so their stories would not contradict each other. One of the officers guided the paramedics to Detective Morales as another approached her. The knife sticking out of her forearm garnered a lot of attention.

M

Chapter
Twenty-Six

Veteran Support Group
Queens, NY
December 2nd, 2005
9:45pm

"Hi, my name is Danny, I am an army veteran who served in Iraq."

"Hi Danny," the group responded.

"Jesus, this isn't a fucking AA meeting," Mara whispered under her breath, but loud enough to promote a reaction. Danny looked over at her and she noticed his confidence shrink from the comment.

"Ms. Torres," Justin said with a deep glare.

Mara rolled her eyes and continued chewing her gum making loud popping sounds as Danny nervously told his story. Danny was much older than Mara and attended all the other meetings she was forced to attend. For some reason, he always spoke at these things and shared his feelings.

Mara's eyes circled the room of broken veterans who had recently come home from service in Afghanistan or Iraq. Each with a different horrifying story of emotional and physical pain they endured while overseas. Danny was a veteran of the first Iraq war, Operation Desert Storm. During her first group session, Mara made a comment about his failure in Desert Storm to kill Saddam, which lead to most of the people in the room going back to Iraq for another war. That comment didn't go over so well with the group.

Mara wanted nothing from this, she wanted to be out with her friends getting wasted and pick up guys. She missed most of her partying days while overseas in Afghanistan and was hell bent on making up for lost time. The exit to the gymnasium was directly behind her, she had signed her name which was probably good enough for the courts. If anyone questioned why she left, she would say she had to use the bathroom and make up a story about being lost in the school they were in.

Her court ordered mandated sessions kept her out of any further trouble. The judge even purposely made her attend evening sessions on a Friday night to avoid her excessive partying, which was what got her in trouble in the first place. Uncle Dave shelled out big bucks for a fancy lawyer to spring her out of trouble and she was lucky the judge only mandated these therapy sessions as a deal to keep her record clean. The judge mentioned something about knowing the price of service and she deserved a second chance. She barely paid attention to the old man as he lectured her before smacking his gavel down to order these group therapy sessions.

Danny also kept rambling on about sacrifice and now the country doesn't care about him or anyone in this room. All this self-pity bullshit made her yawn and slump further into the metal folding chair. She was also disappointed the guy she hooked up with last session wasn't at the meeting. He was probably done with her anyway. There usually wasn't a second encounter, which seemed to become a pattern lately, she had brought condoms just in case.

"Thank you Danny, for sharing, we're all here for you and we honor your presence here," Justin said as his eyes shifted from Danny to the rest of the room. Mara purposely did not want to make eye contact. She hated sharing her feelings, and wanted to sink further into her chair and camouflage herself from her emotions.

"Ms. Torres, I think it's your turn," Justin said.

241

Fuck.

"Pass," She responded.

"You passed last time, and the time before that, and the time before that."

"What, you keeping tabs on me?"

"Well, since you are pushing the situation, yes I am. As part of your court order."

"Fuck," she responded.

"Okay, marking another pass on your sheet," Justin said.

"Alright, fuck," she stated as all eyes in the circle focused on her. She sat up and looked around the room. She hated being the focus of attention like this, so she lied.

"I'm Torres, served in Afghanistan. Joined the Marines to fuck hot guys, didn't think it would lead to war," Mara said in a monotone voice. Danny seemed to grow some balls and sent a comment her way.

"Fucking crayon eating jarhead can't even take this seriously," he said.

"What the fuck did you say?" Mara asked looking directly at Danny who seemed overly confident. Just moments ago, he was pouring his fragile heart out for everyone to feel sorry for him.

"Now now, we need to keep our comments to ourselves," Justin immediately interjected.

"This fucking pussy got something to say!" Mara said standing while spewing attitude and flexing her chest out hoping this would get her kicked out of the group.

Danny also stood but held his ground, their previous altercations were finally coming to a head. Justin got up but did not get between the two veterans as Mara hoped he would. Fuck. Danny sat back down, he seemed cool under pressure and she sort of liked his attitude. Mara was left standing in the middle of the circle with the spectacle she made of herself. She wanted to run, but the circle was closed around her, like an ambush.

She yelled out, screamed at the top of her lungs. Her eyes watered up and her brow dripped with sweat. She turned towards Justin.

"This is all your fucking fault!" Mara yelled. "You fucking set me up!"

She felt herself losing control. Felt her remaining grip on reality slip away. She didn't want their pity or their sympathy. She wanted them gone.

"This is on you!" she said. Her voice becoming deep and growly. "You fucking did this. You set me up! Wanting me to share my feelings, well here they are! You fucking happy now?"

Mara took a few steps towards Justin who remained calmly seated. Other participants stood and motioned to intervene, but Justin told them to sit back down and remain where they were.

"Come on you piece of shit, do something! Sick your pawns on me, come on! Fucking do something!" Mara taunted him.

"Who are you fighting?" Justin asked.

"What?"

"No one here wants to fight you," Justin continued in the same calm soothing voice.

"What the fuck you talking about? Danny boy over there wants to fight. You're too much of a pussy to fight," she said.

"Why do you want to fight?" Justin asked.

"What the fuck?" she questioned. "Fighting is what we do! We fight, we kill, we fuck, we die. That's what we fucking do! That's what fucking soldiers do! Maybe you assholes forgot!"

"Ms. Torres, look around you. No one wants to fight you, no one wants to harm you."

Mara refused to look at anyone else. She wanted nothing more than to rip his head off.

"We're not at war soldier. We're not here to harm you," Justin said calmly.

"What?" Mara responded.

"You're not a deadwood soldier," Justin said. "There are no bullet holes that show your wounds. For each one of us in this room, those wounds are there. Those invisible holes are there."

For the first time, Mara saw him and the soldiers around her. They were all deadwood soldiers. All broken human beings trying to be glued back together from used parts of fallen soldiers before them in group therapy. Most of their scars were internally manifested set to rot their inner core. Some of them, like Danny, seemed to be healed, or in a much better place than the others. Marathon knew each of their stories; she knew their pain, their day to day struggles and often mocked them in private for their weakness.

She stood there in the middle of the circle defenseless. She turned to leave but there was no clear path out of the circle. One of the other participants stood and motioned that she could pass freely, but she paused and stared at the exit.

Tears flowed down her cheeks as her hands trembled. She heard murmurs from some of the other participants. Their expressions of support were welcoming, almost comforting. She knew what they were saying but couldn't hear them.

The exit was still there in front of her, just feet away. She walked towards it, but then turned and sat down in her original seat that was semi separated from the circle. The group remained quiet as she composed herself. The participants tried to avoid looking at her as she wiped the tears from her eyes. She hated this tough attitude she developed since her return home. She felt like this was a different version of herself and wanted desperately to hit the reset button.

"What's your story?" Mara sheepishly asked looking over at Justin. "Why do you fucking do this?"

"What do you mean?" he responded.

"You run these sessions, hear our sob stories, absorb all our pain and agony, for what? Does it get you off or something?"

"I'm here because I am hired through a grant by the US Army to help veterans adjust back into society," he said. She felt broken beyond repair.

"Adjust back to society," she smirked sarcastically knowing full well her adjustment was doomed to fail.

"Many veterans are able to assimilate back into society after their service," he said. "I happen to be a much older version of you."

"What, you serve with Danny boy over there in Iraq?" she asked mockingly.

"There's always hope Ms. Torres, I welcome you to explore the possibilities that everyone in this room has had bad shit happen to them, sometimes unimaginable horrors. They are here to get help and we use each other for support. I only offer guidance."

"Like one big fucking group orgy," she responded under her breath trying to keep her defenses up even as cracks started to form.

"Ask yourself, would you be here if it weren't for the court order?" he asked.

The hour group session started to wrap up after no one wanted to speak after her. A few veterans hung around conversing near the coffee pot. Justin stood and walked over towards the water cooler off in the corner as other participants left the gymnasium.

"Hey, you okay?" Danny said as he hesitantly approached.

"I'm sorry," Mara blurted out. "I was out of line, and, out of my mind."

"We've all been there," he said. Danny was dressed in a flannel deep red shirt with Wrangler blue jeans. He looked like a weathered cowboy from the rough and tumble wild west. Definitely an odd, but attractive look for someone in Queens, New York.

"Why do you come to this shit?" she asked.

"What kind of question is that?" he responded.

"You look fine, you act fine, you seem fine. Why the fuck are you here?" she asked.

"Well, for starters, this thing has done wonders for me, I was spiraling, and this place stopped that."

Marathon bit down on her lower lip with the hope he would pick up on her intentions. He sat down next to her. Justin now made his way over with a cup of water and handed it to Mara.

"Danny, can I get your opinion on something?" Justin asked.

Fuck, he was onto her. No doubt the judge passed on her information as a way of keeping her out of more trouble. Danny stood up and walked away with Justin just out of eavesdropping distance. After a few words, Justin then walked off and Danny came back but remained standing.

"Here," he said holding out a business card.

"What's this?" Mara asked as she accepted his card. "You're an NYPD recruitment officer?"

"Yeah, normally I don't do this here. It's sorta unethical to recruit at therapy," he said.

"So why you giving me this?"

"Because you can't keep going down the same path," he responded. "Most of us in this room have been there and it ends poorly, which is why we are still here. You need to break the cycle."

"So the solution is giving me a gun and putting me on the streets?" she asked sarcastically.

"The NYPD has a veterans recruitment office. It's a different entry point from the general public and covered under the G.I. Bill. This is giving you a purpose and putting you back in the driver's seat."

"I don't know, your recruitment technique is not hitting the spot," Mara said as she stood and got closer to him. His cologne was intoxicating. "Maybe you should try something different."

246

"Wait, what should I do differently, I just offered you a job?"

She didn't mind playing these games, she knew he wanted her. Soldiers were usually not scared of her aggressive desires. Their back and forth from before was standard mating rituals on the battlefields in Afghanistan. He was just being courteous to the environment. It was generally frowned upon to use these sessions a means to find a fuck partner.

"Was that whole thing an act?"

"What the tears and emotional breakdown?"

"Yes that."

"No, that was real," she said. "This is the act."

Mara inched closer to allow her breasts brush up against his body. He looked up and then over towards Justin who was conversing with the group by the coffee pot. Mara saw the gears in his head turn, she knew his other head was starting to take over the thought process.

"So, you going to take me home and fuck my brains out?" she forthcomingly asked.

"Your place, my teenage son is home," he responded.

"Fuck, you married?" Marathon said as the moment was suddenly derailed.

"Divorced," he said. "Part of my spiral."

"Damn, that was close one. I'm usually good at weeding out the married men," she said.

"Oh good, it's nice to know you're not a home wrecker."

"I live with my uncle, he doesn't approve of men old enough to be my father coming home with me."

"You've done this before," he said.

"Is that going to be a problem?" she asked.

"My Tahoe is parked out back."

"Good enough," Mara stated as she pulled a condom from her jeans and placed it in his front shirt pocket.   MI

Chapter
Twenty-Seven

St. John's Hospital
Far Rockaway
August 31st, 2019
Evening

Marathon sat on an examination table in an empty hospital room in Far
Rockaway, Queens. An emergency room doctor had just finished stitching the
numerous wounds littered all over her body. Mara had a surgical gown on, but was
still covered in dirt, dried blood, and god knows what else. Occasionally she
caught a whiff of herself, she smelled like a boy's locker room after a football
game.

Moments before a young doctor and an army of nurses addressed the combat
knife stuck through her forearm. Luckily, the knife went clean through between
the Ulna and Radius bones. When they pulled it out of her, the intense pain made
her few queasy and lightheaded. The young doctor was experienced enough to
have her lay down before he attempted the extraction. He also numbed the area as
best he could and injected her with broad spectrum anti-biotics. Once the knife
was extracted, he jammed another needle into her to update her tetanus shot just in
case.

The young doctor suggested she should see a neurological surgeon to address
potential nerve damage in her forearm, but after things calmed down, she felt most
of her feeling return. He also suggested a plastic surgeon to look at the wounds

around her face saying something about scarring and how a good surgeon would help preserve her "pretty face."

The doctor then left to deal with other emergencies as she waited for his return. The nurses made her comfortable and a meal was brought in from the cafeteria. She was glad no one was in the room to see her scarf it down. Marathon was hoping to get out of the hospital as soon as possible. Detective Morales was brought to Kings County Medical Center in Crown Heights where a trauma team would address his life-threatening injury to his leg. She didn't find out about going to a different hospital until mid-way through her trip in the ambulance. Something about Kings County being full and St. John's hospital being able to treat her immediately. Sounded like bullshit, and she was on high alert, but everything seemed normal so far. All of her injuries were addressed, and she was completely stitched up and ready to be discharged.

Mara felt awkward in a hospital gown, but she would take it over wearing just a bra and suit pants. Her belongings were in a plastic bag over by the counter on the far side of the room, her Glock was still in her possession, but she knew it would be confiscated by detectives for forensics to analyze. The hospital room she was in was reserved for police to question suspects that were brought into the emergency room for both treatment and questioning.

After replaying the encounter with the sniper, she was troubled by what the sniper had said while he was trying to kill her. "Your ass would have been dealt with a long time ago," she whispered out loud. What the fuck did that mean? How long was he, were they, watching her?

The GPS coordinates were definitely significant. That was the bait to get her out to Broad Channel, to get her out in the open so the sniper could do his thing when she showed up. Mara was convinced Detective Morales was also a target, he wouldn't have made it out of the refuge, they were clearly interested in what he found. There was a reason why half of his department called out sick that day, and why he was fed this information. The main question she couldn't answer was about Frank.

Like the sniper said, she was predictable. He knew her well enough to lay a trap and wait. It would have worked if Esposito hadn't warned her about this, about being watched. She would have shown up and once she arrived out in the open the sniper would have dropped them both. Frank was either knee deep in this or completely out of the loop. On one side, being the commanding officer of the 73rd, how could he not know something was up? On the other side, he had his most senior and trusted detective run the case, which showed he suspected something, but was not in on the conspiracy. Until she knew for sure, Frank was on the do not trust list, which seemed to have all the names on it. As of right now, Esposito was the only one she could trust, even though he wasn't being completely honest with her. His warning did save her life.

Mara remembered the sniper mentioning The Farm when she stumbled upon his nest out by her Uncles Ranch in Pennsylvania.

The Farm.

Was that literally what they called themselves? Using code terminology that basically implied what they were doing? She ran with that clue. What were they farming? Drugs? Guns? Prostitution? Detective Morales suggested the jetty out by the wild life refuge was used in a smuggling operation. Evidence of large trucks came and went on a regular basis, and the detective suggested there was further evidence by the beach where it looked like a dock was used regularly.

Going with the assumption that Marley Williams was involved in gang activity, her murder would certainly send a message to anyone involved. Based on the evidence, she was probably killed at the wild life refuge out by the dock Detective Morales found. The way she was killed, where her body was dumped, were all clear signs of a warning. Her death was definitely a warning, her body was dumped in her own neighborhood, even though it was between imaginary gang borders. Was her murder a message for both gangs? She was still missing gaps in

250

her theory about what had happened, but she had more answers now than ever before.

Mara drew a conclusion that the wild life refuge was an access point to smuggle drugs, guns, girls or whatever into the city. Cops were in on it, and they controlled the flow of whatever the product was while local gangs distributed it to the streets. Unless someone was a rat, things would be smooth sailing with cops managing the distribution. Unless there was a rat, was Marley Williams a rat? Did Marley witness something she wasn't supposed to? More questions than answers, she needed to find Esposito. Over an hour passed as she sat alone in the hospital room with just her thoughts to keep her company. Normally she'd be on her cell, scrolling through social media to pass the time.

There was a reason why crime was down in Brooklyn. Mara always thought that it was solid policing and good policies and programs. Crime was down because everyone was getting paid. The cops, the gangs, the suppliers, everyone in their food chain was making bank and at the same time driving violent crime way down because everyone had a piece of the pie. Murders, robberies, assaults, were all on the decline. But, drug use was on the incline, a sharp incline based on the internal data at all of the precincts. Opioid use increased exponentially since Marathon entered the force. She didn't believe in coincidences.

They were definitely smuggling in drugs, probably opioids. The sharp increase was attributed to corrupt doctors selling prescriptions on the open market to anyone willing to pay. There was no way a few corrupt doctors were responsible for the vast increase in opioid use. They could write prescriptions until their hands fell off and that wouldn't even attribute to all the increased use on the streets.

The maintenance building where the confrontation with the sniper finally ended was empty with no signs of anyone being there during a workday. The parking lot was empty, no visitors, no one around, in fact there was a whole lot of nothing happening at that facility. The office itself had ancient computers not even hooked up. It was the perfect front for illegal operations. Cops alone couldn't pull

251

this off. The wild life refuge was run by the city's parks department. She marveled at how complex this conspiracy was. As long as everyone got paid, Marathon reminded herself, that was the status quo.

Marley's murder was never solved because it was never meant to be solved. It was buried in department files because a cop probably murdered her to send a message. Somehow it landed in Russo and Esposito's lap because they were onto this conspiracy. Mara reminded herself to ask how they figured this out, and why they still refused to tell her.

Russo and Esposito were also not who they said they were. Mara was sure of that now. There was no way the Marley Williams file would end up in the hands of special investigations if cops were the responsible party. They obtained the Marley file through a different source. She wondered what parts of the story Esposito told her were actually true. Morales said the FBI was involved and they had the physical file on Marley's murder in their possession. Maybe Russo and Esposito were FBI agents?

She then thought of Frank, her suspicions of him were now drastically different. He was the likely suspect, the likely fall guy for her to focus on. Like Detective Morales said, Frank was like a father to her and he served with Morales in the army, which created that special bond between soldiers. There was no chance in hell Frank would have set Detective Morales up. That meant Esposito was also being played by making Frank out to be the mastermind. His information was also wrong, or he had drawn a wrong conclusion. While the jury was still out on Frank, Mara moved on to other likely suspects.

Before she could go through a roll call of all the possible suspects, there was movement outside in the hallway. A Nurse returned and handed her another bottle of water.

"Here, you look thirsty," she said. "Just here to check your vitals before the doctor returns."

252

"Thank you," Marathon replied opening the bottle. Before the nurse left, nearly half the spring water was gone from the plastic bottle.

Marathon continued her thought process as she sipped the remainder of the bottle. The sniper implied that she was being watched for a long time. He fucking watched her, the thought of that grossed her out. He was special forces and a damn good sniper trained to be undetectable. Who was behind the order to watch her, who was calling the shots? She knew this organization, The Farm, used former special forces soldiers, some of them were linked to her past so she was somehow connected to this. She knew they had infiltrated the NYPD, and she suspected other NYC agencies were compromised, definitely the parks department. But how far down the rabbit hole did this go? She felt like she was just scratching the surface. Her headache had returned and her forearm started to throb. She took the final sip from her water bottle and then tossed it in the trash from her seated position.

A sickening feeling came over her as her gut answered the question plaguing her for so long. Who could have pulled off this elaborate scheme and control things within the department? Only one name connected everything. John, her former partner. They were the ones who found the body. Marley's body was discarded directly on their patrol, so they would find her. Marathon's mind started racing as she was able to connect John to nearly every bad thing that has happened. She knew he was also checking in on her behind the scenes.

He was texting her as she entered her apartment, maybe to let Bowden know she was close. He knew her very well and could have manipulated the evidence to see if she would take the bait. He was still very much connected in the department and could easily pull strings, especially when he was so well connected at John Street Bar. He could practically run the streets from there with the amount of cop traffic coming in and out on a daily basis.

Marathon jumped off the examination table, she wanted to leave desperately. She started pacing around the room as more details emerged since she became a detective. She remembered talking to John about her discovery, he advised her to let it go, to drop it. She did not. He was fucking warning her, was he the one the sniper referred to as having a hard on for her?

Esposito said Frank was trying to recruit her, Mara was now convinced that Frank was not in on this. Replace Frank with John and everything started to make sense. It did seem like John was recruiting her when they were partners. Way back, when John retired, he wanted Mara to join a special unit in the NYPD, something like the SWAT team. Mara refused because of an old boyfriend, Danny. John stopped pursing this after he found out Danny and Mara were once hot and heavy.

Everything seemed to be connected, the way she was recruited to the NYPD. John requesting her as a partner, spec ops soldiers resurfacing from her past, all of this was not a coincidence. It was all orchestrated. Danny was more than a recruiter for the NYPD, he was pulling double duty by recruiting for their operation, what better place to recruit soldiers than a veteran's support group. You get damaged goods that can be molded into the criminal livelihood they had built. Just have them become cops and no one bats an eye.

John was more than a patrol officer, he was a groomer, maybe middle management in this operation, which meant he still had to get his hands dirty. As she paced back and forth in the room, she realized there were many more players involved. Like the detectives in the 73rd that called out sick, they knew what was going down at the nature preserve. She found her pace quickening, and her heart rate jumped to match her emotional intensity.

Of course, Marathon had no evidence to prove any of this. The complicated chain of events was hard enough to map out let alone prove. She was able to piece everything together because she had spent her entire career in the thick of it. She now had the opportunity to analyze every facet through a different lens and pieces started to fall into place. Marley Williams was the catalyst that could bring down their operation. She was murdered because she somehow broke their status quo.

There was something more to Marley Williams, she was sure of that. Add that to the list of questions to ask Esposito.

Marathon heard more commotion outside her room. Shadows under the door showed movement as she heard muted speech on the other side. The door opened and she was surprised to see two men enter the room. They looked like detectives by the way they dressed, but something was off. The men approached her and offered her a bottle of water.

"Thank you," she said as she accepted the generic lukewarm bottle but did not open it.

"Retired Detective Marathon Torres of the 73rd Precinct, is that correct?" the man to her right asked.

"Yes."

Something was bothering her, by the way the detectives carried themselves. They were too upright, polished and robotic.

"We found a body in the maintenance building along with signs of forced entry. Uniforms are still reviewing the crime scene. Can you help us out with what happened?"

"I don't feel comfortable sitting here half naked answering questions," she said.

"We found evidence Detective Morales had collected," the other man stated ignoring her statement. He was standing to her immediate left. Mara decided to cut him off.

"I'll give my full statement back at the precinct after I am formally discharged from the hospital," she stated.

"We need this information, please cooperate," the man on the right said.

Mara looked at both of them, her suspicion grew as each moment passed. The two men were about her age, tall, muscular, angular and focused. They weren't detectives.

"What did you say your names are?" Mara asked. She looked at the left man and saw he was cracking. She assumed the right one was also.

"Please respond to the questions ma'am. Why was Detective Morales interested in that evidence?"

"Give me a minute to think," she said. "This fucking headache is making it hard, not sure about what evidence you are talking about." She cracked open the bottle of water.

"The sand Morales had in the car, marked as evidence," the man to her left said.

"Oh shit, that evidence, that's the same shit we found on a murder a number of years go," she said. The two men looked at each other. That seemed to spark their interest and confirm her suspicion.

"Hey, there's a bottle of aspirin over on the counter over there," she said. "Can you get it for me?"

The man on the left turned and retrieved the bottle. As he reached out to hand it to her, she leapt from the examination table, threw water in the face of the man to her left. The man with the aspirin was then spun around as Marathon disarmed him of his holstered M9. She took position behind him as the man to her left wiped his face and then drew his weapon. Marathon was narrowly concealed behind her hostage as the other man tried to gain an angle on her.

"You guys need to stop sending military hitmen to kill me," she said as she placed her hand on the man's shoulder. She kept the M9 close to her body but pointed it straight at the man she was using as a human shield.

"You move, you die," she whispered into the man's ear as she opened the door behind her. It was locked.

"I need you to stop," Mara stated to the other man who looked like he was itching to squeeze off a few rounds.

"You're not going to make it out of here alive," he said.

"I don't think you want to do this here," Mara stated. "I know for a fact you two won't make it out of this room alive if you try anything."

The meat shield soldier remained perfectly still, but she knew he was going to try something soon. She stood with her back to do the door crouched down just below his shoulders. Her hand released the man and knocked on the door while keeping the m9 trained on the back of his head. Mara felt the door handle turn and created some space for it to open inwards.

In one fluid motion, she pushed the meat shield forward into the man holding a gun at her and spun towards the opening door. By the look on the officer's face entering the room, he was not expecting her to be there. Mara used that to her advantage and spun around him and crossed the threshold into the hallway. She pushed the officer from the hallway into the room while holding the M9 close.

"Close the fucking door," she said to the dirty police officer who opened the door knowing it would automatically lock once it latched closed. Mara kept the officer in front of her as the soldier with the M9 in back tried to seize the moment. She knew he would eventually start shooting.

"Last fucking chance," she said.

The door swung closed locking the three men inside. She took a deep breath and spun towards the wall next to the door. She heard the men yelling on the other side.

"She's out!"

Shit. There will be more of them. Mara made a mental note to invest in a cell jammer while she looked up and down the hallway she was in. It was surprisingly empty.

From where she was, the hospital looked deserted, like out of a post-apocalyptic movie where the hero wakes up alone, only to discover the world once known is now foreign, dangerous and seemingly deserted. The long hallway had double doors in one direction and a dead end in the other. She noticed the hallway was dimly lit, like it was closed off to the rest of the hospital. The double doors seemed to be her only way out.

As Mara crept up to the door, she peered through the small window to see a brightly lit hallway. On the opposite side of the door was a busy hall with nurses and doctors conducting what Mara thought was normal hospital behavior. She tested the door to see if it would open, and it did but she kept it shut. She was not prepared to go through it just yet. She didn't have much time, their backup would arrive shortly, and she was cornered. Marathon couldn't just walk out into the hallway with an M9 handgun in plain sight. The gown she wore would not conceal the weapon either.

She had no choice but to ditch it, she released the mag and popped out a round from the chamber. She then continued to break the firearm down so it couldn't be used and scattered the parts in the abandoned hallway.

She then casually slipped through the double doors, no one seemed to notice her as she walked slowly along the wall down the busy hall. It was like a different setting from where she was. She wondered why that hallway was closed down, it didn't make sense. Some nurses made eye contact as she continued towards the exit on the other side. As she got closer, she noticed the double doors burst open down the hall from her current position. Two men dressed like doctors were heading her way but they walked like cops. Mara slipped into a room before being noticed.

The room was occupied by an elderly woman. Marathon turned towards her and knelt down by her bedside.

"My ex is here," she said.

The woman nodded and placed her finger over her mouth. She then looked closely at Mara and pointed to the corner of the room. Mara heard aggressive footsteps pass the open door.

"There's a pair of scrubs in that plastic bag over there," the elderly woman said. Mara grabbed the bag and changed.

"That's better," the elderly woman said. "You can't walk around here with your tuchas hanging out."

She smiled and thanked the woman. Mara peeked out into the hallway and noticed it was clear. She then continued towards the double doors and grabbed a clipboard along the way to complete her disguise. As she passed through and heard commotion behind her. Her pace quickened down the new hallway following the exit signs. She felt like she was in a maze as the halls had no clear pattern to which direction she was going. She was now jogging as the noise grew behind her. Hospital staff stood to the side as her pace quickened. She felt like the walls were closing in around her and her time was running out.

Around the next turn the hallway opened up to the main lobby. A security guard, roughly sixty feet away, was on his radio and scanning the area like a predator looking for prey. Their eyes locked for a moment and Mara saw him lift his radio and bark into it. Her cover was blown. He was the only thing standing between her and the exit.

Mara knew she had one opportunity to get out and she seized it. She found herself moving forward and her pace quickened until she reached her max speed. The security guard stood firm and his broad shoulders blocked the double doors. Mara knew she had the advantage, her momentum alone would send the man tumbling over, but that wasn't going to be enough to get past him. He looked strong, like a linebacker getting ready to tackle a running back.

Just before Mara reached the security guard, she leaped into the air allowing her momentum to carry her forward. She raised her right hand into a Superman's punch, at least that's what the mixed martial arts world called it. Her height advantage along with her momentum sent her fist down across the security guards' orbital bone and cheek. As the man fell backwards, Mara's momentum carried her further and sent her tumbling through the double doors to the outside world.

Mara got back to her feet and saw a large sparsely filled parking lot that lead to the street. Tall apartment buildings rose up on the opposite side. She needed to get out of the area and off the streets. The apartment building as good an option as any; there she could find a place to hide and get off the streets.

She darted across the parking lot, nearly at full speed as she gracefully navigated the sporadic parked cars. She found a path that led out of the lot. At full speed she ran towards the walkway, which looked like a breach in a fortified wall surrounding the hospital. Mara crossed through and stopped not knowing which way to turn. The apartment building was directly in front of her, but there was no clear path into the courtyard that separated the three main buildings. The complex was also dimly lit, which would work to her advantage as she needed to avoid the authorities.

Out of the corner of her eye, she saw headlights turn on and a car speed towards her. She ran across the street trying to go where the car couldn't. The car came to a screeching stop and she heard a familiar voice.

"GET IN, NOW!"

Not thinking twice, Marathon turned got into the car just as the tires ramped up again into a high-pitched squeal. The sedan sped down Beach 19th street towards the public beach as she saw men burst out the hospital lobby. They noticed the car speed away but could do nothing about it. At this hour of the night, there were no cars on the road and Mara knew they would easily reacquire them if they didn't get off the road. Mara felt the car slow down as she sat up and buckled her seatbelt.

"Lieutenant, how the fuck did you find me?"

"Russo got a call from one of the nurses," Esposito said as he glanced over at Mara.

"What?"

"We knew this hospital was being used, were you in an abandoned wing?"

"Yeah," Their eyes briefly met as she finger combed her dangling hair behind her ears and out of her face.

"That's where they conduct some of their business," he said.

260

"You probably saved my life," she replied.

"I doubt that. Just ask that security guard you ran through."

"You saw that?" Mara asked.

"Yeah, I was in the lobby when I saw you run right through the guy. By the time I got out of the building myself, you were running through the parking lot like a caged animal being set free. I ran to my car and got there just in time to see you dart out."

"What do they use that hospital for?" Mara asked.

"Treat their wounded," he said giving no further details.

"Where are we going?" Mara asked.

"You need to lay low for a while," Esposito said.

"You've got some explaining to do!" she responded.

"Let's get off the streets first. We're not safe here," he said.

"Fuck that, you can drive and talk," she barked back.

"Alright, I am not NYPD, or special investigations" he started.

"Yeah no shit," she blurted out.

"Can I continue?" he asked. Mara gave a slight nod.

"I'm FBI," he said. Mara still looked at him suspiciously.

"Truth," he continued. "A few years ago, there was a cyber security breach in the NYPD. A number of computers were hit with ransomware and it completely shut down their system,"

"I remember that," Mara stated. "We had to roll back to the MS DOS system and file paperwork manually until the system came back online."

"Because this was a cyber-crime, Russo and I were called in," Esposito said as he took the backroads out of Far Rockaway. He drove slowly and followed the city speed limit.

"The ransomware was bad, numerous case files, budget data, payroll, private information, you name it, it was all swept up and locked behind an encrypted password."

"I know what ransomware is," Marathon stated wanting him to get to the point.

"Well, Russo and I took possession of the encrypted files and rebuilt the database to prevent any further attacks."

"So you're a computer nerd posing as a cop?" Mara playfully asked and laughed internally and the absurdity of what he was implying. Esposito merged onto Nassau Expressway and headed north away from Far Rockaway.

"Russo and I closed the case and moved on. A month later I received an encryption key in my inbox. I still had the encrypted files on a flash drive, so I decided to unlock the files."

"Do you know who sent you the key?" Marathon asked.

"No, the IP address was a dead end," he responded.

"So this just fucking drops on your lap?" Marathon questioned with a hint of attitude.

"Well, with the encryption key, there was a set of file names. So naturally I opened them," Esposito said. "At first, it just looked standard police rotation and patrol information." Marathon waited for him to continue.

"Nothing out of the ordinary for normal police work. But something caught my eye," he said. "Patrol data showed a large chunk of high impact areas left vulnerable. Like not a cop for a mile and for several hours."

"That can't be correct. Our patrols overlap and are intertwined to avoid gaps in policing."

"That's true," Esposito said. "These gaps are rotationally patterned to avoid detection. The only way you would notice would be if you had this document right in front of you. We're talking about large gaps in patrols on the borders between precincts all over Brooklyn. Then I took it a step further," he said as they passed a sign for the Belt Parkway.

"I pulled up rotation schedules to see who approved these patrols," Esposito said.

"Let me guess, Inspector Frank," she said.

"Yep, he approved the patrols for the 73rd," he said.

"What does that prove?" she asked.

"It proves involvement on some level," he responded.

"How did you flag the Marley Williams case?" Mara asked.

"The Marley Williams case file was one of the files encrypted in the ransomware. So my contact in the NYPD flagged that name for me, which led me to you." That explained how he had eyes on her in the precinct.

Esposito merged onto the Van Wyck Expressway as Mara told him what she had pieced together. She elaborately defended Frank and pointed out how the evidence was circumstantial at best.

"Where are we going?" Mara asked.

"I have a place, FBI safe house in Queens," he answered.

He wasn't telling the whole truth. What FBI cybercrime agent gets access to a safe house? She believed what he had told her, but there was more, and some details were exaggerated or misleading. The truth was definitely distorted to make a believable non-truth. Mara decided she would play along as she rested her head against the window.

M

Chapter Twenty-Eight

FBI Safe House
Flushing New York
September 1st, 2019
Early Morning

The sedan slowed down stirring Marathon awake as it turned down Carlton Place just off Northern Boulevard in Flushing, Queens. The sedan rolled to a stop as Mara surveyed the surrounding area. There were small houses packed in next to each other on the opposite side of the one-way road. With Northern Boulevard being a block away, the backs of retail businesses occupied the other side of the street. Carlton Place was a short road that only spanned a block. If you tried to find it on a map it would be next to impossible with all the interconnecting streets that littered the borough.

"Are we here?" Mara asked.

"Yeah, just hang on a second," he said.

Esposito was staring out the window as if he were waiting for something to happen. Mara tried to focus on what he was looking for, but the street looked desolate.

"What's going on?" she asked.

"Russo is going to signal when it's clear," he said.

These two were not computer nerds working deep under cover for the FBI. She continued surveying the area, but nothing seemed out of the ordinary. The street was empty, houses were dark, cars parked on the side of the road. If anything, they were the only ones who disrupted the flow of the block. Their mere presence here might actually cause suspicion to anyone watching.

"We should get off the streets," Mara said.

"One sec," he responded.

Mara's attention turned to a light that turned on and off again on a porch to one of the houses further up the block. If you weren't looking for it, like Esposito was, it was easily missed. Esposito smiled.

"All clear, let's go," he said.

Esposito led the way towards the house. They used a narrow walkway between houses to access the back door where Agent Russo was waiting for them. He nodded at Esposito and then led them inside.

The back entrance to the house led to a kitchen that looked like it hasn't been updated since the 1960s. Russo kept the lights off and motioned for everyone to have a seat around the kitchen table in the middle of the room.

"You really stepped in it this time," Russo said, his voice was raspy and tired.

"This is bigger than we thought," Esposito replied.

"I told you," Russo said. Russo was wearing a light brown suit with his tie pulled down. He looked worried.

"I filled him in while you dozed off in the car," Esposito said. Mara nodded.

"We'll focus attention on John Stroman," Russo said.

"So now that we're all caught up, what's our next play?" Mara asked.

Russo looked at her and laughed like she said something completely outrageous.

"Do you know what is currently going on?" he asked as if there were new developments.

Mara looked at Esposito who then turned towards Russo.

"Can you fill us in?" Esposito asked.

"Yeah, sorry, I was busy trying to stay alive," Mara snapped back.

"Well, if you want to remain alive, you need to stay hidden," Russo said. He then turned to Esposito and placed his cell phone on the table. Mara looked at the screen, it looked like a message board, or a chat room.

"What's that?" she asked.

"This is how we monitor their movements. Most of this is coded and sometimes even encrypted and it is sparsely used. We'll see activity that coincides with unit rotations in certain precincts. But tonight, they've got a hard on for you."

Esposito grabbed the cell phone and studied the text. He scrolled up and down while his face became increasingly grim.

"Mara, we've been monitoring this organization for well over a year and we've never seen this much activity. You have a standing kill order," Esposito said. She questioned how long they've been monitoring The Farm. The message board had hundreds of users and seemed extremely active.

Russo grabbed the phone from him and showed another part of the text.

"Fuck, they made the car," he said.

"I'll ditch it, but we can't stay here long. Maybe a night or two but, we need to relocate soon," Russo said looking at Mara. "They'll use traffic cameras to trace your location to this area."

"We're okay for the night," Esposito said. "We disabled the surrounding cameras anticipating this could happen."

"We didn't anticipate this!" Russo said. "We've never seen them put out a kill order like this before."

"How deep does this go?" Mara asked.

Russo held his hand out towards Esposito who remained seated. Esposito placed the car keys in his hand and then left out the back door.

"He'll take care of the car," Russo said.

"Listen, Lieutenant, if you even are a lieutenant. Tell me what the fuck is happening."

"Agent, that's my rank," he said. "You're being hunted. The Farm, that's what you call it right," he said, Mara nodded thinking she might have mentioned it to him.

"The Farm activated local gangs to shoot you on sight. Certain cops are also out there looking for you as well. It's nearly impossible to determine who is dirty," he continued. "We need to lay low for a bit."

"Fucking great," Mara said sarcastically. "I need a shower and a bed."

"The bathroom is around the corner next to the bedroom down the hall. I'll try and find some fresh clothes for you," Esposito said as he stood. He retrieved a towel for her before pulling additional sheets out of the closet. "I'll take the couch, the bed is clean and it's all yours."

Mara nodded, retrieved the towel and entered the bathroom. She had a difficult time taking off her scrubs, her body was bruised and scarred, and every movement hurt. The shower started to steam up the bathroom, that was her signal to get in. She loved hot showers, the feeling of nearly scalding hot water against her body made her feel clean and refreshed. Mara unraveled the bandage around her forearm. She hesitated, but then let the water freely flow over the staples that held her wound shut. Dried blood fell to the porcelain tub and spiraled down the drain.

She took her time in the shower, almost like she was trying to wash away the past few days and cleanse her body of what had happened to her. She stood there in the hot water until it struggled to maintain a consistent temperature. She got out of the shower and gently dried herself off. She didn't have the luxury of air drying here. Marathon slowly dressed her wound using an ace bandage she found in the medicine cabinet. It looked stocked for this very purpose.

There was no way she was going to put on those scrubs again, so she wrapped herself in the towel and left the bathroom. She continued down the hall where Esposito was laid out on the couch. He sat up straight when he saw her and averted his eyes as she drew closer.

267

"No clothes in the house for you," he said. "Russo will drop some off tomorrow morning."

Mara shrugged and sat down next to him on the couch. Clean sheets were spread out making a temporary bed out of the old sectional.

"Let me look at your arm," he said. Mara held it out and he gently removed the ace bandage.

"You cleaned it up nicely," he said. "Looks like it's not infected and should heal in a couple of weeks."

He started wrapping the bandage back up. His gentle hands didn't hurt her as he delicately rewrapped the wound. She was feeling frisky and hiked the towel up exposing her long-toned legs.

"You'll probably have a big scar on both sides of your arm," he said. Mara could tell he was trying to divert his eyes and make small talk. She knew men typically did this before the action started. Marathon let the towel loosen up top as it started to inch lower exposing more of her body and chest. She wanted him to just dive in and take control.

Esposito didn't move, but he didn't prevent any advances either. He finished wrapping the bandage as Mara slowly got closer. She inspected it and used it as an excuse to get closer to him. She felt his body heat and nearly heard his heart beating rapidly in his chest. He was thinking the same thing. Her towel was now on the verge of falling off completely as she leaned in further and kissed him deeply. He responded and the two embraced as Mara turned her body on top of him allowing the towel to fall to the ground as her legs straddled his waist.

She sat back on top of him, allowing him to take notice of her body. His hands started to explore her backside and slowly made their way down. She felt his manhood grow under his pants as she pressed down into him. Her hips started moving slowly as she leaned in so their lips could meet again. She felt him jump as their bodies moved together. She wanted this moment to last, she backed off from the intense kiss. She loved the look in a man's eye right before the action started. She loved being the source of desire. Marathon felt empowered by the amount of control she had. She could be aggressive, submissive, or a combination of both. The end result would usually be the same.

Their eyes remained locked and she slowly slid herself off of him using his legs like a slide. Her knees met the floor and her eyes moved towards his pants. She unbuckled him and exposed his massive hard on. Her hands wrapped around it and it responded with a pulse. Their eyes met again, the look was still there. She kept one hand on him while she removed his pants with the other. He unbuttoned his shirt and exposed his well-defined body and neatly trimmed treasure trail. He had just the right about of hair on his chest that showed he was more rough and rugged than prim and proper.

Mara took him in her mouth and slowly savored the moment. His hands helped her keep her hair out of her face as she started the rhythmic motion of pleasure. Marathon knew this was just the beginning and she took her time getting him completely ready. He started to moan and that was a signal for her to back off a bit. She released him from her mouth and played with him a bit. His manhood stood at attention and would follow her every command. Mara slowly slid back up north, letting her breasts guide her movement.

She straddled him again, but this time his penis was free to explore her body as if it had a mind of its own. Mara eased herself down onto him and he entered her without any guidance, it only had a one-track mind anyway. His hands returned to her buttocks as she took him all the way in. His hips thrust upward into her body as she felt him completely fill her.

Marathon wrapped her arms around his shoulders and pulled his head in close to her body, placing it between her breasts. Her hips controlled the rhythmic motion as he slowly slid in and out of her. She kept a slow and steady pace and regulated the experience. Her breathing gradually grew shorter and her body started to tense up, Mara hummed with pleasure. She was getting close. His hips began thrusting upwards in sync with her steady rhythm. She leaned in and rested her head on his shoulder while digging her nails in his back.

"Oh fuck, right there," she whispered in his ear as their speed increased. She felt his hips begin to thrust upwards with more authority.

Her body then tighten and released into orgasm. She quivered on top of him as she broke rhythm and collapsed in pleasure. Mara felt him slow down, but he kept her in close and supported her body.

"Did you?" she asked trying to regain her senses.

He responded by guiding her on her back into missionary position. She rested her head on the edge of the couch as he positioned himself between her legs. Her body was still recovering, but she spread her legs wide to give him full access as he began his purposeful thrusts back into her. His hands explored the front of her body as he continued his rhythmic thrusts. She knew he was getting close and the sensation of another orgasm started to build. She pulled him in closer and he collapsed onto her. She accepted his full weight and wrapped her legs around him, not wanting him to pull out. His head now dug into her shoulders as his pace quickened.

"Oh my fucking god, don't stop!" she said as each powerful thrust made her exhale in pleasure. The sound of skin on skin contact was like a rhythmic beat of ecstasy.

He moaned in response. She knew he couldn't keep this pace long and she started lifting her hips to meet his thrusts, giving him deeper access. Her body started to tighten up again as she felt her orgasm build.

"Holy fuck, I'm almost there. Keep fucking me," she instructed as his forehead now rested on hers.

He moaned deeply, she knew he was doing his best to last. This consideration sent her over the edge, and she plunged into another orgasm. Her body fell back into the couch as he pushed in as deep as he could. Mara squeezed her legs to pull him in further as she felt him spasm inside of her.

"Holy fucking shit," she said as she embraced his entire body on hers. They were both breathing heavy, as if they had an intense workout. She unwound her legs from around him and she felt him slip out of her as a river of seminal fluid flowed out onto the sheets below.

After a few moments Marathon sat up and stood. She saw he was still recovering so she pulled him in close and then guided him to his feet. "Come on, there's clean sheets on the bed, right?"

All he could do was nod as she led him to the bedroom. He turned on the AC as she climbed in bed and joined her a moment later.

"Jesus fucking Christ!" Mara heard as she was jolted out of her dream. Esposito was next to her in bed as she sat up just as Russo entered the bedroom. Mara used the sheets to cover herself as Esposito slowly woke.

Russo shook his head and threw a pair of clothes on the edge of the bed. He then turned and walked out of the room, "breakfast is in the kitchen."

Marathon looked back at Esposito and smiled at him. She wasn't embarrassed, but she could tell he was. Her smile turned to laughter as he turned all shades of red. She got out of bed, dressed and eventually joined Russo in the kitchen for breakfast.

"I see you two got to know each other last night," he said as she took a seat at the table opposite him.

"What did you expect?" she responded.

"Decency, people are trying to kill you and he should be protecting you."

"I can take care of myself," she said. "Besides, he didn't let me out of his sight," she responded.

Russo shook his head as Esposito entered the kitchen dressed in what he wore the night before. The partners exchanged glances as he sat down and opened the deli bag to find his breakfast. Mara opened her egg sandwich and took a large bite. The three of them sat in silence as Mara scarfed down her sandwich and sipped her coffee.

"So what do we do now?" she said breaking the awkward silence.

"We?" Russo responded. "You are going to get out of the city and we," point to himself and Esposito, "are going to continue our investigation."

"What? Are you fucking kidding me?" Mara said in protest. "No fucking way!"

Russo's eyes rolled "sweetheart, there isn't a scenario out there where you walk away from this with your life!"

"We have no evidence," Esposito chimed in. Mara sent him a glare to remind him he should be on her side.

"I'm an eyewitness, we have the message board, and we have the evidence Morales collected," she protested.

"We have a dirty cop, a message board without any reference or connections, and Morales still hasn't come out of surgery."

"Dirty cop? You referring to me?" Mara asked.

Russo placed the NY Post on the table. Her picture was on the front page. She immediately recognized it as the hotel she stayed at just before she returned to the precinct to retire. Her eyes made their way to the headline.

"New York Under Covers," the headline read. There was a picture of Marathon on the front page entering the shady hotel.

"Fuck that!" Mara said grabbing the paper from the table. She started reading the article. Her blood was boiling.

"Recently promoted Detective Marathon Torres," she read out loud, "was seen providing illegal services to clients on the Lower East Side."

She looked at Russo who motioned her to continue. "Numerous men could be seen coming and going, where an eyewitness stated she was directly involved in a prostitution ring. The NYPD confirmed that she was not undercover and has denied any involvement in Detective Torres' extracurricular activities."

Mara slammed the paper down on the table. "What the fuck!"

"They are trying to discredit you Marathon. No matter what you say now, you'll have these questions always pop up next to your story. Esposito was now reading the rest of the article as Mara stood and washed her face at the sink.

"Fucking a," he said. "They go on to state how you were attacked in your own apartment building and that Bowden was really working for you as one of your pimps."

Esposito then quoted, "New evidence revealed a dispute between them lead to Bowden's death. Originally Marathon Torres was labeled a hero, but this suggests that the criminal herself was receiving her own medicine."

"I don't know how we are going to get you out of the city," Russo stated. "Your face is everywhere."

"No one is going to mistake your face," Esposito said.

"We also can't stay here," Russo said. "The net is contracting around us."

"So what do we do?" Mara asked.

Esposito and Russo glanced at each other. "Remember Boston?" Esposito asked.

He shook his head, "How could I forget Boston."

Mara looked at the two of them. "Cybercrimes my fucking ass," she blurted out.

Neither of them acknowledged what Mara had just said, but instead they explained what happened in Boston and how Esposito had to smuggle Russo out of the city.

"No fucking way," Mara said. "There is no fucking way I am going to get into a trunk."

"Well, that might not be an option anyway," Esposito said as he was checking his phone. He held up an article with Mara's face plastered on it. Mara grabbed the phone as Russo checked his.

Fuck, this couldn't be happening. The article read "Disgraced Marathon Torres is wanted for the deaths of two officers and the serious injury to Detective Morales. Detective Morales is currently fighting for his life at Kings County while police are on a deadly man hunt for Marathon Torres."

Mara then saw a news banner notification pop up on Esposito's screen. She grabbed it and clicked the banner which sent it to a live report. She placed the phone down on the table so Russo and Esposito could also see what was happening.

"We are live from Kings County Hospital where Detective Morales was just pronounced dead. He died on the operating table after sustaining life threatening injuries during what police are saying was an intense standoff between himself and Detective Torres. We are going live right now to the Police Commissioner."

Marathon felt sick to her stomach. Detective Morales was very much alive when they parted ways in separate ambulances. His leg wound was serious, but his chance of survival was pretty high, especially with an experienced trauma team from Kings County Hospital. Marathon was sure he received the same treatment she had at St. John's. The news report continued as Marathon ran the various scenarios in her head.

"At approximately 4:15 this morning, Detective Morales passed away from the injuries he sustained confronting Detective Marathon Torres. She is wanted for his murder and the murder of two other officers, their names are withheld until we notify their families. Before Detective Morales went into surgery, he was conscious and provided a statement linking Detective Torres to his murder."

Mara's head was spinning as she tried focus in on the details of the crime. The commissioner continued his statement. "At this time, Detective Marathon Torres is considered armed and extremely dangerous. She was last seen in Northern Queens just beyond the fair grounds. We are releasing all the footage to the public. Again, Marathon Torres is considered extremely dangerous. If you see her, you are to call 911 immediately."

The police commissioner began repeating himself and Mara stood and went back over to the sink. She felt nauseous. She heard the commissioner take questions from reporters. The topic of Bowden came up and the commissioner stated that Bowden was a known criminal who had criminal ties to Detective Torres.

"There goes smuggling her out of the city," Russo stated.

"They'll be checking vehicles. The citizens app is reporting checkpoints being set up on Northern Boulevard," Esposito said.

"You might end up sleeping here in the basement for a while. We cannot risk being out in the open," Russo said as they heard a helicopter fly over.

"What's your level of risk?" Mara asked.

"Don't worry about us," Esposito said. "We can handle what is going on, however we cannot guarantee your safety if we go mobile right now."

"Where did you dump the car?" Esposito asked.

"By the Whitestone Bridge," Russo said.

"That might give us some wiggle room," Esposito said as the sound of a helicopter got more intense.

"The basement it is," Mara said as she quickly made her way to the stairs.

The helicopter flying overhead created a sense of urgency as Mara descended down the narrow staircase. The basement was dark, only a single hanging light bulb lit the enclosed concrete walls. The ceiling was low, it felt only a few inches taller than she was. There was a moldy, musty smell that hung in the air as her movement scattered what seemed like decades of dust. Russo slowly navigated the staircase carrying blankets and pillows from the bedroom.

"We really thought we could get you out fast, but right now this is our best option," he said as he placed the pillows and blanket down in the corner.

"I'm cornered down here," Mara stated.

"There's a spot over here," Russo said moving an old dresser away from the walls. The back of it was missing and it provided enough space for Mara to hide in case the house became compromised. The front of the dresser was just a façade with fake drawers that made it look like it was fully functional.

"That's clever," she said.

"It works, we had to use something like this a few times over the years," he said as he put the sheets and pillows in behind the false dresser.

"Russo, we should get going," Esposito yelled from the top of the stairs.

"Wait, you're just gonna leave me here?" Mara questioned.

"We've gotta take care of something," Russo said. He extended her a Glock, similar to her service weapon which she left at the hospital.

"At least I'm not defenseless," she said as she checked the weapon and then shoved it into her jean shorts. Russo then handed her an extra magazine and ascended the stairs.

Mara heard the two agents leave the house. Why were they in such a rush to get out of there? Now that she was public enemy number one, she had no choice but to trust them.

"FBI agents my ass," she said to herself as she made herself comfortable down in the damp basement.

With her access to the outside world completely cut off, all she could do is sit and wait. The sheets and pillows behind the dresser looked inviting, at least she could catch up on sleep.

M

Chapter
Twenty-Nine

75th Precinct
East New York
July 17th, 2006

"Hey rook, over here."

Mara looked to where the sergeant was pointing.

"Your locker room is over there," the sergeant said as the boys went to their own room.

"Oh, thank you," she replied.

"I was told locker 142 would be yours," he said. "Put your shit in there and then come back out to the briefing room. You remember where that is right?"

Mara nodded and then looked around to find the path that lead to the briefing room. The 75th Precinct in East New York, Brooklyn was a large two-story building that took up most of the block. The outside of the building reminded her of high school. It resembled the Romanesque architectural style from the late 1800s that was very popular in government buildings. The inside of the precinct felt like a labyrinth of hallways that each led to a different division in the 75th.

"You go down that hallway, make a left and then you make the next two rights and your briefing room is there," he said with a hint of gall in his voice.

"A left and two rights, got it," she said with a polite thank you wink. She wasn't trying to flirt but knew a quick charm would lighten the mood.

Marathon entered the noticeably small locker room as the sergeant went to join the boys. A detective sat at a bench next to her locker. She looked older, close to retirement. Mara went to her locker, placed her duffle bag on the bench, and tried to open her assigned locker. The rusted handle prevented the latching mechanism from moving. She pushed up with all her might but the latch would not budge.

"Hit the top, right above the handle," the detective said. "Give it a good whack."

Marathon hit the top using the meaty part of her palm. The locker popped open exposing the paint worn interior. It smelt like an old tool box as she cleared the dust from her vision.

"Thanks," Mara replied.

"These old lockers are older than I am," she said. "You must be one of the rooks coming in from the academy."

"Yeah, I graduated on Friday," Marathon said with pride.

"And you chose to come here?" the detective asked with a smile on her face.

Mara knew she had little choice other than what borough she wanted to start her career in. The department then assigned her to the 75th because there were plenty of senior officers ready to train the rookies for real police work.

"I think I know who your senior officer is," the detective continued. "He's a good friend of mine."

"Oh, I haven't heard anything," Marathon replied as she fumbled with the zipper on her duffle bag.

"You'll be paired with an Officer Stroman," She said. "That's all he's been talking about lately."

"He's been talking about me?" Mara asked.

"Yeah, each senior officer receives a pool of rooks as they are about to exit the academy. The officers then request their assignment. Stroman usually gets first dibs because he is the most senior officer of the bunch."

"Oh, I didn't know that," Mara said.

"It's sorta behind the scenes stuff you're not supposed to know about," the detective added.

"So, if Officer Stroman had first dibs, why do you think he picked me?" Marathon asked.

"Hmmm, well, for one, you're former military," she said. "He likes that. Means that you can follow orders and you're not lazy. Two, your scores in the academy were impressive, and finally, he's never been partnered with a female officer before. I told him to give it a try," she said.

"How long has he been on the force?"

The Detective laughed. "He should have retired already," she said. "He's an old dog, maybe he thinks this is his last rodeo, maybe he's looking for new tricks. I dunno, he saw your name and credentials and picked you."

"I see," Mara said as she emptied the contents of her duffle bag into the locker, which included a small package of baking soda to mask the musty locker smell. She was glad Uncle Dave gave her a care package for her first official day on the job.

"For what it's worth, Stroman knows what he is doing," she said. "He's old school, but he has served the department well and his trainees become some of the best."

"Thanks," Mara said. The brief conversation brought some relief to her first day jitters.

"You know where the briefing room is?"

"Yeah, the sergeant told me," Mara responded.

"Good, this place can be confusing," she said. "The senior officers try and pull things the first day. Just play it cool and you'll be alright."

Marathon closed her locker and thanked the Detective for helping calm her nerves. She then made her way out of the locker room and joined the others as they made their way back to the briefing room. There she waited.

"Good Morning everyone," the captain said as the remaining rookies filed into the small briefing room. He was the only white shirt in a room full of blue.

The classroom style seating faced a podium in the middle of the room where the commanding officer stood. He was alone with only an empty free standing white board behind him. Mara's desk was tiny, even for her. The narrow tabletop could barely fit a standard piece of paper let alone any books or note pads needed to copy down information. She looked around and saw only the rookies taking notes like they were back in the academy.

Mara expected Captain Frank Davidson to start pairing the rookies up with their senior officers right away. She looked around the room to see if she could spot Officer Stroman, but she could only see a few senior officers line the back of the room.

"We are going to continue our active patrol duties the commissioner wants. Remember to keep your eyes and ears focused while on patrol," Captain Frank Davidson said, as if he were reading from a script.

She started to wonder if the captain knew about the incoming rookies from the academy. His news and announcements dragged on and Mara only sporadically picked up on what was going on. It was like she entered a conversation just before it ended.

"I think that about does it, we all have our assignments," Frank Davidson said. Someone then leaned in from the desks in front and said something Mara couldn't hear. "Oh right, apparently there are new faces in the crowd."

Frank Davidson looked around the room and smiled. Mara appreciated his sense of humor. He then cracked a few more jokes keeping the rookies in suspense as long as he could before he started reading assignments. Mara heard her name and it was paired with Senior Officer Stroman.

"Alright, everyone has their assignment. Senior officers and rookies can pair up for active patrols. Rooks, your senior officers have the assignment and will take it from here," he said before dismissing the room.

Marathon looked around to see rookies trying to find their partners as senior officers stood and left the room. This was clearly done by design. She studied the situation while she remained in her seat. Most of the senior officers were now gone as the rookies looked lost like kindergarteners on the first day of school. Marathon took her time, and allowed the room to clear out.

"Hey rook!"

Mara turned to see Captain Davidson stare at her from across the room.

"Where's your senior officer?"

"Officer Stroman? He's probably waiting for me outside," she said.

"I dismissed you," The Captain said as he approached her.

"Yes, you did," Mara replied reminding herself that this was no longer the Marines Corps.

"So get to work," He said. "Don't make your senior officer wait."

Mara stood and closed her notebook without any new notes added to the empty pages. She then turned made her way towards where the senior officers had gathered outside the briefing room in the narrow hallway. It felt like high school when classes changed and students gathered to gossip in the hallway. The senior officers looked like they were about to pounce like it was freshmen Friday.

"Officer Stroman," Mara said as she approached a group of officers. They conveniently had their name tags covered with a commemorative band honoring fallen officers who died recently from illnesses contracted from World Trade Center site after 9/11.

The officers laughed. Mara didn't find it amusing, so she took a more direct approached.

"I'm sorry, I was looking for someone more helpful," she said before she turned away. They gave her a nasty look, and she smiled back.

"You don't have to be abrasive," someone said as he walked behind her and then turned down the hall. Marathon caught up to him easily as if he expected her to follow.

"You boys love to play your little games," she said as she matched his pace.

"I see you don't particularly care about making friends," he said as he turned towards her and stopped abruptly. The officer was slightly taller than her, broad shouldered with a stocky build. He looked to be in his late forties, and the lines around his eyes suggested he could be a bit older than that.

"I don't do games," Marathon said.

"Any one of those officers back there will answer the call when you request backup. Earning their respect is what could be the difference between life and death," Officer Stroman said.

Mara laughed, "And I was told the NYPD was just like the Marines."

Officer Stroman continued walking and Mara matched his movements. "Who told you that?"

"Google," Mara responded. Senior Officer Stroman shook his head as he continued walking. The two of them continued down the hall in silence until they reached the back of the station. Officer Stroman paused before the double doors that led to the outside parking lot.

"Equipment check," he said as he looked at her up and down.

"I got everything," she responded rolling her eyes.

"Except for any sense, you seemed to have left them in the mountains of Kabul," he said.

Mara was shocked, she knew he had her file and probably details of her service in the Marines, but to name drop Kabul, where she was stationed, was quite surprising. Nothing in her service record was redacted, but those kinds of details required more information that would could be typically found in a service file. Most correspondence only mentioned that she was stationed in Afghanistan.

He then turned away from her and left through the double doors to the parking lot. Mara stood there and watched him leave. The cultural differences between the NYPD and the Marine Corps was strikingly different. Once a Marine, you never had to earn respect from other soldiers. They would come to your defense in any situation. She chased after him through the double doors.

"Officer Stroman," Mara said as she tried to catch up. He turned back to her as if she were a child.

"Listen kid," he said. "I'm not here to babysit. What you are about to do is learn the real-life work police officers do on a day to day basis. Get all that crap from the academy out of your head and shut the fuck up."

"Excuse me?" Mara questioned.

"The shit you learned in the classroom will get you killed out here," Stroman said he moved closer so only Mara could hear him. "I need to know you got my back and the other officers out here need to know the same thing."

"In the Marines, we never had to say that out loud," she replied.

"Don't give me this bullshit about the Marines and leave no man behind. That's not what I am talking about," he said.

Mara remained silent. She tried to think about what she said or did to get him so riled up. Was this a show?

"Out here, the streets will eat you up. I've seen tons of green-eyed rooks like yourself come out here. Tons of soldier boys think they are out here to change the world. Fuck that!" he said. "You're a queens girl."

"Yeah, so?" Mara questioned.

"Well, this is fucking Brooklyn," he said.

"I'm here to learn," Mara replied.

"That's the smartest thing you've said all day. Get in the van and we'll show you what the real world is like."

Mara saw a number of police officers had already gathered in a large transport van. They were all staring at her, seemingly sizing her up. She knew this

283

was a form of hazing, but it was nothing like what she experienced in the Marines. Stroman was putting on a show, but how much of it was an actual show? She didn't know, she could only assume that what he said was his truth.

The crime rate in the 75th was higher than most precincts, and police were often injected into dangerous situations with little to no warning. But, nothing was more dangerous than patrolling the mountains in Afghanistan. She wondered how much Stroman knew about her service record.

Mara approached the van, Stroman clearly wanted to be last in so she found an empty seat towards the front. The van was in eerily silent for the duration of the ride. She felt eyes pierce the back of her head like the other officers were staring her down. The ten minute ride to the corner of New Lots and Van Sinderen Ave seemed to last forever.

Mara, Officer Stroman, and two other officers got out of the van and stood on the corner. This was the official start of their patrol. Their root was to walk up Van Sinderen to make sure kids were in school and to be a visible presence in the neighborhood while checking in with local bodega and business owners. That was considered part of their active patrol, engage the community to serve and protect.

Van Sinderen was a long southbound one-way street that ran parallel to the L train. The tracks were raised above ground and they served as the official separation between East New York and Brownsville. Just on the other side of the tracks, officers from the 73rd precinct were probably doing the exact same thing. Marathon and Officer Stroman started walking north on Van Sinderen as the two other officers made their way East on New Lots for their active patrol.

There was not much to say as they walked in a straight line up the block towards Blake Avenue. Officer Stroman walked slowly, as if he owned these streets. She found it hard to keep pace with him as it constantly changed just as she matched his stride. This whole tough guy attitude was a show, an act that she had to endure, but she was convinced this wasn't a gender thing. It was more of a rookie hazing situation, like when a freshmen joins a varsity sports team.

"When we get to Blake Ave, you'll see a bunch of activity," Stroman said breaking the silence. His tone was much different now, more even and serious.

Mara stopped and waited for Stroman to turn around. She wanted to get this out of the way now before it became a problem. The show needed to end, and she needed to set some ground rules before things got out of hand. She needed him to know she wasn't some rookie that could be pushed around and she didn't need an audience to do that.

"Hey, kid, you listening?" he asked.

"I get you were putting on a show for the other officers back there. They were playing the part as well. I get that I am a rookie and this is my training day, or whatever the fuck that means," Marathon said. Her words were pointed and calculated. She waited for Officer Stroman to turn around and face her before she continued.

"I don't need anyone reminding me about what's at stake when we put on this uniform and patrol the streets," she continued. "I especially don't need to be lectured about loyalty and the bond people in arms share. You can take all of your pomp and circumstance and shove it up your ass," she concluded. Officer Stroman stood there for a second, smirked back at her and then walked towards her.

"Good, now that we got that out of the way," Stroman responded as he turned to walk with her. "We can get to know these streets."

Her instincts were correct, the display back at the station was an act. She knew by calling him out on it, it would give her the desired effect. Doing that in front of his peers probably would have ended poorly. Plus, she wanted nothing more than to be treated as an equal.

Marathon didn't spend four years of her life in Afghanistan to be treated like she didn't know what she was doing patrolling the streets of New York City. Her time in the Marines taught her to be combative and get straight to the point so there were no misconceptions between colleagues. Her time in the academy taught her she just turned in one uniform for another.

285

"As I was saying," Stroman continued. "When we get to Blake, you're going to see a lot of foot traffic. We start our patrol down south over here because we want to get a feel for what we are walking into. Gives us time to get used to the environment. You can usually smell shit in the air before you step in it."

"You speak like Blake Avenue changes from day to day," Mara responded.

"It does," he said as he pointed to the train tracks to his left. "These tracks separate neighborhoods and housing projects. These cross streets here don't bridge the neighborhoods, but Blake does, it runs straight through under the tracks and into Brownsville. You don't see this shit in Queens."

Mara now noticed why Blake Avenue was an important patrol zone. The elevated tracks to their left was a physical barrier. Fences, concrete and debris littered the area beneath the tracks preventing people from crossing over by car. Blake Avenue was the first intersection north of New Lots that allowed people to cross into a new neighborhood.

"The problem here is that the new school system doesn't particularly care what neighborhood you live in," he said.

"What do you mean?" Mara asked.

"The school zones here are district 23 and district 19. They are also divided by these tracks. But, the new Mayor opened up the Districts so kids can now go to other schools in the surrounding neighborhoods if they don't like the school they used to go to."

"So how does that play out?" Mara asked.

"Since the districts are now open, the boundaries between neighborhoods gets intense," Officer Stroman said. Marathon gave him a look like she didn't follow so he continued. "Gangs in this area use these tracks to draw boundaries as well. When schools started to allow kids in from outside their hood, problems started to pop up."

"So if I'm following you, being that Blake Avenue is a major intersection, kids use this point to cross over into Brownsville to go to school."

"Exactly," he said.

"Okay, now I follow."

"Good, because you're going to need to remember faces, names, tags, signs, to get to know these streets," Officer Stroman said. He then pointed to graffiti on a steel pillar that supported the tracks. "You see that?"

"Yeah, the squiggly lines," Mara joked.

"That's an H up sign. That's a warning to anyone that if you pass the tracks, you are going into Hoodstars territory," Stroman said.

"Hoodstars?" Mara asked with a slight laugh. "I thought this was Bloods and Crips?"

"It is. Locale gangs in the area are usually formed in the housing projects. The Hoodstars are part of Marcus Garvey housing and as they started to run the streets on their block, the Bloods and Crips took notice. The Bloods eventually swallowed them up and now they are loyal to them."

"Shit."

"Yeah, and we are walking in it every fucking day," Stroman said.

As Mara approached the corner of Blake and Van Sinderen Avenue, she noticed a group of teens hanging out by a corner store. She checked her watch and they should have been in school over an hour ago. They were clearly eying her as she approached.

"Yo Stroman," a tall teenager said. "You wanna get your bitch on a leash?"

Mara didn't react but stood alongside Stroman and continued to eye the tall teenager. The teens clearly knew who Stroman was and they clearly didn't like seeing new faces in their neighborhood. They kept eying her and she felt like a fish out of water.

"Shouldn't you guys be in school?" he responded.

"Man, fuck that," another kid said.

"Why don't you take your little whore outta here."

"Yeah, it looks like the streets are about to swallow her up."

"Do I look scared, do I look like someone about to be swallowed?" she asked taking a step forward.

"Yo, I got something for you to swallow," the tall teenager said and all the kids burst out laughing.

"Maybe your mamma should have swallowed," Marathon retorted as the kids continued their laughter, now with greater intensity. Kids love a good comeback.

"I believe it is time for your sorry asses to get to school. Now, I can escort you there or you can walk on your own," Marathon continued.

"Bitch, you can escort me anywhere," the tall teenager said trying to win the crowd back over.

"I'm gonna escort your face to the concrete if you don't back the fuck off and get your ass to school," Marathon replied as the kids continued to react accordingly.

The teen then walked up to her and continued passed her nearly brushing shoulders. Mara didn't react and allowed him to pass. The rest of the teens dispersed and followed the leader towards a school building down the block in Brownsville.

"Not bad rook," Stroman said.

"I thought I was gonna have to plant that kid in the ground," she responded.

"Na, he was just fucking with you," he said.

"You know him?"

"Yeah I see him every shift. His brother runs the Garvey projects over there," Stroman said pointing to a housing complex just to the north.

"That would have been nice to know," Mara barked.

288

"You had it handled well kid," Stroman said. "I would have jumped in if you did or said anything wrong. Those kids now know your face and you started to earn their respect."

"This is how you earn their respect?" Mara asked.

"They only know strength and weakness. You showed strength and they respect that. If you had backed down or if you had taken it too far, they would continue to walk all over you," he said.

"This is different than Queens," Marathon said.

"You'll be fine," he said.

"Thanks, Stroman," she replied.

"Call me John."

M

Chapter
Thirty

FBI Safe House
Flushing New York
September 3rd, 2019
3:45am

Marathon woke to the sound of a car alarm blaring just outside the basement window. The echoing sound ricocheted off the interior concrete walls and made it seem like the car was in the basement with her. In the distance she heard someone yell expletives at whoever broke the silence.

She had made the basement her home over the past few days. Marathon used the lay low time to let her wounds heal and formulate a plan to get out of the city. Russo came up with an idea of using smoke and mirrors to distract the hungry police to other parts of the city. Esposito was in the process of renting a boat to get her off the island by crossing the Long Island Sound into Connecticut. Their plans were nearly in place, the only thing left was the execution.

The car alarm stopped, and silence crept back into the air as she laid in her temporary sleeping quarters. There was no guarantee that this plan was going to work. Getting out of the city at the Queens/Nassau border was better, but not guaranteed. She knew the Nassau County PD was on the lookout for her. They loved getting in on the action when events spilled out of the city and into their neighborhoods in the suburbs.

Marathon decided that she couldn't fall back asleep, so she left her basement apartment and went into the kitchen to retrieve a glass of water. The neighborhood seemed to be calmer than the previous days after the news announced she was public enemy number one. Cops were going door to door, K-9 units were out and about leading their masters in all sorts of directions. Helicopters hovered in place for hours as the noose rested firmly in place surrounding the neighborhood, but it didn't contract any further.

The other day, while she was in the basement, she heard the cops knock on the door. She thought they would breach, but she overheard them talk about how the house was in foreclosure and had no signs of being broken into. They eventually moved on once the dogs determined there was nothing there. Marathon remembered the sprinkler system was still active and that masked her scent.

As with most hot topics in the news, without fuel for the fire, the story would eventually die down and become a distant memory. The news media focused their attention elsewhere and even suggested that she had already skipped town. Marathon wondered if her picture would even make today's paper considering it was moved back to page 6 after spending the previous days on the front cover. Normally, that would be a pretty steep fall from grace.

When the story broke, her Facebook profile picture littered the papers. The NY Post, usually witty and even provocative with their cover titles, opened their version of the story with the title "NYPD Fatale," which served to narrowly archetype her as a character from a noir story.

Marathon particularly loved how the Daily News described her as quote, "The Nikita of the NYPD", making reference to a popular Russian spy. The papers had a field day with this, how crazy it got, how absurdly astounding the evidence was fabricated to meet the new narrative that drove her story of crime, lust and power. She was like a mob boss controlling an entire enterprise of criminal activity. Marathon could barely control her credit card bill every month, let alone an entire criminal enterprise.

291

Mara read each story, from each news outlet. She found common trends in each source and was able to confirm her suspicions based on who was quoted in the news reports. She had never even met or had any correspondence with most of the officers who openly provided information to the press. Yet, they seemed to know her very well, one of them seemed to know her intimately well as he described a passed relationship with her that was completely fabricated.

She did, however, know one of the conspirators who provided a few quotes for the paper. The column describing her criminal career was open on the kitchen table from the day before. Her former partner, now retired, Officer John Stroman spilled all the juicy details. He was interviewed at John Street Bar in Manhattan and had described her in very colorful, not so flattering ways. Woven in his deception, he described Marathon as a lustful power-hungry criminal who ruled the streets of Brownsville and East New York disguised as an officer of the law.

John was the one name she recognized, the one name that stood out and the one person that linked everything together. She stared at the article having practically memorized it the day before. His quoted words dug deep and left a gaping chasm of anger and rage. She felt her rancor boil over as her hostility erupted in hatred. In a reactive motion, she sent her glass of water flying across the kitchen and wanted to scream, but instead collapsed to the kitchen floor where her chin rested on her knees as she curled into a ball of ill-tempered ire.

Moments passed but her vexation only festered. She felt her very core change, like her soul was being recast from within. In this moment, she decided she was not going to run, she was not going to give in and let the NYPD paint their narrative.

She found herself standing in front of the bathroom mirror with a pair of scissors in her hand. She was missing large chunks of hair after pulling out some of the weave that covered the scar from Bowden. With scissors in her hand, she felt her body go through the motions of altering her appearance as her long hair slipped into the sink. She couldn't stop herself even if she wanted to. The image staring back at her in the mirror was something different. Altered by her umbrageous situation.

Like a zombie, she moved back to the kitchen table and sat in wait. She knew both Russo and Esposito would never go for her plan, she also didn't much care. From an early age she was taught to meet her problems head on and confront whatever challenge prevented success. Uncle Dave installed the piss and vinegar attitude and the Marines refined it. She missed her surrogate parents, missed their council and had no way of contacting them. Marathon knew she needed to confront John, needed to look him in the eye before she sent his world crashing down on top of him.

Marathon didn't react to Agent Russo as he entered the kitchen, but she did notice the look of shock and confusion. "Mara?"

"Hey, Russo," she said after a brief moment passed.

"Are you okay?"

"I'm not running," she said calmly.

Esposito entered with tray of coffee and a brown paper bag with grease seeping out the sides. At first, he didn't notice her sitting at the table. His primary concern was getting the stained bag to the counter before its contents spilled out onto the kitchen floor. The sound of crunching glass could be heard as he made his way to the sink.

"What happened here?" he asked.

"Looks like Marathon Torres has something to say," Russo said.

"What?" Esposito said looking at Russo and then at her. He looked at her for a good moment before he fully recognized her. "What the fuck?"

"I'm not running," Mara repeated so Esposito could hear. "No fucking way."

"Okay," Russo said as he sat down across from her.

"There is no fucking way I am letting this asshole get away with what he's done!" she continued pointing to the news article.

293

"He won't get away with it," Russo said in response.

"How long have you been working this case?" Mara asked. The two agents looked at each other and didn't comment.

"That's why," she said.

Esposito now sat down and spread out the breakfast he brought. "Okay, Mara, think about this," he said.

"I have," Marathon said cutting him off.

"You got a plan?" Russo asked.

"I'm glad you asked," Mara stated as she glared like daggers towards Esposito. "Did you recognize me?"

"Not right away," Russo answered.

"Yeah, same," Esposito said.

"That's the point. I can get to John," she said.

"What's that going to do? He's going to kill you!" Esposito said. "He'll recognize you!"

"Wait a sec," she responded. "I go to John seeking help to get out of the city." She noticed Russo deep in thought.

"That has about a 50 percent chance of working," Russo said. "You know that right? He fucking ousted you in the papers."

"Those are better than the chances of making it out of New York alive with your plan," she responded.

"Absolutely not, I'm not going to let you do this!" Esposito said.

"You don't get to make decisions for me," Mara responded. "Shit, the only thing you should say is how can I help."

"Alright, with your personal feelings aside," Russo said who glared at Esposito. "This might be the break we are looking for. Let's hear your plan."

Mara nodded at Russo thanking him for being willing to hear her out. She then glanced at Esposito who seemed offended by the harsh comment she sent back at him. Mara didn't care if his feelings were hurt. She felt a connection with him the other night and he barely responded or acted accordingly since then, but those were issues to be resolved later.

"I call him up, plead with him to help me. Plead with him to get me out of the city. He will agree to that. I know it."

"What about this article?" Russo asked.

"You think a girl on the run has time to read an article? I'll play it off like I am completely unaware of what's going on. His ego will overlook all of that because I am presenting all of his problems on a silver platter," she answered.

"Okay, we use a burner phone and we do this away from here just in case they are able to trace it. We'll keep this location as a fall back," Russo said. He definitely wasn't some computer nerd. He had counterintelligence written all over him. She saw his type in Afghanistan whenever she had to work with the CIA as they tried to locate Bin Laden.

"Right, that's a good idea," she said. "Most likely he will tell me to meet him at John Street Bar. He works there and runs the place. Come to think of it, it is probably more than what it seems."

"Okay, assuming that is your destination," Esposito said. "I'll pull up blueprints of the location so we can get in there to support you."

"No, nothing is going to go down there," she said.

"So what do you need me to do?" Esposito asked.

Mara nodded at him. She was glad to see him come around. "Mack, I'm gonna need you and Russo at a different location," she said.

"What?" Esposito said. "He's going to take you out right there. At the fucking bar. There is no second location."

"Hold up," Russo said. "Let's hear her out."

"John Stroman is not going to jeopardize John Street Bar," Mara said.

"Sure he will, what's to stop him from pulling out a gun and popping you off there?" Esposito asked.

295

"His business," Russo said looking at Esposito. "We've suspected something was off about that place. You said it yourself."

"Right, he doesn't want a situation he cannot control in his place of business," Mara added.

"You know, this is a lot of speculation. You are trying to predict human behavior by making a lot of assumptions on what he will possibly do," Esposito said.

"Please continue," Russo said as he sent another glare towards Esposito. This caused him to throw his arms in the air and he stood up.

"I know Stroman. I know him very well. He has a flare for the dramatic. He loves irony and loves coming out on top, but in style. He's going to take me back to Broad Channel."

"No fucking way," Esposito said as he paced back and forth by the kitchen sink. "Why would he go back to that crime scene?"

"He wants me to realize what is going on before he offs me. I promise you this is what he is going to do! He is a man of control, a man of power, and nothing will get his juices flowing more than bringing me to the spot Marley Williams was murdered."

"How do you know this?" Esposito asked.

"I remember this one domestic disturbance call he and I responded to back during my rookie year," Mara started. She had their complete attention.

"We arrived on scene by foot as we were in the area. The wife was beaten so bad that her face had already swelled up beyond recognition. I was afraid for her as the man was completely out of his mind. Stroman entered home as I escorted the lady out and sat her on her stoop. I radioed for backup and tried to administer first aid. The woman called out for her son who was also in the house. I go up and provided support for Officer Stroman. When I entered, I saw the suspect on the ground with Stroman on top of him. The perp was bloodied and crying out in pain as I heard bones in his arm crack from the pressure Stroman

296

placed on them," Marathon said. She stood and went to the sink and grabbed another glass of water. After a few sips she continued.

"Stroman told me to bring the wife in. He told me to get the boy as well. He stood the man up and forced him to look at the lives he was ruining and then he beat him further," Mara recited. "Afterwards, Stroman was extremely proud of himself and said that he knew the stepfather would never touch his wife again. He told me that he enjoyed this kind of justice."

"So the man gets off on this stuff," Esposito stated. "Why do you think he'll bring you specifically to Broad Channel?"

"He needs a place where he can control the narrative," Russo said. "Think about it. They already framed her, now all they have to do is link her to crimes they accused her of. Broad Channel is the place. It's the kind of narrative the media loves to print."

"They set the narrative for Marley Williams, and now they would have an opportunity to tie up all the loose ends," Marathon said.

"What, you think they will also frame you for her murder?" Russo asked.

"Think about it, I'm public enemy number one," she said.

"No fucking way," Esposito said.

"Again, this is not your choice," Mara replied. "You can either sit this one out or do something productive."

"What do you need me to do?" Russo asked.

"I need you, and Esposito," Mara said while she glanced up at Esposito who looked obviously annoyed. "I need you two to back me up at the wildlife preserve."

"I think we can do that," Russo stated speaking for Esposito.

Mara grabbed Esposito's cell phone which rested on the kitchen table. She used his easily cracked numeric password to access the phone. Russo seemed impressed and pointed to Esposito with a smirk on his face.

"Here is Broad Channel Wildlife Preserve," she said. "The best spot to set up is here and here," she said as she navigated the map on the screen pointing out where the sniper had set up a few days before. "I would suspect there'll be more than just John to deal with. You might want to get there well in advance, so you have time to scout the area."

"When do you plan on doing this?" Russo asked as Esposito studied the map on his phone.

"I'm going to call John later this afternoon, and then head to John Street Bar. If all goes according to plan, we'll be there sometime tonight."

"And if it doesn't go according to plan?" Esposito asked.

"Then you add more murder charges to the list," she replied.

"When you have John at Broad Channel Mara, you need to get him to talk," Russo said. "He is a key part to this operation."

"Yeah, I can set up listening devices around where you think he'll take you and we'll be able to listen to what's happening," Esposito chimed in. Looks like he got over his reservations. Mara pointed to the map where they would most likely end up.

"That shouldn't be too difficult," Russo added. "I'm worried about what comes next."

Mara paused for a moment. Her plan was simply laid out up until that point. The obvious implications put both Russo and Esposito in charge of her safety. Her chance of survival was slim, the moment John suspected something was up, what would prevent him from putting a bullet in her? Her silence grew and Esposito took advantage of this.

"You see, you're still in danger and there is little chance you come out of this alive," he said.

"You guys are gonna have to figure that part out," Mara replied. "I also doubt that you two are computer nerds working for the FBI, so you should be able to handle it." They glanced at each other but said nothing.

"There is inherent risk, and I am willing to be used as bait to nail this son of a bitch."

"I don't know how this is going to work," Esposito said.

"The two of you better figure that out before nightfall," Mara said.

"We can come up with a plan," Russo added. Mara got up and walked out of the kitchen to leave the two men to their thoughts and conversation. Marathon made a quick inventory survey and checked her Glock. She knew at some point it would be confiscated and she would be disarmed. What else could she use in a pinch? She quietly studied her wardrobe while she eavesdropped on the conversation in the kitchen.

She heard Esposito get loud and outright reject Russo's ideas. Russo was looking at it as an acceptable risk and Marathon agreed with him, but Esposito kept pushing back. Russo's voice became elevated as it was distinctly heard throughout the house.

"Well maybe you shouldn't've put your dick where it didn't belong. It's clouding your judgement."

"Fuck off.... She came onto me."

"Yeah I'm sure she did."

There was a pause in the conversation. Mara didn't know why she got a kick out overhearing their conversation and she moved closer to the kitchen to catch their conversation as their voices returned to normal volume.

"Mack, this is our best shot!"

"Both of us have lost a lot, how far are you prepared to go Russo?"

"As far as it fucking takes!"

"We are on our own, there is no backup here."

"We have a young lady here willing to do whatever it takes, this is our chance to make a real dent in these assholes."

Mara inched down the hall. The men continued their back and forth shenanigans as she slowly crept out of the hallway and back into the kitchen.

"FBI my fucking ass," she said making her presence known.

Mack Esposito just looked at her waiting for Russo to take the ball and explain. He also turned towards him expecting the same thing.

"Fuck, it's obvious you're not FBI, or internal affairs, or probably even supposed to be here doing this," Mara stated. "You guys are the reason I'm in this predicament! You two fucking show up unannounced and my fucking world gets turned upside down."

Russo held his hands up in defense, as Mack nodded signaling she was probably right. They looked at each other again with disgust.

"You two are also the reason why I am probably still alive," Mara continued. "I've always felt something was fundamentally wrong with the NYPD. I'm glad I'm standing here without any blinders on. I'm glad I now know who my enemy is."

Before Mack could reply, Mara got closer. "Now tell me who the fuck you're working for!"

"We can't," Russo said. "Our agency is compromised as well and ultimately it doesn't matter."

"NSA?" Mara asked. "CIA?"

"Pick whichever suits your narrative," Mack said. "But we'll tell you more about what's going on here and how we are aware of what's happening."

"A few years back we stumbled on transactions that showed extremely large amounts of money being funneled through the NYC area. We thought something big was happening, like another 9/11 type event," Russo said.

"Naturally, we pursued the case and we found no trace of terrorist activity. So we turned our findings over to local law enforcement," Esposito said. "The computer crime stuff I told you about was real, and very much a part of how we found out about their operational plans, but that came well after this.

"We gave our evidence to the NYPD," Russo said.

Mara looked at the men, the both stared back at her. "What?"

"Little did we know that the NYPD was the source. It took us a few days to figure that out. When we followed up with the NYPD, their official response was gang activity and that it was being addressed," Mack said. "Something about gangs purchasing weapons for a brewing gang war."

"Wait, what year was this?" Mara asked.

"Your rookie year," Russo answered.

"We knew the NYPD was full of shit, gangs didn't have that kind of money. We knew something else was going on," Russo said.

"Holy fucking shit," Marathon said. "You fuckers got Marley killed."

The two agents were silent and averted their eyes.

"She fucking died because you two gave up on your own investigation and let the NYPD run with the evidence you collected," Marathon continued.

"Now you know why we are invested," Esposito said.

Maybe Esposito was older than he looked. Marathon sensed regret in his voice as he confirmed what she suspected. More questions materialized in her thoughts. She sensed this was another partial truth, but it did provide more context.

"We were close a few times, but they've been one step ahead of us for many years. Thanks to you, we now have a better understanding of their criminal network. It's extremely complex, and we still only know pieces of it," Esposito stated.

"This is why we suspected you were dirty," Russo said.

"After Marley's death, the case blew up in our faces, we were reassigned," Esposito said.

"I kept the Marly Williams file open on purpose. I knew one of these fuckers would make a mistake," Russo said.

"I was the one who accessed the file," Marathon said.

"Which lead us to John, our best lead," Esposito said.

"So that's why you have shit after all those years?" Mara asked.

"Every opportunity we've had to make real headway was met with extreme resistance. We've had set back after set back," Russo said. "To the point where we are now on our own."

"We did try other things," Esposito replied looking at Russo.

"Yeah, but it all had the same result," Russo stated. "Remember the financial crime database leak of 2017?"

"Yeah, it was blockbuster news," Marathon said.

"It truly was, we leaked it," Russo said.

"It was all of our data since 2006. It was supposed to expose everyone," Esposito said. "Everything we collected, out in the open."

"What happened?" Mara asked.

"Nothing," Russo responded. "Not a god damn thing."

"The public was outraged, but the news cycle quickly pivoted to different stories and the public lost interest," Esposito said.

"Our Hail Mary play failed," Russo added. The room filled with an awkward silence, but Mara still had a question she wanted an answer to.

"Do you think anyone will recognize me?" Mara asked changing the subject.

"I had to do a double take," Esposito said. "As long as someone doesn't stare at you, I think you'll be fine."

"Well, that's good, considering Mack got you see you up close and personal," Russo jokingly stated.

"Come on," Esposito said. Marathon could tell he had regrets about the other night. She wondered how they could move past this, but that would have to be solved later.

"It's hard to cover up a face like that," Russo said. Mara took that as a compliment.

"But you did a good job butchering your hair," he continued as he held up her profile picture from the NY Post.

Esposito leaned in and then looked at Mara. "Your facial features are much different with bangs. It might just work," he said.

"You ever see the picture of Zooey Deschanel with and without bangs?" Mara asked. Russo looked at her like he had no idea who she was talking about, but Esposito go the reference.

"Yeah, the chick from New Girl," Esposito said. "She went without bangs?" he questioned.

"You'd never know it was her," Mara said. "I was going for that look, but with bangs."

"Well, it's hard to recognize you kid," Russo said. "You need to cover your tattoos, and wear baggy clothing. Every picture of you shows your figure, and the papers specifically mention your identifying marks."

"It's not every day you see a chick walk around with Marine tattoos," Esposito added.

Mara got up and from the kitchen table and made her way back towards the bed room. She paused for a brief moment to thank the agents and then she left to get ready.

M

Chapter
Thirty-One

John Street Bar
Manhattan, New York
September 3rd, 2019
9:45pm

Marathon turned on John Street after walking three miles down Broadway from Penn Station. After her brief cell phone conversation with John, he agreed to help her get out of the city. Her act went according to plan, and she knew how to play up to his masculine ego. His response sounded sympathetic and eager to help, he almost sounded genuine.

After making the phone call from Flushing Meadows, she took the Long Island Rail Road from Mets-Willets Point to Penn Station. The Long Island Rail Road offered more concealment than the subway even though it wasn't as direct a route. Walking the streets of Manhattan was also a better option than taking mass transit south to the financial district where the bar was located. She would rather pass many people on the streets who only were able to get a glimpse of her than spend a 20-minute subway ride where people would be able to really get a good look at her.

The only tense moment on the way was when she passed through Union Square. There was a large police presence there and she wondered what was going on. She managed to keep her distance and avoid any confrontation with police.

Mara now stood on the block were John Street Bar was located. John Stroman was no doubt standing behind the bar waiting for her to walk through the doors. She had to get her game face on. John was intuitive and they both knew each other very well. Mara's life depended on deception and not breaking character, she needed him to believe she was really there for his help. She needed to be afraid for her life and desperate to get out of the city. If he were to pick up on an ulterior motive, the situation would go south very quickly. She probably wouldn't make it out of the bar alive.

Marathon pushed forward feeling her hands tremble as she grasped the handle of the door leading to the bar downstairs. The bar crowd on this Tuesday evening would be very light, if even non-existent. She quietly descended the steps as the next set of doors emerged at the bottom. Once she reached that point, there was no turning back.

Each step downward felt like she was taking a step closer to her grave. She felt her heart pound in her chest while sweat started to pool on her forehead. She reached the landing and saw John through the tempered glass doors. He stood behind the bar, in his normal spot like she always pictured him. He immediately noticed her and motioned her to come in.

"Lock the door behind you," he said as Mara entered. Marathon quickly glanced around, the bar was empty.

"Oh my god John, I'm so glad to see you," Mara said as she fumbled with the lock and then hustled over to him.

She planted a big hug around his broad shoulders like she has always done. Mara now had a better view of the bar and looked behind John while the hug ran its course. She noticed the kitchen traffic door rock slightly as if someone recently went through it. There were empty glasses strung out around the bar and the pool table looked like it was recently used. Mara was sure there were men in the back somewhere just waiting for a code word to engage.

"I just closed up the bar, you came just in time," he said releasing the hug.

"Thank you so much John," Mara said as she took a step back. "I don't know what's going on. The entire department is out to get me, they are calling me a killer. I am not a killer, you have to believe me. I didn't do it," Mara rambled trying to remain in character and sound frantic, like a girl on the run.

Her blood was boiling. She wanted to pull out her gun and drop him right here, but she knew the men in the back would come out with overwhelming force and she wouldn't make it out of there alive. The narrative would remain the same and she would have accomplished nothing.

"Slow down, slow down," John said as he kept his meaty paw on her shoulder. "Come on, have a seat and take a deep breath."

John handed her a glass of water, but Mara instead reached for a bottle of Jameson and took a large sip after popping the lid.

"Easy kid, take a seat, take a seat," he said repeating himself again. Marathon could tell something was off with him.

She sat and inhaled deeply. She thought she was being overly dramatic; she was so far out of her own character that she didn't know how to act in this situation. She needed to scale it down otherwise he would become suspicious. She took another long sip from the bottle and then placed it down on the bar.

"I need to get out of the city John!" she said.

"I know, I've made arrangements," he said. "We'll leave soon, just catch your breath."

"Thank you, John," she said.

"Were you followed?" he asked. She needed to be extremely careful with his questions. He was very good at spotting deception.

"I don't think so. I disguised myself and found these old clothes in a charity bin," Mara said. She pointed to her hair.

"Have you contacted anyone?" he asked barely taking notice of her new hairdo.

"I tried calling Uncle Dave, but it went straight to voicemail," she said. "He's in Paris right now and I was supposed to meet him at the end of the week."

It was the truth. She did try before she called John. She did not leave him a voicemail, but no doubt John knew this information already. Their phones were certainly monitored.

"Did you ditch the phone like I told you?" he asked.

"Yeah, I got rid of it after I hung up with you," she answered.

"Good, they're probably monitoring calls, so this location is no good. We have to get a move on it," he said.

"Oh shit, do you think they tapped your number?" Marathon questioned.

"We need to move," he said in response.

Mara kept her eye on the door leading to the kitchen. It was a standard swing door that opened with the slightest push. She saw shadows move on the other side. No doubt John sent the goons behind the door a coded message, she knew she had passed the initial test, she was still alive.

"Where are we going?"

"I asked harbor patrol if I could borrow a boat to go fishing tomorrow," John said.

"You're going to smuggle me out on a boat?" Mara questioned.

"All the bridges, tunnels and mass transit are being watched. You might make it out, but you might not. Facial recognition is a thing at those locations," John replied. "Besides, a few boat boys owe me a favor."

Fuck, facial recognition is what got her before, even with a baseball cap on. No doubt cameras picked up on her location when she reentered the city to retire. They probably tracked her movements to that hotel in the Lower East Side and monitored her movements to use against her later.

John knowing harbor patrol didn't surprise her. With a smuggling operation like this, she was sure harbor cops were in on it. John walked around the bar towards the door leading to the kitchen. He motioned her to follow. Marathon passed through the doors after him. She closed her eyes expecting to be taken out right there, but nothing happened. The kitchen was clear, and John was standing by the exit door.

"Something wrong?" he commented.

"I can't believe you allow food to come out of this kitchen," she said hoping to throw him off. "A fucking fly flew right into my hair."

"Come, on, we need to move," he said as he showed his frustration.

With the amount of time she spent at John Street Bar, she never knew there was a back door that led to an outdoor staircase. John opened the metal door and waited for Mara to exit. He locked the door behind him as he followed her up the narrow grease encrusted concrete stairs. John remained a few feet behind her as she made it to street level and waited for him to catch up.

"There's a sedan over there at the end of the alley, get in the back and put your head down," he said as he moved passed Mara towards the car.

The old sedan looked like an old unmarked car similar to the one Detective Morales used, it might have even been the same one. Marathon tried to remember the plates, and they did seem familiar. As John got into the front seat, Mara noticed dents, scratches and what looked like bullet holes in the side of the car. This was definitely the car he used. John was connecting Marathon to Detective Morales' death by using the same sedan from the scene.

John sensed Mara was taking too long and got out of the front seat and stood by the door. The former partners locked eyes and Mara instinctively drew her Glock from behind her back. John remained standing by the door and simply shook his head. She knew this was her only play. There was no way she wouldn't recognize the sedan Detective Morales used, and if she played it off, John would have suspected something.

"I had a bet with some of my colleagues, that you would notice the car," he said in calm voice. Mara remained focused on him and instinctively focused her Glock towards his center mass.

"You're fucking behind all of this?" she questioned playing into her deception.

"I would drop the gun sweetheart," John said.

"Fuck you!" she said in response as she moved closer to the car. "What the fuck John?"

"You couldn't leave well enough alone," John said as a figure of speech. "I take you in, under my wing, and all you focus on is some dumb bitch found in a dumpster. You let that haunt your entire career. For what? You threw away your entire career."

"Fuck you!" Mara said. "Marley was just a girl."

"Sure," he said. He seemed very calm. "I had your career all laid out, you could've been made. Fuck, you could've owed these streets."

"Why the fuck would I want that?" Mara questioned.

Mara heard movement behind her, the trap was sprung and by the look on John's face, he was certainly happy she had fallen for it.

"This is the last time I'm going to say this, PUT DOWN YOUR FUCKING GUN," he yelled as two figures emerged from the shadows. Mara couldn't see them and remained focused on John.

"Boys, shoot her in the fucking head!" he ordered, but before he could finish his sentence Mara had raised her Glock in the air and let the weapon dangle on her trigger finger. The two men rushed behind her and she felt a sharp blow to the back of her head as her vision went dark for a second. She felt her limp body hit the back of the car and the fall to the ground. The blow to her head was significant, but somehow Marathon remained conscious enough to play the role.

"Pick her up and get her in the back seat," John barked.

The two men grabbed her by the arms and lifted her off the ground. Mara let her body go completely limp as if she were unconscious. One of the men braced her upright as the other opened the back door. Then threw her body into the back seat. They propped her up and sat on each side of her as the car started. She heard the front door open and close as another man entered the car and sat in the front seat.

The car started to roll out of the alley as Mara remained limp and unresponsive. "Check her," John barked as the sedan turned out of the alley.

Mara felt the two men grope her body. One man pried her eyes open, but Mara did her best to remain on responsive. She then collapsed back into the seat as the men finished.

"She's clean," the man to her right said.

"Keep your eyes on her," John said as the sedan started to pick up speed. "She don't look like much but she's the toughest bitch I know."

"Let's get this over with," a man said from the front passenger seat. Mara didn't immediately recognize the voice, but the way he spoke sounded more refined than the meatheads next to her in the back.

The car hadn't stopped for a while and maintained a consistent speed signaling they were on the highway. That was a good sign. The nature preserve was over fifteen miles away from John Street Bar.

"You have everything ready?" the mysterious voice said from the passenger seat.

"Yeah," John said.

"Good, kill her now and we'll plant the car and the body," the voice said. Mara tried not to tense, but she was prepared to fight if it came to it. One of the men grabbed her head, Mara couldn't react yet. She needed to stay in character just a bit longer. She felt the hands around her neck and they slowly started to squeeze. She roughly knew the position of both men and would be able to put up a decent fight.

"Get your hands off of her," John said. If he had waited any longer, she would have needed to act. The squeezing sensation around her neck eased as if they were waiting for further instructions.

"She needs to die at the scene, with a gun in her hand in a shoot-out," John said.

"You and your crime scenes are what got us in this position in the first place," the mysterious man said.

"I know, but it wasn't the scenario that ruined. It was this bitch," John sharply responded. "This is me correcting my mistake."

"Then you also know you should have dealt with your former partner a long time ago,"

"That was my call," John said.

"You were wrong about her," the mysterious man said.

"I've recruited how many soldiers for us?" John said.

"You should have either brought this one in or cut her loose a long time ago. Now I have to personally attend to the situation. They are questioning your resolve."

Mara felt the car occasionally slow down. They were no longer on the highway.

"Sorry to drag you out of your corporate office and get your hands dirty," John snapped back.

"Oh, you think I am going to be seen with a bunch of jarheads like you. You're gonna drop me off," he said.

"Where?" John asked.

"Next red light," he said.

"What? This is the middle of Woodhaven Boulevard," John protested.

"I have a car behind you," he said.

Mara felt the car slow and she heard the man unbuckle his seat belt. "Text me when it's done," the man said as she heard the car door open and then close again. John mumbled something under his breath which made the two men in the back-seat chuckle.

"Hey, Briscoe, Louie, you guys clear on what to do?" John asked.

"Yeah," the man to her left said.

"Good, because last time I checked you worked for me, not that political asshole," John said.

"He gave us an order," the man to her right said.

"The only person that gives you an order is me," John barked back. "If you don't hear instructions come out of my mouth you don't do shit. I don't give a fuck what that asshole said."

The noise of the surrounding city became distant, they were now replaced with the sound of planes coming in for a landing. She knew they were close to JFK airport. Mara then heard the static sound of a CB radio.

"10 minutes out, we a go?" John said using his radio voice.

"Affirmative, you've got green across the board," a voice stated over the radio.

"Alright boys, as discussed before. Drag her ass out, set her up and take care of it," John said. "I'll position the car and we'll be well on our way before her body gets cold."

Mara decided to stir to let her potential murders know she was still very much alive.

"She's starting to wake," the man to her left said.

"We're almost there. Restrain her if necessary," John said.

"It would be so much easier to just off her here," Briscoe said.

"I don't fucking keep you jarheads around to think," John said. "Even though our boys are the ones processing the crime scene, they need to build a narrative that people won't question. Don't fuck with my narrative!"

Mara glanced out of the back of the sedan every few moments. She noticed they were close to the Wildlife Preserve. Her life now depended on Esposito and Russo. Without their support, there was zero chance she would make out of this situation alive. Mara felt the sedan turn into the parking lot where her encounter with the sniper concluded a few days ago.

312

She felt Briscoe hold her as Louie opened a plastic evidence bag. Mara wanted to know what was going on, so she stirred herself awake just as the sedan slowed next to the maintenance building.

"Hey, bitch, you woke up just in time for the show," Briscoe taunted.

"You see that building right there, that's where your boy died," Mara responded.

"Don't let her get to you," John said. "She's always had a mouth on her."

"A mouth like hers could do so much," Louie said in laughter while he squeezed her cheeks together. Mara sent an elbow in his side which broke his grip.

"How many of you clowns have tried to kill me?" Mara said. Briscoe's grip around her tightened, she knew it was personal for him. His arm slid up to her neck and started to cut off the flow of oxygen.

"Don't worry bitch, we're gonna take care of the job," he whispered in her ear.

"None of you fucking morons could quite finish me off. I bet that happens a lot with you guys," she said. Briscoe started to squeeze harder. She felt his bicep dig into her neck making it hard for her to breathe.

"I could end your life right here. Your scrawny little neck will snap like pencil," he said. He released his choke hold which allowed her to take a deep breath.

"Oh come on boy, you're not going to blow your load before we get there are you? You have to last a little bit longer than a few insults to your fragile masculinity," Mara said after her wind returned.

John started laughing, "I told you she's a handful."

"You have no idea," she said as she used the opportunity to elbow Briscoe across the bridge of his nose. She couldn't get enough force behind it to break it, but it served its purpose to show she was not going to go quietly. Louie reacted quickly and restrained her arms while Briscoe reposition his armed around her neck from behind.

313

"Don't leave marks, and no blood in the fucking car," John said. "We're almost there. Then you can do what you want with her."

Moments later, the sedan went off the smooth blacktop and onto the bumpy dirt road leading to the jetty where Marley Williams was probably killed. Marathon saw two NYPD patrol cars waiting for them.

All was going according to plan, she had made it this far. She hoped Russo and Esposito had eyes on her, better yet a scope attached to a long barrel. The sedan came to a rolling stop and other headlights illuminated the interior. Mara noticed there were two NYPD squad cars positioned directly opposite their location. Her attention then turned towards the uniformed officers standing outside the patrol cars. They stood close together in wait, she noticed they were heavily armed in tactical gear.

"Get her out," John said. "Follow the fucking plan."

Briscoe opened the door and stepped out of the sedan. He then reached back in and grabbed Mara while Louie pushed her out of the car. Mara fell to the dirt road below as dust kicked up into the air during the struggle. Briscoe went to pick her up as Louie emerged from the other side.

"Grab her legs," he said.

The two men then coordinated their attack and the more Mara resisted the more pain she received. Eventually their attempt to pick her up overwhelmed her defense and she found herself being hoisted into the air as if she were being lifted by a forklift. Mara was then dropped in front of the sedan. The headlights from the 3 vehicles blinded her and she could only make out silhouettes of the men around her. She knew Esposito would need to intervene soon, she only had a few moments left.

"John, you fucking piece of shit," Mara blurted out. She needed to get him to talk.

"Well, Marathon Torres, this is not how I thought your career would end," John said. "You did this to yourself."

314

"Fuck you! You fucking murderer!" she screamed.

"You can yell all you want, there is no one out here who gives a shit," John said.

Mara got to her feet and brushed off the dust from her shirt and shorts. A gun was thrown at her feet.

"Pick it up," John said.

"Fuck you!"

John nodded to one of the officers, who fired a single around at her feet. Mara noticed the officers were in full equipment with body armor. She then looked at the gun laying in the dirt in front of her. It looked like her service Glock she had left at the hospital. There was a clip in it.

"It's loaded," John said.

"I don't have a fucking chance, I'll be dead before I pick it up," Mara said.

"You've got two options. You can go for the gun and try to survive, or I can just have the boys shoot you down where you stand. Either way I win," John said.

"Is that how you killed Marley Williams?"

John paused, he looked around and at the other officers who held their weapons pointed at the ground. Mara wondered if she could get the Glock and fire off a shot before she was gunned down. She only needed one shot, one chance, it was tempting.

"Marley Williams? You're still fucking stuck on that gang banging whore," John said.

Mara remained quiet and focused on John. She was baiting him to spill more about what happened.

"She was a warning! She was a message!" John barked.

"She was a teenage girl who attended high school, she was a daughter, she was a friend, she had hopes and dreams and you fucking used her!" Mara barked back.

"Yet, you seem to be the only person who misses her," John said.

"Fuck you!"

"Pick up the fucking gun," John said. "I'm standing right here."

Mara looked at the gun, she was close enough to dive for it. She calculated the distance and the speed needed to take John out before the pigs in uniform could get her. She was running out of time, and she was willing to try. Come on Esposito, come on Russo, make your move, she thought.

John raised his gun towards Mara, "Pick up the fucking gun."

Mara took a step closer to it and she saw the officers react by stepping out of the headlights and into the shadows. They were almost invisible in the darkness as the blaring headlights blinded her vision.

Then, Mara heard a thud come from behind her, then the sound of glass from the patrol car breaking and a sound of metal on metal popcorned around her. The world seemed to explode in a torrent of sparks and ricocheting rounds. Marathon saw the officer's react to the incoming fire and their attention turned away from her.

She had one shot at this. Mara took a long step, which turned into a baseball slide. She grabbed the Glock and popped back up like she just stole second base. John was already moving towards cover and she had no shot. Marathon then continued in the direction away from incoming fire. She heard rounds zoom over her head as she dove headfirst out of the lit area and off the dirt road into the brush. She landed hard and the thorny vegetation scratched her exposed skin.

M

Chapter
Thirty-Two

Broad Channel
Wildlife Preserve
Queens, New York
September 3rd, 2019
11:15pm

The gun fire around Marathon slowed down like a bag of popcorn nearing the end of its time in the microwave. She remained concealed in the brush just off the dirt road. She was well hidden in darkness and obscured by the veil of night. The headlights illuminated a kill box for Esposito and Russo, who, just moments ago sprayed the area with enough metal to get her to safety. She checked her Glock and had a full clip. John certainly tried to make her death as believable as possible.

Louie, one of the jarheads who assisted John in her capture, was on the ground motionless. Blood pooled around his head as it seeped into the dirt road. She then heard John bark orders and she was able to narrow down his position. She saw one of the uniformed officers break cover. They were spreading out and that meant Esposito and Russo were now in danger. She questioned if they were up to the task of engaging trained, heavily armed officers and former special forces in a close-range firefight. With all the gun fire and the element of surprise, they still only managed to take out one of the five men. However, the barrage of bullets did allow her to make it to cover, so they clearly knew what they were doing.

The other jarhead, Briscoe, flanked the back of the sedan. Marathon saw him move and aim his M9 in her general direction. He was coming after her, which meant her position was about to be compromised. As she raised her Glock to take him out, she saw John appear behind the car to cover Briscoe. It was a two on one situation and her current position called for a tactical retreat. There was no viable cover anywhere around her.

Before she could find a path further into darkness, she saw John holding something far more substantial than the M9 Briscoe was brandishing and he was aiming it her way. She knew he couldn't see her, but the flash of the rifle suggested he had a general location. The sound of his Armalite AR-15 pierced the midnight air as metal sprayed the surrounding area around her.

Mara dove backwards and rolled a few feet down the decline towards the banks of the Jamaica Bay. She landed on the soft swampy ground as bullets continued to fly overhead. Marathon held her Glock up and made sure a round was chambered. She focused her weapon back up towards the dirt road where the headlights could still be seen peering through the brush. She heard shouting and John's baritone voice organized the men. She needed to move, her position hadn't much improved. There was nothing around her that would stop a round from an M9, let alone an AR-15.

She got up in a crouched position and kept her head low as she navigated the swampy terrain towards the banks of the bay. Marathon was thankful it was low tide, or she would be waist deep in saltwater. A sound of swampy footsteps could be heard to her left. No doubt Briscoe was on her trail. She focused on the sounds and then saw a beam of light flash across her field of view. She dove back down and sank into the swampy water. The beam of light was a dead giveaway as to where the barrel of the gun was pointed. Get caught in the light, you're dead.

"She's down here somewhere!"

"I'll provide overwatch, you get me a target to shoot," John said.

Marathon heard Briscoe's soggy footsteps get closer. His flashlight passed over her location a half dozen times as he slowly scanned the area like a turret looking for a target. Mara slowly crawled back towards the road. She needed to get out of his direct path and use the negative space around her to ambush Briscoe. At this point, it would be futile to try and use her weapon. The flash emanating from her Glock would give her position away and provide John a clear shot. She needed to take him out without giving away her position.

Mara heard more shots off in the distance, towards the direction where Esposito and Russo likely staged their surprise attack. She heard lapping water in front of her and noticed a body of water separating her from the dirt road. The low tide created a small river like water path in the bank before the road ahead.

She then turned back towards the flashlight where Briscoe was and decided to use this to her advantage. All of her training in the Marines and the practical application in Afghanistan was coming back to her. She slowly lowered herself into the water, it was deep enough where she could be completely submerged if she were to lay down.

As she laid back into the water, she made a loud splashing sound to make it sound like she was running. Mara saw the beam of light focus on her general location as this disturbance immediately garnered Briscoe's attention. Mara held her breath, she hoped he would get the location right before she needed to surface for air. At the Depot, she was able to successfully hold her breath for just under four minutes. That was a long time ago.

The light flashed above the surface of the water indicating Briscoe got the hint. She needed him to get closer, but any movement would now give away her position. She had to hold her breath longer, she had to make sure he was in position. The light rippled over the surface and got brighter. The need to surface and take a breath started to creep in. Her body was reacting to the lack of oxygen.

She knew he was getting close, and needed to last a bit longer. Then a shadowy figure appeared above her. He was in position. Before Marathon could strike, the beam from the flashlight poured through the water and illuminated her position, their eyes met and she had him. His gun was out of position, pointed straight ahead instead of down at the water with the flash light. She sprung up from her position and raised her Glock at Briscoe.

Mara fired off enough rounds to get the job done, Briscoe barely had time to process what had just happened as he collapsed backwards into the swampy mess behind him. The light from John's rifle scanned the area. He didn't have a fix on her. Briscoe's body hid the flash and she used the cover of darkness to circumvent the beam of light trying to pinpoint her position. Mara transversed the remaining distance to the slope, which led her back up to the dirt road. She took cover out of the flashlight's field of view behind foliage.

She checked her ammo situation and determined she had sent five rounds into Briscoe. Marathon heard John call out to him, but there was no reply. The beam of light kept scanning the area and then stopped abruptly. John found Briscoe's body. Mara aimed her Glock using the steep incline while laying prone to steady her aim. There was about one hundred yards of open space between them, well beyond the effective range of her weapon. However, her intention wasn't to kill him, it was to get him to move. If the rounds she fired actually hit him, that would be an added bonus, but the three rounds she fired had their desired effect.

John ran back towards the sedan giving Mara the avenue needed to close distance. She used the edge of the dirt road to stay on track as she ran at a steady speed towards the headlights. She knew she could cover the distance before John was able to get back into cover and acquire her as a target. More gun fire sounded off in the distance towards the path circling West Pond. She couldn't worry about what was happening over there, she needed to get John. She finally had him in a one on one situation.

Marathon paused just before the dirt path opened up to the sedan and police cars. More gun fire could be heard, it sounded like a warzone, but her focus had to remain on her current target. Marathon tried to reacquire John's location after he disappeared behind the sedan, but the still midnight air gave no hints of his

320

location. She remained paused and kept a low profile at the edge of the light waiting for a sign of movement. Gunfire continued off in the distance signaling that this was going to remain an intimate encounter.

Her patience paid off. She saw movement at the edge of the brush on the other side of the clearing. John was waiting for her and saw the lethal end of the AR-15 emerge from the shadows. She slowly flanked his position, moving to her right at a pace only hunters would use. She kept her weapon trained on his general location beyond the light. She had seven rounds left in the magazine and needed to make every one of them count.

She was not completely out of his field of view as she was maneuvered her way towards the two patrol cars opposite the sedan she arrived in. She dropped down low and trained her Glock on the barrel of the AR-15. Something wasn't right. There was no way John could remain prone for that long without moving. His bad back, knees and the rest of his failing body would have made it impossible for him to get into that position let alone be able to get out of it. Before Mara could put the trap together, a shot struck the back of her shoulder sending her flying forward.

More shots sprayed her way as the rounds made the metal on metal sound as they struck the patrol car in front of her. Marathon used her forward momentum to roll towards the back of the patrol car as rounds continued to spark the environment around her.

"You still alive bitch!" John said as she heard him change magazines.

Mara inspected her wound. A large chunk of flesh was missing on her right shoulder. By the amount of blood loss, she quickly determined the wound wasn't life threatening. It must have hit her Scapula bone and ricocheted upwards taking a large chunk of flesh with it. The distinct smell of burnt skin and fresh blood flooded her senses. The pain was nothing she couldn't handle.

Marathon responded to his statement by returning fire in his direction. She sent three rounds his way causing him to scramble towards the other patrol car for

321

cover, about twenty feet away from her position. She was now dangerously low on ammo and her shoulder wound slightly affected her aim.

"How many rounds you got left?" John asked as she was thinking the same thing. "Maybe three or four shots I'd guess."

"Why don't you come over here and find out?" Mara responded.

"Maybe I'll wait for my boys to return and then we'll find out together," he responded.

"That's if they're still alive," Mara said.

"Please, who do you have out there, those two agents? What are their names again?"

"By the sound of it, your boys are having a tough time, what makes you so sure they're still alive," Mara responded. She changed position towards the front of the car as she tried to get a better angle on him.

"They're killers," He responded.

"Just like the ones you sent to kill me?"

John stood and fired at her general position. Chunks of metal flew up into the air around her.

"I should have killed you a long time ago," he said.

Mara heard his clip hit the ground as he was in the process of changing to a fresh mag again. She used the opportunity to better her position by sprinted across the open space between the patrol cars and sedan. John barely finished reloading as she slid behind cover towards the rear of the sedan. She then heard rounds impact around her as John was clearly frustrated with her maneuver. Marathon knew the sedan was unlocked, but gaining access to the lever that opened the trunk would put her in a compromising situation. She remembered Detective Morales said there was a field package in the trunk of the car with body armor and a shotgun.

Mara's back slid against the side of the sedan as she made her way to the trunk. The back of the car gave her just enough cover. Mara wasn't surprised John didn't try and change position, he wasn't fleet of foot and was probably winded from this much action.

Marathon aimed her Glock at the locking mechanism sealing the trunk closed. She simultaneously closed her eyes and squeezed the trigger. Her luck had not run out as the trunk sprang open to reveal its contents. The trunk opened to create a barrier between her and John. The contents of the trunk revealed a shotgun and body armor which were part of the field support package Morales had mentioned. Mara grabbed the body armor and flung it over head. The shotgun was next, but it wasn't loaded. Mara rummaged through trunk and found a box of shells under one of the evidence kits. She finished latching the Velcro straps on the body armor and grabbed the shells.

Her moment at the trunk was short lived, bullets started pounding the rear of the sedan forcing the trunk to close from the numerous impacts. This sent Mara falling backwards and the shotgun shells fumbled out of her hand as she hit the ground. The box containing the shells split open sending them scattering all around her. Mara was exposed in the line of fire and felt a few rounds impact her vest. She grabbed her Glock and returned fire until her firearm signaled it was out of ammo. This forced John back into cover and gave her time to scramble back behind the car.

"I heard that clicking sound, you're out," John announced as she heard him reload his weapon.

Marathon looked around. She held the shotgun in her hands, but its ammo was now scattered in the dirt behind the car just out of her reach. She frantically looked around for options, thinking she could use the shotgun as a melee weapon when he got close enough. As she moved, she noticed a single shell resting by her feet in the dirt.

"Come on out and I promise I'll make this quick," he said. Mara heard his footsteps as he started to close the distance. She scooped up the shell and slid the round into place.

Then in one motion, Mara rose from behind cover and cocked the shotgun. Their eyes locked in that brief moment. Mara saw fear and shock in eyes as she squeezed the trigger sending the buck shot straight towards him. John managed to fire of a round as well. His round hit her square in the chest and the vest did its job absorbing the impact. Mara managed to remain standing as she saw John topple backwards off his feet. His M9 was dislodged from his hand as he hit the ground.

The impact from John's shot knocked the wind out of her. She gasped for air as she made her way towards John who had hit the ground hard. She checked her vest to make sure the round didn't penetrate into her as she kept moving forward. She found another round in the dirt and chambered it in the shotgun. Her wind returned as she drew closer. She saw him stir and readied her weapon.

She was nearly on top of him when she noticed small black beads spread out all around him and covering his chest. The buckshot had sent rubber pellets at John instead of the lethal copper or steel traditionally found in the shells. John was clearly disorientated, he had absorbed the full brunt of the shot. Mara could see bruising already form around his exposed skin where the pellets had made contact.

"Fuck," she said, as she held her shotgun steady.

The non-lethal take down did its job. He was completely incapacitated. She desperately wanted to fire the next round into his skull. At that range, even rubber bullets were lethal. After all he's done, he deserved no less. Mara remained staring at him while he tried to regain his composure. He finally noticed Mara standing over him. He followed her hands to the shotgun.

"Do it," he said.

"Fuck you!"

"If it were me, you'd already be dead," John said.

"Good thing I am nothing like you," Mara said as she solidified her stance.

"We're more alike than you realize, why do you think I picked you?"

"Fuck you!"

"You're a killer, just like me!" he said.

324

"We're not-"

"Not what? The same?" he interrupted. "I see that look in your eye. The look of someone who can kill without regrets. That's why I stuck with you all these years. Hoping you'd join me. The Marines trained you to kill, I thought you had it in you."

The rage was building inside her. She felt her finger dig into the trigger, if she applied any more pressure, the shotgun would discharge sending the rubber pellets into his face at point blank range.

"Marathon," Esposito said as he emerged into the light.

"Oh fuck," she said in relief.

"Are you okay?" he asked.

"Yes, where's Russo?"

"He's been hit," he responded. "I called this in."

"Shit, we don't know who is going to respond."

"It's my office, they'll respond. They have everything," he said.

Mara nodded and looked down at John who must have been wondering what they were talking about.

"That's right asshole, this entire fucking area was bugged. We got everything," she said.

John tried to get up, but Mara kicked him back to the ground. She hit him in the same spot most of the rubber buckshot pellets struck, knowing it would send shockwaves of pain throughout his body.

"Stay down, asshole," she said as John rolled on the ground in pain.

Esposito's cell phone rang, he stepped away and answered it. Mara watched John try and recuperate from her strike. She leaned in close to him.

"There is only one thing I want more than to see your life end here," she whispered.

John turned towards her and looked at her with a rage induced intensity. At that moment, she was satisfied with her decision, he was broken, and she had won.

"I want to see you spill all your secrets, I want to see you break over and over and over again," she continued whispering. "I want the entire world to know what you've done! And finally, when your little world knows you're a rat, you'll spend the rest of your pathetic life behind bars looking over your shoulder."

Off in the distance, Marathon heard the sound of a helicopter approaching. Then moments later, sirens from police cars. The sounds were coming in opposite directions.

"Shit!" Esposito yelled.

"I gather those sirens are not for us," Mara said.

"That helo is," Esposito said. "I'm gonna get Russo."

Marathon saw the helicopter off in the distance, it seemed to pick up speed as the sirens sounded closer. She looked around for a possible landing site and saw there was just enough space for the helicopter to land in the middle of everything.

The helicopter was now close enough for Mara to visually direct them where to land. She relayed commands to the pilot indicating the LZ was hot. Hopefully the pilot understood what that meant. Esposito returned with Russo in tow. He had a massive leg wound just above his knee. A tourniquet was placed in the correct spot and controlled the bleeding, but Mara knew the wound was not fatal, it looked like it missed the artery. She took over for Esposito as he went to secure John Stroman and get him ready for transport. John struggled to get up, but Esposito's strength gave him little choice but to comply.

The sirens from the police were now very close and Mara saw the lights from the patrol cars just beyond the dirt road. The white, blue, and red lights flickered throughout the darkness. When Marathon looked back, the helicopter successfully landed, and Esposito was already moving John into position. Mara helped Russo limp over the bird. She saw John try and resist but Esposito placed

326

his firearm in his face. She couldn't hear what was said, but whatever it was, it made John get on the chopper. After he was secure, an agent emerged from the bird and helped Mara get Russo get on board.

The helicopter took off just as the stream of patrol cars got to the site. Their microphones blared out orders as their spotlights fixated on their position. The pilot flew low over the bay and the scene behind them became a speck of light in the past.

M

Chapter
Thirty-Three

Undisclosed Location
September 4th, 2019
Early Morning

Marathon sat alone in a plainly empty room in an undisclosed location somewhere in New Jersey. There was a makeshift cot in the room, and she was provided a shower, a meal, and a new set of clothes after someone who claimed to be a doctor provided medical attention. The stiches in her shoulder were done properly, so he definitely had medical expertise, not Dr. Jenkins expertise, but good enough. He also checked her forearm by redressing the bandage and fixed some of the loose staples.

Last night's intensity was finally catching up with her. Her doubts about Esposito resurfaced. One common denominator kept resurfacing, deception. He was not FBI, not NSA and not Secret Service. These agents were none of these and they certainly were not computer nerds. That only left one possible explanation. One that thrived off of deception, manipulation, and information.

The CIA.

Russo and Esposito were definitely CIA. No chance they were anything else. They weren't lucky against two well trained heavily armed officers, they were experienced. They've always been one step ahead of everyone and now she was finally putting the pieces together. The CIA typically operates outside the

328

United States and they typically have zero jurisdiction to operate against any US Citizen. Yet, here she was, in an unlabeled government building where no one wore any identification and professionally dressed in the same monotone colors.

Spooky.

The doors were not locked, and in no way did Mara feel like she was being detained. But, with the uncertainty of her situation, she couldn't help but feel captive. There were cameras in the room, but she had no indication if they were on or not. Back in the NYPD interrogation room at the precinct, there was a red light just below the camera lens. This indicated that the events in the room were being recorded. However, if the light was off, someone could still access the camera, to watch what was going on in the room.

Mara heard that was a common thing for detectives to do. They would go into an interrogation room, point to the camera and convince the suspect into giving up valuable information because the camera was off, and it was just them in the room. People actually fell for it, kind of the same way people think Alexa isn't listening to their conversations.

She wondered who was on the other end of the camera watching her. Was Esposito watching, observing? Mara went over to the makeshift bed and laid down. She tried closing her eyes, but her mind prevented her body from sleep. She spent the next few hours waiting, trying to sort out the events, piece together information, remember key details about what she experienced. From the moment this nightmare began, when she accessed Marley Williams' case file on her computer, her life has been nothing but a roller coaster.

The army of cops who responded to the nature preserve, were they John's boys or were they legit cops? She had to assume they were there to serve his agenda and that meant this wasn't over. More heads needed to roll. The detectives who sold out Morales by calling in sick, that's where she would need to start if she wanted to get to the bottom of this.

329

Who was that mystery man in the car with her as John brought her to Broad Channel? His voice sounded familiar and she would make it her business to find out who he was. There were many opened ended questions that kept the hours moving without rest.

Her career in the NYPD was certainly over, she did retire after all. What about her situation as a wanted fugitive being framed for murder, conspiracy and a dozen other crimes? The media had a field day with her, she was known as the NYPD Fatale who was the mastermind behind major crimes in New York City. Her life in the big city was probably also over, there would be little chance she could ever live there again without being spotted or followed. Then there was the fact that the NYPD still wanted to kill her, even if she was vindicated by the law and public opinion.

She wanted to call Uncle Dave and hear his voice. She was supposed to rendezvous with them the day after tomorrow in Paris, France. Where they would celebrate her retirement and enjoy life and luxury. That seemed impossible with all the events that have taken place since they made her retirement plans. She had no doubt they heard the news in Paris about the NYPD Femme Fatale. She would be surprised if they were still in France with the sudden turn of events.

Mara's train of thought was suddenly interrupted as she heard knock at the door. She verbally welcomed the person in and sat up in her cot. Macron Esposito walked in with a manila folder and a fresh set of clothes. He cleaned up nicely since the last time she saw him when helicopter dropped them off.

"So, CIA right?"

"Wow, you get right to the point," Esposito said. "How's your wound?"

"It's fine, your doctor knew what he was doing."

"Most of our field medics were trained in the Army," he said.

"I don't like being jerked around," she responded.

"I got that," he responded. He motioned her to sit at the sole table in the middle of the room. His demeanor changed, almost like he dropped the act from before. Marathon sat opposite him and he placed the folder on the table but kept it closed. She tried to focus on its contents, but the exterior of the folder prevented its secrets.

"I think it's time to fully explain everything," he said.

Mara sat back in her chair, crossed her legs and waited for Esposito to begin. Her tired body wanted sleep, but her mind welcomed the coming explanation.

"A number of years ago, well before you were even on the force, Russo and I were made aware of large sums of money being exchanged in the NYC area," he said.

"Yes, you told me that. It was actually a convincing misdirection," she said.

"The best deceptions only provide slivers of truth," he said. "The money was being funneled in through offshore accounts linked to shell companies."

"Again, you kinda alluded to that as well," she responded.

"Our operation, which began overseas in Dubai, tracked large sums of money all over the world. When we noticed NYC being a major hub, we took action. I was just a young agent at the time working under Agent Russo as a field operative. Marley Williams was not just a high school student attending a school in Brownsville."

He paused and Mara looked at him closely. He didn't speak for a while which let her catch to what that meant. If Marley Williams was not just a high school student, then who was she?

"Marley Williams was an undercover agent sent by Russo to get boots on the ground in New York City," he said. "Money was being funneled through gangs in Brooklyn and planting an agent in the middle of it was necessary to find out what was going on."

"What? No fucking way." Mara interjected. "I fucking met with the family, there was a fucking funeral."

"All set up to drive the narrative that the CIA was not involved and to cover our tracks. Marley got close, she got real close, and John Stroman killed her because she was leaking info to her handlers. Thanks to you, we found her killer."

"Did John know she was CIA?" Marathon asked.

"No, her cover wasn't compromised, they thought Marley was leaking info to a new gang on the streets," Russo said.

"Fuck, so her parents were her handlers?"

"It was great cover, we had boots on the ground, a solid story, solid game plan, while being fed solid info," Esposito explained.

"Until my former partner realized what was going on," Marathon said.

"We think John was tipped off about what Marley was doing. She was betrayed by our own agency Marathon. We also thought Frank was the one calling the shots."

"What?"

"Russo was in charge of the operation back then. The only way John Stroman suspected Marley was because information was deliberately leaked to him to fuck up the operation," Esposito stated. "Russo was able to preserve Marley's cover after her death. Her backstory had holes in it. The agency plugged those holes and filled in the gaps with the gang narrative John was fed from the leak."

"If the CIA leaked info to John, why then protect the CIA's cover?" Marathon asked.

"We operate in the shadows, nothing is more important that remaining anonymous," Esposito said. "Even when the agency betrays their own."

"How could you work for an organization without morals?" Marathon asked.

"Well, you work for the NYPD, you tell me?" he responded. Marathon remained quiet and let him continue, his comeback was solid.

"What we do know is that someone in the agency wanted this investigation to end. Russo went dark and that's where I came in. I helped him remain anonymous by taking care of some loose ends. Russo brought me a long for the ride ever since," Esposito stated.

"Who was Marley Williams, who was she really?" Marathon asked.

"That's classified info, but I can say that she was much like you. Former Marine, dedicated patriot, looked like a high school student."

"She fit the part and Russo recruited her for it," Mara interrupted.

"Basically," he said.

Marathon wondered how old Esposito was. He looked to be in his late twenties or early thirties, but he certainly was much older than that.

"There's more," Esposito added. "We've uncovered a lot during our investigation. We know that the NYPD has been completely compromised where we can't even tell the good cops from the bad cops anymore. We know this organization, you heard them being called as The Farm, is just a drop in the bucket compared to the big picture. We are talking global scale operations."

Marathon leaned forward, Esposito was starting to answer many of the questions that have been bothering her for years. Like how Marley's parents dropped off the face of the planet shortly after her death. But one question was burning in her mind. She needed an answer.

"Why the fuck hasn't anything been done?" she asked.

"With the agency compromised, Russo was left with no choice but to go dark. One agent verses an entire enterprise?"

"Bullshit," she responded. "You were recruited, you leaked financial info, played the shadow game, what held you guys back? You're part of the fucking CIA!"

As if on cue the door suddenly opened and Russo appeared at the threshold. He was on crutches and maneuvered his way into the room. Marathon stood and greeted him warmly as he took a seat next to her.

"Sorry I'm late," Russo said. "Took a bullet to the knee."

333

Marathon helped by pushing in his chair and then placed his crutches so they wouldn't fall to the floor. She then joined him at the table.

"I couldn't help but eavesdrop a bit before entering," Russo said. "Let me clear a few things up Marathon. But, before we start, I would like to say, unofficially, hell of a job."

Esposito nodded in agreement as Russo extended his arm and grabbed her hand from across the table. She welcomed the praise and knew it was well earned. By most accounts, she should have been dead.

"So, now that the pleasantries are out of the way, there was no way I could have responded back then. I was on my own, with only a sliver of support from the agency. My circle of trust went from my team down to myself and Mack, we had a close friend at headquarters. But, I felt he was compromised also," Russo said.

"So after Marley was murdered, you were on your own?" Mara asked.

"Yes, my team was compromised and we were about to be exposed. Macron cleaned up the mess, but then went dark after that," Russo said looking over at Esposito. "I recruited Mack after my team feel apart. He was the only one I could trust from my team of five."

"Little did I know Russo would lead me down this rabbit hole," he said.

"After a year or so in hiding, we started picking things back up again. The financial leaks we mentioned before were true, we tried every tactic we could think of to expose this organization."

"When did you decide to fuck up my life?" Marathon questioned.

"You were always in the picture, always a question mark. When we saw that you accessed the Marley Williams file, we decided to act.

"You said 'fuck up my life' wrong," Mara stated.

"It got you here didn't it," Russo said.

"Is John talking?" Mara asked changing the subject.

"He is, at least right now he is," Esposito said.

"He's just a piece, a low level nothing," Russo suggested.

"He's a start!" Marathon said.

"That's true," Russo said.

"You're not telling me something. What's in the file?" Mara asked.

Instead of explaining it, Esposito opened it and spread out all its contents. Pictures of Marathon emerged from all different time periods, all different occasions, from every aspects of her life. The photos looked like paparazzi shots of her going out, while she worked on the job, even shots of her at John Street Bar. Even shots of Bowman, the man who attacked her on the night of the attack.

"What the fuck is this?" Mara questioned.

"It's our file on you," Esposito said. Mara picked up individual photographs and looked at each one. It was like looking at a yearbook that spanned many years. The photos weren't in any kind of an order as pics from all different occasions were scattered around like a mashup of her life's events.

"We just want to lay everything out on the table," Russo said. "It's time you know everything."

She spent a few seconds on each picture and realized how violated she felt as intimate moments throughout her life was staring back at her. Someone took these pictures, someone knew about her life as much as she did. Past boyfriends, random one-night stands, intimate encounters with friends and family were all captured in this photo dossier. Mara felt her face turn red in embarrassment as these moments in time were only meant for herself.

"You violated me in more ways than I can describe," she said.

"That wasn't our intention," Esposito responded.

"We have you to thank for helping us get to John," Russo said controlling the conversation. "John will never be forgiven for what he has done and he will pay dearly."

"Can you stop with the bullshit. I hate having smoke blown up my ass!" Mara immediately stated.

Esposito looked up at the camera as if he were communicating with someone on the other end thus confirming Mara's suspicion about the camera. With both Russo and Esposito both in the room with her, there was someone else involved. She felt like she was now on the other end of an interrogation. Maybe she was.

"We knew you could be an asset," Russo said.

"There ya go," Mara stated. "I knew you two were jerking me around for something."

"Before we get to that, we need to debrief you," Russo said.

"I got John to spill everything on tape for you," Mara said. "Next time just lead with a debrief line of questions."

"Noted, may I continue?" Esposito asked and Mara nodded. "We have plenty of self-incriminating evidence on John. What we don't have is anything on who is calling the shots. John is just a middleman, low level management at best," he said.

The mysterious man in the car immediately came to mind. He seemed to be giving John orders. She recognized the voice but couldn't picture a face or a name.

"On my way over to Broad Channel, there was another man in the car," Mara said.

"Besides Briscoe and Louie?"

"Yes," Mara responded.

"We didn't spot anyone else when you arrived."

"He got out on Woodhaven Boulevard. There was a car following us, wait, his car was following us."

"What did the man say?"

"The basic bullshit about taking care of me and making sure no one finds out. That sorta shit," Mara said.

"He was calling the shots?" he asked.

"He seemed to outrank John, yes," she said.

"If there is anything else, we need to know about it. It's very rare for the higher ups to expose themselves like this," he said.

"His voice seemed very familiar, like I've heard it before," she said.

"Was it Frank?" Esposito asked.

"No, he had a higher pitched voice, sounded younger," Marathon answered.

"Was it someone you know?" Russo asked.

"No, but I did hear his voice before," she responded.

"When it comes to you, please let me know."

"Right," she said.

Mara put the pictures back in the file and closed it. She sent the manila folder back his way across the table.

"So now we're going to get to why I am here?" Marathon asked.

"My field days are done, Marathon," Russo said.

"We're recruiting you," Esposito said bluntly. Mara appreciated the direct response. Any more bullshit out of his mouth would have ended poorly for him.

"Here I thought you were interrogating me, fuck, just a few months ago you were interrogating me," she said.

"Honestly, what's the difference?" he asked. Which was a good point the more she thought about it.

"Your skill set is well beyond the qualifications needed for what we do. You've got great instincts, and you tend to always come out on top. Well, almost always," he said. Mara knew he threw that last line in there for a reason. He had ended on top of her just a few nights ago.

"I am a criminal and probably still public enemy number one," she responded.

"That's been handled," Russo said. "The people on the other side of that camera have new facts for the media; you've been vindicated. It'll probably make the evening news and then die off by the end of the week."

"No more NYPD Fatale? Sounds like you have done this before," she said.

"We know how to control a narrative, sometimes at least," Russo said.

"Can I leave?" she asked.

"You were always free to leave," Esposito said. Mara thought that was funny by the lack of any information she received while she was here, and she couldn't help but give a big fuck you kind of laugh in response.

"What has John told you?"

"You're avoiding the question," Esposito quickly responded.

"I don't make crazy decisions before knowing all the facts," she responded.

"Funny, that's not what these pictures say," Esposito said as he flipped open the folder to a compromising photo of Marathon in her personal life.

She wanted to curse him out but something told her that he was expecting that. There was much more to Esposito than she initially realized. He became very hard to read, as if their previous interactions were all acted out and staged. She felt manipulated by the two men, like they got her to do what they wanted all along.

"John hasn't said much," he stated breaking the brief silence by answering Mara's question from before. "He's received medical attention for multiple fractured ribs."

Marathon knew that was bullshit. John would talk, you put the right pressure on him and he would sing like he was starring in the local opera.

"What's going to happen to him?" she asked.

"He'll continue to be thoroughly interrogated and treated as domestic terrorist," Russo answered. The two men were becoming shady by only answering with vague responses. Marathon read through the bullshit.

"You're not charging him are you?" Mara questioned.

"Have you ever heard of the CIA arresting someone?"

"No, only surveillance and intelligence gathering." She responded.

"There's a reason why we're called spooks," Russo said.

"Fuck, you're illegally holding him." she stated.

"Not yet, we still have a few hours before it turns illegal," Esposito stated like the law didn't particularly affect his decision.

"I have a sworn oath to the constitution," Mara stated.

"Yes, we all do," he responded. "Funny, you just suggested that the CIA should have taken those responsible out years ago."

"This is different, he gave up, John surrendered. The law is the law," Mara explained.

"Funny it becomes the law when it only conveniences you," Esposito said.

"We are all held by the Constitution, Macron. John surrendered which means he is no longer in the game," Marathon said.

"I do solemnly swear that I will support and defend the Constitution of the United States against all enemies, foreign and domestic," Esposito recited. The Marine oath of service resonated deeply with Marathon's beliefs.

"Yes, that's the oath we are all bound to," she said.

"John's a domestic threat?" Esposito asked.

"Yeah, I think he can be considered that based on what we know," she said.

"John took the oath of a police officer?" Russo asked.

"Yeah, he was a patrol officer," Marathon said.

"Then he doesn't have constitutional rights the same way a regular citizen does."

"Bullshit! Every American deserves their day in court," Marathon stated with authority.

"Hold on, when you were in the Marines, what could happen to you if you broke rank and disobeyed orders?"

"John is not in the Marines," she said.

"No but he took an oath just like you did," Esposito said.

"So that means he doesn't have rights?"

"That means he is held to a different standard," Russo responded.

"This is why people don't like you," she said. "The agency. You change the law and wording to fit your needs."

"We do what needs to be done," Esposito said. "Tell me something, On July 29th, 2003, did you do what needed to be done?"

"Fuck you!" she said standing. She was surprised that date came up in this conversation.

"I guess there is room to compartmentalize the constitution when you are in the thick of it," Esposito said. "At least that's what you did anyway."

"You don't get to fucking judge me!" she snapped back.

"I am not judging, I am just stating some truths. Do you want me to spell out what you did on that day? I'm thinking, maybe you forgot, and maybe we are not so different after all," Esposito said.

"We do what needs to be done," Russo said firmly.

"You know what, fuck this," she said.

Marathon stood and went for the door, she wanted to get out of there quickly. The hallway outside was empty, like an office building after hours. She tried to remember the way she came in and backtracked her way out. She came to a staircase and descended to what she thought was the first floor. Instead she emerged into an underground parking garage. She paused for a second and then leaned up against the wall next to the door. Esposito shortly followed and then stood across from her.

"Go away," she said.

"I called you a ride," he said. Mara looked up at him. She knew he wasn't the enemy, but that date was something that stung. He brought it up for a reason and it should have remained buried. He had no right.

"Where are you headed?" Esposito questioned.

"Pennsylvania," she responded.

"I didn't mean to bring up your past like that," he said. "We've all done things that go against the grain. It's why you are here."

"I bet your skeletons are worse than mine," she responded. "But, I can't seem to compartmentalize them like you can."

Moments later a black sedan with tinted windows pulled into the garage.

"My ride?" Mara questioned knowing this was not a typical car service.

"The spooky kind," he replied.

Mara got in the front seat and Esposito gave the driver the address. She then rolled down her window.

"I never did thank you, and Russo," Mara said.

"That's because you don't need to," he said. "By the way, we couldn't vet Frank thoroughly enough to clear him."

"He's clean," Mara said.

"He's entrenched in NYPD affairs. We can't be sure," he responded. "Signing off on those patrol patterns is a major issue. I wouldn't trust him."

"Good-bye Mack," she said. "Make sure you say goodbye to Russo for me."

"Marathon, the offer still stands, even after you leave here," Esposito said as she closed the window. She watched him enter the building as the driver shifted into gear. The route was already queued back to Quincy, Pennsylvania.

M

Epilogue

Uncle Dave's Ranch
September 7th, 2019
5:00pm

"Hey, this Old Fashioned is your best yet!" Marathon said.

"That's your third one," Uncle Dave said from behind the outdoor pool bar. "I'm surprised you can taste anything."

"We should be in Paris right now," she said.

"We should, but we'll throw you a proper retirement party here," Uncle Dave said.

"Adam has been gone a while, where's he getting this pizza from again?" Mara asked.

"I don't know, he's been on this quest to find NY pizza ever since we moved out here," he said.

"There's only one place to get NY pizza," Mara said.

"Yes, we know, but Adam thinks we can come close," Uncle Dave said.

Mara laid her head back down as she rested the Old Fashioned on the table next to her lounge chair. She wanted to take full advantage of retirement before summer was officially over. Uncle Dave and Adam returned from Paris after the news broke about Marathon being a fugitive. Instead of returning to the ranch, they went straight to New York City to get answers. Marathon contacted them from the ranch after the CIA chauffer dropped her off. They were happy to find her lounging by the pool when they returned a few days ago.

342

Adam and Uncle Dave were worried sick and Marathon properly told them everything that transpired since they separated back in late August. After Uncle Dave lost his shit, they both made her promise to never return to New York again. Marathon's retirement was official and her name was publicly cleared. She was offered large sum from the NYPD to basically remain quiet but, she owed it to Detective Morales to tell the truth about what had happened. He paid the ultimate price for his dedicated service and his family deserved the truth about the department.

The radio played soft elevator style music in the background. It wasn't her favorite, but it got the job done. Uncle Dave came out from behind the bar and sat next to her in his lounge chair.

"Adam better come back soon, I'm starving," he said as he closed his eyes to take in as much sun as he could.

At this time of day, the sun provided that healing warmth that Marathon desperately needed. Her bikini revealed the many scrapes, bruises and close calls with death she endured over the last few days. All of which seemed like a distant memory.

Marathon had to screen her calls over the past few days. Noisy reporters wanted to get her on camera, get a quick sound bite over the phone, anything to continue the story. She went from hero to villain to hero and the public salivated over it. Conspiracy theories raged and the news media ran many unverified stories about police corruption. Marathon knew it went way deeper than the NYPD. She knew they were only the muscle behind the operation in New York.

The NY Post had her on the front page for three days in a row. She found the title "NYPD Badass" particularly amusing, especially since the photo was reused from previous editions when she was public enemy number one. Playboy even called offering her a full spread on their November issue, she simply laughed and hung up the phone.

The papers got most of the story correct regarding John, mainly because she leaked the info to them. He was a dirty cop and framed her for many awful things. Marathon spilled the beans about his involvement in the conspiracy and stated he was responsible for Marley Williams' murder. She knew this would put pressure on the CIA to have him formally charged. She knew the CIA wouldn't like that, but she didn't particularly care what they thought. Besides, they owed her one.

Mara got up from her lounge chair and announced she was going to wash up before dinner. It was her way to saying she didn't want to listen to another breaking news story where reporters were regurgitating information fed to them by the CIA. Before she could reach the house, she froze dead in her tracks. She turned towards the radio and ran towards it. She turned the volume up and listened closely.

"What's going on?"

"Shhh!" she said.

Uncle Dave got up and looked concerned. He began listening to the broadcast as well. Mara was in a trance, the voice resonated over the radio like it did when she was in the back of the sedan with John.

"Holy fuck!" she managed to say.

"What?" Dave asked looking confused.

Mara continued to stare at the radio, listening with great focus. The tone of the man's voice sent chills throughout her body, and a cold sweat formed on her brow. Uncle Dave became concerned and grabbed Mara's arm.

"That voice," she said. "I know that voice."

"The Mayor?" Uncle Dave questioned.

"That's the Mayor of New York City," Marathon said.

M

Marathon Jessica Torres will be back.